PENGUIN
GOVARDHAN ̲ ̲.... ̲ ̲ ̲

P. Sachidanandan was born in 1936 in Kerala. His first book, *Aalkkoottam* (The Crowd) was published in 1970. With no formal training in language, he developed his own literary dialect, which suited the themes he selected for his stories over the years. His works traverse mythology, history and contemporary realities and dwell on the mechanism of power and the deprivation and injustice in society.

He has written nine novels, forty short stories, two plays and two major philosophical works apart from numerous articles on contemporary topics.

*

Gita Krishnankutty has translated the novels and short stories of several Malayalam writers including M. T. Vasudevan Nair, Lalithambika Antharjanam, N.P. Mohammad, Paul Zacharia and M. Mukundan. She lives in Chennai.

Govardhan's Travels

ANAND

A Novel

Translated by
Gita Krishnankutty

PENGUIN BOOKS

PENGUIN BOOKS
Published by the Penguin Group
Penguin Books India Pvt. Ltd, 11 Community Centre, Panchsheel Park, New Delhi 110 017, India
Penguin Group (USA) Inc., 375 Hudson Street, New York, New York 10014, USA
Penguin Group (Canada), 90 Eglinton Avenue East, Suite 700, Toronto, Ontario, M4P 2Y3, Canada (a division of Pearson Penguin Canada Inc.)
Penguin Books Ltd, 80 Strand, London WC2R 0RL, England
Penguin Ireland, 25 St Stephen's Green, Dublin 2, Ireland (a division of Penguin Books Ltd)
Penguin Group (Australia), 250 Camberwell Road, Camberwell, Victoria 3124, Australia (a division of Pearson Australia Group Pty Ltd)
Penguin Group (NZ), cnr Airborne and Rosedale Roads, Albany, Auckland 1310, New Zealand (a division of Pearson New Zealand Ltd)
Penguin Group (South Africa) (Pty) Ltd, 24 Sturdee Avenue, Rosebank, Johannesburg 2196, South Africa

Penguin Books Ltd, Registered Offices: 80 Strand, London WC2R 0RL, England

First published in Malayalam as *Govardhante Yatrakal* by DC Books
First published in English by Penguin Books India 2006
Copyright © P. Sachidanandan 2006
Translation copyright © Gita Krishnankutty 2006

This is a work of fiction. Names, characters, places and incidents are either the product of an author's imagination or are used fictitiously and any resemblance to any actual person, living or dead, events or locales is entirely coincidental.

ISBN-13: 978-0-14310-133-8   ISBN-10: 0-14310-133-1

Typeset in Perpetua by Mantra Virtual Services, New Delhi
Printed at Pauls Press, New Delhi

prologue

Not even the most casual visitor to the courts of the mofussil towns of north India could fail to notice one of its features: the vast compounds that stretch around the court buildings with hordes of people camped under trees the English had planted there years before to chase the heat away. Old people, women and children, surrounded by mats and durries, tin trunks, bundles of clothes and makeshift kitchens. You will also see the ramshackle bazaars that have grown alongside these habitats in shanties and shacks. You can easily make out that these people have come from far-flung villages to camp in these compounds while they await the dispensation of justice and that they have come prepared with relatives, friends and witnesses to help them. Take a closer look at their faces and you might be excused for wondering if they have been camping in these places since the time of Warren Hastings or Dalhousie.

In the last few years, I have had to visit courts in many large and small towns as part of my official duties and have never been able to go past these people milling around the grounds without noticing them. As courts began to be established with the evolution of the notions of law and justice, large numbers of people who hoped for justice and waited for it to be dispensed gathered alongside them. As massive buildings, files and lawyers multiplied to serve the needs of the courts, bazaars sprouted around the dwellings of those who came to seek justice. Eating places to feed them, clothes shops to replace their tattered garments, barber shops to shear their growing hair, dentists to extract their rotting teeth, cobblers to take care of their corn-infested feet, palmists to sell them hope, itinerant musicians and acrobats to entertain them... I felt as though these human habitations and bazaars that had mushroomed around the courthouses had woven a pattern of perpetuity into the prolonged wait for justice in the same way as buildings and files had gradually institutionalized the system of dispensing justice. Considered from another viewpoint, did our cities themselves not grow out of the interminable conflict between those whose rights had been violated and those who violated them?

Some time ago I wrote a short story that touched on these matters. It was about an old man who came to court with his little son, carrying all the meagre savings he had in a wallet, to file a plaint against a zamindar who had snatched away from him the tiny piece of land that was his family's sole means of survival. Once he had paid the lawyer's fees, he found that the money left was not enough to even bribe the lawyer's clerk. The old man wandered around the bazaar holding the child's hand, uncertain of what to do. He was soon trying to assuage the child's hunger and thirst. Then he began to buy little household objects that his family had been yearning to possess for years. In the end, having spent everything he had, he went back to the village, the plaint still in his hand!

However, the images of the people in the compounds of the courts that I had by now started to call court-basties stayed with me. I could not push them away by writing a story. The look in their eyes, of a remoteness that defied both hope and despair, continued to haunt me. Time seemed to stand still in these court-basties, stagnating around them. Ancient colonial buildings with wide arches, massive pilastered walls and corniced pillars, high ceilings that harboured the dust of centuries, fans that, suspended from long rods, groaned perpetually, judges seated in dingy rooms, straining their eyes to read the verdicts, stooping clerks who seemed strangers to death, petitioners swimming through a sea of death: these courts transported me not only into the notorious inertia of the Indian legal system but also into the mind of an ancient India devoid of a sense of time and history.

Stories of lakhs of men and women who, thanks to personal enmity or the greed of informers, were incarcerated in jails and condemned to live in them, deprived of the chance to ever see the light of day again, who gave birth to children and died in that darkness were spawned not only by human rights activists who sprang up after the dark days of the Emergency in the seventies but also by the Henry Stracheys, Thomas Munros and Colonel Walkers who worked for the East India Company in the early decades of the nineteenth century. Lakhs of pending cases requiring the examination of millions of witnesses who had to be dragged into the towns from distant villages; judges who did not know the languages the witnesses spoke and were dependent upon wily interpreters; corrupt court officials and court rules that, instead of extending justice to those who needed it, actually prompted them to shun the courts; justice that was auctioned—to this day, time seems to have frozen into this picture Munro drew of Bengal in the nineteenth century. (A judge of the Supreme Court suggested recently that courts need not accept more than a certain number of petitions, somewhat like hotels that put up boards saying 'no vacancy' on their doors!) Would the great Bhartrihari have passed through these still and timeless fields before he wrote: *kalo na yato vayameva yata*[1] and *bhogana bhukto vayameva bhukta*?[2] Or does our world, in which justice and injustice have become so entangled that we can no longer distinguish between them, a world which sees no compulsion to differentiate right from wrong or light from darkness, give a new interpretation to the couplets written by this poet-king who renounced the world to become a mendicant?

This need not be true. The past, which permeates and co-exists with our mythology, history and literature and lives so comfortably with the present does not have to be a casual visitor to us. I thought I could seek it out in these court-basties and indeed, I felt I did—for a society in whose heart the fire of justice does not burn is certain to lose all sense of time!

I speak of these courts only as an example. The problem is not that of the courts alone. And the solution, as many of our human rights activists seem to believe, does not lie in the hands of a bunch of lawyers. Courts which sway from one side to the other depending upon the eloquence of lawyers are not really that different from the arenas of olden days where professionals were employed to conduct cockfights and sword fights in order to settle disputes between contending parties. Nor is it only in

---

[1] It is not time that passes but we ourselves.

[2] It is not we who enjoy worldly pleasures, it is they who devour us.

the courts of justice that the innocent are punished repeatedly. Kings who go to war in order to establish their suzerainty, avatars and prophets who do battle to impose their versions of ethical codes, revolutionaries who swear by ideologies, modern militant outfits that wear the now fashionable garb of cultural and ethnic identities: all of them believe in one thing—the way to prove their correctness is to wield their weapons on the innocent. Each of them, keeping their private goal in mind, passes judgement on the rest of the world. Messiahs and preachers define right and wrong in terms of revelations, revolutionaries according to the tenets of their political ideologies. The success of the few experiments he conducted is the sole criterion for the scientist to proclaim a theory. For the mathematician, everything comes back to the balancing of equations. The judge restricts all that he deals with to the vocabulary of the law, the linguist to the intricacies of grammar, the poet to the propriety of his metaphors, the musician to the arrangement of notes and the artist to the proportions of figures. As for the injustice and cruelty meted out to human beings, everything—from revelations to ideologies, from scientific theories to laws, grammar, metaphors or musical notes— silently condones or accepts them, provides them rationale and respectability.

Walking this path, I do not remember exactly when I arrived at Bharatendu's *Andher Nagari*. This work, described as a light farce, moved me deeply. Every commodity—wheat flour, rice, dal, firewood, salt, ghee, sugar—is sold in the 'fair' markets of the city of Andher Nagari at a rupee a seer. When a man brings the complaint to Choupat Raja, the king of the city, that Kallu's wall collapsed and killed his goat, Choupat Raja first sentences the wall to death. When the minister points out that there is a flaw in this judgement, the king sentences Kallu, who owns the wall, to death, then the mason who built the wall, the chunewala who mixed the mortar for it, the bhishti who poured out water for mixing the mortar, the kasai who sold the goat-skin water bag to the bhishti, the shepherd who sold the kasai a big goat, and finally, the town kotwal who, while patrolling the town, diverted the shepherd's attention, causing him to sell a big goat instead of a small one. However, the noose did not fit the kotwal's neck, so Govardhan, a passer-by, was finally led to the gallows because his neck happened to fit the noose!

Bharatendu Harishchandra, who lived a hundred and fifty years before our time, stands apart from all the writers of his period by virtue of this work alone. As an artist, he must have known that realism was only one of the many ways of understanding reality, which is why he created such a frighteningly absurd situation to illustrate the cruelty and irrationality of all systems of justice. But why, after having shown that the farcical situation he had created was the actual face of reality, did he suddenly deviate and end his play by using a ruse to release Govardhan from the injustice that faced him? Although he lived only thirty-five years, this brilliant and widely-travelled writer who had learnt many languages and literatures, involved himself consciously in social and political activities and edited a journal, must certainly have come to realize that there is no escape, no freedom, for the Govardhans of this world.

I sat in my room for days together and talked to Bharatendu Harishchandra. Since our subject transcended time, the gap of a century and a half that lay between us did not intrude upon us. He was a much greater scholar than I and had written much more than I had ever done. But this did not stand between us either. After all, what we were discussing was beyond the realm of scholarship, something concerning the ordinary lives of ordinary people. One day, he at last accepted my pleas. In the solitude of the night, he got up and walked out through the frozen darkness to the stone-walled prison in Andher Nagari, the city ruled by Choupat Raja, Resident Sahib and Jailer Sahib. Once there, he flung the gates open. Govardhan, who was squatting on the stone-paved floor of his cell, got up and stumbled out on unsteady feet. He was not free. The noose, far more terrible than prison walls, still hung above his neck. While time stood still, hosts of people from mythology, history, literature and society came from either side of the road and joined him.

And thus began Govardhan's travels.

1

Govardhan did not recognize the man who emerged from the darkness outside and walked down the torch-lit corridor. There had been no one like this man among the sepoys or darogas he had seen the last two days. With his long, flowing hair and bright eyes he had a saintly grace that transcended the charm of youth. One by one, the sentries stood up as he approached. When he reached Govardhan's cell, the guard bent down, slid back the bolts and threw the door wide open.

Govardhan had stopped weeping because his eyes had gone dry. He had persuaded himself to accept the death sentence—a royal command completely devoid of logic that no one in their right senses could possibly accept—as the dispensation of fate. He would go to the gallows the next morning sure of not having committed any offence, his innocence attested by everyone. Since a goat passing that way had been trapped under the debris and killed when Kallu's wall collapsed, someone had to be hanged—this was what the sentries who felt kindly towards him had told him on the way here, in an attempt to console him.

Govardhan got up from the cold stone floor. Except for a square of light that moved with every flicker of the torch, the cell was so dark that even the walls were not visible. Hunger gnawed at Govardhan's skeletal frame. Later, fear overcame hunger. He felt as if he was deep in the jaws of darkness. He could not see a thing. And he had nothing to do except what the sentries told him to do. They were telling him to come out now.

When he came out and stood in front of the visitor, Govardhan's eyes turned involuntarily to the man's feet. The man did not say anything. He lifted his right hand and indicated the way out of the prison.

Govardhan failed to understand what the gesture implied and wondered whether he was being taken to the gallows. What difference did it make? And what could he do, anyway? However, when he stepped out into the bitter cold of the night, winding his shawl close around his neck, no one followed him— neither the sentries nor the saint-like man.

He was alone, he and the darkness.

2

Bharatendu Harishchandra walked restlessly around the study on the first floor of his sprawling bungalow, raising a hand now and then to smooth down his long hair, his eyes agonized. Although he was still in his thirties, the man looked about seventy.

It is certainly an unusual experience for a writer to set one of his characters free. However, Bharatendu's problem reached out beyond the limits of literature. For he had not freed his character from the prison he had incarcerated him in but from the tip of his pen. Govardhan was still a convict and the death sentence hung over him. No matter what he did with his newly-acquired freedom, this would remain unchanged. If his condition were to alter, if he were to return to the street from which he had come, Bharatendu would have to continue writing his play. But he had not done this. Instead, he had severed his ties with Govardhan!

Why had he set out in the middle of the night? Everything had looked different the day before. He had been writing a farce on the absurdities of justice practised by Choupat Raja in Andher Nagari and had been enjoying it hugely. His pen had been preparing to summon the mahant to devise a ruse that would save poor Govardhan from the gallows and hang the raja instead. It was then that he had suddenly gotten stuck at the dialogue of a sentry. It would be gross injustice if no one was hanged for the crime of killing the goat that had fallen under the debris, the sentry had said.

All day Bharatendu had wrestled with the knot of that sentence. As he walked through the garden of freshly-bloomed flowers, the mellow sunlight of the month of Magha felt as unendurable as the fierce heat of summer. Except for Bharatendu himself, and a few chieftains who spent their time between gardens and dancing girls, were not all the ordinary people of the country in some way Govardhans awaiting punishment for crimes they had not committed? People who wandered around carrying on their heads the weight of the sentence that each of them had been condemned to, people who had lost their hopes, their way, destined to end their lives one day with a noose around their necks? Bharatendu gasped for breath as if the rope was tightening around his own neck. The entertaining play he had been writing was changing shape on the manuscript he had before him and turning into a frightening tragedy. No, although it would be justice to make the mahant play a trick and free this man, it would not reflect reality. What was the duty of a writer—to make sure that justice prevailed, or to depict reality? Was it not injustice to forsake reality?

Bharatendu does not know even now what answer he arrived at. But he did do one thing—wading through the darkness and cold of that midnight hour, he somehow reached the door of the prison-house, opened it and let Govardhan out.

It was only later, as he paced in his study that he understood what he had done. Where had he led Govardhan in the course of the play? What was awaiting the man now, outside the stage? What was the point of asking these questions? The play, Govardhan and all the other characters had gone so far away from him! So distant that neither his pen nor his imagination could reach out to them anymore. Their fate was no longer in his hands. Nor were any of them familiar to him any longer.

A frightening emptiness surrounded him. He went up to the window, gripped the cold iron bars and looked out into the darkness.

No light burned in any of the rooms except his. A deep and heavy sleep blanketed everything: human beings, animals, trees. Only the law remained awake, the law which punishes the innocent. The cold and the dark did not touch it. Or rather, was not the law itself the cold and the darkness?

3

By the side of the bed on which the raja reclined was an intricately carved sandalwood table that held a bottle of liquor and a glass filled to the brim. The raja had hardly sipped more than a drop. All kings did not drown themselves in liquor as historians and poets seemed to think, particularly not this king. An attractive serving maid stood next to the wall, awaiting his orders. Guards stood at the door and the jester was seated silently on a carpet before him, cross-legged. It seemed as if all these arrangements had been made merely to satisfy occidental historians who chronicle the lives of oriental despots. Anyway, that is what the resident, Henry Williams, who was seated in a high-backed chair, respectfully facing the raja, thought.

The raja pressed his elbow into a round, embroidered cushion, straightened his back and asked: 'What brings you here at this hour of the night?' He added, 'What does it matter, anyway? If you ask, the king has to grant you audience, after all.'

'That's not it, huzur,' said the resident, embarrassed, 'I am a representative of a trading company. And you are the king of…' He stopped, aware of the raja's stern look.

'You came to tell me that the judgement I delivered yesterday was against the law, isn't that so? So you have one more point to support the accusation that my country is not being governed properly. How many points have you listed now? According to your system of law, how many points do you require for the directors of the Company to take over my country?'

The resident sat up straight in the chair. 'Huzur, we can discuss the case if you have no objection.'

'All right, let's do that.'

'Your Highness will have no doubt that the man who is going to the gallows tomorrow is completely innocent of the charges in this case.'

The raja laughed gently.

The indifference of the laugh shocked the resident. Neither his education and training nor his personal sense of justice could help him accept it.

'That man—what's his name? Ah yes, Govardhan. Why are you so concerned with his innocence, resident sahib?'

The raja picked up a flower from a basket on his bed, smelled it and spoke as if he was talking to it: 'As if my kotwal is the guilty one! As if there's nothing wrong in hanging that poor fellow! I know that all of them—the kotwal, the shepherd, the kasai, the bhishti, the chunewala, the mason, Kallu—they're all innocent. But that's not the issue. Though all of them are innocent, the law is right. The law you people taught us. Just as the goddess of justice is blindfolded, the administration of justice has to be impartial; it cannot change according to the victim. The problem that arose when my kotwal was led to the gallows was that the noose would not fit his neck. The executioner suggested that the noose be made larger. But I said the machinery of the law must be impartial. It should not be altered to suit the size of the victim's neck. If we begin to change things according to people's forms and natures, where will we end up, resident sahib?'

The resident stared at the raja, unmoving and expressionless. The raja allowed the flower to drop from his hand, then turned to the resident and said:

'Tell me, will you be able to go back now and cite this case in your records as an example of my misgovernment?'

The resident stood up. 'Huzur,' he said, his voice low and full of emotion. 'Must the innocent suffer in this way in a dispute between you and the Company? Your innocent subjects?'

'Is it customary in politics to discriminate between the innocent and the guilty? If you traders poison me tomorrow and begin to rule the country, just as you killed my brother yesterday to instate me in his place...'

'Huzur!' The resident's eyes darted around, terrified. 'Your servants, your officials...'

Unperturbed, the raja clapped his hands and addressed his servants and officials: 'You've all heard what I said? You can go now.'

Saying no more, the resident took three steps backward, bowed low and walked out.

The raja picked up the glass of liquor and sat staring at it.

4

David Butler, the jailer, was seated alone on the veranda in front of his bungalow with a book he had taken out to read but could not concentrate on. It was about the wild animals of India. Now that he had assumed his new responsibilities as a jailer, hunting—his favourite pastime—had become limited to being read about.

The constable at the gate seemed to be arguing with someone. The voices quietened after a while. Butler got up and went to the gate to find out what had happened.

'It was a man who kept saying something about justice.'

'What did you do?'

'I drove him away saying this was the jailer sahib's house, not the court.'

'Good!'

Butler went back to the veranda. The jail was not very far away. From where he was seated, he could see it in the glow of the lights in the compound, a black granite building. He sat staring at it, his mind heavy.

When he had been transferred from the police department of the Presidency, ruled directly by the Company, to this princely state to take charge of its jails, Butler had thought that life here would be quiet and pleasant. So far, his work had mainly involved hunting down thugs and, in his spare time, wild animals. He had decided he would hunt here purely for pleasure.

Making up his mind, Butler called the khansama and asked him to tell memsahib, who was supervising the smoking of the rooms to drive out the mosquitoes, that he was going out. He went to the stable, untied a horse, stroked it for a while, then mounted it and galloped to the resident's bungalow.

'This is like jumping from the frying pan into the fire!' he blurted out, venting his anger on the resident. 'In the Presidency jails, we had prisoners who languished for years waiting for trial and who finally died in their cells. We knew they were innocent victims lodged there by informers who wanted to settle a personal score with them. But we still operated within the law. But here we have a man who will be hanged tomorrow merely because his neck is slender enough to fit the noose. And it is I who must issue the order to pull the rope!'

'Sit down, David,' Resident Williams said, pointing to the glass of whisky the khansama had brought. 'Cool yourself down a little.'

Although he sat down and drank the whisky, the jailer's anger did not abate. His short, stocky body heaved up and down in the chair keeping time with his breathing.

Henry, who was himself exhausted, essayed a smile and asked, in an ineffectual attempt to reason out things: 'David, how long has it been since you came here?'

David looked at him and said as if he could not have cared less: 'Long enough to realize it is time the Company took over the administration of this state.'

Henry shook his head and leaned back in his chair. 'You know, don't you, that everything in this state bears the same price tag? Rice, bran, silver, straw... Our people say that a state that does not understand the value of things is doomed. But the Raja has an answer to that. He says that if gold and rice cost the same, people's desire for gold will be curbed, and everyone will buy only what they need. And needs have limits as desires do not. He thinks people should demand justice according to their needs. He calls this one-rupee-a-seer market a market of justice. Don't you see this monarch is not the fool we imagine him to be?'

'We have never rationed justice in our country.'

'I've heard you're very good at hunting,' said Henry. 'What law do you follow when you hunt animals? You are right—we have one law in our country, and another in this country. Have you ever seen the Company's account books? Revenue receipts on one page and expenses on another. That's the beauty of our bookkeeping. Do you know David, the Company took two hundred thousand pounds as a bribe to have the older brother of Choupat Raja, for whom you and I work, killed and to place him, the younger brother, on the throne? Naturally, you now have to hang anyone he sentences to death. We used to laugh at him once, now *he* laughs at us!'

'I do not know who laughs at whom, sir. But I do know who weeps...'

'Tomorrow, when this man's neck breaks, you too can shed a tear or two with him. But it is certain that you will give the executioner the order to pull the rope!'

David gulped down three drinks in quick succession, put on his hat and made ready to leave.

The khansama arrived at that moment and said that a constable had come from the jail with a message. The constable followed him in. It took him a couple of seconds to regulate his breathing.

'Sahib, the prisoner is missing. The cell is still locked, but there's no one inside.'

Henry and David looked at each other.

'The walls are intact and no tunnel has been dug,' continued the constable.

'All right. You can go,' Henry dismissed him.

'This is real trouble.' David got up from his chair. Henry smiled. 'Don't you mean the trouble is over?'

'No, sir. This is just a beginning, a big beginning.'

Henry signed to him to sit down.

'I can't sit down, sir,' said David. 'Although I am only a jailer, I had an explanation to offer if I did not pull the rope: that this man is not guilty in the eyes of the law. But now, he is guilty, according to the law. It is my duty to hunt him down. My problem has just started, sir.'

Henry watched David salute, march out, get on his horse and ride away. When he was completely out of sight, Henry asked the khansama to bring him another whisky. He drank it silently. Then he put on his coat, untied his horse without a word to anyone, sprang onto it and rode into the darkness.

5

There was another person who was not destined to sleep that night. Ramchander—mathematician, social worker and Urdu journalist. He was working on his thesis late into the night by the light of an oil lamp.

As Ramchander leaned back in his chair to rest for a while, he suddenly wondered when he had chanced upon his subject. At the time when Westerners were pushing mathematics into the realm of geometry, the Hindus had continued to dabble in algebra. The Greeks could conceive only what was concrete, whereas the Hindus had managed to assimilate abstractions and hypotheses into a science like mathematics, whose function was to factually analyse the distinction between correct formulations and erroneous ones. They had made zero and infinity operational numbers. One day, while lecturing to his students, it occurred to Ramchander that Western imperialism could be combated spiritually by reviving the algebra-oriented attitudes of the Hindu mind. Accordingly, instead of going along the path of calculus familiar to Western mathematicians, he tried to solve mathematical problems with the help of algebra.

All this was fine, but, in the matter of political and social issues, had he arrived anywhere in his thesis? Ramchander felt that his efforts were plunging him deeper and deeper into the aesthetics of mathematics itself. And solely into mathematics— whether it was algebra or geometry, everything ended in mathematics.

Suddenly, a thin, hunched figure burst in on him. He moved like a sleepwalker, his eyes like those of a hunted animal. As if he had no control over himself, he came and squatted on the floor in front of Ramchander's table. Adjusting his blanket so that his hands and legs were covered, he glanced around quickly and began to speak to Ramchander: 'Babu, when I looked through the window, I saw you reading a book. I realized you must be an educated man. I cannot write or read at all and am completely ignorant. Tell me, what work does a hangman do? Does he fit a noose around the neck of a sentenced man or does he go in search of a man whose neck will fit the noose he has prepared?'

Ramchander felt the man was in a hurry. But he could not quite follow what he was saying. He asked, 'Who are you? And what is your problem?'

'It is just as I thought—you educated men can never understand a direct question. You always ask for explanations.' The stranger's displeasure was clear. 'In any case, how would you know the difference between one human being and another? You just echo what the sepoys and darogas here say: that there is only one principle in arithmetic, that two and two make four. In the bazaars in this place, rice, bran, silver and straw are all sold at the same price, a rupee a seer. The judge said to me yesterday that the gallows here has only one noose and that it is too small to fit large necks!'

Ramchander was alarmed: was this man trying to force his own problem into the realm of mathematics? It was all very strange. However, Ramchander was troubled—the man seemed to be grieving deeply.

'Tell me, who is going to be hanged?' asked Ramchander gently.

'Who? This Govardhan,' said the man placing a hand on his chest, 'who is nothing, no one—whom could they get hold of to hang but this Govardhan with a scrawny neck? Kallu's wall collapsed and killed a goat. The raja found the kotwal guilty. But his neck was too thick to fit into the noose.'

Ramchander abandoned his papers, got up from his chair and went up to Govardhan.

Govardhan had got up by then and was straightening his blanket.

'Wait, Govardhan,' said Ramchander. 'If this is your problem, we might be able to do something about it. We have an association that consists of writers, journalists, teachers and so on. We call it Kayastha Sabha as a joke. Tell me which court pronounced this verdict.'

'Forget it, babu. I didn't ask you to save me. And you won't be able to, anyway.'

Govardhan began to walk away. He turned at the door and looked at Ramchander.

'All I asked you was whether all that is happening here is just or unjust, right or wrong, according to your science. That is all.'

He went down the steps and melted into the night without waiting for a reply.

Ramchander was stunned—he felt as if someone had intruded upon his solitude, slapped him and walked out. Would he have been able to save Govardhan? But Govardhan had not asked to be saved. From the moment he had walked in, he had had only one question: was the fate hanging over his head just or unjust? Ramchander should have given him a direct answer, the way a teacher, who evaluates the problems his students work out, does. He realized sadly that he had not done this, that he had unnecessarily thrown one futile question after another at him instead.

Guilt assailed Ramchander. Govardhan had come in the dead of night and left him and all scientists—who felt that issues of justice and injustice were not their subject—a burden to shoulder. Govardhan's neck would probably be broken when this night ended and his questions silenced. But Ramchander's night would continue and he was not sure of its dawn...

Parvati appeared at the door.

'Who was that, clamouring here at this midnight hour?' she asked, her eyes heavy with sleep. 'Or were you talking to yourself about some new problem you have?'

'There's been a mistake in my calculations, Parvati, a serious mistake.'

'Was it a problem you had to solve in steps? Then you might have missed a step!' Parvati tried to help him as much as her learning would let her.

Generally, her inconsequential chatter infuriated him, this girl that his parents had entrusted to him when she was just a little child. The years had only distanced her from him. But today, somehow, he was not angry.

He placed his hand on her shoulder and said gently: 'The steps we work out in arithmetic are not the same we take when we walk, Parvati. In arithmetic, the steps must bring us back to the question we started from together with, of course, the answer. I feel, after I heard what the man who forced himself into this room said, that the answers I found to my problems are taking me somewhere different. Like the steps we take when we walk, they are leading me farther and farther away from the point at which I started…'

6

It was long past midnight when, groping his way through the darkness, the mahant arrived at the high gates of Bharatendu Harishchandra's palatial kothi. For a minute he stood at the iron bars, barely visible in the soft starlight, gasping, trying to recover his breath. But only for a minute. He soon pushed the gate open, walked through the vast garden, trampling over the flowering plants, passed through the kothi's many doors one by one and unhesitatingly made his way to Bharatendu's room, like a familiar visitor. Recognizing him, the guards did not attempt to stop or question him either.

His eyes red from the lack of sleep, his hair wild and dishevelled, Bharatendu got up from his chair to greet him. 'Why have you come here now, guruji?' he asked in a tired voice.

The mahant's eyes widened in astonishment.

'All day yesterday, he wept, calling out to me to help him,' he said. 'Had I not promised to go to him if he was in trouble? Where is my Govardhan?'

Bharatendu noticed the sweat dripping from the mahant's matted hair even in that terrible cold. Yes, he was right. In the third act of the play, the mahant had promised he would go and rescue Govardhan if he was in trouble.

Bharatendu shook his head. 'Guruji,' he said. 'Go back, you cannot save Govardhan now. Go back.'

'What has happened to Govardhan?'

'He's beyond our reach now. Not only that, you and I know that Govardhan cannot escape his punishment. That which cannot happen, we cannot make it happen. You and I cannot deceive ourselves, guruji. Please go back.'

'But it is my dharma to save him, to see that justice is done.'

'Guruji, I set Govardhan free from my pen. Just as he has been freed from the ink in my pen, he has also been freed from the lines and columns of space and time that we use to construct our stories. He is now the Govardhan of all places, of all time. He will go on weeping, asking you for help, that is certain. And your dharma will twist and turn in agony, wanting to save him. But you will never meet each other…'

Mahant stood with his eyes lowered, as if trying to reconcile himself to what Bharatendu had said. Both froze in their stances. The mahant's shoulders sagged and he turned and began to walk away slowly.

A wet circle of the sweat that had trickled down the mahant's body had formed at the spot where he had been standing. Bharatendu stared at it as if waiting for it to evaporate.

The mahant went out the way he had come, passing through the many doors and trampling over the flowering plants. When he came to the road, the eastern sky had begun to glow a silver-grey.

·Govardhan's figure drifted before him like a log caught in a flood; sometimes clear above the water, sometimes awash in it. The mahant wondered—what link did he have with the world? There was a metaphor for it in the manuscripts on dharma: a drop of water on a lotus leaf. Both evident in themselves and touching each other, but connected only by a tenuous bond. What lay before him was the dharma he was ordained to carry out. And as for him, he did not have the capacity to carry it out. What metaphor would illustrate that situation?

7

Covering himself closely with the blanket that came up to his neck, Govardhan walked over the rough, uneven road. Darkness enveloped it like the waters of a flood, drowning all sense of north, south, east or west. He had not chosen the road: he had seen it in front of him when he came out of jail. He had had no choice of any kind before him.

He had found no answer at either of the two places he had knocked at. He had been driven away from the gate of the first. The second, he thought, had been a waste of time. And guruji, whom he had called for all night, had forgotten his promise and not come. Justice, knowledge, dharma: they had all abandoned him with equal callousness. There was only the road, rough and dark, before him to ask for help.

In the pale light of the morning, he saw a small group of people coming towards him. As they came closer, he detected the words 'Ram nam satya hai' from the hum of their voices. They turned into an open field on the side of the road just before they reached him. Govardhan realized that they were not carrying a pall although they were chanting the chant of pall-bearers. It was as if the dead body they had been carrying had fallen down somewhere on the way, but they continued oblivious to the fact. As they melted into the shrubs and their chanting grew faint, Govardhan went on.

The east grew brighter and the hills and trees in the distance took clearer shape. Govardhan discovered that there was no road beneath his feet, that, at some point, it had disappeared into the desert like a river just as the dead body had slipped from the pall-bearers' shoulders.

He thought he could see Salma and Mannu climbing up the slope of the hill. He realized with a sense of guilt that they had not been in his mind at all the last two days. Mother and daughter seemed to be returning with pots of water from a river he could not see. Salma had pots balanced on her head and waist. Little Mannu had one on her head. Govardhan had come to the city with them just a few days ago, after spending days on the road and in wayside sarais until the head of a muth had allowed them to put up a hut on their land.

How long would he have to journey to get to them? He was surrounded on all sides by a wilderness filled with rocks and shrubs. The morning light, growing steadily brighter, increasingly accentuated his helplessness.

8

The roar of hoof beats came to a sudden stop behind him. The man seated on the horse that had come right up to Govardhan was resident sahib.

The resident did not dismount and was evidently in a hurry. He bellowed: 'Govardhan, the moment I knew you had disappeared from your cell, and that its locks and walls were still intact, I knew that you had been freed only from the play. The noose still hangs over your wretched head. Besides, there are hunters on your heels. Run! Hide somewhere if you want to stay alive.'

The resident turned his horse and sped away without even waiting to make sure Govardhan had heard him.

Govardhan stood where he was and looked all around. Barren land lay everywhere with not a single path in sight. He could not even tell which direction he had come from. Who could tell where his safety lay in a place like this that had no front or back, left or right, past or future? Was he himself aware of what the resident had come and told him as a matter of duty?

Govardhan had always known that what he had achieved was not deliverance from his fate but an extension in the distance towards it. One more extension.

The rise and fall of the hoof beats of the resident sahib's horse recreated like magic for Govardhan a scene from the past associated with this very place. He recognized the gravel-covered area, the barren piece of land that did not have a front or back, left or right, past or future. Yes, he was sure he had been associated with this place.

It was here that he had encountered once, long ago, a similar paradox of freedom, freedom from slavery. And the malik who had freed him had said the same thing to him: 'I am freeing you from my ownership. It was my duty to protect you when I was your master. But now I am no longer your master. Try to find ways to protect yourself!'

It was here that, in the course of the years, the centuries that had engulfed their strange lives, Govardhan had been separated from his brother for the second time. Govardhan and his brother, Ali Dost, had sat open-mouthed in front of their malik. Understanding nothing the malik said. Later, when they understood the implications of what the malik had said they parted not only from him but from each other as well.

Govardhan looked down: at the stones, the earth, the stunted shrubs, the tufts of brown grass. And the little insects threading their way through them. It was those little insects that had explained to the brothers what the malik had meant by freedom. And it was this knowledge that had encouraged them to part from each other.

Each of them had something at that time to help them choose their paths—the other one. You go this way and I will go in the opposite direction! And today, Govardhan was alone with only the light for company, the light that flowed in filling all the directions, that exposed him to the whole world.

9

'The mission is over,' murmured Ibn Battuta to himself, seated on a rock jutting out of the deserted land over which nothing seemed to be moving.

The two slaves, Govardhan and Ali Dost, squatting in front of him, heard what he said and looked at each other, understanding nothing. Then both looked at the malik.

Ibn Battuta saw them and grinned. The slaves were baffled by his laughter. They got up and bowed.

Ibn Battuta mulled over all that had happened. He had started the journey with a thousand horsemen and three thousand foot soldiers. He had been going to the emperor of China as the messenger of Mohammed Tughluq, the sultan of Delhi. He had had with him, as presents from the sultan, a hundred carefully chosen horses, a hundred white slaves, a hundred beautiful Hindu dancing girls, fifteen eunuchs, gold, swords, pearls and corals. These two slaves were all that were left of them. The sultan's enemies, robbers, hunger or disease had looted or destroyed everything else. The night before, there had been four slaves.

Two had died in the course of the night.

'Fools,' he said, 'I am setting you free! You can go wherever you like.'

'Aka!' cried Ali Dost and Govardhan, not comprehending what he said.

'Yes, you fools. The mission the sultan sent me on is over. You were part of the gifts I was taking to the emperor of China. You are of no use to me now!'

'Aka!' cried Ali Dost and Govardhan again.

Ibn Battuta got up. He gave the rock on which he had been seated a kick with his boots, then stamped on the ground below, on the shrubs and the grass. The little insects that lived between them emerged and scattered here and there, confused, not knowing where to go.

Squinting his eyes against the glare of the sun and staring into the distance, Ibn Battuta called the slaves by name for the first time and said: 'Ali, Govardhan, I am giving up my position and the honours I held and going back to my old job. I do not know where you will go from here. Maybe all I am doing is setting you free from myself. I am doing this because you have become a burden on me now. In a way, each of us is now a burden on others. On one side we have the armies and robbers of the local kings attacking us; on the other, the wrath of the sultan. If each of us is alone, we can merge into the crowd. If we are together, everyone will recognize us and finish us off.'

'But what can we do, aka? Where can we go?'

Ali and Govardhan had never been anywhere on their own. They had never done anything because they wanted to. It is only when their malik tells them that slaves even eat or drink.

'How will we find food to eat?' asked Ali helplessly.

Hunger and thirst were gnawing at all three of them.

Ibn Battuta said: 'Friends, that is not your problem alone, it is mine as well. In a sense, that is what freedom is—having no one to provide you with food and shelter. I was a free traveller until I came to Hindustan. One who had no kitchen or well or farmland of his own...'

Ibn Battuta was lost for a while in pleasant and unpleasant memories.

Govardhan mustered the courage to ask: 'What does "traveller" mean, aka?'

'Leave that alone,' said Ibn Battuta, coming back to the present. 'Search for food and water now, like me. And learn to protect yourselves. Let us agree that none of us will offer the others food or try to protect them. Each one for himself! It's the only way to survive.'

Clutching the shrubs for support, Ibn Battuta climbed down the rock on which they stood. There was a well below. When he came to it, he uprooted a creeper, took off the tunic he wore and tied it to the tip of it. The slaves covered their faces with their hands when they saw their malik naked. Through their fingers, they watched the malik lower the creeper into the well, wet the cloth in the water and draw it out. He wrung the wet cloth into his mouth and drank the water. Then he wrapped the cloth around him again and walked away.

When he had gone, Govardhan and Ali Dost climbed down holding on to the shrubs like the malik had done.

10

Ali and Govardhan wet their clothes in the well, wrung them out, drank the water, spread their clothes to dry and huddled side by side, naked, like little children.

After a while, Govardhan turned, touched Ali's shoulder, drew closer to him and called out: 'Brother!'

Since the days when they had played together as little children, and over this long period they had spent as slaves, it was the first time Govardhan had addressed Ali this way. It was not that they had not remembered they were brothers. Slavery had effaced many bonds.

'Brother,' said Govardhan again. 'First we lost our parents. And now our malik.'

Govardhan pressed his face into Ali's back. Ali's eyes filled with tears. He embraced his brother.

Long, long ago... the first time they had been separated...

Two children trudging through the passes in the Hindukush ranges. Two brothers. There were many children and all around them rode soldiers wielding long whips. White snow covered the passes and an icy wind that pierced the bone blew over them. Was it day or night? Where were they being taken? Hunger, pain and exhaustion made such questions meaningless.

It was the army of a sultan from Central Asia on its way back after conquering and looting Hindustan, an army that had collected, besides vast quantities of gold and gems, a great number of children to be sold as slaves in their country. Every now and then, a child would drop dead. The soldiers would move on, kicking the dead child away and driving the living children on.

Too tired to walk, the younger brother clung to the older one's shoulder. The older one tried to heave him onto his back, but could not. Slipping further and further down, Govardhan gripped his older brother's fingers. Losing his grip on one finger after another, he finally caught the last one after the little finger, Ali Dost's sixth finger.

The children had already forgotten the parents who had bestowed brotherhood upon them. The sultans of Central Asia had, with each invasion they made, caught and driven hundreds of slaves before them and called these mountains the 'Hindukush', meaning 'the slayer of Hindus' because they had killed half their booty while crossing them. Not only had these mountain ranges killed many slaves, they had even erased all memory of their past from those who survived.

'We lost our father and mother, younger brother,' said the older one, 'and now we are losing our bond of brotherhood as well. We will soon be slaves, nothing but slaves.'

The younger one's grip on his older brother's sixth finger loosened and he fell down. The older one moved on, unable to stop or to listen to his moans...

Now they were no longer slaves and the master who had

held them together had vanished. Like a child, Govardhan fondled Ali's fingers one by one. The first five, then the sixth. It was to this one that he used to cling and walk as a child. And it was from this one that he had finally been separated.

'Fate separated us,' said Govardhan. 'And fate reunited us again.'

'No Govardhan,' Ali corrected him. 'Fate only gave me another name. A new name—Ali Dost. Slavery united us, freedom now separates us.'

Govardhan stared at Ali, bewildered.

'You remember what the malik told us?' continued Ali, looking at Govardhan's fingers fondling his own. 'He gave us liberty. But that does not mean we are going to get our parents back, or our past. Nor will it make us brothers again. We are going to be something else to each other, Govardhan.'

'And what is that?'

'I don't know. Anyway, we are going to find out, each by himself. You remember what the malik said. Our ways will be different.'

Ali slowly withdrew his fingers from Govardhan's. For the second time. Their eyes moved from their fingers to their bodies. To their nakedness. They were ashamed.

Ali said, 'Our clothes must have dried. Come, Govardhan, let's put them on. It's time to go.'

They got up and put on their clothes. Reading the suggestion in Ali's eyes, Govardhan began to move forward. Ali waited until Govardhan took a few steps, then walked in the opposite direction…

11

Ali Dost's wife, Salma, and his daughter Mannu waited two whole months for him to return from the battlefield. No one ever waited that long for sepoys who had gone to war. If they were defeated, they were either put to death or forced to join the enemy army. If they won, they went off to plunder the enemy cities. Sometimes they came back with the loot but most times they stayed where they were. This time, the fact that Timur's army appeared at the gates of the city the very next day made it clear that the army had been defeated.

These two months were for Salma and Mannu, as much as for the other inhabitants of the city, a period of terrible suffering. As Timur moved, his army traced patterns on the ground with dead bodies. It was with the corpses of those who had attempted to flee that he built the first wall around the city. When Timur left after two weeks, not many living beings—human or animal—were left behind. He had plundered everything he could in the name of wealth or honour and made sure that smoke no longer rose from any hearth.

Once the army withdrew and silence spread in the wake of the massacre and famine, the pestilence that had been waiting outside the city took over. At the end of two months, Salma and little Mannu, surprised to find themselves still alive, set out in search of another city.

The survivors of every war, famine and plague go out in search of new pastures, wasting no time waiting for those who have disappeared or weeping over those who have died. Journeying over the banks of rivers that have gone dry, over fields that have been abandoned and temple courtyards strewn with the bones of the dead, they stop when they can no longer walk any further and build a hearth at whatever spot they have reached.

Transformed into a soldier of sorts, Ali Dost too was looking for a new abode in the wasteland of his freedom. He did not consider any army alien to him nor look at any king with anything except respect. He was ready to fight any battle. He made a home in whichever city he went to. Sometimes he would take a woman and establish a family. Sometimes he would just plant his seed in an unknown womb. When the next battle was announced, he would abandon everything and go.

When Sultan Mahmud, defeated by Timur, fled to Gujarat, Ali Dost went with him. It was a sultan of Gujarat who first discovered the induration of this soldier's heart. All soldiers on the battlefield kill to save their own lives. But to kill or maim a man who has done them no harm, who can do nothing to them because he is himself in chains—not all soldiers can do that. Therefore, kings did not send soldiers with such skills to the battlefield, they retained them as their palace guards. This was how Ali Dost found his way from the battlefield into the palace.

Ali Dost's duties began after the war was over. He was trained to behead people, chop off their limbs, castrate them with boulders, impale them on stakes, tie them up to pillars and set fire to them. While performing these tasks, he never asked his victims who they were, what crime they had committed or even whether they had committed a crime at all. Like civilians who flee from one dwelling place to another, he neither rejoiced in nor grieved over his new mission. He accepted everything as it came, unquestioningly.

12

Govardhan too had to discover the nature of his freedom in the waste of a city from which no sound emerged, where nothing that had life remained, from whose hearths no smoke arose. With this difference, that this punishment had been meted out to the population not by an enemy army but by the ruling sultan himself.

It was a punishment that no monarch before him had ever tried out on his people: to order the entire population of a city to move with all their belongings to another city a thousand miles away, leaving no family, no individual, no sick or disabled people behind.

The sultan had reason for being so cruel, for inflicting this ordeal on his people. It was not the kings of other countries he saw as his greatest enemies but his own people. Hundreds of them who had broken his laws were brought before him every day, fettered and chained by his qazis. He would order that they be beheaded, dismembered, flogged or tortured. Yet there was no decline in the number of people brought before him every day. And that was how the sultan decided to punish a populace that had no faith in him in a way they would never forget.

Govardhan was one of the crowd that swelled steadily as more and more people came out of their houses, their belongings stuffed into bundles they carried on their heads. Horsemen were breaking into the houses and chasing people out with whips. Cats and dogs ran out, terrified. The cries of human beings mingled with those of animals.

'Victorious sultans used to punish us for the crime of having lived under defeated sultans. But why should our own sultan do this to us?' Govardhan asked the men walking with him. No one replied.

After a while, he wiped the sweat off his forehead and murmured again, this time half to himself: 'Why is the sultan punishing us at all? None of us have defied any of his orders.'

No one answered that either. Which sultan was punishing them or why: this question had ceased to be a problem for them.

All right then, if that was how it was. Perhaps free people, like slaves, had no voices, thought Govardhan.

After a while, he heard a little child speak. In a soft voice, as if chanting a mantra. A little girl with dusty, matted hair and a sunburnt face, seated on her mother's hip, was pointing at a horseman twirling a whip and whispering: 'Abba, abba...'

The horseman came right up to them, his whip in the air. Govardhan suddenly turned and covered his face with the end of his turban so that the man would not see him. Galloping through the crowd, the man vanished as he had come.

Govardhan moved close to the child, touched her cheek which was rough with dust and asked, 'Was that your abba, child?'

Frightened, the child did not answer. It was her mother who replied: 'Yes, it's her father. My husband.'

'And my elder brother!' added Govardhan.

They began walking together through the crowd. Govardhan offered to carry the child after a while. She did not object. Gradually, the city from which all life had been drained got left behind. As they moved on, the sultan's horsemen began to disappear as well and they were at last on their own.

'Ali will never come back,' said Govardhan, 'to be your husband or this child's father or my elder brother. That's not his fault. It is the nature of the different paths we take.'

Like a swiftly-flowing river entering the plain, the crowds slackened speed slightly. But each person still clutched his or her belongings or relatives as if they feared they would fall apart if they didn't.

Govardhan, Salma and Mannu held on to one another too, forging the bonds of a new family.

13

Seated in audience, listening to complaints and issuing orders, the sultan of Java took a break to drink a cup of fruit juice. A slave with an unsheathed knife in his hand suddenly stood up at that moment. The sultan gave him permission to speak and provide entertainment during the interval. Gesticulating and bowing his head from time to time in a dramatic manner, the slave delivered a lengthy speech. Ibn Battuta did not understand what was being said at all. The courtiers seated next to him explained that the slave was expressing his respect and affection for the sultan in this speech and that such acknowledgements of gratitude were common in the intervals between the hearing of complaints. When the speech was over, the slave gripped the knife tightly in both his hands and slashed his own throat with lightning speed so perfectly that his head fell on the ground and rolled away. The sultan laughed. He turned to Ibn Battuta and said: 'These are my slaves. They kill themselves for the love of me!' He ordered that the body be carried away and burned and that a generous pension be given to the slave's wife and children.

This ghastly scene haunted Ibn Battuta until he left Java. Wherever he went, he saw ordinary people, soldiers, slaves and women lay down their lives for those whose property they believed themselves to be. When the emperor of China was laid to rest, not only courtiers and slave-girls but even horses were placed in the grave. In India, when he saw wives willingly enter their husband's pyres, he fainted and fell off his horse. Every time he boarded his ship, he sighed deeply, comforting himself with the thought that he was, after all, only a traveller.

This traveller had sometimes accepted high positions under the sultan of Delhi. He had fought for him, amassed great wealth, built mansions and a harem for himself. There were periods when he had renounced everything and become a mendicant. Then, because the sultan had wished it, he had gone as his envoy to the emperor of China. Now he was a fugitive, fleeing from the spears of the attackers and the wrath of the sultan.

He wandered through forests and over hills. One night, he hid in mustard fields, eating mustard shoots to dull his hunger and dozing in the company of snakes in the moonlight that blossomed from the yellow flowers. In the morning, he came upon a herd of cattle who led him to a village. The villagers not only refused to give him anything to eat, they even took away the clothes he was wearing. When he was thirsty, he had to use his shoes to draw water from a well.

He finally reached the shores of the great Arabian Sea, where rows of coconut palms stretched their heads out towards the water. He sat down on the white sand and brooded over the ludicrous game fate had played on him, transforming him from a traveller who had been free into a hunted animal.

Why had this scholar-poet, who had left home at the age of twenty-one to become a traveller, decided to play such bizarre roles? Anyway, which character really decides on his own role in a play? Lured onto the stage by the director's magic wand, each one of them has to dance to his whims or those of the prompters and accompanists in the wings. Every soldier in this great play, every slave and dancing girl, even every horse, has been enticed out of some hidden hole or corner of life onto the stage—including the traveller Ibn Battuta who was drawn from the desert of Morocco by the power of Muhammed Tughluq, the sultan who sat on the throne of Delhi. Suddenly, cruel realities materialize from nowhere, drive out the director, his prompters and accompanists, and take over the stage.

Those who attacked the sultan's entourage claimed that they were avenging the cruelties he had perpetrated, stories of which had reached even distant Morocco. However, punishment was inflicted, ironically, not on the director, but on the characters, who had already been punished much earlier. The audience must have applauded. But every lash of the whip fell on the naked backs of actors stripped of their costumes. Was not the freedom he so generously granted the two slaves left with him as much of a falsehood as this strange dispensation of justice? One of the two was now seated on a horse wielding his lance and whip on his own family. While the other one was running all over like a madman, knocking at every door in a vain attempt to save himself from the noose hanging over his head.

The sun rose over the straight line of the calm sea, beyond the turbulence of the heaving waves. It seemed to Ibn Battuta as if he could hear the sound of bells ringing and conches blowing from everywhere around him. An old man who had just had his bath in the sea and offered prayers to the sun appeared before him, making the dark thoughts in his mind seem irrelevant. He had long hair and the grey beard of an ascetic, but his eyes did not have the peace an ascetic should have had. Ibn Battuta, who resembled him not only in form and expression but also in attire, got up and stood respectfully before him.

'Who are you?' asked the ascetic gently.

'A traveller,' replied Ibn Battuta.

'What I see in your eyes is not the curiosity of a traveller but the fear of a hunted animal.'

'Mahantji, I do not see the peace of an ascetic in your eyes either.'

The mahant's restless eyes became even more anxious.

Ibn Battuta went on: 'You are right. Renunciation and detachment are what the laws of the world have ordained for us. And yet, what disturbs us is something entirely different. We meet at that point, although we have come from different poles.'

'Are you the traveller who freed Govardhan from the bondage of slavery?'

'What I have seen everywhere, mahantji, are slaves who cut off their own heads and offer them to their maliks, or those who follow their masters into their graves or pyres. I am afraid to call the condition of the people whom I freed freedom. Perhaps both of us are performers of futile deeds that bear no fruit.'

A wave rose towards them, drenched them to their knees and receded. The mahant waited until it went back, then said: 'You are a traveller. Do I have to tell you that the problem is the road, not the destination? My way is that of dharma and therefore I pursue it. My dharma is to oppose adharma and injustice.'

'Mahantji, I was just a character in a play who tried to free another character from the play. Like the human being who is subjected to injustice, you, who work for the establishment of dharma, are a character in a play as well. All your playwright has assigned you is the role of a character.'

A smile appeared in the mahant's eyes, dimming the restlessness. He laid his hand on Ibn Battuta's shoulder.

'Traveller,' he said, 'the countries you passed through may not have done you justice. But you cannot abandon travel. Have you ever thought of how you can free another character from a story while you yourself remain in it? Why do you see yourself as the one who carries the burden of the role? You are the traveller seated astride your dharma, riding it!'

Ibn Battuta held both the hands of the mahant in his own and kissed them.

By this time the sun had risen.

14

Ramchander was walking up and down the yard when Parvati brought milk and fruit for his breakfast and summoned him. He washed his hands and feet mechanically with water from a brass pot while Parvati waited. It was a day of fasting for her. She had finished her ablutions and puja in the morning.

'Do you know what I was thinking of, Parvati?' asked Ramchander although he had no faith in her capacity to take part in a discussion on his problems. 'I was wondering to what extent our actions are really our own, or how far they are subservient to the laws the universe has ordained for us. That is to say, are we the riders of horses or just the carriers of burdens...'

Parvati did not say anything, nor did Ramchander expect her to. He peeled a banana, ate it and went on as if all he wanted was to give expression to what was in his mind: 'If everything happens according to a predetermined pattern as the scriptures say, would it not mean that our actions cannot be judged—that there is no right or wrong, no sin or virtue?'

This time Parvati answered: 'It's not like that. Virtue, sin, heaven, hell, they all exist.'

Ramchander looked at her with admiration.

'How right you are!' he said. 'It's just as I thought. Our Puranas point to the rising and setting of the sun, the sequence of days, nights and seasons, as examples of the mechanical and cyclic nature of events. But Yama, the son of Surya, went beyond the mechanical nature of events and discovered that they had characteristics and attributes. He separated them into right and wrong ones. Are not the account books of the heaven and hell you spoke of, where every individual's actions are recorded, in the possession of his assistant, Chitragupta?'

At a loss for words, Parvati simply smiled.

Lost in the conversation, Ramchander forgot his breakfast. 'Like the scriptures, the physical sciences also say that the sun, the moon and all the planets move along paths dictated by certain fixed laws. But it is different with a human being. If he walks on a straight path along the rounded surface of the earth, he will come back to the spot from where he began, like the planets. But he is at liberty to take a path that is not straight. What do you say?'

Ramchander laughed to himself, shaking his head. A cat came up to him, mewing impatiently, and he poured out some milk for it on the floor.

'This means that although these rules and dictates exist, there is also right and wrong on the earth and the need to judge actions. Do you know, whenever our Kayastha Sabha meets, we discuss the same things: mistakes in grammar, deviations in metre, the breaking of customs and rituals, violation of laws, lapses of government—why even printers' devils in books! But what stays insistently in my mind is the wrong done to that man, Govardhan.'

The cat mewed asking for more milk and finally sprang up and overturned the glass. Ramchander looked on curiously.

'It was milk that had been offered to the goddess on this day of fasting!' exclaimed Parvati, annoyed. 'I know. All this started after that man barged into your room at midnight. You used to sit quietly in the same spot working out your mathematical problems. Now you speak as if you're delirious, walk up and down like one possessed… I think it was a ghost who came here!'

'No, Parvati, it was a man. Perhaps the one person who can answer all my problems. I even suspect that he might be the man who pulled our Chitragupta, the guru of the kayasthas, out of his house and left him on the roadside. The greatest thing human beings can achieve, Parvati, is to understand the pain of the wounded, the suffering of the helpless. Who but the wounded and the suffering themselves can describe that to us? That is why I say that the answers to our problems lie on the path that man took. Because his path is that of suffering.'

The cat was busy licking up the milk spilled on the floor. Parvati watched, uncertain what to do. Ramchander got up and went back to walk in the yard.

15

Even as little children, Chitragupta and Yama had come to realize that history was not simply a collection of days, seasons and years.

Dandi, who sat beside Surya in his chariot and calculated the passage of the months, the solstices and the years according to the movement of his master's chariot, was Chitragupta's father. One day the child Chitragupta, asked his father: 'What good are these records of the passage of the solstices, the years, the eras to us, father? What are we going to do with them?'

'This is history, child,' said Dandi, placing his hand on his son's head. 'These books record the passage of time without leaving out even a moment. However you measure it, there will not be a single mistake. Whether you add up the columns horizontally or vertically, the answers will always tally.'

'Father, mathematics is not merely addition and subtraction,' the son countered, mustering his courage. 'It is differentiating between right and wrong. Think of all the happenings in this world: deceptions, betrayals, frauds, cruelties...'

Dandi smiled. 'You do not know, son. There is no event in this world that is not recorded in my chronicles.'

Chitragupta shook his head. 'Events do not exist simply as events, father. They have characteristics and attributes.'

'Do you think Surya, who observes all events, does not note their characteristics as well? He witnesses everything, child.'

'Can justice be enforced only with witnesses, father? Do you not need plaintiffs, judges, officers, to execute the verdicts?'

That is how the child Chitragupta, the son of Dandi, decided to put an end to the long days he had spent with his father in argument and discussion and leave his house. As he went on his way, he met Yama, the son of Surya, who was the same age as he was. Yama had disagreed with his father as well, got down from his chariot and come to earth. Together, the two boys started a movement to find out the characteristics of events, to provide meaning and significance to history. They established a city called Samyamani as the headquarters of this movement.

'Looking back, Chitragupta, how dreadful the path we took was!' said Yama, the Dharmaraja, while walking one morning in the garden in front of Samyamani. 'The perpetrators of injustice laugh at us derisively. Those who wield power hate us. Even the well-meaning try to exercise control over us, discourage us from administering justice. We were forced to build a strong fort around this city to ward off attacks. Only I know how I escaped from the fire that the great Mahadeva himself prepared for me in one of his usual outbursts of anger.'

'Why look back, my lord?' said the more mature and mellow Chitragupta. 'Let us look ahead. Think about the many changes taking place in the world, about the spiritual and practical challenges these changes throw before us. On the one hand we have war, tyranny, oppression, revolution. On the other, the defective laws and ideologies that human beings have invented to deal with sins and virtues. Look at the case of this Govardhan. A king who is deliberately unjust and behind him, the Company. Trade, the thirst for power, treachery—the kayastha that I am, I search for the sinner amongst them and am soon lost in the wilderness! I am in despair, my friend, I do not know what to write against this case in my book!'

Yama walked up to the fence at the end of the garden and stopped. Beyond was a sloping valley. Human settlements were scattered right through this valley, far into the distance. In the bright light of the rising sun, each one stood out clearly.

'Chitragupta, you too kept going farther and farther back, searching for the sinner behind the sin. Look the other way, at the innocent man who has been sinned against. He stands alone on the road, bearing the burden of suffering, at the very spot where the sinner abandoned him. What reply do we have for him in the books of Samyamani? Or in the laws made by human beings?'

'Forgive me, my lord,' said Chitragupta. 'Although I have started to note down the characteristics of events, this servant of yours is inherently only a kayastha. A keeper of accounts. While your mind reaches out beyond that, to the human being. However, reality does not change. In the books of Samyamani, there is provision only to punish the sinner and reward the virtuous one. No relief is offered to him who suffers for the sins of others either in our books or in the laws invented by men. Everyone abandons him on the road or buries him under the debris or writes him off.'

'This is my greatest worry, my friend. We have only been able to invest events with characteristics. We have not been able to give history any meaning. Do not the protests that gather momentum against us every day prove that the movement we began to punish sinners and reward the virtuous has failed to generate confidence? Even those who have not sinned mock the system devised to punish those who have. Remember the stories they circulated about Samyamani? That scourges have built houses to live in around the city. That demons with long canine teeth and protruding eyes stand guard at our gates, armed with swords. Chitragupta, we tried to administer justice. But why could not the people of the world conceive of a need for justice?'

Yama's voice faltered.

They stood facing the valley, which was by then completely bathed in sunlight. They saw guards leading sinners and virtuous people along the long path that wound towards Samyamani.

Yama looked up and saluted the sun: 'Father, you have given me abundant light. But my eyes are once again unable to see everything properly. Behind what is visible, father, how much more there lies that is invisible!'

'Sinners seek places to hide in, Dharmaraja. As for the virtuous, they come forward without feeling ashamed. The innocent and the wronged who are neither sinners nor virtuous slip behind our range of vision.'

'Look carefully, Chitragupta,' said Yama, pointing to human beings who could be seen only as specks in the distance, 'do you see a sanyasi there? He knows he is helpless, but he has taken a vow to free his disciple, the innocent Govardhan, from the gallows. Do you see a writer who has put his pen down sorrowfully because he has realized that the canvas is larger than the creation he is attempting? A scientist who searches for the variable of a moan which he found entangled in the

equation of his algebraic problems? These men give me hope,
Chitragupta. Somehow, I have a feeling that they will claim
our legacy. As we claimed that of our fathers...'

16

By the time Salma made her way back to the village with the bundle of firewood she had gathered in the forest, dusk had fallen. Utterly exhausted, she put her load down on the platform built around the banyan tree, outside the village temple. She drank some water from the tank nearby and squatted on the ground.

Her kameez was so drenched in sweat that it had to be wrung out. The lower part of her pyjamas was torn in several places and her feet were flat and cracked, knocked as they had been against stones and thorns. She wiped her face, her head and her neck with her chunni, then sat back against the platform. Suddenly, her eyes filled with tears but she did not try to wipe them away as she had wiped her sweat. She gazed at the shattered image of the world before her through a film of tears.

Devotees streamed into the temple. There was only one temple in the village and people flocked to it, tired after their work, tired of coping with life. The sant who was seated in the glow of a lighted oil lamp sang to those who sat before him in the dark:

> *Jog biyog bhog bhal mamda*
> *Hit anhit madhyam bhram famda*
> *Janm maran jaham lagi jag jalu*
> *Sampati bipati karm aru kalu*[3]

Salma had a lump in her throat. The tears dimmed her eyes, reluctant to flow down. The shattered face of the world became as mystifying as the sant had described.

Days had passed since Govardhan had disappeared. She had no idea how much time had passed since Ali Dost had gone away. If coming together and separation were illusions, what was reality?

The truth was that human beings were always alone. If there was a truth beyond meetings and separations, likes and dislikes, birth and death, it was that a human being is ultimately alone. Salma was alone again. Salma and Mannu. At the end of each long day spent in hunting for food, firewood and water, mother and daughter withdrew into the narrow lair of night. With vacant minds in which no images took shape.

Salma laid her head on her knees and wept bitterly.

Her tears spent, the shattered world unified again.

The temple bells rang, then fell silent. The lamps flickered in the wind. Having explained the first few lines, the sant went on:

---

[3] Meeting, separation, good things, bad things, friends, enemies: these are all illusions of the human mind. Birth, death, wealth, calamity, action, time: these are only creations of the mind, lost in the darkness that is the absence of knowledge.

Dharani dhamu dhanu pur parivaru
Sargu naraku jaham lagi vyavaharu
Dekhiyo suniyo guniyo man mahi
Moh mul paramarth nahi[4]

Standing up on her exhausted legs, Salma lifted the bundle of wood onto her head again and walked on. There was no one on the footpath that wound through the shrubs. Except the evening and its fading light.

Suddenly a fear took shape in her mind. Whirling inside her mind like a cyclone, it blew away her fatigue. It was just two days before that some pandas had come to her with a demand. A young, unmarried thakur was dying. His soul would not attain salvation if he died unmarried. They needed a girl who would marry him. The girl they had found to marry him and burn on his pyre after he died was Mannu. They thought they could carry out this plan by enticing Salma and Mannu with money or threatening them since they were poor and helpless. Salma had scolded them and chased them away, but she was afraid now. Pandas were not the sort who would go away so easily. They would lurk in the vicinity, waiting for their chance. Salma quickened her pace.

She collapsed with the firewood at the door of the hut. There was nothing but darkness inside. When she lighted the lamp, the cruel face of reality appeared. The hut was completely empty. Not only Mannu but the pots she had taken that morning to fetch water were missing. Which meant that she had been

---

[4] Things we see and hear and think about like land, a house, wealth, family, heaven, hell, have their roots in the desires of the mind and are not real at all.

waylaid on the way to the river. A curtain fell before Salma's eyes, blocking the light entirely.

The village, never having been in the habit of lighting lamps in the evening, had sunk into sleep long ago. Not only the preparation of food and eating, but all other activities, movements, sounds, had ceased with the setting of the sun. Denuded, completely drained, Salma walked through a dense darkness, with no knowledge of where she was going. There was no path to tread, no destination to reach: all was darkness.

17

What first attracted Govardhan's attention were the street dogs that kept stumbling against the walls and the objects that were either lying on the ground or falling down. If any of the children threw stones at the dogs, as they often did, they would run helter-skelter and dash into things. He wondered what disease it was that had invaded this town and inflicted blindness on all its dogs. In a little while he realized that not only the dogs but the cattle, the pigs, the cats and even the rats of the town were all afflicted with the same ailment.

An intimidating silence permeated the town. Aloofness and apathy were apparent on every human face. No one spoke. They seemed as indifferent to beauty as to ugliness. There was hardly anything beautiful to see except the odd tree that had flowered or an ancient house with vestiges of traditional architecture. The houses and streets were filthy and stinking. People walked along as if they did not want to look at or think about anything. As if they were blind and deaf.

As it neared noon and the air of lethargy that hung over the town thickened, Govardhan caught sight of a handful of boys who had gathered on the platform in front of the immense gates of an old, fort-like mansion. He thought at first that they were sheltering there from the heat of the sun. But he realized as he went nearer that, seated in a compact circle, they were silently immersed in some kind of work. Suddenly, a cat jumped out of their hands with a piercing cry that startled Govardhan. It did not take long for him to realize that the blood that lay spattered everywhere as the creature rolled on the ground and flung itself into the air from time to time was flowing from its eyes. Watching it twist and turn, the children followed it, imitating its cries and dancing.

Govardhan's head spun and unable to endure this sight, he fainted. When he opened his eyes, he saw the children sprinkling water on his face. He screamed and the children drew back, frightened. Govardhan could still hear the cat wailing and, above it, the thudding of its body as it writhed in pain. A blind dog that had heard its cries crept towards it, sniffing the trail of blood. It went right up to the animal and caressed the twitching body with its face, as if to comfort it.

Govardhan wondered whether what he had witnessed was a figment of his imagination. For a moment, he felt that he himself was blind. As if speaking from within darkness to those who stood in the light, he blabbered something to the boys, his voice both angry and sad. The boys looked at one another, confused.

Govardhan could not understand what these children, who considered catching helpless animals and blinding them a pastime, found so frightening about him. He was certainly not stronger than them, nor did he have the power to take them to task. Later, when he was able to talk to them, he came to know that what had scared them was just the fact that he was older than they were!

The children of the place were terrified of older people because they had the authority to thrash and even mutilate them. The panchayat tried and sentenced wrongdoers and the task of hanging the guilty was carried out by the parents themselves. Baby girls were suffocated to death as soon as they were born by stuffing sand into their mouths. Children were thrown into flooded rivers to propitiate the angry waters. Girls were rare in the town and the boys sought strange and unnatural ways to satisfy their natural urges. Animals that had been blinded proved useful for this purpose.

The practice that the strong indulged in, of stealing light from others to illumine their own darkness, was not new to Govardhan. But of what use was it to attack the light? Ultimately, only the darkness would remain. A darkness whose widening depths appeared to him like gaping pits. Govardhan was afraid of everything he saw there: the silent adults; the capering, noisy children; the blinded animals groping their way. Every creature walked suspiciously, as if there might be a pit hidden in the space before the next step...

A cow stumbled towards him and, almost about to fall, dashed against his body. He stepped aside to avoid treading on a rat that lay exhausted on the road. The sight of a blind dog and bitch mating by the wayside haunted him for a long time after he had seen it.

By evening, Govardhan arrived at a cremation ground at the edge of the town. A place that lay unattended, with no watchman, no gate, not even a fence around it. Morsels of rotting cloth, empty liquor bottles, vomit and drying human excreta lay scattered on the rocks and among the bushes.

Pinpoints of light flickered here and there in two pyres that were almost burnt out, like eyes opening from within the dark grey ashes.

A feeble moan led Govardhan behind a huge rock. He saw a girl seated there, weeping with her head on her knees. He could make out her face in the faint light of a crescent moon that was about to set even before night had fallen.

One of the pyres, the girl told him, was that of her father.

'Did he love you very much?' Govardhan asked her.

'He used to come home drunk every day, close the door and attack me. If I protested or resisted, he would thrash me with a whip,' she said between sobs. 'As soon as I gave birth to his child, I stuffed sand into its mouth and killed it.'

Why was she weeping, then?

Whatever the reason for her grief, it was the first person in that town whom Govardhan had seen crying. In a place where the chasm between the generations, between the strong and the weak, was so wide, he thought it was an extraordinary thing to witness a person grieving over her own sorrow. He pressed his hand against her head, turned and walked away.

He picked up a blind cat from the roadside. A black cat. Happy to have found a companion, he fondled its head and walked on.

18

Ali Dost followed the soldiers into the room.

Kamran was lying on the floor. There were no shackles on his hand, no chains on his feet. His head rested on a thin, oil-stained pillow. He gazed at the soldiers, his eyes wide with apprehension.

There was one other person in the room—a priest who was huddled in a corner, terrified. His lips chanted the name of god feverishly. In obedience to a signal from Ali Dost, two soldiers came up to Kamran and pressed his hands down tightly on the floor. A third soldier tied his legs together and sat down on them. The fourth one held his head, crushed a piece of cloth into a ball and stuffed it into his mouth.

Ali Dost then sat down on the floor near Kamran's head, folding his legs under him. He took out two needles from a bag he had with him, lifted Kamran's eyelids with one hand and jabbed each eye fifty times. The five normal fingers of each of his hands participated in some way in this act, but the sixth ones hung limp and only bore witness to it.

Ali Dost then took out a lime from his bag and squeezed it into each eye socket as the blood kept spurting out. Kamran screamed as loud as the gag in his mouth would let him.

His work done, Ali Dost got up and went out. The four soldiers were still holding down Kamran's hands, legs and head. The priest huddled closer into his corner and chanted louder and faster than before. The soldier removed the cloth from Kamran's mouth and he groaned.

It was a very hot day. Coming out of the room, Ali Dost stood for a while in the bright sunlight, looking at the blood that had spattered his hands and clothes. Although he had carried out many strange forms of punishment, it was the first time he had blinded someone. The blood that had spurted out when he lowered the needle the first time had sprayed into his face and almost blinded him. He had wiped the blood from his own eyes and continued his task. When he had looked at Kamran's face after he finished, the first thought that had come to his mind was that his victim would no longer be able to see him. When he chopped off someone's hands and threw him down or drove a stake through his anus, the victim's eyes always stared at him. The present situation should have given Ali Dost relief, but somehow, it did not.

Ali Dost was only a possession that had been transferred from a defeated monarch to a victorious one—like the canopy over a royal throne, or elephants, or slaves, or court poets or the women of the harem. Positioned between the king and the subjects, between he who punished and he who was punished, he had no responsibilities, no obligations towards anyone. Then why did the darkness that had fallen between him and his victim today disturb him so much?

The slaves waiting outside poured water on his hands. He

washed them mechanically and wiped them with the towel the slaves held out.

After performing such tasks, soldiers like Ali Dost were treated to a session in the tavern. But he did not go there. He made his way to the barracks but did not enter. He untied his horse and led it towards the road.

He walked some distance, then got onto the horse. He kicked its sides to make it gallop.

When they left the town, the roads became tracks and soon these too vanished. The horse galloped over open meadows and through woods.

As he rode on, listening to the horse's hoof beats, Salma and Mannu suddenly came into his thoughts, he did not know why. On an earlier occasion as he had sat astride a horse, cracking his whip to drive out the people of a town from their homes, he had caught sight of Salma and Mannu among them and quickly turned away. He had ridden all the way from Tughluqabad to Daulatabad and, months later from Daulatabad to Tughluqabad, on horseback. But after that occasion, he had not once seen them among the people who walked before the horsemen's twirling whips. Each time they had been driven out, the number of people who had reached their destination had been less than half of those who had set out.

Ali Dost experienced a great loneliness.

At sunset he came to a village at the edge of vast wheat fields. Both he and his horse were utterly exhausted. Ali Dost dismounted and sat down, leaning against a haystack. The hay and the earth were cool, probably from the previous day's rain. Suddenly, he wanted to throw up. He retched violently and felt very relieved when he had brought everything out. He breathed deeply to overcome his exhaustion.

Hearing him throw up, an old woman came out of a hut nearby. When she realized that he was a soldier, she was furious. Flailing her hands, she screamed at him: 'Did you have to come here to empty out your bile after plundering the poor of the few coins they have and getting drunk?'

Still gasping for breath, Ali Dost said: 'I'm not drunk, Mother. Someone else is, and it's for him I'm throwing up.'

It was the first time he had spoken to a person after torturing his victim. But he would not have been able to explain what he meant. He was not sure what it was that was troubling him. The words had spilled out of him like the bile he had spewed, that was all.

19

On the day after he had been blinded, Kamran sent a message through their mutual friend, Munim Beg, to Emperor Humayun that he wanted to meet him. Humayun, who was planning his campaign to recover Hindustan after having subjugated his younger brother, laid down a condition for the meeting: Kamran would betray no emotion before him. When he was told this, Kamran laughed aloud even though his head was splitting with pain.

As Kamran had expected, it was Humayun who burst into tears when he saw his brother's bandaged face. 'I stained my hands with my brother's blood for the sake of the vanities of this transient world! I did not keep the word I gave my dying father!' he lamented.

'If this is how you feel, why did you do what you did?' asked Kamran unemotionally.

'It was not my decision, Kamran, it was that of the law. Just as I am a brother, I am an emperor as well. I too have to obey the law.'

'How fine that sounds!' Kamran smiled. 'It is the emperor who finds it necessary to safeguard his throne, Humayun, not the law. As far as the law is concerned, whoever is seated on the throne at a particular moment is the emperor. The law does not punish or safeguard anyone, it is you and I who do that. I have beheaded people, Humayun, and burned them at the stake. I did not have to consult books to do so. I did not come to you today, Humayun, to hear about the loopholes in your philosophy.'

'What have you come for?'

'To congratulate you! To celebrate the death of brotherhood! I spat on its face long ago and today you did so too, although for different reasons.'

'Don't say that, Kamran. Your greed for power has made you forget that you are my younger brother. And yet, in spite of that, I saved your life.'

Kamran made a gesture of despair. 'You will never understand, Humayun. You keep polluting politics with your silly arguments, destroying its purity by inducting fathers, sons and siblings into it. I thought you would have freed yourself from all this at least today. After all, I have ceased to be a threat to your throne.'

The act of speaking was a strain on Kamran's muscles. He groaned, pressing his hands tightly on either side of his head and sank to the ground.

Humayun could not endure Kamran's agony. Nor did he understand his brother's words. He called the guards and asked them to take Kamran away. When they had left, Humayun plunged into thought. In a way, he felt it might have been better to have killed this brother. He could not bear the way he had looked, the words he had spoken. If Kamran had died, he might

have haunted his memory. But where would an emperor find
time to remember? And if memories did come back to him,
there were always opium pills...

Hindal had been killed, Askari imprisoned, Kamran blinded.
Humayun felt lonely once more as, seated on his horse, he
moved the next day towards Hindustan in the midst of his army.
The Mughal army was a mobile city that included not only
soldiers, officers and ministers, but also wives, servants, cooks,
traders, dancing girls, courtesans and even moneylenders. It
raised a deafening clamour and clouds of dust. Humayun had
led this army many times, sometimes as victor, sometimes as
fugitive. None of these three brothers had been with him then.
Maybe these brothers had been worse enemies than Sher Shah
or the sultan of Gujarat or the Rajputs. They had attacked him,
separately and together, even when his enemies had driven
him out of the country and he had been wandering alone through
the Thar and Sindh deserts. And yet, it was not while he was
fleeing from pillar to post that he had yearned for the brothers
who had been killed, imprisoned and blinded—it was now, when
he was on his way to recover all that he had lost, bearing the
flag of victory.

Once, as children, when he had been riding with Kamran,
they had come upon a dog urinating against a tombstone in a
deserted garden. Kamran had said: 'The man laid to rest there
must certainly be a heretic!' Humayun had replied, 'And the
dog's soul must be fanatically orthodox!'

Humayun was full of complexities and contradictions. He
was not orthodox, neither was he a heretic. No king and none
of his brothers had given him any help when he fled from
Hindustan to Iran. The shah of Iran asked him to embrace the
Shia faith, but Humayun would not. The shah pointed to the

fireplace where a fire blazed to drive away the cold and said, 'You will burn here along with the firewood, to give me heat.' Humayun wasted no time, he asked for a piece of paper and signed on it to say he had accepted the Shia faith. Humayun could melt with brotherly love; he could also be frighteningly cruel. Over and over again, he forgave the brothers who had raised their swords against him. Whenever he won a battle or captured a city, he would put on a red robe and sit on his throne. Until he put on his green robe again—which would sometimes be after many days—his soldiers would kill, plunder, burn and rape the inhabitants of the captured city. Humayun was an excellent soldier but a totally inefficient ruler. He always delayed taking decisions. His intelligence had been blunted by opium. He enjoyed the arts and a life of pleasure, but could never find the time to stay in one place and rule in peace.

However, there was one thing he believed in implicitly: empires should be ruled by dynasties and, when the ruler dies, the right of succession should belong to the eldest son. He was not prepared to compromise on this matter. He considered those who did not agree with him and those who were not loyal to him wrongdoers and sinners.

Unlike Humayun, Kamran looked at the world not in terms of right and wrong, but in terms of success and failure, or strength and weakness. Once he learnt that Humayun would spare his life and only have him blinded, he had lain unprotesting before them. All he had requested was a pillow. This did not mean that he had accepted that he had done his brother wrong. Kamran had never been one to give up anything willingly. From the time he was a child, he had firmly believed in his own capacities and skills. He had never doubted that he was better than his brother, Humayun. And this was true in many ways.

He who is victorious in battle kills the vanquished. Kamran had done this. The aim was to make sure the enemy did not gather enough strength to attack again. While the aim of the vanquished is to somehow escape with his life, so that he can attack again. Babar built an empire with his strength. Sher Shah Suri wrested it from Humayun, Babar's son, and drove him out. Had fortune favoured him, Kamran would have achieved what Sher Shah had. Kamran had not staked his claim to the throne as Babar's son or as Humayun's brother but as a strong soldier like Sher Shah. He therefore did not understand why people said it was a crime for him to desire the throne or to fight against Humayun. If an Afghan, who was not a Turk or a Mongol, could defeat Humayun and become the emperor, why couldn't he? If either of them had been captured, Humayun could have beheaded Sher Shah or Sher Shah could have beheaded Humayun without a trial. They would not have had to discuss this with a lawgiver, or seek an opinion. Neither the Turk nor the Mongol tradition laid down anything about the claims and obligations between brothers or between father and son. They recognized only victory and defeat, not sin and virtue. He who was strong and capable won and the land and people became his. Kamran was, therefore, at a loss to understand why this army of amirs, imams and qazis was ranged against him.

Kamran thought of his failure as a mistake he had made in military strategy. Whereas, for Humayun, it was the success of a doctrine and he was on his way to celebrate it. Behind him lay the fallen bodies of his enemies within the family, before him were the enemies of the empire, ready to fall.

Shrugging off loneliness, Humayun marched forward. It was a cloudy day. It would be raining all over Hindustan, he thought.

The rivers would overflow, cities and villages would be submerged. Until the rains subsided, until winter set in and the Hindu festivals were over, he would spend his time on the banks of the Indus, training his soldiers, collecting weapons, planning operations. He tried to compose a poem in his mind.

Faraway in Pirhala, guarded by soldiers he could not see, surrounded by physicians, plunged in darkness and pain, Kamran was trying to compose a poem as well.

According to Gulbadan, the chronicler sister of both Humayun and Kamran, Kamran was a better poet than Humayun. These two brothers could not understand each other. One believed that only a dynasty had the right to rule a people, the other that this right belonged to the strongest person. Two blind men who opened their eyes only before mirrors!

20

Choupat Raja and the Company Bahadur were not very different from Humayun and Kamran: they too looked at their own images. But they did not call the frames they looked into 'mirrors'; they thought of them as windows opening on to the countryside. And of the faces they looked at in them as the actual faces of the people.

Resident Henry Williams and his younger brother, General John Williams, however, were looking out through real windows. Out of the windows of the bungalows their Company had constructed for them, towards the people of the country their Company was in the process of acquiring. For they were, after all, officers of the Company.

It was not for Henry or John to decide who should rule these people, or whether the Company should rule them or just carry on trading with them. The Company had decided to govern them anyway. How the country was to be ruled: this was the point Henry and John deliberated and on which they held different views. Each guarded his own views passionately, as they did their images in the mirror.

Whenever they met, Henry and John tried to illumine the darkness that lay between them. They were not sure they succeeded in this. But as brothers, they were not like Humayun and Kamran. They valued and respected the relationship between them. As they did now.

'Zamindar, jagirdar, talukdar, sardar... how many of them do you have on your list, Henry? Each one a bigger clown and villain than the next. I cannot even remember their names,' said John, waving his hands.

The journey from where John worked to Henry's residency was long and tedious, and it was getting dark when he arrived. But, as usual, they started discussing state matters as soon as they met, without taking any rest. Henry answered John's remarks with a smile, he did not reply to them.

John went on: 'Kings who search for convicts whose necks will fit the noose. Kotwals who run around trying to save their own lives. And our officers, who pull the strings for these clowns!'

Henry still did not say anything. He walked up to the window and gazed at the deserted landscape outside, wrapped in darkness. A hot breeze blew in through the window, proof that the heat had not subsided even though the sun had gone down.

John went up to Henry and placed a hand on his shoulder. 'Forgive me, Henry,' he said, 'I realize how you feel. When I look at the situation here, I find it difficult to control myself. I do not know why we've come here, to live in this hellish place. Where people worship gods who have four hands and elephant heads and wear garlands made of skulls; where they burn widows along with their dead husbands; where mosquitoes, flies and hundreds of diseases breed plentifully; where districts are governed by dacoits and highways scattered with dead bodies; where every British officer is welcomed with a row of corpses...'

Henry spoke at last: 'Do you know why we are still drawn to this country, John? Because ordinary English people like us are looked up to and obeyed as if we are lords. Because our orders are carried out. Every one of us wants to play the role of a lord, John.'

It was John's turn to be silent now.

Henry went on: 'These kings and zamindars whom you call clowns—that's what they want too, to be respected and obeyed. Actually, we are as clownish, as cruel, as them. We compete with them and swarm over every inch of these people's bodies like mosquitoes or flies.'

'Don't compare us with these kings, Henry. What we are trying to do is to free these people from the oppression of the local overlords. Once they are brought directly under the Company, the people will be able to save that portion of the taxes which their overlords now take from them as middlemen.'

Henry shook his head and turned back from the window. 'I hope all our calculations come out right,' he said. 'Unfortunately, John, the arithmetic we learnt from the Greeks does not add up or subtract in the same way in this strange country.'

Henry got up and poured out two whiskies. They sat down at a table in front of a shelf on which was arranged an odd collection of objects: books, stone and terracotta figurines and seeds from trees in the area. A servant began to pull the rope of a long cloth punkah above them.

Henry picked up an old terracotta statue that had recently been excavated. 'John, do you see the infinite sorrow, the endless endurance, in the eyes of this figure? These people here have gone through so much more than we ever have. And the misery we inflict on them now makes what the overlords and dacoits made them suffer trivial in comparison. Whenever it attacks and subjugates a country, our Company, which keeps meticulous accounts, recovers from its king whatever they spent on waging the war. The king in his turn extracts it from his subjects. Tomorrow, when our government buys this country from the Company, these people will have to pay that price as well! The taxes we collect from them now and will be collecting from them later will be far higher, John, than what these despots have been taking from them. I am sure you know that the methods of torture we employ in the provinces we rule directly are of a kind that no tax collector or native ruler here has ever used.'

They sat without speaking for quite some time, each in his own world, while the punkah moved lazily.

'Henry, although I live very far away, news reaches me steadily. I know how that clown of a king treated you. It hurts me to think of the shameful situation you are in. Whatever the Company and its policies are, you do not deserve this, Henry.'

Henry laughed. 'Leave that alone, John. Consider it the irrational reaction of a ruler to immoral behaviour on our part. Isn't that all it can be?'

John poured more whisky into the glasses.

'This was not the reason I came rushing here today,' he said. 'I wanted to warn you about certain intelligence reports the Company has been receiving. A restlessness that cannot be explained seems to be brewing among the people—not the kings this time, but the people. They seem to think that the measures we have taken against the inhuman practices here are attempts to destroy their religion and convert them to Christianity. For example, we heard that a few secret organizations are burning widows and sacrificing infants solely in order to break the law. Worse, there is a rumour going around that the fat of animals, considered holy by one section of the people and impure by another is being used on the guns we have given the sepoys. If all this snowballs into a revolt, it will not be one that rises from the kings or nawabs but from within, from our own army.'

Looking into the emptiness, Henry said quietly, 'What I see before my eyes is the picture of a terrible holocaust.'

'We are in the proportion of one to ten in the army.'

Henry shook his head. 'A moment ago, we spoke about an innocent man who is going to be hanged only because his neck is thin enough to fit the noose. Look at the figurines on this shelf. How attractive their necks are! Whoever is victorious in the rebellion, John, the ones who will lose are these people here. The holocaust I see is the one that will destroy them.'

The fan began to move slower and slower since the man who pulled the rope had dozed off. After a while it stopped altogether. Both the brothers watched the man, making no attempt to wake him up.

21

'If we were to take the series $1/0=\infty$, $2/0=\infty$, $3/0=\infty$ and so on to its start, we would arrive at the result that $0/0=\infty$. Similarly, the series $0/1=0$, $0/2=0$, $0/3=0$ would again imply that $0/0=0$. Reversing the expressions, $0 \times 1=0$, $0 \times 2=0$, $0 \times 3=0$, we arrive at the result, $0/0=1$, $0/0=2$, $0/0=3$ and so on. In other words, we come to an absurd conclusion that $1=2=3$ and so on. In order to avoid such mathematical absurdities, when 0 and ∞ stand alone or are used in expressions like $0/0$, $0–0$, they are left undefined or treated as indeterminate.' Ramchander was speaking at a meeting of the society of intellectuals who lightheartedly called themselves the Kayastha Sabha.

The poets, artists, journalists and historians who formed the audience found Ramchander's examples attractive but did not ask any questions. Only the handful of students who sat in the rear since they were not members of the Sabha were restless. They generally attended only special occasions like this when someone gave a speech.

Ramchander went on: 'I spoke at this Sabha once before on a subject connected with mathematics. I said on that occasion that while Westerners, attracted by the concept of the concrete, were pushing mathematics in the direction of geometry, algebra was taking shape in the minds of Hindus who liked to wander around in the regions of the abstract. I was engaged at the time in solving the problems of maxima and minima using algebra, thus diverging from the path of calculus that the Westerners had chosen. My ambition was to revive the algebra-oriented slant of the Hindu mind and to re-establish traditional mathematical methods in the field of education, making it possible to combat Western imperialism with spirituality.'

Syed Ahmad Khan frowned and shifted in his chair. Mirza Ghalib watched him with his habitual smile.

'I have abandoned that project,' continued Ramchander. 'What I am anxious about now is not just Western oppression but all forms of oppression under which human beings lie groaning.'

This time, Syed's smile mirrored Ghalib's. But the students at the back were agitated. One of them shouted, 'Sir, you are contradicting yourself! You're unnecessarily complicating things.'

Ramchander said to the students: 'When I said that I preferred algebra to geometry, I did so with the intention of exposing your minds to a world of complexities, contradictions and uncertainties. We cannot think of mathematics or science as perfect and absolute, standing beyond complexities, contradictions and uncertainties. I, however, do not ask you to abandon reason and objectivity and embrace eternal contradiction. At one end, we have reason and logic; at the other, the reality of life, teeming with contradictions. While mathematics and science turn towards reason and logic, our lives themselves are plunged in absurdities. What I ask you to do is, on the one hand, to carry the contradictions of life into the realm of mathematics and science, and on the other, to use logic and reason to resolve the absurdities in which our life is plunged. I have tried to show how mathematics, when faced with contradictions and uncertainties, calls these indeterminates. I am not giving up my fundamental proposition. I am actually developing it so that our area of activity can be enlarged.'

Ramchander stopped. The students appeared to be satisfied but the members of the society in the front row were not. Whether it was a question of foreign domination or social reform, they did not share similar views. Many of them were keen on pursuing their own materialistic concerns along with scholarly ones. They therefore viewed Ramchander, who was known among them as a scientist, with suspicion. They feared he would trap them in endless arguments. So none of them said anything.

The unpleasant silence in the hall, which was lavishly decorated with arches and pillars with cornices, seemed a reflection of the decay of history. Ramchander let his eyes rest on each person in the audience. Some smiled at him, others avoided his eyes. He asked himself why he had said all he did. Maybe, he thought, these people were asking themselves the same thing. Ramchander resumed speaking.

'Friends, you must be wondering why I said all this to you.' He went on to explain: 'A strange incident occurred a few days ago. It was late at night, and my wife had gone to bed. I was in my room immersed in the project on maxima and minima that I was working on. I was alone with my lamp and my papers. Suddenly, this scrawny, hunched villager burst into my room. He had the eyes of a hunted animal. He flung a whole lot of questions at me as soon as he came in. Then he opened the door and left without waiting for an answer. I do not know where he came from or where he went to. But what he told me shattered my peace of mind.'

Ramchander paused. This time the entire audience looked eagerly at him. He went on: 'He was a convict condemned to be hanged. Do you know what his crime was? He had a thin neck! Someone else had actually been sentenced to death, but when it was found that his neck was too thick to fit into the noose, the king sent his men to look for a person whose neck would fit it. And it was this wayfarer whom they caught. Our king believes that the machinery of justice should be impartial and above suspicion. That the size of the noose should not be changed to suit people's necks. Where will we end up, he asks, if the devices and instruments of the law are changed to suit different individuals? He has therefore fixed the diameter of the noose. Friends, the absurdity and hypocrisy of this system of justice were what fascinated me. My nocturnal visitor asked me: is not the principle that two and two make four the only arithmetic you know? Mathematics and science are efforts to separate right from wrong. Do not the systems of religion and justice attempt to do the same? And yet, how is it that we cannot find reason and logic in our lives, that they are trapped in endless absurdities and hypocrisies? Why is it that our scholars and scientists are not concerned about this?

'I know there are innumerable hounds chasing that man—among them, the law, mathematics, science, society and so on. I see his sorrowing wife and children following him. Uprooted by the whirlwind he has provoked, I see many people, including myself, following him. I called this meeting to tell my fellow members about my journey. I am about to leave now. I am not certain which way he went. I do not know in which direction I should look for him, in front of me or behind, to the left or to the right. I could meet him anywhere. All this makes my journey difficult. Or maybe easy.'

Ramchander came down from the stage without waiting for a reaction from anyone. Not looking at any of them, he walked past the arches in the room, went down the long flight of steps outside and onto the road which was crowded with noisy pedestrians, horsemen and palanquin bearers. The sound of the muezzin's call to the evening prayer rose from a mosque in the distance. A platoon of the company's soldiers, keeping time as they marched, went past him.

22

Bharatendu had performed his morning ablutions and was coming down to the garden in front of his kothi. A man seated on the bench on the lawn caught his attention. He realized from his clothes and his features that the man was a foreigner. A hennaed beard that spread in a semicircle around his chin. A huge turban on his head. A shirt with numerous frills. Shoes with upturned toes. A large bag on his shoulder. A radiance full of energy that belied his age and tiredness and made it clear to everyone that he was a habitual traveller. Bharatendu stood thinking for a moment, and then asked: 'Ibn Battuta, I presume?'

Smiling graciously, the visitor stood up and offered his respects.

'We have not met before. Then how did I know you?' asked Bharatendu.

'We know each other through the wisdom and experience that is common to us, thakur,' said Ibn Battuta with humility.

'Do they not differ, since we follow different professions?'

'There is only one kind of wisdom and experience in this

world, thakur—what humanity gives us. What makes the difference is whether we accept them or not, or to what degree we accept them.'

The poet's sharp eyes were fixed on the traveller's face.

'I heard that you set Govardhan free,' Ibn Battuta went on. 'I did so long ago.'

'The thought that the power to free a man lies only with his creator occurs to me often,' said Bharatendu, almost to himself.

'Liberation is not for the one who is liberated, but the one who liberates. For no one gives up anything until it grows so large that his hands can no longer hold it. Look at me. The director disappeared and we, the actors, had nothing to do. At that point, I could free myself only by freeing the others. For at least on the stage, they had been my slaves and I their master!'

Still lost in thought, Bharatendu said: 'These people have always been given directors who have failed to understand them. In a sense, all kings are always foreigners to their people! Do you know, janab, we writers too were a lot like kings in that respect—always foreigners to their characters!'

'And you say this to a traveller, an eternal foreigner! But, unlike the emperors, we never subjugate people, it is they who conquer us! As for litterateurs, we differ from them in that while we approach people with curiosity, you appropriate them with the arrogance of your scholarship. Ultimately, it is the people themselves who are the truth: they turn kings into fools, they defeat us and—forgive me, thakur—reduce you writers to mediocre creatures. They transform the experience of a traveller into knowledge and the knowledge a writer possesses into experience. It is people who are really supreme— these insignificant beings who drift over a sea of plunder, arson, massacre, rape and humiliation. You pluck your characters out of that ocean and I leave my hosts behind in it as I get ready for each new expedition.'

Bharatendu walked to and fro, shattering the dewdrops that the blades of grass bore on their tips. Seated on the bench, Ibn Battuta followed his moving figure with his eyes.

'There is truth in what you said,' Bharatendu admitted finally. 'Take a look at history. At these people who are punished over and over again for no fault of theirs. They are not just floating over the sea of suffering—they struggle with it, fight with it as they row over it, not knowing where they are going. There is no need to define their acts as courageous or cowardly since all they are doing is just living. But is living such a trivial act, Ibn Battuta? Each farce we writers roll out turns without our being aware of it into a tragedy. Each swift brush we have with life burns our fingers. Think then of the human beings who live in that fire! It does not matter whether they are courageous or cowardly, all of them burn in it the same way.'

Ibn Battuta held a full-blown rose in his hands and moved his fingers down, fondling the thorny stem.

'Thakur, do you know how many times a day I touch my head? To make sure it is still there? It has become a habit with me.'

'Freedom eludes the liberated and the liberator in the same manner, Ibn Battuta.' Bharatendu stopped walking and stood before the traveller. 'Possibly, freedom is not freedom at all! If the liberated Govardhan is condemned to wander around with the death sentence hanging over his head, the punishment meted out to this Bharatendu, who liberated him, is a life sentence. A story writer can know no peace until he brings his story to an end. As for me, having allowed my character to escape, I cannot now write an ending. Tell me, traveller, will you be able to cease travelling even if your feet are stuck in a pool of stagnant blood?'

Ibn Battuta got up, smiling, and took Bharatendu's hands in his own.

'Thakur, both of us are helpless creatures who cannot shake ourselves free from the mystery of life,' he said. 'Your imagination will never let you rest. You will keep picking up characters from this sea of blood and tears and making them journey in whatever way you want. As for us travellers, we journey through it, burning and wounded. This is our fate. Our kind will never know respite. Nor will we die.'

23

'Freedom is not freedom at all—who said that, Ruswa?' asked Umrao Jan, lifting her eyes from the floor of the terrace to Ruswa's.

It was a moonlit summer night. The terrace of Umrao Jan's kothi, so clean that there was not even a speck of dust on it, had been sprinkled with water to make it cool. Surahis so fresh from the potters' that they still smelled of earth were filled with water and lined up on the parapet. Delicately scented paan leaves lay on a platter and beside them, hookahs with strands of jasmine wound around them, their smoke pervading the air like heady incense. A candle flickering under a carved glass shade cast an enchanting glow on Umrao Jan's face.

'Bharatendu Harishchandra said that while speaking to the historian and traveller, Ibn Battuta,' said Mirza Mohammed Ruswa, bowing courteously. 'But why do you ask, Umrao?'

Umrao Jan did not answer. Instead, she asked another question: 'Mirza, do you remember, you once recited a couplet to me?

I went to Kaaba on a pilgrimage, but in vain
My sinful feet found the path of human love again.'

'I certainly did,' said Ruswa, 'but you changed it to:

I turned my back on Kaaba with great disdain
Gave up my faith, took the path of human love again.'

'How marvellous life is, Ruswa! And how full of sorrow! No prophet, no poet can ever understand that! I read as far as you have written of the novel based on what I told you of the story of my life. It is time now for us to part, Ruswa. Do not write any more. I am setting you free.'

Mirza Ruswa looked at Umrao Jan in disbelief. The garlanded hookah he was puffing at was still in his hands.

'Mahatarma, if you were just a courtesan without education or culture, I would have accepted what you said. Do those with knowledge have to display undue modesty?'

'Do you mean that education destroys modesty?'

'Wouldn't it be better to go on with the story and not waste time arguing?'

A wry smile appeared on Umrao Jan's lips. She sent back the servant maid who had brought her paan. A dry breeze grazed the cold floor of the terrace, drank in the moisture and clung there, reluctant to leave.

'That's not the thing, Ruswa. You are turning me into the heroine of a novel. I do not wish to have a new birth in literature. Let me live this life.'

'What kind of life is this, Umrao?' asked Ruswa, full of emotion. 'What has it given you? Just humiliation wrapped in flattery! In literature, you will win esteem. Even after centuries, when the nawabs and kings who come to see you dance and listen to you recite poetry lie at rest under the soil, you will still be alive in people's minds...'

'What is life, Ruswa? The answer to that question can only be found in life. Not in literature. The novel you are writing is trying to liberate me from life. Every word, every line of my poetry was a lie. If I am to correct my poems, I can do so only in life—through a new poem. I want to bring literature into my life, not the other way around.'

Umrao Jan's voice trembled. It took her a few minutes to collect herself. Composed again, she went on: 'There is only one colour, Ruswa, in my Satrangi Mahal—black! It took me a whole lifetime to understand that. It doesn't matter. By the time I understood, it had become very dear to me. Let us part now, Mirza Ruswa. You with the lightness of freedom. I with a load in my heart.'

Ruswa puffed at his hookah many times. Between him and Umrao Jan, the minutes flowed by. The moon slanted in the sky. The molten wax from the burning candle shaped the outlines of a sculpture.

Ruswa said: 'What Bharatendu, the Master, said was right. Freedom is not freedom at all. I am going, Umrao. But what I have now is not the freedom of a bird in the sky. For that matter, is what the bird has freedom? We need not argue about that either. Let the knowledge that fantasy is heavier than reality remain Ruswa's alone!'

> *'She'll rue the day she loved you, Ruswa of evil fame*
> *For you will not let her go until she gets as bad a name'*[5]

---

[5] The word 'ruswa' means one of evil fame

Umrao Jan who had learned, through life, the permanence of partings and the transcience of meetings sang a verse to make their parting a pleasant one.

And then she added: 'Umrao too earned a bad name—but then that is her fortune!'

24

The king's herald stopped at the crossroad near the marketplace and adjusted the drum hanging around his neck. He beat it for a few minutes, then took out the proclamation and read it aloud:

'Hear, hear! The orders of the king! If Govardhan, the culprit who escaped from jail, is not apprehended in fourteen days from today, the sentence of death to which he was condemned will revert to the kotwal. If the kotwal escapes meanwhile and is not caught in the next fourteen days, the ganderia will be executed. If the ganderia disappears and is not caught in the next fourteen days, the kasai will be executed. If the kasai absconds and is not caught in the next fourteen days, the bhishti will be executed. If the bhishti escapes and is not caught in the next fourteen days, the chunewala will be executed. If the chunewala flees and is not caught in the next fourteen days, the mason will be executed. If the mason disappears and is not found in the next fourteen days, Kallu bania himself will be executed. Since Kallu's wall collapsed and killed a goat, someone has to be punished. Hear, hear! His majesty the king also decrees that henceforward all executions in the country will be carried out by beheading the culprits, not hanging them.'

The herald beat his drum again, then moved towards the next crossroad.

All the people in the houses and shops and at the gates listened to what he said. Then they all went back to their work, telling themselves that this concerned only the kotwal, the ganderia, the kasai and so on and not them.

However, three men seated on a deserted platform in front of the one-rupee-a-seer market listened to the proclamation with rapt attention—the mahant, Butler, the jailer, and Ramchander, the mathematician. The king's order was important to each of them in a different way.

As the herald moved away with the drum, the mahant spoke, his eyes wide and dreamy between his long hair and beard, his voice solemn: 'Fourteen days! If fourteen days pass like this, my Govardhan will be saved.'

Butler sounded reflective: 'So the king has decided to use the sword instead of the noose! So much the better. He has realized then that the law is not to be played with at least as far as the instrument of justice used is concerned.'

Ramchander moved in between them and placed his hands on their shoulders. Looking at each of them in turn, he said: 'Friends, the problem here is not what you think it is. While you concentrate on keeping the culprit hidden or improving the instrument of execution, you forget that you are indirectly justifying the irrational nature of the verdict. And that makes you guilty yourself.'

'The task my creator has given me is to save Govardhan from the gallows.' It was clear from the mahant's voice that he was not happy with this. 'This is the pact Govardhan, I and the writer who created us made among ourselves and I have to abide by it.'

'A pact made by three people!' Butler laughed aloud. 'How simplistic! This is an issue between two countries or rather, two continents; between two systems, two philosophies or two eras. Between primitive and modern law.'

'You deceive yourself, Butler sahib,' said Ramchander. 'Look into yourself and you will see where the problem lies. Not between two laws but in the concept of law itself. It is the law that has provoked your anger against the hanging of an innocent man. And it is the same law that compels you to hunt that innocent man down now. You are trapped not between two systems of law but within the inhumanity, the irrationality of law itself.'

'Master,' said Butler, brushing Ramchander's hand off his shoulder, 'you speak as if you are conducting a class for children!' He hurried towards his horse without waiting for a reply and rode away. The other two watched him silently. As he disappeared into the distance, Ramchander shook his head sadly and said to himself: 'We believe that the law protects the helpless and punishes the wicked. But how cruel, how blind, that law itself is!'

The thud of the herald's drum faded slowly and the din of the marketplace grew louder. Traders were spreading out the groceries and vegetables they had brought in bullock carts and on the backs of donkeys. As more and more wares arrived, the number of buyers steadily increased. The bazaar seethed with people. Cries of 'One-rupee-a-seer!' rose everywhere, in varied registers.

Actually, it was unnecessary and meaningless for the hawkers to cry out. In a market where grain, straw, oil and oilcake, fresh or rotten vegetables were all sold at the same price, it was unnecessary for traders to attract buyers or for buyers to bargain with traders. The only valid measure the king permitted in the country was a seer; it was forbidden to weigh by length or in numbers or by any other measure. And yet the whole market kept shouting, 'A-rupee-a-seer!'

Looking displeased, the mahant said to Ramchander: 'Master, why did you hold forth to the jailer about being trapped in absolute law? Do you not see that I am bound to absolute dharma and you to absolute reason in the same way?'

'Mahantji, it was you who tried to reduce your dharma to a mere pact with Govardhan.'

Mahant shook his head. 'The law the jailer upholds, the reason and the dharma that you and I acclaim are all devalued currencies in this market. If you give it deeper thought, you will understand that it is the way commodities are measured, not the values or prices attached to them, that is the tragedy of this market. Everything is weighed by the same measure—law, dharma or reason. Not that we do not know this, master. It was in an absurd attempt to escape helplessness and humiliation that the jailer reached out to cling to the perfection of law. I reduce dharma to a pact between two people and you grow garrulous about the irrationality of law, all in the same manner. We are all trying to give a fake identity and respectability to coins which have lost their original sheen and markings and begun to look alike. As you said earlier, in doing so, we lend our support to the system which measures all of life with a single weight, that of the seer... The biggest problem, master, is how to get out of this market. I had warned Govardhan when he came in, but he did not pay any attention...'

The mahant looked around in despair. Placing their hands over their ears, he and Ramchander struggled forward, weaving their way through the insane calls of 'A-rupee-a-seer.'

25

The six of them squatted in a row on the floor of the kotwali, covered with square terracotta tiles—the ganderia, the kasai, the bhishti, the chunewala, the mason and Kallu bania, in that order. The floor was uncomfortable, since the criminals and policemen who walked incessantly over the tiles had worn them out. The eyes of all the men burned with fear and from lack of sleep. They had arrived in the morning and it was now late night.

Kotwal Moinuddin's eyes strayed for the umpteenth time to the row of men seated before him, their faces alternately illumined and shadowed by the flickering flame of the torch fixed on the wall. From the ganderia to Kallu bania and from Kallu bania to the ganderia. Each time, his gaze rested awhile on the face of the last person at each end of the row.

'You have nowhere to go? Have you stopped selling goats?' he finally asked the ganderia.

'Whether I stop selling goats or not, kotwalji, my punishment will not be lifted.' He shot a look of hatred at the kotwal. 'But if Govardhan is not arrested in fourteen days, you...'

'I know, I know.' The kotwal raised his voice, 'You're afraid that I'll run away. Did you look at the kasai sitting next to you? Look at the hatred in his eyes.'

'This is not the time for suspicion or hatred, friends!' It was Kallu bania, who sat at the end of the row, who spoke. 'In that case, I should suspect and hate all of you. We all share the kotwal's anxiety. Even I, who am at the end of the row, share it. To find Govardhan, whom the king has condemned to death, is now the duty of each of us, not the kotwal's alone.'

The tired, irritated kotwal stood up, his tall, broad body like a wall in front of them. The sharp eyes under his thick eyebrows caught and held them like a magnet. The kotwal said: 'It is very late, the night is in its second phase. You can all go home now. You can do your own work, whether it's selling goats or slaughtering them. All of you forgot your responsibility to your own profession and tried to shift the blame onto someone else. But I did not do that. The reason being that I am your kotwal. The kotwal does not blame other people. Nor does he abandon his work and run away.'

Kotwal Moinuddin looked on stoically while the row of men from the ganderia to Kallu bania filed out of the room and the space before him became empty. Exhausted, he took off his cap, placed it on the table and sat down on the single chair. The emptiness before him stared at him, but he dismissed it. Pulling out the drawer of the table, he reached for the grubby sheets of paper inside. The couplets he used to scribble on them in his free moments looked at him pleadingly. He ran his fingers over them, his eyes wet.

'Don't call out to me! There is no poetry in me now.'

26

It was while Mannu was on her way back, her pot filled with water, that the pandas hiding behind the bushes pounced upon her. They dashed the earthen pot on the ground and broke it, gagged her and dragged her away. None of the other women who looked on did anything. They did not even utter a cry.

The pandas rushed her to the thakur who lay on his deathbed and forced her to marry him. The ceremony was over in a few minutes. The thakur died next morning and they started the preparations for the cremation at once.

Mannu was in a state of shock and hardly knew what was happening around her. When it was all over, they left her alone in a room and closed the door. She sat on a sheet spread on the floor, driving the mosquitoes away and dozing off from time to time. Outside the closed door, people spoke in hushed voices. At first she paid no attention to what they were saying but at some point, she began to listen. What she heard wrenched her out of sleep.

'The burning ghat is flat and deserted. There's no place to hide,' said one of them.

'There's no need for anyone to hide. We only have to hide our weapons. Let everyone merge into the crowd, we'll be taken for relatives,' counselled another.

'The crowd must take their places early. The police must not receive any information until everything is ready. If they get wind of it, they'll arrive there with guns. If only our leaders had given us some guns!' said yet another person.

'We must perform both the tasks together—the revival of our sanatan dharma and the declaration of revolt against the foreigners. The same act will be carried out in several places today. Performing sati in defiance of orders, trapping white policemen and killing them...We must succeed at all costs.'

The last speaker spoke with authority. He was perhaps their leader.

There was a quick drum-roll announcing their arrival. The clamour of the crowd increased. It was like a festival.

Opening the door to the room where Mannu sat, a group of women pushed their way in, followed by children. The women began to dress Mannu up like a bride while the children looked on enviously.

Mannu's heart stopped beating. She wanted to fight against the women seated around her but her limbs would not move, they were paralysed.

They did not take long to dress her up. Gripping her arms tightly to prevent her escape, they led her out. The relatives of the dead man were quarrelling loudly with one another over his property and possessions. They were soon at each others' throats. A group of men armed with knives and swords suddenly appeared and took charge. They set out with Mannu, the drummers in front with the women following them. The sati procession had started.

When the procession arrived at the burning ground, the body had already been laid on the pyre. The women accompanying Mannu grabbed her and began tearing off her jewels and clothes, each trying to outdo the other. Mannu fell down and the women tugged and pulled at her limbs and kicked her. Finally the pandas drove them away and lifted her onto the pyre, setting it on fire amidst a frenzied beating of drums and invocations to the goddess.

Mannu woke from her stupor to hear the thudding of horses' hooves. Fanning away the smoke rising from the pyre, she saw a white man and a group of native policemen. She shouted to them that the rebels had laid a trap for them and that they should watch out. But they did not pay any attention to her. Men armed with swords rushed out of the crowd and attacked them. The next thing Mannu heard were gunshots. Shooting continuously, the white man rode up to the pyre, pulled her out and seated her on his horse. He smothered the flames on her clothes while she clung to him.

The rebels were still fighting with the policemen. Resident Henry Williams' horse sped along the deserted bank of the river. The Resident, whose arm was bleeding from a wound and Mannu, whose skin was burnt in several places, sat on the horse, not speaking to each other.

27

A chill ran down Kotwal Moinuddin's spine when he realized that the raja's ravenous eyes were fixed on his neck. He lowered his head as though to hide it.

'You can never conceal your neck from my eyes, kotwal,' said the raja, noticing his gesture. 'No subject can keep his neck hidden from the king. It was to remind all of you that I changed the system of punishment from hanging to beheading.'

'I seek your pardon, huzur,' said the kotwal humbly. 'I am innocent.'

'You should be ashamed, kotwal, instead of being frightened!'

'Hukum.'

'You are a kotwal. You know the law. You are aware that every one of my subjects, from Kallu bania to Govardhan, is innocent. And you are still not ashamed to plead your innocence and yours alone to me! Where have they gone: your honour, your pride, your sense of brotherhood? Each one of you hunts the one next to him, ready to destroy him in an effort to save your own neck. I am disgusted with you shameless people! But enough of that. I called you here today for another reason.'

The raja took his hookah from the servant maid and began to puff at it. The kotwal waited respectfully for the royal command, which did not come for quite some time.

'Kotwal,' he said at last, 'you know, don't you, that the chain of chapattis has reached our country as well?'

'Yes, huzur.'

'What do you know about it?'

'Our spies have no clue as yet, huzur, what it is about. From where it started, or for what reason—'

'There is no need to find out. I called you here to tell you to break the chain. The white men feel that it involves a conspiracy against them. And we need their trust.'

'Yes, huzur.'

'You may go now.'

The raja sent for his minister as soon as the kotwal left. The minister waited respectfully before him.

Signalling to the servant woman to bring him wine, the Raja asked: 'Is the chain of chapattis moving as it should, mantri?'

'It is, huzur. As soon as a messenger reaches the headman of a village with the chapattis, he sends chapattis to five other villages within the next five days, as the message has instructed him to do. No one has dared to break the chain.'

'Excellent!'

The raja got up and began to pace up and down. The maid followed him with the goblet of wine.

'What do you think, mantri—will Moinuddin be able to break the chain?'

'Huzur, the kotwal is more concerned about trying to save his own neck.'

A smile appeared on the raja's face: 'That is why I have

made a chain of necks that runs parallel to the chain of chapattis! A chain of slender, beautiful necks as tempting to the sword as chapattis are to the palate!'

The mantri suggested to the court poet, who was seated cross-legged on a mat on the floor, that he compose a poem extolling the king's intelligence.

The raja picked up the goblet of wine from the tray the servant maid held, so that she could stop following him around. He drank a long mouthful, then asked the minister: 'Mantri, are we too not trying to liberate our subjects, just as these foreigners claim they are doing? Who will save this Andher Nagari ultimately: they or we?'

28

When the artillery led by the Ottoman Turks and the Portuguese soldiers destroyed the walls of the Chittor Fort, Bahadur Shah, assured of victory, did not think that he was setting the people inside the fort free. Ali Dost and his friends, who stood outside waiting for the sultan's orders, did not think so either. Those who were inside the fort themselves did what the sultan and Ali Dost had expected them to do. Under the leadership of the rani, Karnavati, all the women in the fort gathered whatever firewood was left, set it alight and jumped into the flames. All the men without exception rushed out of the open gates of the fort and sprang on the swords the sultan's soldiers held drawn. Only children were left behind. Ali Dost and his companions counted their bodies as they were lifted out of wells and ponds after the battle, stopping when the numbers went beyond three thousand.

Later, when Humayun's forces defeated Bahadur Shah and captured Champanir, Ali Dost became Humayun's property, part of the loot of war. In a mood for celebration, the emperor wore red and gave orders that some of the enemy prisoners be paraded before him. Ali Dost and his companions, who had been comrades of these prisoners until then, were appointed to torture them. As the emperor watched the prisoners being tortured and the sound of their shrieks merged with the hiss of fires and cries of the people in the streets, he broke into a dance, his red robe swirling around him.

By evening, silence fell over the deserted fort. Seated in the glow of a candle in a corner of the durbar room which had been washed clean after the day's macabre activities, the lonely imam on duty read a verse from the Holy Book. The verse that described how Allah had sent birds to shower lumps of clay on the elephant army and the army had turned as limp as straw. Dazed by opium, Humayun imagined that the imam had selected this particular verse in order to criticize his cruelty. Furious, he ordered that the imam be trampled under an elephant's feet. Ali Dost's strong hands twisted the imam into a ball and carried him to the elephant. Since he stood at a safe distance, Ali Dost's body was not soiled, but filthy morsels of brain and intestine splattered all over the mahout.

While the Choupat Raja and Company Bahadur argued about which of them was more competent to liberate the people from their oppressors, Humayun and Kamran about the right to rule and Henry Williams and John Williams about methods of rule, all of them kept talking to their reflections in the mirrors in front of them. But Ali Dost, who had grown up as a servant of them all, who had tortured and killed in obedience to whoever his master was, did not possess a reflection and could see everything except himself. It was of no concern to him whom he served—an Afghan, a Turk, a Hindu, the king's son or just a strong soldier. He did not care if his master was going to win or to lose. He did not wonder whether what he did was right or wrong. Even his own pain and pleasure did not enter his thoughts.

Ali Dost stood among the huts in the village and watched Humayun's army march over the maidan in the distance. Horses, elephants, foot soldiers were all completely enveloped in dust and slowly became a moving cloud of dust which raised thunder but no lightning. The villagers shuddered as the thudding of the horses' hooves rose above the din of the drums. When they realized that the army was moving away from them, they went back to their huts, relieved. Only Ali Dost stood where he was.

'Whose army was that, son?' asked the old woman who gave him his food, pressing his arm.

'I don't know, amma. Maybe Humayun's,' said Ali Dost indifferently. He added, 'Or Mohammed Ghori's... or Alauddin's... or Akbar's... or Nadir Shah's...'

Noticing the uneasiness in his eyes, the old woman caught his hand and asked: 'What is troubling you, child? You haven't told me.'

'Do you see the sixth fingers on my hands, amma?' he asked her. 'They do not take part in any of the acts my hands perform. But they are witnesses to all of them.'

'Is it the fear of sin that haunts you?'

'What is sin or virtue to a slave? Even my victims may not hate me. I have never been one of the five fingers of my hand, Amma, I have always been the sixth, the outsider.'

'Allah knows you cannot be punished for your deeds, Allah who made you a slave.'

'I seek responsibility for my deeds, amma, not forgiveness. I want to own them, whatever they are. All my masters were cruel. When they were defeated, their conquerors put them to death. But I was never punished. The conqueror quietly made me his property. Everything I did was for others. I was only a witness to even my own deeds.'

'Is freedom from slavery the freedom to be cruel?'

'I do not know, amma. When I watch armies led by kings march past me one by one, I sometimes think that what concerns this world is not cruelty or kindness but accountability or unaccountability.'

The old woman allowed him to withdraw his hand from hers. As she turned and walked away, she murmured to herself:

'I do not know either. I grew up seeing only tormentors everywhere. And then I saw people tormenting others in order to escape being tormented themselves. And now those who torment themselves in order not to give others the privilege of tormenting them. Who knows on whose side Allah is! Does He know Himself?'

29

The man coming from the opposite side looked as if his feet were not touching the ground. His eyes were fixed on a spot somewhere in the distance. His hands, held slightly away from his body, seemed like the stiffened wings of a bird. No part of his body moved except his legs which wavered and fumbled, trying to get a grip on the ground.

All he wore was a piece of cloth around his loins. Even that stayed in place only because, soaked in blood, it had stuck to his lacerated flesh. The blood that streamed down from the wounds on his body left a trail of red footprints behind him. The man did not seem to have noticed the dog following him, licking the bloody footprints.

It was a terrible sight.

Govardhan was terrified when he saw the man. In order to make sure that what he saw was real, Govardhan called out to him many times when he came up to him. But the man went past him, paying no attention, his eyes still fixed on a spot in the distance, his body as stiff as before. Govardhan stood still, following him with his eyes.

The man walked a little farther, and then collapsed on the ground like a tree that had been felled. Frightened, the dog moved some distance away and waited, looking at the man and Govardhan in turn. The man lay convulsed for a few moments, then became still.

Govardhan did not know what to do. He ran up to him, lifted him up and turned him on his back. He was dead. There were only two creatures that Govardhan could consult—the blind cat that he had been carrying in his hands and had now set down on the ground, and the dog which was still looking at him questioningly. The cat, sensing what had happened, turned in his direction blindly.

Govardhan pulled out the man's hands from under the mass of lacerated flesh that his body had become and placed them on his chest. He was startled to see that there were no thumbs on either hand. He got up abruptly, picked up the cat and walked away quickly.

The setting sun cast a reddish hue on the flat terrain that was covered with dry grass and stunted shrubs. The entire length of the footpath running through it was marked with the man's blood. There were no human beings or dwellings anywhere in that area.

He came upon a tripod after he had walked a short way. Abandoned by the scourgers and the scourged alike, it stood isolated on the ground, its three legs piercing the sky. Govardhan did not know whether to feel anger or compassion towards the silence and immobility of those three legs. His hands moved forward to touch the logs from which they were made, still fresh from the jungle, the branches and leaves having just been chopped off them.

Feeling something crawl up his legs, Govardhan looked down and saw black ants running all over the ground, the only sign of movement in that place. They were rushing up and down picking up the tiny morsels of flesh that the whip had scattered every time it struck its victim.

30

The sun had set by the time Govardhan reached the village. There was commotion everywhere, as if some calamity had taken place. In the bazaar, shopkeepers were hurriedly pulling down the shutters. Hawkers were bundling up the objects they had put out for sale and rushing away. In the melee, people jumped over the rice and wheat that had been piled up in cones. The voices of women calling out to children and the slamming of doors could be heard everywhere.

Was a cyclone threatening the place or had an attacking army arrived? Govardhan could not make out anything and no one had the patience to speak to him. In despair, he caught the hand of a man who was running and stopped him. But as soon as he saw the man's hand, he let go. It had no thumbs! Govardhan sensed that the man was equally shocked by the fact that he, Govardhan, had thumbs on his hands. As he bolted, the man cried: 'Run!'

The marketplace was on the bank of the river. Govardhan saw a few boats that were flying the Company flag coming ashore. Some were empty, others were filled with goods. Govardhan now understood why people were running away. The officers of the Company, their gomastas and dalals, were coming to sell their goods and buy goods from the villagers. Whatever the transaction, bargains would be made at gun point.

Govardhan noticed an open door at the rear of a house and rushed towards it. The woman inside was frightened at first but eventually allowed him to enter. Her children brought him water to drink. There were no thumbs on their hands either.

Govardhan gradually came to terms with the frightening fact that no one in the village had thumbs. Just as he had accepted the blindness that the cat he carried in his hands had constantly reminded him of.

Govardhan said to the woman: 'I come from a town where blinding helpless animals is a pastime for children and inflicting torture on children is a pastime for older people. I found it impossible to seek shelter there. I thought it was better to flee from the policemen who were after me.'

'The people here will not give you shelter either,' said the woman. 'We cannot even protect ourselves.'

'Yes, I know. Moreover, I have all five fingers!'

Govardhan gave the cat a piece from one of the chapattis the woman gave him and ate the rest with slices of onion. While eating, he said: 'I had an older brother, long ago. He had an additional finger, a sixth one, on each of his hands. Fingers that remained only witnesses and did not participate in any of the acts he performed. I used to walk along with him when I was a child, clinging to those fingers. The people I see here have four fingers, but no thumbs on their hands.'

'We were all born with thumbs, but we cut them off,' she explained to him. 'We were weavers by caste. The officers of the Company often came and camped in our village with their gomastas. They would convene a cutchery in the village and force us to sign contracts to sell the cloth we wove to them at prices that they decided. The prices were ridiculously low but we had no alternative. If we refused, they would tie us up and flog us to death. In order to escape this fate, we cut off our thumbs, threw them into the river and gave up our trade. It became a ritual with us to cut off children's thumbs and offer them to Ganga-ma. But they did not spare us. When we abandoned weaving and took to farming the land and fishing, they arrived to buy our rice, our jute, our fish, and forced us to buy their salt, their tobacco, and their opium. It was they who decided on the prices for everything they bought and everything they sold. If we did not agree…' she broke down.

'I saw a man on the way here. He was a heap of mangled flesh. He fell down on the road and died.'

The woman was silent for a while. Then she began to weep. The two children, who were seated in the corner eating chapattis rushed up and threw their arms around her.

It was then that Govardhan noticed that her clothes were white and that there were no bangles on her hands. If the Company caught a man and took him away to flog him, he did not usually return. It was assumed that he had died. The villagers would go on with what was left of their own lives.

'All you saw on the way was one tripod,' she said when she had composed herself once more. 'Tomorrow, you may see many of them. So many women are going to be widowed tonight!'

Cries and screams rose from the bazaar late into the night. The gomastas and dalals of the Company kept forcing the villagers to open their shops and sell their goods. The sounds subsided gradually and the night of the tripods began.

The wife and children of the man who had died the day before lay huddled in a corner of the one-room mud hut, their arms around one another. Govardhan and his companion, the blind cat, lay in another corner. The cool night-breeze brushed gently over them, trying to soothe their pain. As the darkness deepened and the tumult created by the empire-builders faded away, sleep came to them like a blessing.

The village of those without thumbs was peaceful again by morning. The boats had left with their cargo.

31

Kotwal Moinuddin raised the lantern he held in his hand in order to look closely at the face of the woman at the door. Who was she, this woman who had come alone at this hour of the night? Even as he was looking at her, she slid down along the door frame and collapsed on the floor.

Moinuddin lifted her up, laid her down on the bench in the room and sprinkled water on her face.

There was not even a constable in the thana. He had sent everyone away and had been sitting in the same posture alone in his room, his eyes red and swollen from lack of sleep. He had not gone home for days nor eaten a proper meal. He had not gone out in search of Govardhan. Nor had he gone to investigate the affair of the chain of chapattis, he had only sent havildars to look into it. All he had done during this period was attend to the daily routine in the station. Kotwal Moinuddin did not want to give anyone occasion to say he had run away to save his head.

When she recovered consciousness, Salma looked at the kotwal and wept. 'Kotwal babu, save my daughter, my little one! The pandas have kidnapped her, to burn her along with some old man's body!'

Moinuddin understood at once. There had been so many cases of late. Rebellious Hindus had been registering their protest against the laws the firangis had passed banning sati, while Muslims, not to be outdone, had begun to stone fallen women in their community to death. All of them believed they could register their protest against the white man's rule by breaking their laws, even if it meant punishing their own women!

'Don't worry,' he consoled her. 'The foreigners will give up their lives to see that the law is maintained. From the resident downward, they would have gone all out to fulfil their duty. Perhaps they have already rescued her by now.'

No sooner did he say this than the kotwal clicked his tongue. What law was he talking about? Had he forgotten the fate that awaited Govardhan? The fate that might become his?

Moinuddin dismissed all such questions from his mind, returned to his duties and took out the register to record the woman's complaint.

'What is the girl's name?'

'Mannu.'

'Her father's name?'

'Govardhan.'

The kotwal was devastated. This woman was asking him to find Govardhan's daughter! Did she know that he had been commissioned to find her husband and have him beheaded? And that if he did not succeed in his task, he himself would be beheaded?

Moinuddin bit his lips, opened the register and wrote the report. Then he took Salma to his quarters, just behind the thana.

He had not been to his quarters in many days. The constable

who was in charge of the house was asleep on the veranda. He woke him up and made arrangements for Salma to stay there. Then he lay down on his bed.

He felt as if rain had fallen on the fire that had been burning within him for days. He did not think about the death sentence hanging over his own head and Govardhan's. All there was in his mind was the image of a small girl whom the pandas wanted to burn alive and her agonized mother. The happiness that had come to him because he had been able to accept another's pain instead of his own brought him the kind of sleep that had eluded him for days.

32

David Butler felt far more exhausted than the horse that had been running for hours, carrying him on its back. Exhaustion had always been for him an experience to be deeply enjoyed, to be celebrated by relaxing, but it did not seem so to him now.

Butler was on his way back from a tiger-hunting expedition that had proved fruitless. He had not been able to spot the animal anywhere. Reluctant to come back empty-handed, the party had shot a few deer. Then, dismissing the others, Butler had chosen to ride alone through the countryside.

Spring had just ended and the days were getting warmer and longer. Darkness had not fallen, but the dense foliage of the mango trees that surrounded the village made it seem as though it was already night. He walked in, leading the horse. The dogs began to bark frantically but the villagers drove them away when they saw that he was a white man.

When he saw these people, Butler's thoughts flew to the fugitive Govardhan, apprehending whom he now considered his particular duty. So far, he had not come across him. But then, any of the people he had seen could have been Govardhan, for he had never seen the man himself. It was easy to make out a tiger from a deer, but how could he distinguish one tiger from among many?

As he entered the village, he saw more and more people. Actually, all the people of the village had gathered on the open ground before a dargah, around a huge banyan tree. A fakir stood on the platform built around the tree. Everyone, including the fakir, was singing, palms outstretched in an appeal to God. But it was not a prayer and the words were strange:

> O moula who gives
> Water to plants,
> Grains to living creatures,
> Why do you give human beings
> Only thirst and sorrow?

Tears streamed down everyone's cheeks as they sang, whether they were old or young, men or women.

Butler stood leaning against a tree outside the circle and watched them. Torches began to glow brightly as the darkness slowly deepened. A village where everyone wept! Butler found the scene mystifying. Why were these people crying? What disaster had overtaken them?

He suddenly caught sight of another person who stood like him outside the circle of people, leaning against a tree. He was not crying.

Butler went up to him and asked: 'Why aren't you crying?'

'You're not crying either!' countered the man. 'But I know why you're not. You're searching for someone in this crowd. It is victims, those who are preyed upon, who weep, not hunters.'

'That would make you a hunter and all these people victims?'

'These people have given me refuge.'

'From whom?'

'From my victims.'

Butler ruminated over what he said for a while before he spoke: 'Hunters who flee from their prey! Prey that gives refuge to the predators! Are you a poet or a fakir?'

The stranger came out from under the tree's shade and began to fondle his horse's neck and sides.

'Butler sahib, the person you are searching for is my younger brother, Govardhan. An emperor ordered me to gouge out his younger brother's eyes and I have just arrived after completing that task. The victims whom I tortured and wounded are all around me. The people of this village which gave me refuge have been the victims of innumerable hunters for centuries. And yet, I had decided very long ago that my place would never be among victims...'

'I do not understand you,' said Butler gently, 'but I am sure you are not a poet. I dislike poetry anyway. However, the problem that both of us face has something in it which is not quite prose. Look, it is not my aim to hunt down your younger brother like an animal. All I need to do is to arrest him in my capacity as an officer. Enough of that. Tell me, do you know why all these people, from children to the very old, are weeping like this?'

'I do not know, sahib,' Ali Dost said, turning his palms up. 'Perhaps it is the thought of a great calamity approaching that makes them weep. They may not be able to tell you themselves what it is if you ask them. Victims have a singular capacity to foresee impending disaster even without being able to explain what exactly it is. You must have noticed that as a hunter.'

'Oh God!' A chill coursed down Butler's spine and he felt his hair standing on end. Fear, anger and pain assailed him in turn. This man who was fleeing from his victims to take refuge among other victims was certainly no fool. Nor were this crowd of people fools either. History had not written its final verdict on those who were weaker, those who were ruled or those who ruled. Butler felt his own eyes growing moist.

It had grown dark and the torches glowed brighter. The fakir danced as he sang:

O moula who gives
Water to plants
And grain to living creatures...

The whole crowd sang and danced with him.

Butler asked himself anxiously: what disaster threatened them?

Ali Dost, who had begun to walk on, leading his horse, asked himself the same question.

33

It had grown dark by the time Henry got back to his bungalow, covered in dust, sweat and dried blood. The knife-wound he had received on his arm had stopped bleeding, hurting only when he moved the arm. But the girl who sat with him on the horse seemed in a bad state. Her clothes and hair were singed and her skin burnt.

Henry was astonished that this ten-year-old girl had endured the pain of her wounds so quietly. She had not wept or lost consciousness. Seated amidst the flames of a pyre that had started to blaze, she had called out to him to try and save himself. A girl of ten! He had not spoken to her on the way, only holding her as close as he might have a beloved daughter.

He took her straight to his reading room. He washed and dressed her wounds, applied medicine to them and gave her new clothes.

'Do you know why I brought you to my reading room?' he asked, trying to put himself at ease with her. 'Books are the greatest marvels to me and you are a marvel like a book.'

She did not say anything.

He asked: 'Why did you call out and ask me to save myself? Even though you knew I was the only one who could have saved *you* at that moment?'

'Sahib, they were burning me as a trap to kill you,' she said, with the innocence of childhood. 'I overheard them talk about it. They wanted to raise a revolt against you.'

She did not seem to see him as a foreigner, an enemy.

'I know,' said Henry. 'I knew when I got the news and set out to save you. It is wrong to burn widows alive along with their husband's bodies. It is my duty both as the resident and as a human being to prevent that. Even if it means adding fuel to the revolt against the Company.'

'Then why didn't you save my father? My father too is innocent, just as I am. And yet, your police hunts him like a wild animal, they want to catch him and hang him.'

Henry sprang up. 'Your father! Are you Govardhan's daughter? My God!' He was completely taken aback. He thought to himself, 'A book is a marvel to me until I read it. When I finish reading it, it becomes a greater marvel! The more I begin to understand you, the more perplexed I become!'

Mannu began to cry. Henry placed his hand on her shoulder and said affectionately, 'My child, you do not know. And I don't know how to make you understand. As far as saving *you* is concerned, the law is on my side. But in your father's case...'

'The law says an innocent man must be hanged?'

'No, child, the law does not say an innocent man must be hanged. The jailer is searching for Govardhan because he escaped from jail. It is a crime to escape from jail.'

'Yes, yes, and he is to be hanged if he is found, even if it is against the law!' Mannu had stopped crying. Her words were sharp, her voice far more measured and calm than that of a child. 'If I had jumped off the pyre and run away, would you have caught me and handed me over to those brutes?'

'You do not understand,' said Henry, shaking his head.

How could the mind of this child, trained in simple methods of reasoning, comprehend the complex twists and turns of the deceitful law that played hide-and-seek in the murky alleys frequented by trading companies that encouraged fraud, unscrupulous empire-builders and local chieftains with dubious reputations? Nor did she understand how he had sneaked through those alleys and tried to save Govardhan. He could not tell her that story. Loyal and obedient servant of the Company that he was, he could not find the courage to say that to this innocent child.

It was not a pleasant experience at all for Henry to find himself, the representative of the most powerful and ruthless empire on earth, fumbling for words and contradicting himself at every second sentence in front of this unlettered little girl who came from a people who had been slaves by birth and caste over centuries. But he had no alternative.

Mannu had fallen completely silent. She did not cry or ask questions, but sat like a closed book in a corner of the reading room. Henry, however, had not finished with his explanations and justifications, which poured out of him as he paced up and down in the spaces between the shelves, glancing at the child every now and then from the corner of an eye.

34

Not just the dispensation of law and justice but governance, trade, gambling and even lovemaking were conducted in the narrow, murky alleys of the city of Delhi, thought Mirza Ghalib. Everything assumed a clandestine nature in this city. Seen from above, it was as if nothing noteworthy ever happened here except the eternal and regular passage of time from morning to night and night to morning. It seemed that nothing here was meant for those of noble birth, whether it had to do with governing or trading or lovemaking or drinking or gambling. When Colonel Brown asked Mirza Ghalib whether he was a Muslim, he replied: 'Half a Muslim! I drink wine but don't eat pork!'

And yet, the story of how his clandestine exploits had taken him to prison became the talk of the town. People ridiculed him and composed lampoons about this famous poet of Hindustan. Friends turned away from him.

It was while he was gambling in a godown, hidden away behind a paan shop, that the law reached out through its back door and caught him. That was the second time it had happened. The first time, the police had let him off with a warning. This time, he was sentenced to six months in prison. He was reluctant to tell them he was a poet. And when he did tell them, there was no change at all in the daroga's attitude. If he was caught the next day in the bedroom of some rich man's wife, it would be the mullahs who would draw their swords against him. The city had turned against the poet.

Ramchander had once narrated the story of a poor man who was caught as he was walking down the road and taken to the gallows for the sole reason that he had a slender neck. The poverty-stricken fellow had gone to the rupee-a-seer market to buy bran. Seeing that every commodity was being sold there at the same price, he had decided he would buy rice instead. It was then that the sepoys caught sight of his neck. If they wished to, they could have charged him with the crime of having bought something he was not worthy of. But they did not do so. It was the law itself that the law had caught here, the law that had placed itself behind bars!

Ghalib paced up and down the stone floor of the prison. He was furious with everyone, with everything. The poem he had been about to write burned itself out in that anger.

The guard heard his footsteps, came to the door and struck his stick against the bars. 'You cannot walk up and down like this, this is not a garden. Go and sit down quietly.'

His pride wounded, Ghalib sank down on the floor. He hated the guards, the police, the darogas. And the paanwalas, the tavern keepers, the sakis, the dancing girls, everyone who walked through the streets of this city. He felt deeply resentful of the friends who had deserted him in these evil days. None of them had the capacity to understand a poet. The love and intoxication, the pleasures that touched a poet's heart to life could only be obtained here by lurking in by-lanes at midnight, knocking furtively at back doors and throwing dust in the eyes of sepoys and darogas and mullahs. He hated even Urdu, the language of this rabble. He had been born in a noble and ancient Turk family, he decided he would write henceforward only in Persian. Picking up a pencil and a piece of paper, he began to write his new credo:

Sham'a har chand bahar ja:rid aassazn soozad
Khushtar a:nst ki bar kit'adar aivaan so:zad.
U:di man harj maso:zi:d gar so:khti:ast
Baravari:d ki dar muzmari sulta:n so:zad
a:h zi:n kha:n ki dard na tuva:n ya:ft hava
juz samu:me ki khaso kha:re baya: ba:n so:zad[6]

As he put aside his pen and lay with his head pillowed on the stone floor of the prison, a question troubled him: whom would Ghalib serve then? Which sultan, which king? The gem-studded walls of which emperor's palace would he brighten? Hindustan was in the throes of a complex power struggle. Passing from

---

[6] The candle's flame with equal ease puts
  Darkness everywhere to flight
  But better that it burn for kings
  Filling their palaces with light
  Ghalib is precious frankincense
  If he must burn then it were right
  To burn him in a costly censer,
   Symbol of a prince's might.
   Alas! that he lies here where
   Never comes the cooling breeze of morn

the durbar of one king to that of another had been as simple as opening one's eyes from one day to the next for Amir Khusru and Kalidasa. For there had been only one king and one durbar at a time in the country. Whereas war, mutiny, governance, commerce were all entangled here. And not only kings but even traders held durbars here.

To drive away his worries, Ghalib thought of a pure love poem.

35

The geography of the landscape changed as Govardhan left the village and the fields behind it. There were hills thick with trees. Tracks made by woodcutters wound through the woods and there were small clearings here and there beside streams. The tracks too would soon disappear once the forest became dense. He had been instructed to skirt the forest and follow the woodcutters' tracks until he reached the next village. Most probably there were wild animals here. There were plenty of snakes anyway.

The headman had given Govardhan a task to do in return for two days' food and shelter. He had to carry a packet of chapattis to the next village and the headman there would grant him safety for another two days.

Govardhan did not know the purpose of carrying chapattis from one village to another in this way. All that the headman had told him was that his task had to be carried out in the utmost secrecy. It was obviously a task fraught with danger. Which was why the headman had risked providing shelter to

Govardhan, a culprit wanted by the government. What offence could there be in passing on a few chapattis which could have been easily made anywhere from one village to another? But Govardhan asked no questions. Each of them had to safeguard the other's crime, that was all. Since he himself had been charged falsely, Govardhan thought that the headman's crime could be a misplaced one as well.

He went down to the stream and drank some water. Then he picked up the packet of chapattis and his cat. That was when he heard voices. Instinctively, he ran to hide among the trees.

A group of people were walking along the woodcutters' track. Six men: all carrying sticks, spears and long knives. They were talking among themselves and looking around apprehensively. They walked in single file, the edge of each one's dhoti tied to the dhoti of the one in front of him. Govardhan recognized them as they came nearer. Kallu bania led the line, followed by the mason, the chunewala, the bhishti, the kasai and the ganderia. Each of them had been pursuing their independent lives in the city and now, because of this case, they were bound together by a chain. There were two people left to complete the chain: the kotwal and Govardhan. Govardhan suddenly had an overwhelming desire to join them and become part of the chain. Injustice bound him and these men together. However, the nature of the mission he had undertaken drew him back. He sank deeper into the bushes.

'Didn't I tell you he would never hide in a jungle like this?' said the ganderia. He gazed all around fearfully as he spoke. 'If we search for him here, it's morsels of clothing we should look for! The tigers will have finished him long ago!'

'What clothes would he have worn?' said the bhishti. 'The

idiot had come from his village to see the city!'

'He's no idiot. He jumped jail, remember. He'll do anything to save himself. I think he's part of a gang of robbers...' said the chunewala.

The kasai fondled his knife. 'Isn't that why we've come prepared...'

Govardhan was shocked. He had thought they were all united as victims of injustice. But these men seemed to have united for another cause—to hunt him down. They had been pursuing him all the way, weapons in hand, thirsting for his blood! Fear coursed through his nerves like lightning. Aware of everything that had happened, they seemed to think of themselves as innocent and of him as a criminal who wanted to implicate them.

'Did you know, his wife is with the kotwal. He's locked her up in his house.'

'Strange fellow, this kotwal! He knows he'll lose his head if he doesn't find Govardhan in ten days' time. And he wants to share his bed with the rascal's wife those ten days!'

'The kotwal is playing a different game. Maybe he thinks that if the word gets around, that fellow will come and fall at his feet.'

'What about his daughter? I heard the pandas married her off to some old, dying thakur in order to burn her along with his dead body.'

'That's an old story. I believe the resident sahib himself arrived at the spot, lifted her from the pyre and took her away on his horse.'

'Like the kotwal, the resident too needs a woman to warm his bed.'

'Imagine! Ten years old and the little flirt already has two men!'

'As is the rascal, so are his family!'

'That's not the problem now, fools. Can we trust the kotwal? Our lives hang on that question. If he…'

As the men moved away and disappeared, still talking among themselves, Govardhan felt terribly alone and abandoned. Although he had not seen them, the thought that there existed this chain of victims who were his brothers had comforted him. The chain had broken and he was alone now.

Not only the chain but his family too had broken up. It had shattered in pieces. Govardhan was afraid even to think about them. What if he went and fell at the kotwal's feet to plead for Salma, as these men had suggested? But the kotwal was already helping her. The resident sahib who had lifted Mannu out of the pyre was the same person who had come on horseback to warn Govardhan to run away from the policemen who were chasing him. The kasai and the bhishti did not know that. It was a consolation to Govardhan that Mannu at least was in safe hands.

Govardhan was afraid to come out even after the men disappeared. There had to be a gap of at least a day between him and his hunters. He had to spend a day by himself in the jungle and allow them to move well ahead.

Before him was a chain of chapattis, in place of the broken chain of victims. A chain in which the links were petitioners or culprits, he was not sure which. No one knew where the chain had started or where it would end, but he was certainly a link in it. He wondered whether being part of this newly-acquired chain would be a consolation, whether it would quell the horror of isolation that surrounded him now.

The blind cat mewed, reminding him that he was not alone. It pushed its legs into his lap, rubbed against him, curled up, stretched itself, raised its head and looked at him with sightless eyes. Govardhan held it close to his chest and felt his eyes grow moist.

The cat was hungry and so was he. It was very late and night had fallen. The night of the forest. There were chapattis in the packet. What if he ate them?

Govardhan released the cat, so that it could search for prey of some sort, whatever its blind eyes would allow it to find. It did not come back.

He tightened the knot on the packet of chapattis and sat on it. Something in him told him that he should not break that chain.

36

Ramchander dozed against the stone platform on the wayside that was used to rest loads. On either side of the wide highway that ran through the deserted area were huge trees, these stone platforms at frequent intervals and a few sarais where travellers could find water and food. It was noon and the sun was high in the sky.

Ramchander opened his eyes to find two young men sitting beside him. They wore white clothes and carried bags and sticks. They looked like brahmacharis from some ashram.

They offered Ramchander water and fruits at once, as if they had been waiting for him to wake up. Ramchander was hungry and thirsty, so he accepted them eagerly.

'Thank you, children,' he said.

'It is we who should thank you. We've been looking everywhere for you.'

'Why were you looking for me?'

'We were in the audience when you spoke at the meeting of the Kayastha Sabha. We were seated at the back, so you may not have seen us.'

Ramchander sat up straight and looked at them carefully. No, he had not noticed them.

'It was what you said about right and wrong that attracted us most.'

Ramchander did not say anything.

They continued: 'It was so inspiring! It's not just sums that go wrong. Notes in music can go wrong, or colours in a painting or grammar when writing. Ideas, history that has been recorded, good and bad, justice and injustice, dharma and adharma, knowledge and ignorance, memory and forgetfulness. The whole world is held in the balance between right and wrong. It made us curious to hear you present a problem that we had been struggling with for years.'

'Where were you seated?'

'A little faraway, in the Samyamani.'

'The Samyamani...' Ramchander turned the word over in his mind. He glanced at the bundles of paper they held in their hands.

'You are...?'

'Yes, we are accountants,' said the more talkative of the two. 'I am Chitragupta, son of Dandi, the progenitor of all kayasthas and historians. And this is my friend Yama, son of Surya, the witness of all things. Our fathers perceive the world as a collection of living beings and history as an anthology of events. We quarrelled with them, arguing that events are not just events alone, that they have characteristics and attributes.'

'There is a science above all sciences,' said Ramchander. 'The faculty that human beings possess to distinguish right from wrong. And there is something beyond that as well: having distinguished right from wrong, the resolution one makes to act upon this. It is the combination of these two that makes a human being truly human.'

'But, masterji, things often have a way of becoming complicated. For instance, even when people recognize right as right and wrong as wrong, their courses of action vary so widely. You, a teacher of mathematics, give your pupil five marks if he does his sum right and zero if it is wrong. In other words, you do not award him anything if he does it wrong. A judge on the other hand awards the accused a punishment if he finds him guilty, he sends him to jail. And he lets him go if he finds he has acted right—in other words, he gives him zero. So you see that although the teacher and the judge have similar notions of right and wrong, they react to them in very different ways!'

Ramchander congratulated them: 'Brilliant!' He continued, very seriously: 'You said, didn't you that events are not events alone, that they have characteristics and attributes as well. That they, therefore, have to be separated into good and bad events, right and wrong ones. I want to go one step further. We have to investigate the circumstances and the environment in which those circumstances occur as well. For example, the result of a mistake a boy commits when doing a sum affects only him. But the person found guilty by a court cannot escape with zero marks alone, for other people have to suffer for his wrong deed. Tell me now, what was your experience when you launched your expedition to differentiate between the right and wrong of man's deeds?'

'Look at us, masterji. How do we look?'

Ramchander smiled at them: 'You are handsome boys!'

'Yes, we were born handsome children to our parents. It was the time when history was just beginning and there were only accountants in the world... If you follow this route, sir, you will reach Kashi. Or Puri, Dwaraka or Sringeri, all abodes of scholarly men. When you get there, ask them what we look like. They will all tell you how ugly and awful we look, they will speak of our long, protruding teeth, our reddened eyes and clawlike nails, the spears and ropes we carry with us to torture people. Our journey has been extremely tedious, masterji. There is no limit to the hate, the hostility we have provoked. We set out to investigate the characteristics of events, while you are looking at the nature of those characteristics. We extend our good wishes to you. Even though we know all about the rows of stakes and crosses erected on this road for those who endeavour to unite truth and justice, logic and science...'

The young men picked up their bags and sticks and got up. Ramchander watched silently as they disappeared down the long, endless road.

37

'Mantri, who is the greatest trader in this country?'
'You, huzur.'

'How dare you say that?! I am the king of this country, the god of its people.'

'Huzur, you became king through barter. By trading two lakh pounds. No bigger bargain has ever been made in this country.'

'You are right.' Even though it was he who had paid, the raja complimented himself on the enormity of the amount. But his expression suddenly changed. 'How dare you say that! I'll have you hanged!'

'Huzur!'

'All right. From the moment you became my minister, you've had a noose around your neck. I'm not going to pull it tight now.'

'Huzur, the native merchants are waiting outside with their grievances.'

'The patwaris complain that when they go to collect the

taxes, the Company's gomastas drive them away, threatening them with guns. The native merchants complain that the patwaris collect levies only from them, not from the Company's men. I don't want to listen to any of them. The king's duty is to rule, not to listen to complaints. Send them away and call the resident in.'

The resident came in and paid his respects.

'Um... what have you come for?' asked the raja.

'Huzur, you sent for me.'

'So you will not come unless I send for you? The Company's gomastas have let destruction loose everywhere. And the resident sits in his bungalow as if he knows nothing. I have exempted the Company from taxes only as far as external trade is concerned. As far as trade within the country goes, the Company and its gomastas have to pay my taxes. Is not that my firman?'

'You are right, huzur.'

'And yet the Company's men threaten my tax collectors with guns. They fix their own prices for buying and selling their goods in the market. They torture my merchants with their whips and guns if they protest.'

'Huzur, I have written to the directors of the Company asking them to take action against the erring officers.'

'Excellent! Our resident has sent a report to the directors of the Company against the Company and its officers! Your work is over now. You may go.'

As soon as the resident left, the raja sent for a bottle of wine, poured some into a glass and sat there looking at it, not drinking.

'Mantri!' said the raja softly. 'The wine in this glass has the potential to intoxicate me. But I will not become intoxicated unless I drink it, will I?'

'That is right, huzur.'

'Ruling a country I do not have the ability to rule seems like trying to enjoy this wine that I have not drunk yet. Why then do I feel inebriated?'

'It is not just the act of ruling that is intoxicating, Huzur, even the greed to rule can be so. Those who fight for power can be as blind in their behaviour as those who wield power.'

'I have heard that being involved in trade can be as intoxicating as ruling a country. Are we not witnessing the transformation of trade into government in this country? When I look into the future, my cursed eyes see a time when governance will turn into trade, mantri. Today or tomorrow, my head will roll on the ground. But on the day that happens, my statue will go up in every marketplace in every city. But wait... didn't you say, mantri, that those who fight for power can be as intoxicated as those who wield power? How much lies in store for my subjects to see!'

The raja swallowed a gulp of wine, got up and began to walk about. Silence fell between them for a few moments.

'Huzur,' ventured the minister hesitantly, fearfully. 'Do you love your subjects?'

'Do I not?'

'Why do you punish them all the time? Even when they have done nothing wrong?'

'Mantri, where else does the intoxication of power lie but in the act of punishing?' The raja swallowed another mouthful of wine, went up to the minister, placed his hand on his shoulder like a friend and said gently: 'Tell me mantri, what if I release my subjects from punishment for a change?'

The mantri stared at him as if he had said something blasphemous.

The raja went on: 'Why should I apply laws that I cannot enforce on the foreigners on our own subjects? Since we have become incapable of collecting taxes from foreign traders, from today I exempt all my subjects from taxes. Send out men at once to proclaim this order throughout the land!'

The mantri stood astonished and as the minutes passed, his bewilderment gradually changed into fear. His lips trembled. He looked at the king's throne and saw that it was trembling. While trying to sit down on it, the raja slipped and fell down. The glass in his hand rolled to the ground and the wine streamed over the floor.

38

The sky had been overcast since morning, with clouds racing across its expanse. From time to time they dipped to bathe the city, then rose again to rush across the sky. Caught in the exhilaration of the monsoon's arrival, Umrao Jan and her sister courtesans went to the mango grove near the lake to celebrate, accompanied by Nawab Chabban, Ali Akbar Khan and Gauhar Mirza. They hired carriages, loaded them with cooking utensils, provisions and tents and drove out. The countryside was beautiful, its lush green washed clean by the rain.

They lit a fire in the summer-house in the mango grove and began to fry puris and cook vegetables. Gauhar plucked a basketful of mangoes straight from the tree. When they had eaten enough of the fruit and littered the place with the skin and seeds, they began to smear mango juice on one another. One by one, they fell down in the slush. Some dived into the lake, others preferred to roll in the mud. A group of gypsies arrived and began to sing and dance. As the mood of celebration reached its zenith, the rain came down in torrents. Huge raindrops rippled over the surface of the lake as the wind made the trees dance wildly.

It stopped raining by evening and the sun came out. Everyone changed into dry clothes and set out for a walk in the forest. The nawab and his friends took their guns and went to shoot birds. Umrao Jan left the group and went away armed with her sorrow and a sense of loneliness that had descended on her when the celebrations ended.

The sun went down behind the trees and the sky and the surface of the lake shimmered like liquid gold. Umrao Jan did not know how far she wandered. The sun sank lower, touching the sky with delicate hues of red, while the clouds kept changing colour.

She came to a narrow muddy path over which a couple of peasants were returning home, their ploughs on their shoulders. A girl went past her, herding cattle. The path became deserted after that. She walked on and reached a fakir's dwelling where some people were seated, smoking hookahs. They showed her the way back—it led through a wood full of thick trees. Umrao Jan took the path, making her way back in the semi-darkness. After a while she heard someone digging. Following the sounds, she came upon a man in a vest and a dirty dhoti, digging under a clump of trees. Their eyes met. Though it had been years since she had seen him, Umrao Jan recognized Dilawar Khan at once. She stood frozen, unable to move or speak, faced with the man who had abducted her and sold her in Khanum's kothi when she was a little girl of ten. Recognition, however, eluded Dilawar; frightened by her expression, he dropped his spade and ran away.

Unable to control her agitation, she described the incident to the nawab the next day while they were having their meal.

'Why didn't you tell me at once?' asked the nawab sadly. 'If you had, we could have caught the rascal. He's a notorious dacoit; the government has fixed a price of a thousand rupees on his head. But it is too late now anyway. Having learnt of the king's proclamation exempting the people from taxes, Dilawar Khan has declared that he wants to reform. He is going to surrender himself before the king at a function tomorrow in the rupee-a-seer market. He will hand over all the loot he has extracted over the years to the king. In return, the king will appoint him a subedar in his army!'

Umrao Jan said nothing, nor did she weep. She had ceased to weep long ago. Ever since the younger brother whom she used to feed all the things she liked most to eat, going without them herself, had pulled out his knife and fallen on her when she met him after an interval of years. And her mother had peered out for an instant from behind a torn purdah of sackcloth and withdrawn as suddenly, to become the memory of a sob in the dark. She told herself that fate had cheated her once more; that was all.

The nawab continued: 'The whole city will gather tomorrow to felicitate the king. We nawabs and mirzas cannot stay away. We will have to do something too.'

39

Ramchander was not present at the celebration that took place in the rupee-a-seer market. Butler and the mahant were there, but they did not speak to each other. Once the proclamations and announcements had been made, the king got into the royal chariot and drove to the palace. Dressed in the new green robes the king had given him, Subedar Dilawar Khan proceeded on horseback to the cantonment to inspect the troops. Reluctant to disperse at once, the crowds stayed awhile.

The society of intellectuals mockingly called the Kayastha Sabha met that evening. The Town Hall, embellished with richly carved arches, pilasters and cornices, was full, proof that the city was in a festive mood. However, the speakers remained speakers and the listeners remained listeners as usual.

There were two points on the agenda. One was the fate of Govardhan and the other the surrender of Dilawar Khan. The speakers expressed deep sympathy for Govardhan. There was absolutely no doubt that it was incompatible with logic and justice to punish an innocent man. However, the sentence the king had passed on Govardhan was a clever slap in the face for the system of law the foreigners had imposed. Even while disapproving of the way the king dispensed justice, it was not right to condemn what he did—the problems that individuals faced could not be placed on par with larger interests. Intellectuals had to take a balanced view. They could suggest that Govardhan plead guilty and ask the raja's pardon; they could appeal to the raja to be lenient and sympathetic to Govardhan.

All the speakers felt that Dilawar Khan's surrender was to be welcomed, regardless of what his antecedents had been. There was no one who had not heard of him. The sufferings he had inflicted on people through murder, dacoity and kidnapping were endless. His name had struck terror everywhere, in the cities, and throughout the countryside. Still, he could not be denied the right to repent. And to surrender himself before the king at this juncture was definitely good for the country. He was prepared to donate the wealth he had amassed over the years to the treasury to compensate for the losses it would suffer from the withdrawal of taxes. The speakers hoped that other dacoits would follow his example.

At the beginning of the meeting, some friends of Ramchander announced their resignation and left.

Most of the remaining members thought that these matters were not their concern. Being poets, teachers, journalists, officials or historians, they were afraid that it would affect their neutrality if they took sides and expressed a firm opinion. Therefore, once they understood the viewpoint of the speakers, they too left the hall.

Those who remained did not understand what was happening at all. Idle curiosity had brought them there. They sat through the meeting and left without making any comments.

That was how that day's meeting of the Kayastha Sabha ended. Circumstances in the city did not permit a meeting for many years after that. And by the time the situation changed, the Kayastha Sabha had ceased to exist.

The same day, the Company's army surrounded the raja's palace at midnight. A few shots were fired, but no battle took place. No one ever saw the raja after that. The Company's trade was transformed completely into the government of the country.

40

Two telegrams. Both said the same thing: that he had to take over the post of commissioner. But they were different in that one was an order from the Governor and the other a request from his younger brother, John.

As soon as the king was arrested and the Company took over the government, Resident Williams had made it clear that he would resign and return to his country. The two telegrams were a reaction to this. A decision was urgently required. The country had no king.

Holding both the telegrams in his hand, Henry paced up and down the room. He put the papers into his pocket from time to time, and then took them out. Finally, he went up to the door of Mannu's room. Although the door lay open, he knocked on it twice, hesitantly. Mannu came running up.

'Can I come in, child?' he asked. She moved aside for him to enter.

He went in and said shyly: 'My child, I have come to seek your advice on a certain matter—a personal matter.'

As he began to speak, the resident was astonished at himself. He had so many friends and colleagues in this city, citizens of repute with whom he could have discussed this problem, but he had not approached any of them. It was to this ten-year-old illiterate girl that he had finally come, looking for the answer to his question. And with so much fear and humility. As if her decision was final.

Naturally, Mannu did not understand what he said about trade, government, the difference of opinion he had had with the Company. All she understood was this: that this foreigner whom she had begun to call 'uncle' was a good man; that no matter how bad a piece of work was, it was better that a good man did it than a bad man.

'A good man could destroy himself doing a bad deed. But uncle, will not the deed itself become better when a good man does it?'

Henry stared at the little girl who barely reached up to his waist. The wisdom and logic of what she said astounded him. He had saved her and was caring for her now. And yet, she was thinking of how to alleviate the tragedy that threatened all human beings in general rather than just him, her saviour and protector.

He had just turned to go after thanking her for having helped him take a decision when David Butler's horse came flying like a bullet and stopped before his bungalow.

'The battalion has risen in mutiny, sir,' he said, without alighting. 'The native sepoys have left the barracks and are attacking the officers.'

'And your jail?' asked Henry, trying to look calm.

'It's been broken into. The prisoners are out, they have joined the mutineers.'

Henry's reaction was clear: 'Something must be done immediately. We have to save the magazine at once, and also the families of the civilians and the officers.'

'We do not have a single battalion we can call ours, sir,' said Butler, wringing his hands in despair. 'There are only officers in the city, no soldiers. Officers who know only how to give orders, not fight.'

'Never mind, David. Let us go.'

Henry Williams, taking over as commissioner in this way, went out with Butler the jailer. Mannu, who was left alone in the bungalow, stood at the door watching them go. In the confusion of the moment, they had forgotten to tell her what to do or not do.

41

One more army appeared on the maidan before the village, raising dust and noise. The villagers came out of their huts and looked at it fearfully. As the horses drew nearer, the clatter of their hooves on the ground sounded like deafening drumbeats.

However, this army was different. Ali Dost's eyes, that had seen several, detected the difference at once. There were no commanders, kings, queens or dancing girls with it. It was just a regiment without a leader. There was not a single sixth finger moving on its own. Every horseman had his sword drawn as if the enemy was directly in front of him. As they came closer, Ali Dost heard their war cry clearly: 'Sitara gir padega!'

Almost unaware of what he was doing, Ali Dost rushed into his hut, took his sword and ran to his horse. Untying the animal, he sprang on it hurriedly. In a few moments, he was behind the horsemen. Battling the dust they raised, he kicked the horse on its side, trying to catch up with them and shouting: 'Sitara gir padega!' although he had no idea at all what it meant.

The old woman stared at the emptiness that Ali Dost and his horse had left behind and muttered something in the name of Allah the Merciful.

42

The potter stuffed clay into the frame of the Durga image he had fashioned from straw wound around a bamboo pole, to flesh it out. Inserting bits of clay into the figure, shaping them delicately, taking off whatever excess material there was, he fashioned elegant hands, breasts and buttocks. As he worked on the figure in the thatched shed on the bank of the river, the village children gathered around to watch silently, full of respect and admiration. Each time the figure took shape in his hands, the potter would see the respect his audience felt gradually transform into a feeling of devotion for the goddess. He did not know whether this was a loss or a gain, but he never failed to witness the change.

The boatmen rowing across the river that was like a sea, with the farther bank invisible, sang as they rowed. The breeze that wafted in from the river caressed the potter and the image. Whenever he sat back for a while to rest and to allow the clay to dry, he heard and felt these things.

When he had finished shaping the body and head of the

image, he started to shape the fingers of Durga's many hands which would hold her weapons.

'Kumhar-bhaiya, kumhar-bhaiya,' the children gathered around him called out. 'There are only two folds in these fingers. They are all thumbs!'

'Yes, children,' said the potter, with the detachment of the artist who has almost finished his work. 'I do not know how to make fingers. I am attaching the fingers I found floating in the river. After all, it is Ganga-ma who gives me the clay and water I need to make the thakur.'

'Kumhar-bhaiya, how do these fingers come floating through the water?'

'I do not know, children. Someone must be chopping them off and offering them to Ganga-ma—the thumbs of Ekalavyas who are being forced to give up their own knowledge of a trade.'

'If all the fingers are thumbs, how will the thakur wield her weapons and do battle?'

'The thakur is only a lifeless image, children,' said the potter, going down into the water to look for the remaining fingers he needed. 'If they are thumbs, let them be. After all, are they not the only things in this straw-and-clay image that represent human beings?'

43

A lone horseman appeared on the dusty road that was baking in the heat. The wounded, exhausted animal limped along, close to collapse. As they came nearer, Moinuddin realized that the rider, like the horse, was wounded and exhausted. He waited.

The sky was enveloped in dust. The May sunlight pricked his skin everywhere like needles. He felt intensely uncomfortable inside his uniform, with a turban over his head.

The rider and his horse stopped when they reached the kotwal. All the man wore was a tattered shirt and underwear. Blood dripped from many places on his body and his head drooped. The moment he halted, flies settled on his thin body. A stray dog appeared from somewhere and looked at him expectantly.

Moinuddin drove the dog away, went up to the man and took a close look at him. 'Jailer Sahib!' he cried, hardly aware of what he was saying.

Jailer Butler nodded his tired head. He managed to tell the

kotwal in broken sentences that a huge band of mutineers was advancing towards the city. He had encountered them on the way and somehow escaped them by running into the woods. Since they were headed for the city, they had not pursued him. 'But they snatched my gun,' he said. 'Fortunately, my wounds were not fatal. Moinuddin, you must give me a horse. And a sword. And a kurta-pyjama. It's the only way I can escape. They must have reached the city now. There are a lot of valuable things in my bungalow that I collected during my stay here. And my wife and daughter as well. I do not know how I can save them. Moinuddin, will you be able to?'

Moinuddin escorted him to the next village and procured water and food for him. Then he arranged for a horse for him and a set of Indian clothes. Butler set out for the city disguised as a native with no one to help him except himself.

By the time Moinuddin arrived in the city, riots had broken out everywhere. No one knew exactly what was happening. However, no one wasted the opportunity to loot and plunder.

Moinuddin turned towards the thana where many people had gathered. They were not only carrying away the guns, but also ripping out the doors and windows of the building and taking them away. Moinuddin raised his gun and fired a few shots, successfully dispersing the plunderers. He learnt that the mutineers had taken the city and were hunting down the white men and killing them.

As his tired eyes took in the carnage that was taking place, he noticed that a crowd had gathered around the collector's office, preparing to attack the women and children from white families who had taken refuge on the roof of the building. Moinuddin admonished the daroga who was looking on, not doing anything. The daroga turned away and spat contemptuously.

Moinuddin shot him down. By the time he turned towards the crowd, a number of mutineers had arrived on the scene. Realizing there was nothing he could do, the helpless kotwal abandoned the women and children to their fate and walked back to his quarters.

44

Salma was still standing at the door waiting for Moinuddin. Though no words came out of her mouth, her fragile frame itself was a question mark. Mannu, Govardhan and, above all, the riot that blazed over the city: what would she ask him about?

Moinuddin went straight in and sat down on the cot. His mind and his body were equally shattered. He drank greedily from the pot of water that Salma brought him and poured some of it over his head.

'The resident sahib rescued Mannu, Salma. She is at his bungalow but...'

'But?'

'What a fate, Salma! The mutineers are attacking the white men's houses. All their menfolk have gone off to guard their weapons and the magazine. Their women and children, alone in the houses, are at the mercy of...'

At that moment, a crowd of bearded men roared into the house. Moinuddin reached for his gun. But they were not mutineers, they were local mullahs and members of the ulema. They had come to take Salma away and submit her to a trial for living with a man who was not her husband. Once before, when they had come to him demanding that she be handed over, Moinuddin had dismissed them saying that implementing the law was the business of the state. Taking advantage of the absence of authority, they had returned. Not to ask for her, but to take her away.

Moinuddin took only a few minutes to settle the matter. He did not talk to them. He grabbed the gun and fired twice into the air. Then he shouted: 'The next shots will not be fired into the air!' They fled.

'Hum!' Moinuddin's laugh was actually an expression of anger. 'Salma, I have been fighting criminals for twenty years with this uniform, this gun and this horse to help me. Today, I have acquired some new knowledge about these things. I came back here abandoning a number of helpless women and children to the wolves. In order to save Butler sahib, whom the rebels had left half-alive, I had to find a kurta and pyjama.

'The Company dismissed the king. And now the Company itself has been dismissed by the rebels. Whoever comes to power, there is no difference. Leave aside the governance of the new rulers, their arrival is itself as bad as the governance of the old rulers. The rebels climbed to the roof of the collector's office in front of my eyes and attacked the women and children who had sought shelter there. I saw one of those ruffians run his sword through a baby and hold it up for everyone to see… We cannot allow these things to happen, Salma… Perhaps it is during these twilight periods between light and darkness that we can do something. While sultans and kings and companies rule, we are nobody, we cannot aspire to be anybody.'

'That means then that when another king comes, you will become a policeman again and implement his laws?'

'We are small people, Salma—small and weak. We are just Govardhans, Salmas, Mannus and Moinuddins. The designs on a length of cloth that comes out of a weaver's loom. Pieces of coloured cloth that people snip and cut and sew together to make their flags. Bits of coloured thread that people snip and cut and sew together to make pictures that establish the right and wrong, the beauty and ugliness of philosophies, religions, various forms of art.'

Salma went up behind him and placed her hand on his shoulder. He leaned his head on her breast.

45

It was not easy to make one's way through the heap of bodies. First there was the shock and the difficulty of extricating limbs that were interlocked. Then there was the fear of being found to be still alive and being attacked again. Mannu stayed in the same position for a long time. Meanwhile, the blood kept flowing. Not all the bodies were dead—small sounds emerged from some of them.

It was an old, isolated house standing in a large compound on the outskirts of the city. Bibighar, they called it. There were several rooms but all the women and children who had been herded out of the bungalows of the white sahibs were thrown into one room. Not all of them were white. There were women who had been staying with the whites—women of mixed descent as well as natives. The room was packed. A window with broken shutters was the only opening to the outside world. The heat from outside and from the bodies inside had turned the place into a furnace. There was the added stench of sweat, excreta and vomit. Every day one or two people died of diarrhoea and dehydration and their corpses lay there, decomposing.

And then, one afternoon, men armed with sabres entered the room. As soon as they came in, they began to strike out, right and left. Mannu did not remember how long the carnage lasted. Since the room was packed with people, some of those who were behind or underneath others escaped. When the attackers left, locking the room, those who had not been killed were not sure they were really alive. As far as they were concerned, the difference between being alive and being dead had become very slight.

The door was opened again the next day. This time those who came in had no weapons. They threw the bodies out, then dragged them and flung them into a well in the yard. Those who wore clothes that were worth taking were stripped. Some of those who were thrown into the well were still alive. Three little boys who were still alive ran round and round the well until they were caught and thrown in. A few who seemed to have no wounds at all were kept apart. Once their work was over, the men dragged and pulled these survivors to the gate.

One of those who escaped both death and the well was Mannu.

46

From the palace of mirrors that Kaiqubad had built at Kilokari for his famed orgies, you could see the bustling new city of Siri and the beautiful Yamuna flowing past the magnificent gardens of the palace. But that day, the mirrors of the conference hall within the palace reflected only three figures.

Three people on whom rested the power of the present sultan, Sikander-i-Thani Alauddin Khilji. Kamla Devi, whom the sultan had acquired from the harem of Rai Karnadeva of Gujarat after defeating him in battle and to whom the sultan had given the title of queen was in charge of the discussion. The other two were Malik Kafur the eunuch, also acquired from Gujarat as a slave and then raised to the post of the chief of the sultan's army, and Amir Khusrau, the court poet whom the sultan had inherited from his predecessor, Jalaluddin, after the latter had been betrayed and killed by him. The sultan, gravely ill and confined to his private chambers in Siri Fort, was obviously on his deathbed and the three had assembled to discuss the situation.

All three participants were at a loss as to where the discussion should begin. The queen broke the silence at last, looking at the mirrors around them: 'These mirrors are amazing! Their loyalty is boundless!'

Amir Khusrau padded out this statement at once: 'Rani sahiba, their loyalty can cross all limits and turn into disloyalty when they start to reflect the images of what we wish to be rather than of who we really are.'

'None of us chooses an image for ourselves, Amir,' said the queen curtly. 'Slaves, court poets and queens are not permanent assets for any king. Like the royal canopy, the crown and the throne, they pass from one king to the next. The images you say we wish to acquire are really our own, a particular image of ourselves at a particular point in time. That is all.'

'Whom does the rani sahiba mock—herself, or the army chief or the court poet?' asked Malik Kafur in his usual roughshod way. 'Still, there is some truth in what the rani said. Sultans come and go but we stay on. What the rani sahiba does not know is that the likes of the three of us—slaves with their physique, court poets with their words and queens with their beauty—sustain the might of not only Sultan Alauddin Khilji's but every sultan's sultanate.'

At that moment, some of the mirrors suddenly cracked, fell down and shattered. All three were taken aback. Furious, Malik Kafur summoned the guard and ordered him to catch hold of the man who had thrown stones at the palace and bring him in.

'Perhaps it was not a stone,' said the queen doubtfully. 'There is a battle going on somewhere between the firangi Company's forces and the native rebels. It could be a bullet that was shot from there.'

Khusrau grew uneasy. 'Where is it? I wonder who is going to win this battle...'

'Don't worry, Amir sahib,' said Kafur in a mocking tone. 'They have Mirza Ghalib, another poet of Turkish origin like you, to shoulder their worries. Think about our sultan lying in bed with his body all swollen instead. What do you care about anyway? When Alauddin marched into the city holding Jalaluddin's head aloft on his spear—the sultan who loved you and gave you the title of the Parrot of Hindustan—were you not one of the first who waited to greet him with a poem praising him, composed for the occasion?'

'Every new sultanate is built on the grave of a history destroyed by wars and words.' Amir Khusrau attempted to evade the jibe directed at him and take refuge behind a profound philosophical statement. 'You and I, Kafur, erase the blots on the past for every new sultan and prepare a clean, freshly-washed new world for him.'

The rani leaned back slightly, looked at the mirrors facing her and said: 'Mirrors do not reflect the past. For the sultanates, there is only the present, Amir. We queens decorate with our beauty the palaces that you cleaned thoroughly with blood and tears. Wine never fails to intoxicate, no matter how it is served or who serves it.'

'When the beauty of the present is all that matters, we condemn the past to eternal ugliness. To erase the past is also to acquiesce in wrongdoing.' Khusrau cast his eyes into the distance. 'Mirrors don't do this.'

'All right, it is we who do that. But just as we approve of the wrongs done to the people, Amir sahib, we also approve of the wrongs done to us.' The memory of the cruel experiences she had undergone appeared as furrows on the queen's aged face. 'The stench of lust I have to bear each time… the bitter fluid you swallow each time at court, Amir, while singing the praises of the wicked… the wounds of humiliation you had to receive, Kafur, each time the regime changed… it is these that give us the right to speak on behalf of the people. No sultan can claim this right.'

'That is why, rani sahiba, I told you that we are the real masters of the sultanates,' added Kafur, reverting to the point he had made.

For a few moments, all three wandered over the pastures of their pasts: bedrooms that stank of perspiration and foul mouths, courts where drunken courtesans and buffoons sang and danced, battlefields resounding with groans and cries.

They were brought out of their reverie as another panel of mirrors crashed down. Infuriated, Kafur summoned the guard again. As soon as the man appeared, Kafur drew his sword and cut off his head. The head rolled over the floor like a ball and came to rest at Khusrau's feet, tracing a red semicircle of blood from the spot where the man's torso lay thrashing to where it had stopped.

Amir shuddered and drew back. He said: 'Kafur, why did you send this to me?'

'Didn't you once write a poem describing the beauty of heads lying scattered like pots of money over the battlefield and comparing the redness of the lips of the wolves who came to lick the blood to lips stained with paan?'

Disregarding Kafur's jeer, Khusrau said: 'Kafur, this is not the guard you sent to catch the man who threw stones at the palace. This is the guard who replaced him.'

'His head too would have rolled exactly like this, wouldn't it?' said Kafur calmly. He wiped off the blood on his sword on the clothes of the dead guard, whose body had by now become still. Putting the sword back into its sheath, he went on: 'That is not the point, my friends. In a way, it is just as well that these mirrors fell down and broke. We did not come here today to look at our present images. We came to think about the future. Sultan Alauddin Khilji lies in a palace not far from here, feeling the filthy fluids he accumulated over the twenty years of his rule gradually fill every organ in his body to bursting point. Yet here we sit, wasting our time talking about the past and the present.'

'Yes, we forgot that,' admitted Amir Khusrau.

'*You*, the queen and the court poet, forgot. Malik Kafur did not forget. The poison he injected into the sultan's veins a little while ago is now flowing through them. Soon his skin will crack open, the filth will flow out and the sultan will become clean and whole again, ready to meet Allah. None of the sultan's children will have to witness this painful sight. Malik Kafur had arranged earlier for their eyes to be gouged out... Malik Kafur has not abandoned the sultan as the two of you have. How can he abandon him? He is a loyal slave, isn't he, and a eunuch?'

'Kafur!' cried the queen and the poet together.

'What is this, Amir Sahib? You must have already composed a poem for the new sultan. Just put Malik Kafur's name into it. And rani sahiba, Malik Kafur has always thought that shifting from one bed to another is like jumping from one tombstone to the next. Kafur may be a eunuch, but he too needs a bed to sleep on!'

The guard came in just then and reported that the man who had thrown stones at the palace of mirrors had been caught. He withdrew and two soldiers dragged in a man forcefully and stood him in the centre of the red semicircle between the dead guard's head and his body. It was the kotwal.

Kafur unsheathed his sword at once but the queen raised her hand and stopped him.

'Don't, Kafur,' said the queen, 'your sword may be a long one but it will act only in Kilokari. Its reach will not extend to Civil Lines. Dilli is bigger than all of us.'

She turned to the kotwal. 'Kotwal Moinuddin, what you did was unworthy of a policeman. Why did you do it?'

'Kotwal?' Moinuddin seemed astonished. 'How can there be a kotwal in a city where there is no sarkar?'

'The sarkar has not disappeared, Kotwal. It is still here. The sultan is still alive.' As she said this, the queen cast a quick glance at Kafur, who lowered his eyes.

'Rani sahiba, chief of the army and respected court poet, the humble person who stands before you is the self-appointed nawab and subedar of the city of Dilli, where riots are now taking place. In his mind he is a poet as well.' Moinuddin bowed to each of them in turn and continued: 'I walked all this way to request you to come out of this palace of mirrors in which you have been trapped. If you do not shatter these mirrors, you will have to look at your ageing faces forever. It is true that Moinuddin threw a few stones at this palace. He seeks your forgiveness for doing so.'

'But why should we come out?' asked Khusrau in panic.

'The people are waiting for you outside. The people of a city ravaged by riots.'

'What for?' asked all three together. Even Kafur sounded terrified.

'Because they all think you belong to them.'

'That is true,' said Kafur, relieved. 'We made a resolution to that effect a little while ago. We are prepared to make it a firman.'

'That is not necessary, chief. If you break these mirrors that reflect only old age, if you come out and walk through the streets... as you used to do in your younger days...'

'But Moinuddin,' the queen addressed him by name. 'The sultan is on his deathbed. The country...'

'The country can wait, rani sahiba. The mutiny is raging now in Shahjahanabad and Civil Lines. There is no king there either. The Company's men and the local overlords are hunting down people and killing them in the same fashion... or maybe, in cities where people live, there are always riots. And unending massacre, plunder, looting, arson, rape... In the streets where you used to walk before you came to the palace of mirrors, people are crumpling up and falling just as they used to do in the old days. The armies of kings, dacoits, trading companies, mutineers, rebels: none of them allow the people to sleep in peace even through one night...'

Moinuddin's voice faltered and gradually faded away. Exhausted, he sank down on the floor, in the middle of the semicircle of blood, with the dead guard's head keeping watch on one side and his torso on the other.

47

As he came out of the palace of mirrors and walked towards Shahjahanabad, anxious and restless, Moinuddin came upon Mirza Ruswa flying a kite, seated on the balcony of a recreation shed put up on the banks of the Yamuna.

'Ruswa sahib?' Moinuddin went up to him. 'The whole country is entangled in a state of anarchy and you sit here flying a kite. Have you any idea how many people are being killed on both sides every day? Blood is flowing through the streets…'

'What else is left for me to do but this, kotwalji?' asked Ruswa, smiling, not taking his eyes off the kite in the sky. 'I had thought for a while that I could enter reality and write something. But that obstinate Umrao Jan is determined to lock herself up in the dark interior of her Satrangi Mahal and not allow words to flow into my pen.'

'The mob has looted Satrangi Mahal as well.'

'I know.' Ruswa took his eyes away from the kite and looked at Moinuddin's face. Moinuddin saw that his eyes were moist.

'Tell me, kotwalji,' he said, 'what did the triumvirate in the palace of mirrors tell you? Didn't you go there because you could not decide between the Company and the rebels just like those unfortunate people who have to make beds, tune their lyres to varied pitches and divert their forces to suit the needs of each new king?'

'That is not right, Ruswa sahib.'

'Maybe I'm wrong. But the question here is not one that lies between the Company and the rebels, it is one that lies between fantasy and reality. And in this matter, it will be fantasy that will prevail in the end!'

'Whether it is fantasy or reality, Ruswa, those who have to live must live,' said Moinuddin, walking away.

Ruswa gazed at him for a while. Then he fixed his eyes on the kite again with a sorrowful smile and began to pull the string with greater force.

48

The street was deserted, and the houses were dark as if the city had suddenly been abandoned. In the cities in the plains of the Ganga, no one stays inside the house on summer nights. People come out and stroll around to see whether the leaves on any of the trees are moving, hoping to catch a whiff of some breeze that might have strayed in. But tonight, everything was absolutely still and silent.

As he passed through the street of the carpet weavers and entered the street of the artisans who engraved designs on brass, Amir Khusrau listened carefully, trying to make out if any of them were at work. The sound of a chisel moving over brass was one that had always attracted him. He had always yearned to invent a musical instrument that would recreate that sound. The sitar, like the veena of Hindustan, made a chain of individual notes while the chisel produced a continuous sound as it moved over brass, like the sound one string makes as it rubs against another.

The streets were narrow and the galis even narrower. When

he came to a spot where a street and a gali crossed, Khusrau suddenly stopped. He strained his ears as if he had caught the outline of a raga. Yes, he could hear it distinctly, flowing out without any obstruction. It was so faint that he could not make out whether it came from a stringed instrument or someone was singing it. Its magical quality matched the disturbing emotions it evoked. What astonished Khusrau most was that the raga seemed very familiar to him.

He searched up and down the street. He went into the gali that crossed it and looked on both sides. He peered through windows and into balconies. But he could not find where the raga came from.

At last he came upon a man, thin as a creeper, seated on the veranda of a dilapidated building. The loincloth and shawl that covered him were tattered. There was no instrument in his hand and his lips were pursed. Strangely, the music that still hung in the air stopped the moment their eyes met.

The man bowed his head respectfully to Khusrau. Khusrau hesitated, then turned away to continue his search. Changing his mind, he looked at the man again. He felt he had seen him somewhere, that this was someone he had wanted to meet.

'Who are you looking for?' asked the man.

'Did you hear a raga?' asked Khusrau hesitantly.

'What kind of raga?'

'Maybe you wouldn't understand if I told you. I'll describe the notes. You know the individual notes you hear when you strum a veena with your fingers? And the continuous sound one string makes as it rubs against another? What I heard was something between the two. And the sound was full of pain.'

'It was the cry of a cat,' said the man in his simple idiom. 'A cat's unbroken cry when it is cruelly tortured.'

Khusrau looked at him suspiciously. 'Where is the cat?' he asked.

The villager shook his head. 'In a distant town where it is a pastime for children to blind the poor animals. You would have heard it very faintly. But wait... I had abandoned that cat in a jungle.'

'Then this must be the jungle.'

Govardhan laughed. 'This is not a jungle, sahib, this is a city. The famous city of Dilli, in whose courts you sing your odes in praise of murderers and torturers, just as you sang them for their victims. And this is the street of the brass workers of that city who engrave designs on vessels with their chisels...'

The man got up as he spoke and walked away, gradually disappearing into the darkness. Khusrau stared at him as he went. Was he the owner of the raga he had heard, he wondered. Although the man had disappeared, the raga or its soul at least still seemed to hang in the air of the street, robbing him of his peace of mind.

The now silent strains of the raga began to pull him, drag him far away beyond cities and villages, beyond mountains and jungles and rivers, to a distant battlefield on the dry Deccan plateau. And there, like a flash of lightning, he recognized it.

He had accompanied Malik Kafur there on a campaign, heading a battalion himself, to wage war against the king of Devagiri, a non-believer. After a long and fierce battle in which thousands had perished, the king had surrendered and agreed to convert. The victorious army had camped on the battlefield for the night. The moonlight had had a magical whiteness that lay like a fine muslin cloth over the black rocks and the undulating land which curved like a woman's naked body between them. Khusrau had shed his soldier's role and journeyed through poetry into the realm of music. Taking out the sitar he always carried, he had sat down in the moonlight and plunged into the composition of a new raga. Capturing the faint and subtle sounds around him, he had found notes to weave bridges between them. When he finished, his eyes had overflowed, he did not know why. He had fallen asleep on the spot.

It was when day broke that Amir Khusrau had realized that the sounds he had used to compose the raga were the cries and moans of the wounded soldiers who lay on the battlefield waiting for death. He had forgotten the night before that he was seated on the battlefield.

49

Someone patted Amir Khusrau on his shoulder as he slept leaning against the wall of a house on the street. 'Amir sahib, Amir sahib,' he called.

Opening his eyes, Khusrau looked at the man before him and the daylight that spread behind him. The street was still deserted.

'Mirza, what has happened to these streets?' asked Khusrau.

'What are you doing in these streets? Why have you come here looking for people?' countered Mirza Ghalib.

'I don't know... I was suddenly searching for... for many things.'

Khusrau's eyes were restless. He went on, his voice faltering: 'It was right, Mirza, what you asked me. I served seven kings, spending my days in their palaces; I sang in seven courts. I varied the pitch of my sitar to suit the tastes of each court. I praised murderers exactly as I had praised their victims. I wrote about whatever happened in front of me and whatever I saw at each particular moment, not caring to see the difference between the one and the other. But that does not mean my soul was not searching for something, Mirza.'

'You are the poet of poets, Amir.'

Khusrau paid no attention to this praise. He went on with what he was saying: 'I met a man at night here. An extraordinary person. I was chasing a familiar raga that had suddenly come floating out to me from the street. The raga, its melody, its identity, eluded me. And yet that man pointed it out to me with the greatest ease. He even made out who I was! But the most amazing thing was that I felt he was the person I had been seeking for years, subconsciously, without even being aware of it.'

They began to walk along together and Khusrau continued to describe his experience.

When he finished, Ghalib said: 'I too was searching for someone the whole night—you! Wondering how I would find you, who were so far away, here in this street.'

'Why were you searching for me?'

'Amir sahib, you said that you wrote about whatever appeared before you by chance—kings, palaces, dancing girls, precious gems, dishes prepared in the royal kitchens, paan, drinks, acrobats, rope walkers... I wrote about the calamities that happened before my eyes: the mutinies and the blood baths. Yesterday, I completed a poem on Queen Victoria, who rules the world. But all these were topics I consciously selected. In fact, while I lay on the stone bench in prison, suffering the bites of mosquitoes and bugs, I decided I would burn my flame only to strike off a thousand reflections from the glass columns of the royal palaces.'

'What are you driving at, Mirza?' Khusrau's tone betrayed irritation.

'My question is, do not you, me and all poets write on subjects that we consciously and willingly search for and select? To be honest, we are not just mirrors, Amir sahib.'

They had arrived at Nizamuddin. Khusrau stopped. 'You know I cannot go beyond this point, Mirza.'

Ghalib, who had walked two steps ahead, turned back. Khusrau stood with one foot resting on his tombstone. Ghalib laughed, came back to his own tomb and placed a foot on it.

'I too have a tomb here,' said Ghalib. 'The truth is that when questions come up that are difficult to answer, we poets and thinkers search for excuses to take refuge in. In death, in the limitations of space, in the framework of time that we claim to have lived in...'

'And what about the man I met at night? What do you say about him?'

Ghalib did not answer immediately.

Standing on their tombs, they looked at the swarm of huts which had sprung up around the dargah of Nizamuddin Aulia and their own tombs. A slender spiral of smoke threaded its way towards the sky from one of the roofs. A flock of birds flew in perfect formation from one end of the sky to the other. Faint human voices made gashes in the frozen silence.

Pausing every now and then, Ghalib said: 'What actually matters is what we explore and what we select for ourselves from a world filled with all that we do not explore or select. Because I choose to burn my flame so that it will reflect in a thousand glass pillars in the royal palaces, it does not mean that the slums outside are not steeped in darkness. What that man in the street saw was something that we did not—the blind cat. Look around you, Amir sahib, the streets you had thought were deserted are now...'

Ghalib pointed to the basti, which was becoming steadily noisier. People kept coming out of the houses. The streets were bustling with activity and shrieks and moans arose from them. Men ran through the streets with knives drawn. One house caught fire, then many houses. A riot had broken out—it could have been between foreigners and natives, between Hindus and Muslims, between Bangladeshis and Indians, between the soldiers of Ghiyasuddin Tughluq and the believers of Nizamuddin Aulia, between peerzada wholesale dealers and ragpickers who went from door to door collecting empty bottles, old newspapers, polythene bags...

50

When they went out, closing the door of Bibighar behind them, the cries of the women followed them. The screams of Ali Dost's victims had always pursued him and it was a habit with him to not heed them. Like him, Ali's four companions also walked on without paying heed to these cries.

Once they passed the gate, the five of them went in five directions. They did not speak to one another. Strangers, they had come together as if they had been destined to and worked side by side for two hours. After that, they went their separate ways without sparing a backward glance. All Ali Dost had understood was that they were the same sort of people. They had come in the same way, carried out the same task by the same method and gone back the same way. They were all Ali Dosts. It had been a revelation to him that they had been five in number. There had been no sixth person!

Ali walked alone down a track furrowed by the iron wheels of bullock carts through an area scattered with shrivelled trees and ruined tombs. He still held his bloody sword unsheathed.

He scrubbed off the dried blood from his hands and feet. His clothes, soaked in blood, had become as stiff as if they were starched. His beard and hair had become matted. His hands ached terribly from the force he had used to stab his victims.

Force, the application of force, was the important thing. But to behead or mutilate a victim in compliance with a malik's orders was like performing surgery. To tie up a victim's hands and legs, disarm him and then work on him required skill, not force. Ali Dost thought that it was the fact that he had held himself accountable and owned up to his deeds that made him, who had all the while been just a sixth finger, one of five fingers. Even if the reward he had received for this was the terrible ache in his hands. He massaged and comforted each aching hand with the other.

There was one thing that still disturbed him: no one had told him or his companions to go to Bibighar and cut up the women inside to pieces. No one had even given them an inkling that so many women and children had been locked up in such a place. How had they all arrived there at the same time? And begun to work in the same seemingly preordained manner without exchanging a word with one another? What had impelled them to go there as if they were bound on a mission? Had there been another invisible malik behind the non-existent one?

Floating and drifting through the heat that still rose from the burning earth although the sun had gone down, Ali repeatedly questioned himself: who was that malik? Where was he hidden?

A horse came galloping up from behind and suddenly stopped near him, almost touching him. The rider said to Ali: 'I am the malik. Malik Kafur. What do you want?'

Ali was very frightened. He said, his lips trembling, 'Malik, you're the army chief...?'

'Not the army chief, the sultan. I've sent my malik and his children packing. Now I am the sultan, the badshah ruling over Hindustan!'

Ali stepped back and bowed deeply.

'What was the doubt you had, Ali?' asked Sultan Kafur kindly. 'Are you wondering who the malik is who hides behind the deeds you think are yours alone?'

'Huzur, I did not take orders from anyone to come to Bibighar. And yet I always have the feeling that I did not come there by myself, that I was sent.'

'Ali, I too was once a slave like you. Today, I have become the malik. But behind the malik that I am and the slave that I was, there was always another malik. As there is a malik behind you who thinks you are the owner of your deeds.'

'And who is that, huzur?'

'Power! It drains out the ownership from behind every deed that you think you are doing yourself. Leaving you impotent, a eunuch. Like every sultan, I am a eunuch.'

'Forgive me, huzur, for talking too much. When the sixth finger becomes one of the five on a hand, when five fingers join to make a fist, a faith... Or maybe what you said is true. I felt that I saw, among the women I chopped in pieces, the face of my daughter Mannu. Maybe my sword slashed through her as well...'

Ali's throat choked. Sultan Kafur waited for his emotion to subside. When he was sure that Ali was his calm self again, the sultan said: 'Ali, there will be no future generation for those who walk our path. The path of power is also that of impotence. Anyway, why do we need another generation? Do you or I have a father, a progenitor? We walk alone!'

Malik Kafur waved his hand towards Ali and kicked his horse

on the side to make it move. He and his horse moved into the darkness that had already taken shape.

Three or four horsemen came galloping up from behind. As they passed Ali and Kafur and overtook them, Kafur's body fell to the ground. A spear belonging to one of the pursuers had pierced him.

Ali Dost stood on the road for a moment, then went on.

51

Deprived of her possessions, Rani Kamla Devi walked out of the palace at Kilokari alone, her purdah in place, through the streets Kotwal Moinuddin had told her about, towards the fort of Siri. That was where Devala Devi, the daughter she had had by Karnadeva, and Mirza Khizr Khan, the sultan's eldest son, to whom she had been given in marriage so that she would be made the next queen, were. However, the eunuch Malik Kafur had gouged out Khizr Khan's eyes...

Although she wore purdah, the palki bearers recognized the queen. When they parted the curtains of the palki for her, she could not refuse to get in.

Walking in step and changing shoulders in unison like soldiers, the kahars walked along. The pace at which they walked had the speed of running. And yet they only walked. If they ran, the palki was sure to jolt and whoever was seated inside would feel uncomfortable.

As they alternately spun out this process of walking into running and curbed that of running into walking, the kahars channelled their breaths, splintered by the activity they were engaged in, into prolonged cries of 'hiyano...' Their efforts turned their gasps into song:

Hai doli, hai doli,
Hai doli, hai doli,
Doli drowned in song
Doli wrapped in silk
Hai doli, hai doli.
Doli sinking into shoulders,
Doli drenched in laughter,
Hai doli, hai doli.
Doli wearing out the feet,
Doli slumbering in dreams,
Hai doli, hai doli
Hai doli, hai doli,
Hiyano... hiyano...

The rani did not listen to the song of the ḳahars, she only felt its rhythm—a rhythm that created pleasure out of pain, mirth out of sorrow. But in truth it was not the laughter the kahars sang about that was on the rani's lips.

The kahars crossed the streets of the city of Siri one by one. Busy streets giving way to desolate ones. Finally they put the palki down at the gates of the new city of Jahanpanah which came up at the end of Siri.

The rani got down and walked. All she saw on the vast maidan were stones and lumps of mortar scattered here and there. The fort of Siri and the palace had disappeared. Khizr Khan with his gouged-out eyes and Princess Devala Devi with her tearful ones had turned into earth long ago. Dilli had increased in length and breadth.

When she turned back to look, the rani saw only shrubs and undergrowth where the city had stood. Kilokari had also gone up in a cloud of dust. And the Yamuna had altered her course leaving the gardens to dry up.

The rani removed her purdah in order to get some fresh air. She could find the spot where she had got down from the palki only by counting the number of steps she had taken. The palki had disappeared. Someone had taken it away.

52

All she could hear were loud noises. In the cacophony, the poem that Umrao Jan was trying to tune to the melody of a raga with the help of her tanpura evaporated in the air.

Another gang of robbers, she said to herself.

Many days had passed since a song or the sound of a tabla had been heard from Satrangi Mahal. The plunderers had broken all the tablas in the house as well as the new ones that had been brought to replace them. Fear choked the throats of the dancing girls and would not allow them to sing. It was in this situation that Umrao had dared to set the poem she had in her mind to music with the help of her tanpura.

No one in Umrao's kothi had taken sides in the mutiny. And yet, people kept attacking the house. At first she had wanted to know who they were. Later, she had given up. They were just robbers, she said to herself.

They took away whatever they could lay their hands on in Satrangi Mahal. Nothing was left behind. Among the guards and musicians who worked in the palace, three had been killed.

The dancing girls had been raped. Soon there was no oil to light the lamps. And no food to eat.

When the plunderers left, Umrao got up. Having been beaten and kicked around by the thieves, angry at not having found anything to loot, the servants lay on the floor, moaning. Umrao went up to the door and gazed outside, her eyes vacant.

Faiz Ali was standing on the road. The man who had been visiting her for some days now, about whom she knew nothing. He signalled to her to come out. She went down at once, not even thinking whether she should or not. They walked along together.

There was a palki waiting at the crossroads. And kahars. Faiz Ali opened the door for her. Umrao got in first, he followed. The kahars lifted the palki on their shoulders. They sang:

Hai doli, hai doli,
Hai doli, hai doli,
Doli drowned in song,
Doli wrapped in silk
Hai doli, hai doli,
Doli sinking into shoulders
Doli blossoming in thoughts
Hai doli, hai doli,
Hai doli, hai doli
Hiyano... hiyano...

53

The only valid reason Moinuddin had for placing his services at the disposal of the badshah whom the rebels had installed as their head in Dilli was the hope that this would pave the way to end anarchy, bring back the rule of law and save the innocent from the atrocities they were being subjected to. Whether they were rebels or men who worked for the Company, they had all behaved like thieves and wolves. It was no longer men who walked the streets but swords that cut down everything in their way. Moinuddin was prepared to serve whoever could restore the rule of law. To this end, he longed for someone to win the war as quickly as possible. After all, he was a policeman.

However, the problem was that although the city had come under the control of the rebels, the decrepit old badshah knew nothing about governance. It had been months since the soldiers who had conducted the mutiny had received their salaries or rations. The badshah did not even have enough money to pay his own servants' salaries. The soldiers therefore went around the city looting and plundering. Men like Dilawar Khan who

had taken part in the rebellion had been plunderers even in the
past.

Moinuddin could easily have pretended to see nothing, taken
off his uniform and withdrawn with Salma to some safe place.
Many had done so. Moinuddin had thought about it seriously.
Taking both sides in turn, he had argued with himself day and
night for some days before deciding to take the plunge. He
would have never agreed to become a rebel, but he now became
the police chief of the rebels. And therefore the virtual ruler
of the city. People addressed him as Nawab Moinuddin.

Salma was frightened of Moinuddin's new identity. He visited
the quarters less and less and on the occasions when he did, she
avoided being in his presence. When he was not there, she
feared the mullahs and the ulema; when he was there, she
feared him.

'Why do you hide, Salma? Are you afraid of me?' he asked
one day.

'The kotwalji has become a nawab now,' she said from behind
the door. 'When the mullahs came asking for me once, you
drove them away with your gun. Now the firangis and their
law have gone away and the law of the ulema has come back.'

'Are you afraid then that if they come now, I will hand you
over for them to stone you to death?'

Salma did not reply.

Moinuddin went up to her and said, 'Salma, as far as
Moinuddin is concerned, he's always been Moinuddin whether
he's a kotwal or a nawab. Moinuddin has been a loner, Salma,
from the time he was born to this day. But now, he can no
longer carry the burden of himself. Can you not share some of
it?'

Salma continued to be silent. Her eyes wandered faraway,

to where the earth caressed the sky. The moistness in them glistened, but she did not weep.

'I know what you are thinking about, Salma.' Moinuddin placed his hand on her shoulder. His form came between her and the horizon on which her eyes were fixed. 'I tell you again, Salma, we are small people. Small and weak. We have no laws, no rights. Our appeals and complaints do not get anywhere. All we can do is survive. We fight one another, support one another, mate and reproduce in order to survive. Why think of Govardhan any more? Or of Mannu? Journeying over their narrow paths, crossing their tunnels, they are out there somewhere, trying to survive along with the fellow human beings they have met...'

54

Mannu opened her eyes to the awareness of an excruciating pain in her groin. Her whole body was a mass of pain and shame.

They had been travelling in a bullock cart. She had learned from their conversation that the two men who accompanied her were called Balbir and Agha. At first she had thought they were good men. They had given her some of the bread and water they were carrying. One was driving the cart, while the other sat behind with her. When the cart reached an isolated path in the middle of a forest, the man beside her suddenly caught hold of her. She had screamed and tried to resist him, but he had bound and gagged her and then raped her. He had then taken the reins and the other man had repeated everything he had done.

They had reached a deserted shed late at night. The men had pushed her into a room and bolted the door from outside. Mannu had neither the strength nor the interest to find out where they were. Overcome by pain and exhaustion, she had dozed off.

Sunlight filtered in through the half-open window. She saw that it was quite a large room. The floor and walls were made of earth and the roof thatched with grass. She had been in a room like this with a half-open window the previous night, with a large number of corpses for company. Here she was alone. Thinking of that night and the day that had followed, she wondered whether she was better off then or now.

Although she found it difficult to walk, Mannu slowly made her way to the window and opened both the shutters. She saw before her a number of litchi trees loaded with clusters of red fruit. The shed stood on top of a low hill. Through the gaps in the trees she could see fields below. No houses were visible nearby, nor people. Only the sun shone harshly in the sky. Though it was warm, the gentle breeze that wafted in made her smile for the first time since her ordeal had begun. Having nothing else to do, she stood there holding the bars of the window and gazing out. She wanted to howl into the silence outside but did not.

After a while, she heard the animated chatter of children and their heads soon appeared above the slope, then their full, active bodies. Mannu's mind leaped with happiness. As they came nearer, she realized that she had been shut up in a madrasa. She clapped her hands and called out to the children. They ran up to the window.

They drew water from the well in the madrasa and brought it to her. They vied with one another to give her the litchi fruits they plucked from the trees. From their excited chatter, Mannu gathered that two men had been found lying dead at the foot of the hill with bullet wounds. Listening to their description of the men, she guessed they were the men who had brought her here. Suddenly, the children wondered why they were speaking to her through the window. Shouting, they rushed to the door, unbolted it and started out with her for their village without bothering to wait for the maulvi who would come to teach them.

When they arrived at the village, the children began to argue about whose house they would take her to. As she stood among these good-hearted children, she was suddenly aware of her own wounded, abused body, wrapped in tattered, bloodstained clothes. Shame and a sense of loss filled her as she thought of how she too had been an innocent child like them two days earlier. She began to weep.

The child who finally won the argument took her to a house where she learned even more about the value of goodness. There was only a middle-aged woman named Ayesha there, the mother of the little boy who took Mannu to the house. Ayesha bathed her, gave her new clothes to wear and made her Mannu again. Occasionally she talked about her younger brother, Altaf, who was not there at the moment, as if Mannu was a member of the household and knew everything about him.

55

Blasting open the city gates with dynamite, the firangi forces came down from the high ridge. Very soon their rifles and cannons began to echo through the city.

Dilawar Khan's robber gang changed sides immediately and presented themselves at the gates, ready to receive the firangis. The firangis needed their help to locate and identify the rebels. In return, they were allowed, at least for the time being, to plunder and loot the city unchecked.

Only two things rose from the city inside the fort walls: smoke and screams. And only blood flowed through its drains. Dead bodies hung from the branches of every tree, from the rafters of every house. The army was not prepared to pardon anyone except those who agreed to carry out the duties of firangi executioners. And there was a great demand for executioners.

Moinuddin watched the spectacle silently. Somehow, he was not able to summon the usual argument about the establishment of law and order to his aid this time, or to join the firangi forces. All his logic and reasoning, his intelligence, his very consciousness, forsook him. Seated inside a crumbling tomb, shielding their faces against the violent fluttering of bats, Salma and Moinuddin argued for a long time. Both knew Moinuddin was a prized catch for the army and that they would spare no effort to find him.

'Kotwal Moinuddin was the one who gave his word that he would never betray the men of his thana by running away in order to save his head from Choupat Raja's executioners,' said Moinuddin, his eyes darting from one end of the tomb to the other. 'What a game fate plays!'

'But even now the kotwal is not running away from his word,' said Salma, placing her hand on his shoulder. 'The kotwal has never betrayed anyone.'

'Choupat Raja disappeared and the Company made its appearance. Then the Company disappeared and the rebels came. Now the rebels have gone and the Company is back again. The warrant on the kotwal's head still remains—what does it matter if it's in the Company's name now!'

'Didn't the kotwal once say that the very arrival of an aspiring ruler could be in effect far more fierce than the rule of the old one?'

'Butler sahib and Resident Williams were incensed that the innocent Govardhan was going to be hanged purely because his neck was thin enough to fit the noose. Now they no longer research law, they are busy looking for branches high enough to hang people from. They catch hold of whoever they find near such branches and hang them. People run away as far as they can from trees. They do not need laws, Salma; they need only a branch to hang Kotwal Moinuddin, who saved the lives of Jailer Butler and several other firangis. Truly, Salma, it is not human beings who betray us now but trees! The trees that give us shade!'

Salma pressed her face against Moinuddin's chest and wept. She had begun to admire this man. She no longer spoke of Govardhan or Mannu. She had abandoned all the questions she had about the past, one by one. Both had only one question before them now, that of their own safety.

Finally Moinuddin shaved his head and his beard, disguised himself as a Brahmin and Salma as his wife. Somehow evading the swords, the bullets and the hangman's noose, they escaped from the city.

56

They brought the clay idol of the goddess Durga in procession to the accompaniment of drumbeats and chanting and set her down on the bank of the river. The drummers took off the slings from their shoulders and sat down for a much-needed rest. Most of the devotees who had been dancing and shouting 'Jai!' to the goddess under the influence of frenzied faith and liquor had broken off from the procession at various points on the way. The few who were left carried the idol silently to the river's edge and toppled it into the water. While doing so, one of them called out 'Jai!' three times in ritual fashion. They immersed the idol fully in the water, turned and went away.

The kumhar watched all this, standing under a tree some distance away. Casually and dispassionately.

When everyone left, the idol floated to the surface once more and began to flow along with the current. In a little while, its garlands and decorations and the clothes it had been wrapped in slipped away. Soon, the clay started to dissolve in the water and the idol disintegrated. By the time it drifted up to the kumhar, it had become just bamboo and straw. The only parts that remained were the fingers—all thumbs with two folds. Fingers that had been cut away from the idol by the current. They drifted slowly over the calm waters of the river in search of some other kumhar waiting somewhere faraway...

57

After many days, the cantonment was quiet again. Most of the houses were still vacant. And in many of those that were occupied, there were no women and children. People were afraid to come out although there were lighted torches at junctions and the armed forces were keeping watch all around.

Henry Williams stood on the veranda of his deserted bungalow—even the servants had run away—and looked out. The rebels had taken away Mannu while he was out. She must have met the same fate as all the women and children who had been snatched away: a collective death that left behind no names, and a well or river for a tomb. The bungalow had always been lonely. But the loneliness which returned to it after the few days when Mannu had brightened it with her presence felt different.

He took a sip from the glass in his hand. He liked the bitterness of whisky and before swallowing each mouthful, he held the liquid in his mouth for a few seconds.

John had gone with the forces for a mopping-up operation. Gunshots could be heard in the distance. It was John's regiment that had saved the cantonment. But it was only because of Henry's strength of mind and confidence that the men of the cantonment had been able to hold out until John arrived. Everyone said that but for him, not only the cantonment but the weapons and the magazine would have gone to the rebels. As for Henry himself, he felt no pride or pleasure in this praise.

Henry could not help wondering: the displaced king, Jailer Butler, the officers he used to know and their families, Kotwal Moinuddin who had saved so many innocent civilians—where were they all now? How many of them were alive and in what condition? Some people enjoyed making these calculations after a war or a revolution, some disliked it. But more than any of these, Henry's mind was obstinately fixed on the villager, Govardhan, who had barged in one night some months ago and disturbed first Butler's sleep and then his own. Everyone who had tried either to harm him or help him had disappeared from sight. Only Govardhan, who had been nothing to him at all, remained. Where was he now? In what condition?

Throughout the operation, John had congratulated him on his courage, his fortitude and his presence of mind. His younger brother was honest and gracious, but when he cursed the rebels, Henry had protested.

'Empires are not built by accepting other people's point of view, Henry,' said John. 'Once it occurs to you that what you are doing is wrong, you will not be able to fight.'

'Let us not say who is right and who is wrong,' said Henry. 'It is not the theories evolved by rulers or rebels that decide right and wrong. What matters is how their deeds affect the innocent. How we, then they, and then we again, treated them, are treating them now.'

'Many innocent women and children were killed. We managed to save at least a few.'

'That's right. Your regiment saved a few of the innocent. And now, John, which regiment will come to save the lakhs of innocent people who are going to incur the wrath of the white men? I saved some of the white Govardhans who were attacked. But I have no hope of being able to rescue even one of the lakhs of black Govardhans from the noose which is already around their necks.'

Henry's eyes wandered beyond the cantonment which was sleeping quietly in the glow of the torches. He saw villages which had turned into blazing balls of fire, countrysides that had become deserts. Going beyond them, he saw trains that had been blasted and overturned and people lying crushed to pieces inside their compartments. And maidans where crowds of people, surrounded by the armies of generals, were trying to conceal themselves helplessly behind one another to escape the bullets raining on them. Two savage races that had thrown away all pretence of justice or mercy and were bent solely upon exterminating each other. Members of the sub-races within each larger race cutting each other down, burning one another, throwing bombs, raping... Columns of smoke, rivers of blood, rows of hanging bodies stretched as far as the eye could reach, leaving no gap between them. Henry's eyes moved slowly along these paths that no longer differentiated between the thirst for power and the longing for freedom, resting on sights that gave no clue about whom the conflicts were among.

John did not answer any of his doubts. He was caught in the task of retrieving the empire.

Somewhere in the distance, a shot was fired.

The moon had risen here, over the lives of an unfortunate people.

Leaving the cantonment and the empire to decide their own affairs, Henry Williams stepped out from the veranda into the yard and then onto a road drenched in moonlight. And from there he walked on and on, towards the vast tracts of land where his feet led him...

58

Mirza Ruswa was coming down the stairs of a courtesan's house in the red-light district of the old city. His mind seemed to be suspended from the string of a powerful kite in the air. At times he felt that he too was floating in the air under its influence.

The name of the kite that held Ruswa afloat was Khuni Jhoru. A name so attractive that anyone was certain to grab it from a bookstall. A name that gave off so much heat that even the silver screen would be set ablaze if it was made into a film. Khuni Jhoru was actually a prostitute. But Mirza Ruswa was very particular that his heroine should be very different from any of the prostitutes he knew in the city.

Suddenly an explosion shook the entire building, shattering the lower portion of the stairs, showering pieces of glass and brick all around.

Ruswa got up slowly from a part of the stairs that hung down and tried to find his way down the steps, but failed. This time the kite lifted him a foot above the steps. Floating in the air, he thought: why not make Jhoru the member of a suicide squad belonging to a terrorist organization fighting for the creation of a theocratic state? Or the central figure of a revolutionary party engaged in guerilla warfare in the cities in order to establish a communist state? He also needed an idealistic journalist in the terminal stages of cancer, who was in the process of revealing the heroine's extraordinary story to the newspapers, part by part...

Although he still floated on air, Ruswa managed to come down.

A huge commotion had taken over the street which had been full of the fragrance of flowers and sweet music a short while ago. People were running helter-skelter. The car in which the bomb had been placed had become a mass of crushed and twisted metal. Corpses and limbs detached from bodies were scattered everywhere. Police jeeps, reporters and photographers had appeared out of nowhere. People who had escaped unhurt and gathered to watch were arguing among themselves: had the bomb been exploded by Islamic fundamentalists? Khalistanis? Communist revolutionaries? No, no, they were firangi forces. The Meerut Regiment. Nadir Shah's army...

The string of the kite snapped and Ruswa landed on the ground. He saw a group of horsemen by the roadside. Dilawar Khan and his gang! Dead bodies lay on the ground, probably of people who had been selling flower garlands or paan, who had been shot at or cut down. Looking at the houses on either side, where lamps flickered here and there and the sounds of the tabla and ghungru had suddenly ceased, Dilawar Khan shouted: 'Every badmash will be ground to powder and scattered to the winds! Remember that, all of you!' He and his men then kicked their horses on the side and galloped away.

Ruswa realized that the string of the kite had snapped because a villager had collided with him. The man was searching for something among the dead bodies. Ruswa lifted him up by his shoulders.

'You?' asked Ruswa, trying to remember where he had seen him before.

'Yes, Govardhan. Do you have any doubts?' countered Govardhan, sounding irritated. He looked Ruswa up and down. 'So you are after me as well?'

'No Govardhan, I'm done with all that. Ever since Umrao Jan dismissed me so unceremoniously from the Satrangi Mahal, I have not looked down on the earth. I no longer catch my characters from the earth now, but from the sky, with an angling rod.'

Govardhan looked him up and down again. 'Wait here,' he said.

Govardhan continued his search. When he came back, he held a dead cat in his hand. Its mouth hung open and its teeth protruded.

Ruswa was astonished. 'Was this what you were searching for?'

'I had abandoned this blind cat in the forest. Surprisingly, the animals there left it alone.' Govardhan stroked its unresponsive back. Then he said: 'What I was searching for, Mirza sahib, were my wife and daughter.'

'But why look for them among these corpses? Who would have had any enmity towards them?'

'This is why I repeat: you poets, writers, intellectuals, you will never understand what this illiterate Govardhan understands so plainly. Do you really think there was enmity between those who lie dead here and those who killed them? Why were this poor cat's eyes plucked out? And why does a noose hang above my...? My wife and daughter did not do anyone any harm, babu. The poor souls gave no one any trouble. This is why I continually search for them among the victims who were attacked or punished.'

'Govardhan, I might have written about you if it were still the time before I walked out of the Satrangi Mahal, before I took an oath not to pick up characters from real life. The world is full of villains, cowards and clowns. But the characters I create are intrepid, courageous and victorious. I write about shrunken and wretched urchins like you fighting and winning their battles, I weave false dreams for you. Mirza Ruswa weaves dreams, Govardhan, dreams! And everyone likes them. As long as suffering, misery and injustice exist in this world, there will be buyers for the dreams that Ruswa sells, no matter how false, how unreal they are. I sell them heavens of freedom, of revolution, of scientific wonders, theocratic states, ethnic fantasies, miraculous powers... If you walk a short distance, you will see elegant bookshops that sell beautifully printed translations of my books in many languages like hot cakes. You will see huge cinema halls playing films made from my books and people waiting desperately in front of them, hoping to get in, or rioting, fighting among themselves because they didn't get seats...'

Ruswa began to walk along as he talked, forgetting Govardhan as the torrent of words poured out. Govardhan watched him from behind. Mirza's feet were a foot above the ground...

The lights in the courtesans' houses began to come on. Gradually, the sounds of the tabla and the ghungru floated out from them. Vendors selling flower garlands and paan reappeared in the streets. Chewing paan, wearing flower garlands around their necks, men climbed up the stairs once again.

59

When Ramchander knocked at the door of the muth, fully drenched, the force of the rain had not abated at all. He thought no one would hear him knocking since the shutters of the door were themselves clattering loudly in the wind. Besides, who would bother to come out on this cold, wet, dark day?

However, astonishingly, the door opened at once. It was the acharya himself, the head of the muth, who opened it. A slim, tall Brahmin, full of radiance. An aura of great scholarship shone around him. He was a young man who did not seem to have passed the stage of brahmacharya.

'Are you the pariah?' asked the acharya.

'I...' Ramchander shrank back in awe. He found it amazing to think of the head of a muth waiting at the door for a pariah. Why would he do that? To pour molten lead into his ears because he had heard the Vedas being recited unawares? Or to tear out his tongue for having dared to learn his letters?

But there was no anger on the acharya's face. He repeated very gently: 'Yes, the pariah who was to come to bestow knowledge on me?'

'Acharya, what knowledge can a pariah bestow upon you? The great Sri Sankara who has travelled through all of Aryavarta, defeated all the scholars in the land in argument and finally scaled the ultimate peak of knowledge, the sarvajna peetha: what can he expect from a pariah?'

They stood on either side of the gate, the acharya in the shelter of the gatehouse and Ramchander in the driving rain. The acharya did not invite Ramchander inside or even into the gatehouse. Through the curtain of rain, Ramchander glimpsed the huge hall where the inmates of the muth recited the Vedas and the four-pillared quadrangle of the building where they stayed until they completed their brahmacharya.

'Foresight told me that a pariah would come to impart knowledge to me. The knowledge he would impart is not something I do not already know. Still, oh pariah, it has been ordained that I cannot use this knowledge unless you impart it to me. Therefore do not waste my time. Stand where you are and perform your duty, then go your way.'

Ramchander realized that the acharya was not prepared to invite a pariah inside even if he had come to impart knowledge to him.

'Teacher of the world,' said Ramchander, 'You, who are the protagonist of Advaita, you are the universe as well as the knowledge of the universe. You are the acharya as well as the pariah. Therefore no one, not even a pariah, is different from you.'

'Pariah, you are testing my patience,' said the acharya, sounding irritated and impatient, 'you know there is nothing in this world that I do not hold within myself. Still, even as Brahma, the ultimate knowledge, needs human beings as instruments to know itself, I need a pariah to become myself.'

Ramchander confronted the acharya: 'In that case, acharya, the pariah will not come to you. Somewhere along his journey towards the muth of self-born knowledge, the pariah has ceased to be. The powers that be and the centres of self-born knowledge have snuffed the life out of pariahs. All along the way here, I saw the bodies of pariahs hanging from every tree, their necks broken, their mouths open, their eyes protruding. And not only their bodies but those of their parents, their wives, their sisters, their children. The pariah you expect cannot hope to reach here. His knowledge and life lie outside the purview of this muth. He has, therefore, ceased to be on the way here. I am a poor accountant, a kayastha, who came to tell you that you need not wait for him anymore.'

Having already begun to close the door, the acharya closed it firmly as Ramchander finished speaking. Ramchander stood there for a while, looking at the closed door, the strong walls, the thick forest of coconut trees rising behind them and, above it all, the heavy rain pouring incessantly over everything. Then he continued his journey along the bank of the river that ran beside the muth, the turbulent, swiftly-flowing river that the monsoon rains had made arrogant.

60

A woman's voice called out from inside the inn: 'Please wait, traveller!'

Govardhan stopped. He saw a woman's face in the square of the window of the inn that he could glimpse through the thick mango trees surrounding it. Although it was late evening, there was just enough light for him to see that she had made up her face carefully. Govardhan went up to her.

She came out to the veranda. 'Traveller, can you buy me something to eat?' she asked. 'There's not a soul here, not even a watchman.'

There was no one in the inn and it was situated in a deserted region outside the town. The forest lay just beyond it.

Govardhan said: 'I will have to go to the town to get something. I'm coming from there.'

She did not reply to that.

'All right then, give me some money,' said Govardhan.

He went back to the town and bought rotis and vegetables. She thanked him and he was about to leave when she stopped him. 'Wait, you good man. My name is Umrao Jan. You must have realized what my profession is. If you do not mind, keep me company. I know you are hungry and there is plenty here.'

They sat down on the floor and she served him like a good housewife. He was so hungry that he began to eat without waiting for the usual formalities. She watched him eat with great enjoyment. After a while, she said: 'You did not tell me anything about yourself.'

'Govardhan has nothing to say, he has only things to ask.'

Umrao Jan laughed, then suddenly grew thoughtful. The laughter faded from her face.

'Umrao Jan never asks anything, she only tells,' she said. 'In our profession, we usually sing and our guests listen.'

'Baiji, when I said I ask questions, I did not mean it is part of my profession,' said Govardhan with an indifference born of experience, giving all his attention to the food. 'I was suddenly separated from my profession one day, I do not know how or why. And that is how I began to ask questions. If you begin to ask questions, maybe you too will have to give up your profession. Look, baiji, I asked questions all the way as I came here. Everyone I met was knowledgeable and skilled in their own profession. But none of them could give me an answer. What I learned was that our own professions make us incapable of understanding the problems of others.'

'I needed you to make me understand this.' A happiness mingled with pain spread over Umrao Jan's face. 'The number of people who have come to me! Nawabs, ustads, lawyers, government officers, even domestic servants! This time it was a highwayman—Faiz Ali. I had run away from my house to escape the dacoits—how was I to know that I had come upon another dacoit? And one who even had a price on his head!

When we arrived here, the police arrested him and took him away. Even the palki in which he brought me here was carried away by someone... Do you know why they all came to me, from nawabs to dacoits? To listen to poems about love! It is prostitutes, Govardhan, who have been appointed by our cities to compose and sing poems about love! No one has found this strange or unnatural. I never asked any of these people what brought them to me. The truth is that there were never any questions between us.'

'You are not eating, baiji. You keep looking at me and talking. At this rate, I will finish all the food.'

Umrao Jan smiled and drew her plate towards her.

'How strange!' she remarked, putting a piece of roti into her mouth. 'In this desolate jungle, in an inn where there is not even a watchman, on an evening when the sun is beginning to set, two people who came from different places and are each going their own way, sit and share a meal together. One has only questions and the other only answers... And yet, there is no connection between your questions and my answers. Deep chasms gape between the words we exchange.'

'Baiji, you have begun to recite poetry now. But poetry is lies. There is only one question in the world: the question of injustice. No matter how many gaps you feel there are between my question and your answer, they are about the same thing, injustice. Look, though I have done nothing wrong, and though everyone had admitted to this, they have decided to hang me! And the punishment meted out to you was for a fault you certainly did not commit, wasn't it?'

'Yes,' said Umrao Jan, the piece of roti still in her hand. 'While you became a fugitive to escape punishment, I accepted it. I not only accepted it, I made use of it and even enjoyed it in my own fashion. I once tried to take revenge on the dacoit, Dilawar Khan, who had abducted me when I was a child and sold me into this profession. Of course I failed. Imagine, fate, that plays such cruel jokes on us, made me realize that the man whose help I sought to escape from that profession was himself a dacoit! Dilawar Khan now goes around the country tightening the noose around the necks of hundreds of innocent people! My dear Govardhan, while you became a fugitive to escape the noose, this sister who sits beside you is a person who dared to transform nooses into poems! What a game life plays with us, brother! Who will Umrao take revenge on? Who will she run away with? There is no way Umrao can go out. In any case, there are still so many people who wander through the Chowk in search of deceptive poems and songs on love. The long stretch of my life that began and ended with dacoits has taught me that this mural, like the wall on which it is painted, has no end. The wall goes on and on, not allowing the mural that incorporates Govardhan, Umrao, Faiz Ali, Dilawar Khan and Ali Dost to come to an end... I sent away Mirza Ruswa, who wanted to transform my life into a story. Poor Umrao did not realize that her life itself is a huge palace of stories...'

Govardhan got up. Placing his hand on her shoulder, he addressed her by the name she had had as a child. 'Ameeran didi, I walked out of that wall. Or the painter who drew me peeled me off the wall and made me walk down this road. The fact that you sent your painter away does not mean that you have to stay on the wall. One day you too must come down to the road which, after all, does not need to be different from the wall. This place too is full of fear and pain. Still, to know that both of us are walking along this road, to hope that we may meet someday, is a great blessing.'

Govardhan walked towards the forest as if welcoming the darkness that came down from it. Umrao Jan stood like a painting on the wall watching him.

61

'So we have another child here,' said Altaf when he saw Mannu. He did not ask who she was or from where she had come. He was delighted to see a child at home when he came home from his sojourn.

Everyone in his house was a child to him. Although Ayesha was older than him, he called her 'ladki'. Ayesha and Mannu were 'ladki' and Ayesha's son was 'ladka'. He behaved as if he was the oldest of them all, the most knowledgeable—and yet, he was actually a child himself. He would laugh and joke with all of them and stage mock fights. Mannu realized that Altaf was seldom at home and that, when he was, it was like a festival.

There was, however, one aspect in which Altaf was very mature. He seemed to hold much more strength within him than was visible and the elders of the village discussed matters of importance with him. Yet, what was in his mind was beyond the comprehension of these elders. Which was why none of them knew where he disappeared from time to time or for what reason. He would sometimes fall silent as he laughed and joked, go out by himself and sit down somewhere, gazing into the distance.

Ayesha had told him everything about Mannu. But he did not ask her anything about her tragic circumstances. Nor did he show her particular sympathy or advise her on what she should do. He behaved as if she was a younger sister who had always been in the house.

One day, as he stood outside by himself, Mannu went up and stood just behind him. It was growing dark and a cool breeze was blowing. The darkness made everything around them obscure, but the stars shone brightly in the sky.

'Bhaijan.'

Altaf was not surprised. He said, without even turning around, as if he knew she would be there: 'Tell me, child.'

Mannu did not say anything.

'Child...' Altaf decided that he would speak himself. 'Once upon a time, a man kidnapped a girl from her house. He locked her up and raped her. Her father filed a case against him, but thirty years passed before the police apprehended the man. By that time, he had married the girl and they had become a couple living together happily. They had had children and their own daughter had been married and given birth to a child. The woman he had kidnapped, his wife, was no more; she had passed away. The father who had filed the complaint had died as well. When the police handcuffed the man and took him away, his children stood by helplessly and wept.'

'Why did you tell me this story, bhaijan?' asked Mannu.

'Why did I think of this?'

Mannu had not asked him that. Still, she said, 'Why did you think of this, bhaijan?'

Altaf turned. Mannu thought he looked shocked. His face

was pale, as if he had committed a crime of some kind. He caught her hands in his.

'Forgive me, child,' he said. 'I suddenly remembered my abba. I don't know why, your own experience reminded me of him. I should not have told you that, though.'

Although Mannu's heart had grown dry and shrivelled, her eyes filled with tears. She held his hands to her face. They stood silently like that for some time, a chill breeze blowing through them.

'It's not like that, bhaijan,' she said at last. 'Who can you speak to about the sorrow I awakened in you except to me? But it is your own burden. Let mine stay separate from it.'

'I no longer know, child, whether there are such things as mine and yours, old and new, right and wrong. Sometimes I feel I am completely blind. My abba who committed the crime and my mother who was the victim, both survived that incident. And the person who accused him has disappeared from the scene as well. Only the crime itself remains. And Ayesha and I, the result. Turning it over in our minds, first upside down, then downside up, looking at it from this side and that, we had tired ourselves out. It was then that you came, bringing back the horror to us in all its starkness. I suddenly feel reason and the ability to make judgements draining out of me like a flood.'

'Do we have to make judgements, bhaijan?'

'Failing to make judgements would mean condoning injustice and cruelty.'

'Sitting in judgement is a luxury to be enjoyed by those who do not take part in events. History is a wonderland for those who distance themselves from its experience. Is it not enough for us, bhaijan, to react to our experiences as they happen?'

Altaf raised the face of the girl he had been holding close to him and looked wonderingly at it. As if he doubted whether these words really came from this girl who had not even learned her letters. Where had she found such wisdom at her age? He was afraid to call her a child any longer.

'Mannu,' he said, 'I feel afraid of time. If we allow time to have its way, we will have to see things that are wrong become right and things that are right become wrong. If we don't, we will all reach a state where we become mere pictures on a wall. Only those who pass before us will have the prerogative to move. Mannu, I am a living being who tries to react constantly to wrong. But all this history may be rewritten tomorrow. And I might then be adjudged a criminal or a hero. I am neither of these; I am just an ordinary human being with a heart that beats. Our helplessness is not limited to our own times, it extends into the times that are to come. It is only by chance that a person succeeds in becoming what he really is. Most people live lives which are not theirs and will be remembered for what they were not. Mannu, my child, either time should not exist or there should be no dividing lines between right and wrong, sin and virtue. Is it not a good thing that human lives are so short?'

'Altaf bhaijan, how old are you? And how old am I? Is it not unsuitable for us to talk of how long life can be?'

'My child, you are pure gold.' Altaf embraced her. The cold night enclosed the small globe of human warmth that they were.

Altaf left that night. He never came back.

62

David Butler had lost everything he held dear in the rebellion. A hunter by interest and a policeman by profession, Butler's greatest pleasure had been to collect beautiful things. From the horns and stuffed heads of the animals he had killed to valuable sculptures, paintings, chandeliers, carpets, jars, carved platters of gold, silver, brass and stone, he had collected innumerable objects with which he filled the palatial bungalow he had built for himself. But what he had considered most valuable were his beautiful wife and their equally beautiful daughter. Everything had been wiped out at one blow. The house and all in it had been burned and looted by the rebels. They had dragged away his wife and daughter, hacked them to death and thrown them into the river where they had turned into food for fish and crocodiles. He too would have become prey to the vultures had that policeman not appeared to save him.

When he emerged from hiding after many days, Butler was an embodiment of blazing anger. It set him on fire to see the burnt ruins of his house. All of humanity stood before him divided into two categories—black and white. Colour became the only criterion by which he would judge them. The rest of his life was to be a mission dedicated to carrying out these judgements.

He hunted those who were black instead of the animals of the jungle. In the jurisprudence he practised, doubt replaced evidence. Anyone on whom the shadow of doubt fell, whether it was an old man or a woman or a child was condemned as a rebel and hung from the half-burned beams of his bungalow. The dead were allowed to hang there, rot and fall down. The living were brought in and hung among the dead. The stench of rotting flesh spread for almost a mile around the bungalow and the clouds of vultures circling above plunged the region into a perpetual darkness where worms fed on the rot and decay. People said that even the ghosts of the dead would not survive there. They named it the Bungalow of Dead Ghosts.

While the burnt mansion thus became the Bungalow of Dead Ghosts, the mansion that Butler built in its place assumed an entirely different character. It became an enormous harem that he filled with all the women he had acquired while quelling the rebellion. Butler soon came to be known as Butler Nawab and the harem as the Jail of Beauties. From outside, the structure itself and the number of guards around it made it look like a prison. No one knew exactly what went on inside it. None of the women who went in ever returned. It was rumoured that they had strange chores to do and that they were subjected to endless punishment and torture. In the minds of the people, the fate of the inmates of the Jail of Beauties was no less dreadful than that of the inhabitants of the Bungalow of Dead Ghosts.

Among the nawab's acquisitons was an old and uniquely-designed palanquin that he had snatched from the streets of Lucknow. He renovated it with smooth sheets of sandalwood. Curtains of silk brought from Benares and Kanchipuram were hung on its Persian-style windows and Gothic doors. A red flag flew from the golden spire on top of it. The bearers of this unique palki were ordinary native kahars, thin, barefoot, half-naked, with sunken shoulders and flat feet. A contingent of armed horsemen accompanied them as escorts.

Nawab Butler stood on the balcony of the mansion and let his eyes wander. Barren land lying dead and motionless in the hot sun stretched as far as the eye could see. He saw a palki crawling along the road that led to the gates of the Jail of Beauties, obviously on its way back from a mission.

The trail of dust raised by the horsemen and the kahars followed the palki like the tail of a comet. As it drew nearer, he saw the golden spire on top shining in the sun and the flag fluttering. The humming of the kahars gradually separated itself from the hoof beats of the horses and the footsteps of the men and wove itself into a song punctuated by their breathing:

Hai doli, hai doli
Hai doli, hai doli,
Doli wrapped in song
Doli sunk in pain
Hai doli, hai doli.
Doli sinking into shoulders,
Doli sinking into pits
Hai doli, hai doli
Hai doli, hai doli
Hiyano... hiyano...

The palki entered through the gates that the watchmen had opened and stopped in the courtyard. The kahars put it down and stood aside, gasping, melting in sweat. The chief of the horsemen came and stood before Butler, who had come down by then, and saluted him.

'Huzur, two girls. One the daughter of a nawab and the other of a peshwa.'

Butler moved the purdah of the palki, looked carefully into it and delivered the verdict: 'This one to the new bungalow and this one to the old.'

63

There was a deep well that had run dry at a spot by the side of the Uttarapatha. Covered by bushes and surrounded by rock-formations, it had for some reason attracted the attention of kings. Used initially by the people of a nearby village who threw rubbish and the carcasses of animals into it, guards were soon posted all around it up to a distance of about half a mile. It was said that emperors from Asoka to Aurangzeb flung their brothers and opponents into it. The guards were posted to ensure that no one would hear the wails of the unfortunate beings who were thrown in and to convince them in turn that no one from the outside world would hear them either. In spite of this, the forsaken souls inside it wailed incessantly.

At some point, the guards disappeared. No one dared come near the well at first, but gradually dacoits began to frequent it. It became a custom with them to throw a part of their loot into the well as an offering.

Continuing this custom, traders and travellers passing that way began to throw coins into it to ensure that their journey be blessed. It was said that screams were heard from within whenever the offerings fell in. If they were heard, it was considered auspicious and a good omen for the journey; if they were not, it was considered inauspicious.

As time passed, the prestige of the well grew and spread far and wide. It became a holy place and a large number of pilgrims gathered there every Thursday. Shelters were constructed for the pilgrims to stay in and trees planted around them. A fair and a market were held there on Thursdays. The area around the well was cleared and a path laid for pilgrims to circumambulate. Men and women, old people and children, would walk around the well many times, throw offerings in and go back with their minds at peace.

The difference between Asoka's well, as it came to be called, and other places of pilgrimage was that people did not come to seek something new but to pray that they would not lose what they already had. Chanting the names of the things they wished to keep safe in their possession, they would throw coins into the well. The screams from the well would assure them that their prayer was answered. However, as time passed the screams grew increasingly weaker. Withdrawing into the shade of the trees after they prayed, the devotees would argue in their minds: had they heard a wail or not? Ashamed to say that they had not heard anything, they would keep the secret to themselves. Many of them, therefore, returned with the doubts they had brought with them when they came.

One Thursday afternoon, the traveller Ibn Battuta waded through the cries of the hawkers and the cacophony of the loudspeakers and came to the well, where it was relatively quiet. He had walked a long way and was extremely thirsty. He asked many of the people who were circumambulating whether they would draw some water for him. Busy sharpening their ears to hear the wails from the well, they did not answer him. Finally, he sat down on the edge of the path, waiting for a devotee who would be willing to help him quench his thirst.

As he sat watching the people who were circumambulating, he noticed a group of six who seemed different from the others. While each one of those on the path seemed plunged in the depths of their own anxieties, this group of six were connected to each other, the end of one person's cloth being tied to that of the person next to him. They looked distracted and their eyes were vacant. He felt that they had already lost whatever they were praying to keep safe. They went past him several times and suddenly, in a flash, he recognized the man who was leading the chain—it was Kallu bania. The next time they appeared, he recognized the second man as the mason. Each time they passed him, he recognized the rest one after the other as the chunewala, the bhishti, the kasai and the ganderia. Each time, Ibn Battuta called out to the person he had recognized on that round by name and asked him for water. But they walked past without responding. The seventh time the chain appeared, he played a trick on them. He called out the name of the person who should have been at the end of the chain but was not: 'Govardhan!'

When they heard that name, all six of them turned, their faces pale. 'Where is Govardhan?' they asked in one voice.

'I'll tell you if you give me some water.'

'Don't you know, traveller, that there is no water in this well?'

'I should have known that,' said Ibn Battuta bitterly. 'There is no water in this well, there is only thirst!'

'Now tell us where Govardhan is!' they pressed him.

'You still need an answer to that after having circumambulated so many times? Govardhan, my companion, is within you. He is within you, screaming...'

All six of them fell silent and looked at one another. Ibn Battuta left them and went towards the well. When he came up to it, he took out a few coins from his bag and threw them in.

The six men were watching him from behind. They called out, 'What do you have, traveller, that you do not want to lose?'

'Thirst,' said Ibn Battuta without turning back.

64

The drumbeats and cries grew louder as Govardhan walked along, evidently towards the place from which they originated. His heart began to beat faster, but, for some reason, he kept walking through the jungle in the same direction. As he drew closer, he realized that the cries rose from devotees who were calling out 'Jai!', victory, to Kali-ma. The rhythm of the shouts and drumbeats quickened to a frenzy from time to time, then slowed down and stopped and started again after a while, gradually waxing faster and faster.

Suddenly, there was the sound of a gunshot, then a few more. The drumbeats stopped completely and the jungle fell so silent that even the chirping of the crickets stopped.

Walking through the silence, Govardhan came to what looked like a cave. He saw that it was a Kali temple. The torches still burning inside revealed that the devotees had fled abruptly, leaving behind their drums, the articles they had used for worship, the sacrificial animals, even the goddess herself. The sound of the guns must have frightened them.

The idol of Kali, glistening black, holding aloft her curved sword, with fierce eyes and a red tongue that stuck out, naked except for a garland of skulls, seemed to be staring at the sacrificial lock made of iron planted in front of her. Goats' heads were piled up in a pit to the side of the lock. A goat that had been caught in the lock and could not extricate its head struggled wildly, its limbs flailing the air. A large number of goats stood awaiting their turn. The odour of turmeric powder and burning incense enveloped everything, while the torches flickered wildly.

At the start of the ritual, drums were beaten as each goat was led into the lock. It was believed that the mounting rhythm and the shouts of the devotees would drown the cries of the goats and erase any pity the spectators might feel or any fear the man who wielded the sword might experience. Before the animal was trapped in the sacrificial lock, it was given a banana to eat and some water to drink from an earthen pot, but since both these were only rituals, neither was properly executed. Bananas from which just a bite had been taken were scattered everywhere. Once the animal was locked into the device, the drumming and the cries of 'Jai!' would rise to a crescendo. At the climax, the man with the sword would raise the weapon, the animal's head would roll down into the pit and the drums would fall silent. Slashing off a small bit of flesh from the writhing body and collecting a little blood in an earthen pot, the man who had killed the animal would run quickly towards the goddess as if he feared the flesh and blood would lose their warmth. A row of earthen pots was lined up in front of the idol. The blood was still warm in some of them, while it was cold or starting to clot in others. The drumbeats started up again only when the next animal was led in for the ritual.

Govardhan walked up to the animal caught in the lock and set it free. He released each of the goats waiting on the other side, slashing through the ropes that bound them. When he reached the end of the row, he screamed in shock—the last of the sacrificial animals was a woman. A dark-skinned woman who had been bound hand and foot, gagged and tied to a post. Unable to utter a sound she was thrashing violently and trying to say something with her eyes, dashing her head against the post.

Govardhan released her as well. She was a tribal woman who had been recently converted to Christianity by the missionaries. The freedom her new religion offered had proved to be her death warrant. When he untied the ropes that bound her, she collapsed on the ground in a heap, unable to stand. He lifted her up and said to her, lowering his voice: 'Come, we must escape from this place at once. The moment they realize that it was the hunters who fired those shots and not policemen, they will be back here.'

Not saying a word, she walked along beside him. When they came up to the idol, she stood for a moment looking at it. The glow of the torches had dimmed and the eyes and tongue looked even more furious.

Govardhan knew what she was trying to ask the idol. Who was this goddess angry with? Why was she demanding the blood of the innocent? How could killing helpless animals bring victory to her?

'What shall I call you?' asked Govardhan.

'Mariam,' she said.

'No one can answer you, Mariam—neither these men who hail the goddess nor the goddess herself. Men are helpless. In order to destroy some evil people who had been cruel to them they created a goddess and filled her eyes with anger, her mouth with blood and thirst. But the goddess could not destroy their enemies. In the end, the men had to line up sacrificial animals to satisfy the thirst of the goddess. Tomorrow she may demand the blood of those very men. Govardhan has traversed so many strange paths, seen so many strange things. Come, let us get out from this place quickly…'

By the time they left, the torches had burned out. The figure of Kali had melted completely into the darkness. Only its red eyes and bloodstained tongue looked steadily at them from within the dark.

65

The rain and gale had abated by morning. The sun had come out and the sky was clear. That was not the only change—Ramchander was no longer seated under a coconut tree but beneath a large umbrella fixed on a platform on the bank of the river. And the river was different as well: it was not the Periyar but the mighty Ganga!

A group of Pandas rushed in, jostled him out of the shade of the umbrella and pushed him down. He had a hard time trying to avoid being trampled by the pilgrims who were going down the steps for a dip in the sacred river. Scrambling up, he managed to weave through the crowd that swelled as the day advanced and make his way to the burning ghat.

The men who worked at the burning ghat were as busy as the pilgrims, but they did not drive him away. He realized that they did not have the time to even turn around and look at him, that they had simply taken him for one among them. One of them handed him pieces of firewood to stack on a pyre. Another entrusted to him the long pole he had been using to push back pieces of firewood which had fallen away from the pyre, and went away to attend to something else.

Someone touched Ramchander on his shoulder at that moment. He turned and saw that it was a woman.

'Come, masterji, let us leave.' she said, 'Neither the path of the seeker of knowledge nor that of the ascetic is yours.'

Ramchander did not know her and said nothing in reply. He followed her obediently.

They walked past the bathing ghats and entered the narrow galis that criss-crossed the town. There were rows of houses on both sides. Human beings and cows passed them in both directions. He caught up with the woman, who was walking ahead of him, and asked: 'Where are you taking me, devi?'

'I saw you struggling for your life at the bathing ghats, masterji, while the pandas rained blows on you and the pilgrims kicked you around. After all that, why did you accept the pieces of firewood and the pole that the domes at the burning ghat, those people of the lowest caste whose profession is to cremate bodies, handed you, to help burn the bodics of people you did not know? I could not understand that.'

'Where are you leading me?' Ramchander asked again.

'As if all the roads in the world are spread out before you! Didn't the ashram of wisdom shut its doors in your face? The wise guard their knowledge as a secret, masterji, they never divulge it to others. Mine is the path of pleasure, one that is open to all people at all times.'

She gave Ramchander food to eat. While he devoured it hungrily, she said: 'Do you know why my path always lies open? No one ever stones a prostitute to death. Nor is she ever burned on a pyre with a man, or locked up in a harem. A prostitiute is beyond all laws. She is free to offer pleasure untainted by emotion to every man.'

Ramchander, however, felt that the purity of that pleasure was too bizarre.

'Your ashram too does not allow me beyond its gate,' he said.

'Masterji!' She sounded despondent.

'That is not your fault.' He caressed her as she lay in his arms, her face pressed to his chest. 'Your mansion has only a gatehouse and it is there that we are making love.'

'We women of pleasure do not carry happiness into the hearts of men, masterji.' She ran her fingers lightly over his lips. The arrogance he had heard in her voice as they walked through the galis had drained out completely.

'And pain?' he asked.

She did not answer.

'Not only you but I too am outside the gate. You, me, a number of people like us. Only knowledge shuts itself up inside the inner courtyards of mansions. I too was in an ashram like that once—until a man burst in one night and dragged me out. Ever since, I have been wandering around in search of that man. You are right, our knowledge does not have a life beyond our experiences. Tortured cruelly by our senses, we have to find our pleasure in the weird ecstasy of these gatehouses.'

He drew her closer to him and let his lips run down the length of her body. They forgot themselves completely for a while. When they came to, he saw the glow of tears on her wet face.

'You did not tell me about your sorrows,' he said.

Once again, she did not answer.

'Is not this pleasure a beautiful layer of passion wrapped around our sorrows?' he asked again.

'I do not know whether sorrow or happiness is the real

essence of a human being. Perhaps ashrams which are the storehouses of knowledge should debate and determine whether happiness is a layer that collects over sorrow or sorrow a layer that collects over happiness. Those ashrams, however, are out of bounds for us.'

Ramchander wiped the tears on her face. 'Tell me about your sorrow,' he said again.

'Masterji, what layers, what coatings, does a prostitute have? Her sorrows are as naked as her pleasures.'

When Ramchander was leaving in the morning, she asked, 'Masterji, may I come with you?'

'You told me that prostitutes live outside the rules of society,' he said, placing his hand on her shoulder. 'That means that women who are burned along with their husbands' bodies or stoned to death in the courtyards of mosques or locked up for life in harems are dealt with by the jurisdiction of the law. But do you think it is the body of law that is applied to them—rather, is it not lawlessness? Once again, you were speaking like the wise men who live behind closed doors in their muths. Those women are just as much outside the law as you, devi. There is no need for you to come with me. You are already with me.'

Although his form was dissolving into the vast expanse of the world outside the gate, she did not feel that she had lost him.

66

Moinuddin, who had taken the name Acharya Uddalaka, lay with his head in Salma's lap and looked at her face. Salma, who had become Savitri, let her fingers wander over his shaven head and the tuft of hair left on it and over his face on which hair had begun to grow again, and then drew out the sacred thread from beneath his shawl.

Around them was a green stretch of land, an oasis that had taken shape in the middle of the desert thanks to a canal that some king had dug long ago. The fresh greenery and trees emphasized the long contours of the desert region that lay beyond. Shifting sand dunes lurked just beyond the canal, as if waiting to swallow up the green earth with its vegetable farms and hutments the moment they found a chance to do so. Beyond them, clouds of dust misted the horizon that united earth and sky.

Uddalaka and Savitri had taken shelter the night before in a small temple that the farmers of the oasis had erected. Once the priests and devotees who assembled there in the evenings after the day's work sang a few bhajans, rang the bells and departed, the temple usually lay silent and deserted. The arrival of the couple at that spot in the course of their escapade was like the start of a dull chapter in their long story. Although their days were dull, they were however full of disquiet. The intervals of rest in each changing chapter of their story were like oases in the desert.

Leaving the heat of the day behind, the desert was sinking into the cold of the night. The soft moonlight made the cold more intense.

'Will this sacred thread and shaven head protect me from danger, Savitri?' asked Uddalaka. 'All they will do is hide my name, Moinuddin—and maybe they will not do even that. Uddalaka means he who split the bund and came out. He who lay across a field like a raised bund to prevent the water seeping in.'

Savitri did not say anything. Her hand let go the sacred thread and wandered over his chest. He realized that her hand was warm. He lifted his head up from her lap and made her lie down beside him. Then he opened out the blanket and covered both of them with it so that the heat of their bodies would remain with them and not escape.

'Acharya, I had a dream today while walking along the road,' said Savitri, putting her head down on his chest.

'A dream...?'

'Yes, a dream. It was not a thought, panditji. How can anyone think such things?'

'What was the dream?'

'That Mannu was running towards me, exhausted, bleeding, her clothes tattered. A number of people ran behind her wielding sticks—native sepoys, white sahibs, men in white khaddar, people with guns and bombs... Mannu was crying out loudly for help.'

'And then?'

'She suddenly stopped. Govardhan was hanging from a tree in front of her. Ali Dost kept pulling the rope but Govardhan refused to die. He had caught the rope in both hands and was trying to prevent the noose tightening around his neck. Forgetting her own plight, Mannu asked him: "Abba, how long can you keep hanging like this? How long? For what length of time?"'

How long? For what length of time? The question turned from Govardhan to Uddalaka. Uddalaka did not answer. He drew Savitri closer. He curled into her oasis and she into his.

Savitri woke him up before day broke. 'Kotwalji! Acharyaji!'

Uddalaka sat up and looked around. The yellow light of morning was advancing towards him from the edge of the desert like a cavalcade. He realized that it would not take long for the coolness of the morning to evaporate. Another day of escapades and hunting had begun.

'Savitri, while walking along yesterday, you saw a dream. Of Ali pulling the noose tight around Govardhan's neck,' said Uddalaka. 'Do you know what I dreamt when I was asleep last night? I dreamed that Acharya Uddalaka betrayed Kotwal Moinuddin and Kotwal Moinuddin betrayed Acharya Uddalaka. And that Savitri was chasing Salma and Salma, Savitri.'

Savitri looked at him, her eyes wide.

'Do you remember, Savitri, the government proclamation we heard in town?' Uddalaka went on. 'The price on my head that the messenger announced while he beat a drum? One thousand rupees! Who knows what price they have set on Govardhan's head! The king's reign is over, so is the badshah's.

The queen herself has taken over the reins of government. But the price on Govardhan's head still remains. Later, when the natives take over and the claimants among them change the system of government, the price set on Govardhan's head and Moinuddin's will still remain. Heralds will continue to beat their drums and proclaim the prices set on the lives of innocent people, the lives of Salma and Mannu. Kings, sultans, companies, revolutionaries and heroes have always hunted us. Philosophers and intellectuals will stand behind them from now on, filling their emptying quivers with new arrows. Artists and poets will continue to describe the daring deeds of this hunt in beautiful colours and words... What distresses me now, Savitri, are the prices they have set on our heads and the many names, adjectives and markings they give us. This brings the hunt down from the areas of the rulers to the spaces we ourselves inhabit. In the dream you saw yesterday, wandering through the desert looking for food and water, there were so many people in the bizarre crowd pursuing Mannu that we had never seen before. How many more like them we are yet to see! Savitri, when I send my eyes into the deserts that stretch before us, I see even stranger things. I see people hunting each other, lynching each other. The new names and qualifications we are going to be given, the markings that are going to be imposed upon us, the signs and features by which we will be known, are the biggest curse that will fall upon us. The faith we follow, the colour of our skins, the shape of our noses, the language we speak, the food we eat... Look there, Savitri, at that maidan, at the desert...'

'But panditji, all of us belong to the same class, the class of innocent, unjustly punished human beings.'

Uddalaka shook his head. 'No Savitri, we are becoming

different... Come, let us get out of here quickly. These people here are innocent too. But that is of no use. When day breaks, someone may recognize us.'

They climbed hurriedly down the steps of the temple, had a bath in the canal, dried their clothes and set out.

By this time daylight surrounded them. Peacocks soared down from the trees and passed them, screeching, paying them no attention. But the people who were coming out of the huts had started to take note of them.

67

On one of the first days of the month of Ashadha, Kalidasa discovered a beautiful dark cloud that had the majesty of an elephant frolicking in a mountain valley. But for some reason, the gentle cloud was not prepared to take up the mission he had wanted to assign it even after Ashadha had passed, and Shravana, and then the month of Bhadra arrived. Although the message to be sent to the yaksha's beloved in a poem filled the poet's mind, the muse of poetry did not bless him.

The poet knew the reason for this. For the past few days, visions that were quite different from the yaksha, the yaksha's beloved and the rain cloud had been disturbing him. He had been coming across some very strange people in the streets of Ujjaini. Foreigners with long hair and beards and restless eyes, women whose faces were swollen with weeping, babies hanging from vultures' beaks. He no longer saw scholars who greeted him with their heads bowed or young women inviting him from behind shy eyes. Instead, people stared at him with eyes full of hate from behind bushes in gardens, through cracks in the walls of crumbling ruins, from derelict steps beside old ponds that had dried up, through the clouds of dust raised by herds of old, sick abandoned cattle that roamed the streets. Strange people, though they had faces that seemed familiar.

The poet walked to and fro in the terraced garden of his mansion that had been cooled by frequent showers, drinking in the fragrance of the flowers and enjoying the companionship of liquor. None of the verses of the poem containing the message of love to the beloved had come out right. No wonder the rain cloud had refused to carry them. The poetic tastes of the cloud were in no way lower than his. He tore up verse after verse while the faces that haunted him left the broken walls, the ruined steps, the clouds of dust raised by cattle and dared to climb right into his terraced garden!

Angry and discomfited, the poet came down, unmindful of the deepening night. The street was deserted and silent, even the guards seemed to have withdrawn. The taverns and brothels were asleep. The torches planted at the junctions gleamed dimly, the oil in them having burned out. Walking on and on, the poet arrived at the mansion of his friend Amir Khusrau in Kilokari.

The evening assembly had dispersed and Khusrau was seated by himself on the balcony, lost in thought. He had not taken off the clothes he had worn at the assembly. When he saw the tall, handsome figure of the poet of Ujjaini coming up the stairs, Khusrau got up quickly, received him and led him to the seat reserved for guests.

The poet's robe and head dress had become slightly wet in the rain. He took them off and wiped his head and body with the fresh towels Khusrau handed him.

The poet courteously sent away the saki who had appeared at the door in response to Khusrau's signal. Evading most of the required formalities and rushing through the rest, he plunged into his subject:

'Amir, what really baffles me is that these people's faces seem very familiar to me,' said the poet. 'I do not understand the expressions on their faces, whether they be sad or angry. Perhaps if I peeled them away, I would be able to recognize the faces. For some reason, this makes me afraid.'

Khusrau took a wad of paan wrapped in thin silver foil and held it out. 'Great poet,' he said, 'It is not long since I too had an experience as extraordinary as the one you describe, in a deserted street in Dilli.'

'Tell me!' Kalidasa leaned forward impatiently.

The moon, moving from behind clouds, suddenly spread its radiance over the balcony. Although they were speaking of dark streets, the companionship of a shared experience touched the space around them with light.

'Mahakavi, while coming one night along a street in Dilli as lonely as the one you described, I suddenly heard a raga flowing out of a narrow, dirty corner of it. I had just crossed the street of the carpet weavers and come to the street of the brass workers. It was a spot where I would never have expected to hear a raga like that. And what is more, just as you said, the raga seemed very familiar to me.'

'Who was singing it?'

'The strange thing was that no one was singing.'

'Meaning that...?'

'It was a man who had taken on the form of a raga for the moment, to confuse me.'

'Amir, you are joking!'

'You must believe me, mahakavi. It was only later that I knew who the man was. The sultan's soldiers had issued a proclamation at various junctions between Kilokari and Jahanpanah to the effect that a reward would be given to whoever apprehended a certain prisoner who had escaped from jail. They said further that they had information that the criminal was wandering through the streets of the city troubling the people, that he was a magician who had the power to take on various forms...'

'You are right,' said Kalidasa, trying to refresh his memory. 'A proclamation of the same kind was made by the king's soldiers in Ujjaini as well. I did not pay much attention to it then.'

'Listen to the rest. This man had not actually run away from prison. His cell was opened one night and he was set free. By a dramatist like you!'

Kalidasa leaned back in his seat, lost in thought. In the end he said, half to himself, 'Amir sahib, we have both written poems and plays. But we have never broken the law or rebelled against kings and sultans.'

'No, our kings and sultans have never had occasion to issue proclamations against us.'

'On the contrary, they praised our poetry to the skies and gave us rich gifts.'

'To tell the truth, I was reading one of your poems a few minutes before you entered. How vibrant your verse is!'

Amir Khusrau got up, went in and came back with a book. He opened a page he had marked with a peacock feather and said: 'Look, when I came to this stanza, I kept reading it over and over again.

Sa nirvasya yathakamam tateshvaleena chandanow
Stanaviva disastasya sailow malayadurdurow

Asahyavikrama sahyam duranmuktamudanvata
Nitambamiva medinya srastamsukamalamghayal[7]

I bow my head before this peerless imagination. What magnificent metaphors! What depths of resonance!'

Kalidasa was visibly moved by this praise. But the poet noticed that Khusrau's voice was becoming softer and his face growing clouded.

'What is the matter, Amir? What has happened to you?'

Amir Khusrau began to pace up and down the terrace, his finger still between the pages of the book. Every time the branches of the kadamba tree which had grown to the height of the first floor touched his head, he turned back and came up to the poet. When he replied, his voice trembled: 'I do not know why I suddenly remembered the raga I heard that day by the roadside. I did not tell you the whole story. It was a raga I had composed myself. The raga had come to me long ago on a lonely night on a battlefield, after the battle was over. I had woven it from the notes I picked out among the sounds I heard around me, not realizing that they were the moans of men who had been wounded and were dying slowly…'

Khusrau stood where he was, frozen in silence. A tremor of fear ran through Kalidasa's spine like lightning, freezing him as well. Trapping them in these postures, the moon and the clouds kept playing hide-and-seek with each other over and over again.

---

[7] The heroic one, filled with the unquenchable spirit of conquest, embraced the Malaya and Durdura mountains, heavy with the fragrance of sandalwood, as if they were a woman's full breasts; after having enjoyed this pleasure to the full, he fell upon the Sahya from which the fabric of the sea had retreated as the clothes fall away to bare a woman's buttocks.

'Amir!' Kalidasa broke the silence at last. 'Whenever we meet, we lose ourselves unawares in discussions on literature. But it is not an occasion for that today. Come, let us go and ask that dramatist why he performed such an odious act.'

Both the poets came down from the Kilokari mansion. The night had progressed well into its second half. Since the moon had set and the torches at the crossroads had dimmed, darkness enveloped the streets. Although they tripped over a body lying on the path, the poets managed not to fall down. They thought it was perhaps the body of a thief the soldiers had killed. Dragging their feet, which kept slipping on the sticky blood flowing over the ground, they went on their way.

Bharatendu was still awake, seated by the lamp as if he was waiting for the visitors. He came down and led them inside.

The poets' silence could not hide the uneasiness that was eating into them. At the same time, they sensed the storm raging in their host's heart behind the calm and courteous exterior he turned towards them.

'Do you see this circle?' Bharatendu drew their attention to the wet circle on the floor. 'When the mahant went away, this circle was left. It is the perspiration that dripped from his body. How many years it has stayed here, refusing to dry up! Poor the mahant could not save Govardhan. He had to go back the way he came.'

'Govardhan...?' Kalidasa's curiosity grew.

'Didn't you come to speak to me about Govardhan?' asked Bharatendu calmly.

'The man for whose capture the soldiers have been proclaiming a reward! Yes, we came to find out about Govardhan,' said Khusrau.

The light dimmed from Bharatendu's face.

'What news you've brought!' Bharatendu shook his head, pained. 'God! I did not expect this. So they have placed a price on his head! Now even his own people will hunt him down!'

'You let him out of jail. Are you trying to save him from the police as well...?'

'My revered guests, please sit down. You are not in a hurry, are you? For one thing, it is night. And you are tired. It gives me no comfort to see you stand like this.'

The poets sat down. So did Bharatendu.

'Look, my friend, let's come to the point,' said Kalidasa. 'The man you freed from prison is roaming around Ujjaini and Dilli, disturbing law-abiding citizens. He has become a problem to everyone.'

'The problem is not yours alone, it is mine too,' said Bharatendu firmly. 'Govardhan is a character I created. I did not let him out for fun. I had no alternative except to set him free. Look, you are men of letters and you will understand even if other people don't. A time comes in our lives when we have to free the characters we created, the ragas we composed, the sculptures we fashioned. My turn came first, yours has not yet come...'

Kalidasa and Amir Khusrau stared at Bharatendu with great interest and quite some disbelief.

Bharatendu went on: 'Look, wise men, these characters, ragas, sculptures that we create do not, as we think, belong to us. Nor are they our slaves. If they become persons of dignity, if they split our pens at the tip and walk out into the world, should we not feel happy in a way? Even if cruel hunters lurk on their paths, even if we can only sit back and helplessly watch them...?'

Bharatendu's voice was choked. His eyes moved down from

their faces to the circle of perspiration Mahant had left on the ground. A shadow fell over his face. He had suddenly forgotten himself as well as the honoured guests who sat beside him.

Kalidasa and Khusrau got up. They went down the stairs. They knew that their host had not noticed them get up or leave. But they did not wait for him to do so. Lost in themselves, they walked in silence through the streets that had begun to be touched by the slivers of morning light in the east. One walked towards Dilli, the other towards Ujjaini.

68

Kalidasa paced up and down the courtyard of his mansion in Ujjaini, steeped in thought. This was all he had done since he came back from his meeting with Bharatendu. He would walk on the balcony for a while. Then he would descend and pace up and down the courtyard. Once more up to the balcony, then down to the courtyard again. Two days and two nights had gone by in this way.

It was nearly time for the sun to rise. Having risen twice, the sun was preparing to rise once more. The poet saw the flowers in the garden open out one by one. He shuddered every time one of them broke open, as if each had made a thundering sound as it blossomed. And now, birds were making real sounds, followed by the ringing of bells from the temples and the recitation of stanzas from the Vedas. The world was reverberating with sound and growing radiant with light.

The king must have been annoyed at not seeing the poet at the evening assemblies. The dancing girls must have wept until their eyes hurt. He would have to answer all of them. But meanwhile, he was distressed, wondering how he would answer himself.

The poet's heart was full of the verse Amir had quoted to him. All the scholars without exception had praised him for it. Amir too had praised him and then suddenly fallen silent.

Sa nirvasya yatha kama...

The poet recited the lines to himself again. At the time when he had written them, there had been a full day's discussion over the words '*vikramam*' and '*langhanam*' that he had used. It had been pointed out that the words implied the physical pressure a man applies in order to rouse a woman's passion and that no one with an awareness for art would fail to be delighted by their dhvani, the meaning they implied.

The question the dramatist had asked—whether a writer should not feel happy if his characters walked out of his pen and became dignified people—pierced him like an arrow. In the verse, it was the act of a king attacking and subjugating a territory that he had compared to an act of copulation with its connotations of lust and passion. Why had a poet of his stature not thought about the dignity of the people who had been attacked and subjugated?

The face of the king who had been enraptured by the verse and the image of the courtiers who had nodded their heads in time to the rhythm of the words came to his mind. It was clear that all of them had perceived the cruel act as one of love. He could, if he chose, argue that his poem was true to that extent. But he had not chosen that imagery to expose the vulgarity of their minds. He had wanted to delight, to titillate them. Therefore, he had really been on the side of those who looked at an act of cruelty as an act of lovemaking and delighted in it; he had not been on the side of those who had suffered it in agony. As a poet, had they not been characters he had created?

The poet ran into the house like one possessed. He came out again holding in his trembling hands his most acclaimed poetic work. His heart thudded like a drum. He was afraid to open the book. How many ghosts like this he might find in it! But he could not help opening it. He stood there helpless, drenched in perspiration. His shawl slipped from his shoulder.

Sadayam bubhuje mahabhuja
Sahasodwegamiyam vraje diti
Achiropanatam sa medinim
Nava panigrahanam vadhumiva[8]

These were the words that his eyes fell on when he opened the book. Once again, the courtiers' heads nodded before him, keeping time with the rhythm of the words. It was not because he was not strong enough but because he feared that the virgin he had just married would grow frigid if he used force that the king was gentle with her: wasn't it to imply that you used the word 'mahabhuja' to describe the king, asked Emperor Vikramaditya. King of kings, can I call you weak? said Kalidasa without thinking, forgetting that the lines were attributed to Aja, the son of Raghu. The emperor roared with laughter—not as Vikramaditya, but as a character the poet had created… The poet's hands crushed the page.

'Be gentle, did you say? Be gentle and kind?'

The poet shuddered when he heard the voice. A group of

[8] Drained of strength, he handled his newly-acquired territory with gentleness, as if afraid that, like a newly-married young girl, she would be repelled by him if he used force.

men with long hair and beards parted the bushes and came towards him. One of them came right up to him, snatched the book from the poet's hands, placed his finger on a page and ordered him to read: 'Read! What the king who was a mahabhuja did after he had disrobed the virgin's body with gentleness and satisfied his lust—read, what did he clothe her with? Read it out loudly!'

The poet read the lines he had written, obediently:

Bhallapavarjitaistesham
Sirobhi smashrulairmahim
Tastara sarghavyaptai
'sa kshoudra patalairiva[9]

The moment he finished reading, Huna women whose faces were red from weeping for their dead husbands came and stood on his left.

'Look, poet,' they cried, turning their reddened cheeks to him, 'forget our sorrow and pain. Think of a verse to describe the beauty of the exciting redness of our cheeks!'[10]

Another woman came up quickly and stood on his right. Pulling off her clothes, she showed him her naked breasts.

'Not there, poet, look here!' She turned his face towards her. 'I have taken off my necklace because I lost my husband. Instead, to provoke your imaginative faculties, I have put on

---

[9] He covered the land as thickly as flies would cover a beehive with the bearded faces that his swords and arrows had harvested

[10] *tatra hunavarodhanam*
bharthrishu vyakthavikramam
kapola pataladeshi
babhuva raghucheshtitham

my sumptuous breasts an unthreaded necklace made with the pearls of my tears.'[11]

All the bushes suddenly disappeared from the garden. The crumbling walls on the roadside collapsed one by one. Cattle-dust settled over the earth with magical rapidity. The strange characters who had been lurking around and behind him for days came and surrounded him without any hesitation. He recognized every one of them without exception.

'Get out, get out of here!' he shouted in a moment of madness.

They did not go away. He had known they would not. He had wished secretly that they would not go. After all, they were his characters. His own creations, his own children. They had come before him after such a long time! People whom he had written out, treated like material for enjoyment. Who had lain flat, waiting to be raped. The patterns of cloth used to cover violated bodies. Red cheeks, full breasts... The objects that had provoked delighted laughter at the court of the king had come back now to stand before him as dignified people with bold voices. Shedding his fears and doubts, he stood in front of them humbly, his head bowed.

And then suddenly, another group of visitors arrived—a number of severed heads suspended in the sky by their hair behind the men and women lined up before him. Their eyes bulged, their mouths were wide open. Blood dripped from their necks. And yet, this terrible sight did not frighten the poet.

---

[11] *Anena paryasayatasrubindun*
  Muktaphala sthulataman staneshu
  Pratyarpita shatruvilasininaa-
  Munmuchya sootrena vinaiva hara

For they too were familiar to him, they were objects he had used with glee to embellish his poems.

Hanging in the sky, each of the wide-open mouths began to laugh. The sound of their mirth took shape as a verse in his mind:

Adhorananam gajasannipate
Siramsi chakrairnisitai kshuragrai
Hritanyapi shyenanakhagrakoti-
Vyasaktakesani chirena petu[12]

The heads began to talk: 'Great poet, you have raised your eyes now not to look at us, but at the high points of your imaginative faculty and poetic excellence. But do you really see the vultures your imagination has summoned? The vultures who picked us up from the battlefield and now suspend us by our hair from their beaks? No, all you see is us. The vultures are elsewhere.'

'My children, my beloved children,' the poet pleaded with the men and women surrounding him and with the heads that hung in the sky. 'The day that Bharatendu spoke of has arrived for me as well. I free all of you. Be liberated! Journey wherever you like! It does not matter whether your freedom is my ruin or my tragedy in the eyes of the world. My poetry finishes here. It is time for you to take over.'

The heads interrupted him. 'No, Mahakavi, our journey will not give you freedom. The vultures you are searching for, that

---

[12] In the war of the elephants, although the heads of the mahouts were sliced off by wheels that looked like sharp, pointed razors, they did not fall down for a long while because their hair was caught on the toenails of the vultures.

tore us apart, are within yourself. Even if you give us freedom, we cannot give it to you. Because we are actually suspended on *your* nails. We are neither lustful kings embracing virgins nor are we soldiers who draw our swords in order to kill innocent people at the bidding of kings. We are not even the elephants who carry soldiers. We are just mahouts who stand at the farthest end of the long line of rape and plunder. And yet your cruel quill used our terrible destiny for your pleasure. Hanging us from the vulture-claws of your pen, you won praises and gifts from kings. No, we do not have the power to leave you. Will you be able to throw away your quill? We can go away only if that pen is with us...'

69

The firangi platoon arrived in the dead of night, unbeknownst to the sleeping villagers. By the time day dawned, hardly anyone remained to find out.

They set fire to the houses in the village as soon as they came. Those who tried to escape from the fire by running out of the houses were either hung from the trees or bayoneted by the soldiers who waited outside. Men, women and children—all were killed.

Only one house was not burned. Altaf's house stood firm while every other house fell. They did not kill the people inside it—Ayesha, her son and Mannu. Instead, they beat them up and tortured them in their attempts to know where Altaf was. It was soon obvious that they had come to the village in search of him and that it was because of him that they had set fire to the village. As for Ayesha, Mannu and the child, they had no idea where Altaf was but quickly realized that the sarkar did not approve of what he was doing.

The torture that began at night had taken on many varied

forms by the time day broke. The soldiers tore up the victims' clothes and rained blows on their bare bodies. They bundled them up on the floor and kicked them. Since all of them were in different rooms, they knew of one others' presence only through the moans that echoed through the house. The women heard the child's loud cries gradually weaken before they stopped altogether.

The clouds that had gathered over the sky opened out only after the flames had gone down. Once the rain started, it poured heavily, turning into a storm. It washed away all the signs of devastation in the scorched village and made it clean. And bore mute testimony to the torture being carried out in Ayesha's house.

The roof of the house was partly blown off and the earthen walls began to crumble. Suddenly, a soldier cried out that a bund had collapsed somewhere and that the river was in flood. Even as he said this, the water flooded the village and the walls began to collapse. The soldiers abandoned their victims and ran for their lives.

By the time Mannu extricated herself from the debris of the roof and walls, she was afloat on the water. Hanging on to a piece of the roof, she managed to climb onto the branch of a tree. Binding herself to the branch with whatever bits of cloth she could find, she drew her knees to her chest as the water level rose. Perched on the branch, she watched human beings and animals drift over the water, Ayesha among them.

70

On a night when not only human sounds but even the voices of animals and birds had fallen silent, Govardhan heard only one sound. Mariam's sighs. He felt that the sighs—or were they sobs—of this slave girl, who did not know how to speak or even cry properly, were full of every kind of emotion, even happiness. At that moment, however, he did not want to identify the sounds. Accepting them in a wider human context, he drew her face onto his shoulder, and pressed his own against her hair, matted with sweat and dust.

The floor was bare, there was nothing to sleep on. So they took off their clothes, spread one person's on the ground and covered themselves with the other's. Between these two layers, they were no longer Govardhan and Mariam. They were just a man and a woman, communicating with each other through the shared warmth of their bodies.

The night had grown cold. They knew it would get still colder. All that the world around them seemed to be doing was to heat up by day and cool down at night. This pattern had been going on for days. In the midst of this, Govardhan felt that after years, he was moving on the edge of something that could weakly be termed happiness. Mariam too felt the same way.

Actually, a dead body lay in the room with them—if their surroundings could be called that. The roof had burnt down and it was just a space with walls around. As for the corpse, it was so charred that it could barely be recognized as that of a human being.

The village was located in the path of the Company army's victory march. Like a storm or a flood, the army had razed everything in their way to the ground. Corpses lay scattered everywhere. When Govardhan and Mariam arrived, even the cinders had burned out. Since the army had already passed that way, they felt they could spend a night there in safety, although they were surrounded by dead bodies.

There was even some food in the house they had entered. The army must have arrived as a meal was being prepared. A few rotis had already been made, the rest of the dough still remained. The people in the house had probably rushed out, for all the bodies except one lay outside. The bayoneted women and children lay with their limbs outstretched, drenched in blood. Two men hung from the trees.

Walking past the corpses, Govardhan and Mariam entered the house and ate the rotis they found there. It was many days since they had come upon food like this. And a safe place to sleep. The warmth of the day was soon replaced by the cold of the night.

Govardhan and Mariam lay with their arms around each other. Their soft sighs quickly turned into gasps. In the small enclosure guarded by dead bodies and ashes, the chill of the night was dispelled by the heat of their bodies.

As their gasps gave way to sighs again, they heard an anguished cry outside. Were jackals attacking a body that was not completely dead?

Govardhan felt that the cry was full of pain, not sorrow. He could not have said at what stage sorrow and pain became separate emotions. Nor when, having grown separate from each other, the mind reached a state where it could not feel sorrow; but the body sensed pain...

Govardhan and Mariam realized that they were both just short of this state. But they wondered how long they would continue to be on this side of it.

Overwhelmed by their selfishness they clasped each other more tightly, afraid of the frightful groans that came from outside or the cry that waited to emerge from themselves.

71

'Tell me, Umrao, what is that man like, the one who pulled you out into the streets?' asked Bharatendu anxiously.

Umrao's eyes peered into the thick curtain of rain in front of her as if searching for the man. She said: 'What is he like? Like an ordinary man. Like anyone you see on the road. He could even be from my village. Maybe that is why I thought of him as a brother.'

Bharatendu walked on, plunged in thought.

He had seen her standing on the veranda of a shop waiting for it to stop raining and invited her to shelter under his umbrella. Walking together under the umbrella, they had recognized each other at once, even on that dark and cloudy afternoon.

The rain kept growing heavier and lighter by turns. There were no street lights and as the darkness intensified, the rain became an invisible presence.

'I know why you are so worried, guruji,' she said. 'Your

mind is full of Govardhan. And the man I saw was your character, Govardhan. Are you happy now?'

'It is certainly a relief,' said Bharatendu placing a hand on her shoulder, 'to know that you met him and accepted him as a brother. My mind is now at peace.'

'You are still not telling me what you think. Will this really give you peace of mind?'

'My friend Ibn Battuta, the eternal traveller, told me that travellers and writers can never be at peace.' Bharatendu walked a few yards. 'There is nothing they can call their last country or their last work. You are right, Umrao. In my case, even this work is destined to be left unfinished. Govardhan has escaped from me, but I keep searching for him. I should not do so and yet... Sometimes, at midnight or at times like this when it rains heavily and everyone wants to stay home, I take an umbrella and...'

'The same encounter with reality which compelled you to put your pen down while you were halfway through the farce you were writing was the one I was swimming through aimlessly until I found I had jumped into the trap of Ruswa's literature. I sent him away at once and went back to the bitterness, the stinging fire of Satrangi Mahal. It is amazing that the very character you set free has now come to pull me out of there!'

Bharatendu laughed. 'How amusing! While I wander through these streets in search of the character I set free, you, who have resisted being drawn into the imagination of a writer, walk into the shelter of my umbrella by yourself! There is no end to wonders and coincidences in this world of ours. In a way, is it not these wonders and coincidences that encourage us to go on with our bitter, searing lives?'

Dramatist and dancer had gone quite a distance, leaving

behind the dark, narrow streets of the old city. They were now walking through a plaza in a modern city, flooded with electric lights as bright as the light of day, full of multi-storeyed buildings, concrete thoroughfares and glittering shops. The rain had stopped and people had begun to come out. Bharatendu folded up the umbrella and they stood on the roadside. The electric lights threw hundreds of reflections on the wet road.

Bharatendu pointed to a huge cinema house festooned with gleaming neon signs and larger-than-life posters.

'Plays used to be performed here once upon a time. There used to be one or two shows a week on a small stage illuminated with oil lamps. Many of my plays were staged here the first time... Umrao, have you ever acted in a play?'

'You forget that I used to be a dancer,' said Umrao, lowering her eyes. 'A courtesan.'

People coming out of the cinema hall after the evening show flooded the street. A large-screen Ruswa fantasy filled with passion and violence was showing there. The spectators' faces still reflected the delight they had felt while seeing it. Cars and buses honked impatiently as if they wanted to drive all the people away.

His eyes moving idly over the crowds, Bharatendu said: 'What do you think? Did people see a courtesan in you... or did they see Umrao in a courtesan?'

'Why do you ask me this?'

'I don't know. All kinds of questions keep coming up in a dramatist's mind.'

'What kind of questions?'

'About his characters, for example. About the actors and actresses who play those characters. About the images that enter the minds of the spectators through those actors and actresses.'

Umrao's voice grew sombre, as if the world she had left behind was again casting a spell on her. 'Honoured playwright, do you know what the tragedy is? That, before they come to see a play, the spectators have no particular images in their minds for the characters. An audience watching the *Sakuntalam* does not see the woman on the stage as Sakuntala; they see Sakuntala in the actress.'

'Only one who has lived her life as if it is a play can say that, Umrao,' said Bharatendu, placing his hand affectionately on her shoulder. His brow suddenly grew furrowed. He said with infinite sadness: 'We writers are like jailers. Until it is completed, each work is like a prison in which we torment our characters. It is the readers who throw open the prison and free them.'

They turned back, the plaza slowly receding behind them. The rain had stopped completely. Muddy country roads of earth began to replace the wide thoroughfares as they walked farther away from the town.

'Umrao,' said Bharatendu, 'do you know who I was thinking about before I saw you on that shop veranda?'

'Who?'

'About Mannu.'

'Who is Mannu?'

Bharatendu laughed. 'You wouldn't know! Mannu is not one of my characters. She is a girl from real life. The real-life daughter of Govardhan, a character in a play. Think, Umrao, how many people there are who are related to our characters but who do not appear in the play!'

'You are right. But what were your thoughts about Mannu?'

'Maybe I was all wrong, but as I was walking through these narrow streets in the rain, the sounds of the tabla and the ghungru came to my ears from a kothi. I suddenly feared that some Dilawar Khan might have taken that little girl and left her in the same kind of place as you were. There was no reason to imagine something like that, but it could have happened, after all. In the dark streets of Pataliputra or Chowk of Lucknow or Sonagachi of Calcutta or Kamatipura…'

'Umrao has seen much, Bharatenduji. But what she has not seen exceeds what she has. There are so many doors besides those of Chowk and Sonagachi for hunted animals to curl up in. Our thoughts can wander around groping in the darkness and mist among the many possible squares on the board… then, sometimes it occurs to me that everything need not always be dark and foul. Because I could not capture laughter, it does not mean there is no laughter in this world. You yourself spoke some time ago of the things which encourage us to live…'

'See where we have reached!' Bharatendu caught Umrao's hand to make her stop.

They had not noticed that they had crossed the field and reached the village, that they had come to a stage in the middle of the village. A satsang was in progress there in the light of oil lamps. It was the thudding of the drums and the rhythmic clapping of the villagers that had brought them to a halt. Washed by the rain, the trees around breathed new life. The earth beneath their feet was moist and as soft as velvet.

Santo, andhadhundhi andhiyara[13]

Kabir sang, standing in the midst of the people, using all the strength of his voice.

Isi ghat andar bag bagicha

---

[13] Oh gentle folk, why do you grope in the dark?

Isi mein sirjan hara[14]

Kabir sang a line and the villagers listened very attentively. When he repeated it, they sang with him:

Isi ghat bhitar sat samundar
Isi mein now lakh tara
Isi ghat andar hira moti
Isi mein parkhan hara
Isi ghat andar anhad baja
Isi mein uthat phuvara[15]

When Kabir rose, the villagers rose as well. When he moved in rhythm to the song, they did so too. They became immersed in the song just as he was. Eternal music flowed out of each of them as in the song and fountains of happiness sprang up. The happiness spilled into the village, enveloping it and spread into the jungle. The trees began to sway and lightning flashed through the sky.

Unaware of what she was doing, Umrao began to move into their midst and Bharatendu caught her hand to stop her. 'No, Umrao,' he said. 'Let's stay here.'

She obeyed.

'So many people in the world consider others their own property,' said Umrao. 'Kings, political leaders, brothel-keepers, writers... they make people kill each other for their own purposes, make them dance, weave stories using them. This

---

[14] In this body is a flower garden and the benign creator stays there.

[15] All the seven seas are in this body. Myriads of stars glitter inside it. All the precious gems are within it and it is the tester as well. Eternal music swells in it and fountains of life spring from within.

unattractive man here is also doing the same thing. But what a difference there is! When he sang, I could not help singing as well. When he danced, I began to dance along with him. Why did you stop me?'

Umrao's eyes filled. Bharatendu drew her head down on his shoulder. He looked up at the large raindrops which had begun to spatter down, then at the villagers who were dancing to the rhythm of the rain. He said:

'Gardens, oceans, galaxies, musical waterfalls... my feet begin to move too, as you described. But if we take even a step forward now, we may fall down. There is still a great distance between us and this stage we see before us. You have just stepped onto this path. You might have left behind court singers and poets. But there are singers and singers, Umrao—so many, many more of them. Aren't you still among those who do not have a final place to stop?'

72

The streets of the city had been decorated as if for a festival. Although he had no penchant for fairs or celebrations, Shahanshah Alamgir Aurangzeb had decreed that this occasion should be memorable. Earlier, the soldiers had gone round the city and announced to the beating of drums that everyone who lived in the city had to be present on the main avenue that started at Chandni Chowk and encircled all of Shahjahanabad to reach Firoz Shah Kotla.

The emperor had described the unhappy situation that had been prevailing in the country the past year as a rebellion. How else could the attempt to single out archaic theories of dynasty and family to pollute politics be described? Since the emperor wanted to maintain purity and simplicity in affairs that concerned power, he preferred to use accurate weights like strength and weakness in his balance rather than vague norms of right and wrong. He had ruthlessly quelled the rebellions organized by his old and infirm father and by his older brother, Dara Shukoh, who spent all his time with books and fakirs. He arrested his father and incarcerated him in the fort at Agra. As a formal closing ceremony to mark the end of a rebellion that had actually crumbled much earlier, he issued a proclamation announcing that Dara Shukoh, who had been running from pillar to post for more than a year, be captured, brought back to Dilli and beheaded in public. However, at that moment, the shadow of a grand-uncle made a sudden appearance, stumbling unsteadily out of the darkness of three generations. It was not the dark of forgetfulness but his own blindness that made the old man totter in this way—by rights he should have rushed in on horseback, brandishing a sword. 'Long ago, son, when I argued like you on the side of strength and not tradition and was defeated, my brother declared me a heretic and ordered that I be blinded. Today, following the same ideals I did, you have been victorious. Mubarak, my son, mubarak!' Uttering these words the shadow groped its way back stumblingly, just as it had come.

The darkness the visitor left behind had stayed with the emperor for two full nights. When he groped his way through it and reeled out at dawn on the second day, Aurangzeb had changed. The qazis, the imams, the muftis, even his sister, Roshanara, said he looked like a mullah. He started to call Dara Shukoh, whom he had described until then as a rebel, a heretic. While speaking at the council of ministers, he used the words 'right' and 'wrong' instead of 'strength' and 'weakness'— with the difference that he meant religious rights and wrongs, not those of the hierarchy or the dynasty. The mullahs who had quarrelled with him and distanced themselves from him earlier welcomed him now as their saviour. Aurangzeb had summoned his trusted qazi, Abdul Wahab, and issued an urgent order to arrest Dara's friend Sarmad, who had been walking naked through the streets of Dilli, singing songs, and behead him along with the prince.

The city burned in the sweltering heat of August. The previous day's shower had only made it sultrier. A haze of dust, black in certain areas and yellow in others, hung in the air. People lined up to watch the procession along the royal avenue from Chandni Chowk to Firoz Shah Kotla under the cruel sun which offered no shade at all, not even to a crow. The soldiers had been ordered to go from house to house and drag out those who had stayed away, with no wish to witness the gruesome ordeal. People's skins had blistered in the heat and sweat poured down the cracks in the skin. Many collapsed. No one dared attend to them for fear of the soldiers' whips. They were even afraid to talk to one another. As the day advanced they began to ask themselves: to whom was this punishment being meted out, to Dara Shukoh and Sarmad or to themselves?

Among the spectators were people who had come from distant places, who had been trapped along with the crowds that were driven to the place: Umrao Jan and Gauhar Mirza, Henry Williams and David Butler, Bharatendu Harishchandra and the Portuguese trader Nunis, Ramchander and Galileo, Savitri and Uddalaka, Mariam and Govardhan. Standing at various spots along the route, each one talked to his or her companion about the astonishing spectacle that was being celebrated.

'Gauhar, didn't you always describe yourself as a mirza?' Umrao teasingly questioned Gauhar who had been her constant companion ever since she had come to Khanum's house. 'See what happens to the mirzas! It is a shahzada who is going to be taken this way today to be beheaded.'

Gauhar Mirza laughed thoughtlessly.

Umrao stopped joking and went on gravely: 'Gauhar, you were first my mischievous classmate, then my attendant in the house. Some nights when I had no visitors, I even welcomed you to my bedroom. But why did you come here to witness such a terrible sight? What is the bond between you and me?'

'Umrao, no matter what light I considered you in, you were always distant from me.'

'How many connotations do closeness and distance have, Gauhar. I, a dancing girl who sang and prostituted herself, know that. I felt as close as a sibling to an unknown and illiterate villager I chanced upon in a wayside sarai a few days ago. I even began to imagine that he hailed from the same small town I was born and brought up in until Dilawar Khan snatched me away from it. Do you know what he said when he took leave of me? That even if we did not meet again, it was a great relief for him to know that we both walked the same path.' Umrao broke off as the crowd started cheering slowly. 'See, Gauhar, we are waiting here to witness one brother behead another. The emperor's orders are that we cheer the act loudly as it takes place. The procession seems to have started, listen to the uproar...'

'Why have we been brought here to witness this drama?' David Butler asked Henry Williams angrily. 'In what way are we responsible for it?'

'David, do you not have the responsibility to be present at the ceremony that marks the end of a revolt?' Henry pretended to be surprised. 'Besides, we are participating in something that proves the victory of our philosophy!'

'Well, today marks the end of all claims a family or a dynasty might have to rule a country.' There was faith as well as doubt in Butler's voice. 'But what is it the beginning of? They have announced that one more person will be beheaded today, Henry, one who is not in the race for power at all.'

'The beginning took place long ago, David. Maybe you forgot all about it when you set foot on this soil. Try to remember the time we went to watch the auto-da-fe in Madrid. Sixteen persons were burned at the stake that day. Scaffolds were erected on high platforms in the plaza. Heretics, Protestants, Jews with dunces' caps on their heads, women accused of being witches who were dragged along with lighted torches in their hands and ropes around their necks. I can still see all of it clearly before me. We put on our best clothes and took musical instruments along as if going to a festival. And we went early, to get the best seats. When the inquisitors proclaimed the sentences, we shouted with everyone: let them set fire first to the beards of the dogs! And when the executioners stood below the scaffolds and actually set fire to their beards with torches attached to long poles, we screamed like children at a circus...'

'But these people are not screaming the way we did. They are shouting because of the blows the soldiers standing behind are raining on them. They know that if they do not cheer, the Company's army will hang them. I can see them weep furtively when the soldiers are not watching, and pretend that the tears flowing from their eyes are drops of sweat!'

'What you see is the truth, Butler,' said Henry, looking into the distance. 'But I can see more: at festivals of this kind, after a while, when the army is no longer behind them, these people will shout even without being prodded, not caring whether the victims are heretics or rebels or patriots, just as we did that day at the auto-da-fe in Madrid...'

'Why are you silent, Nunis?' asked Bharatendu of Nunis, who was seated with his head bent as if in meditation.

Nunis raised his head just as much as was needed to answer.

'It's nothing,' he said. 'I suddenly thought of another procession I saw while wandering through Vijayanagara after selling my horses. A procession which was leading a Hindu wife to the pyre of her dead husband. She was seated on a donkey, facing backwards. People followed beating drums and she was singing some kind of song to the rhythm of the beats... Tell me, Harishchandraji, is it true that Shahanshah Alamgir Aurangzeb has banned the practice of sati?'

'Yes. But so did William Bentinck of the Company, among many others.'

Encouraged, Nunis raised his head and asked: 'People say that the emperor has banned the mujra dance and prostitution and driven singers and musicians out of the kothis. What about that?'

'It's true.'

'And the consumption of alcohol?'

'Has been completely banned.'

'That he has given up all ostentation and is content to dress simply and eat frugally?'

'That is true as well.'

'That although Islamic law allows him four wives, he does not have that many?'

'So I hear.'

'That means then that he has fewer wives than Dara Shukoh and Amir Khusrau?'

'Nunis, I sense some crooked intention behind each of your questions.' Bharatendu was annoyed. 'Is it your aim to cast a halo of purity around this cruel emperor's head?'

'Do you think he needs such a halo? The emperor is beyond haloes and images. I was just indicating different possibilities.'

'Let me ask you a question, Nunis. Does the fact that Dara Shukoh and Amir Khusrau had more wives than Aurangzeb prove anything?'

'It does. At least it proves that simple fact.'

'Nunis,' Bharatendu shook his head. 'You are a traveller and historian. You must look at things in their right perspectives.'

'It should be the other way, Harishchandraji. Does current thinking not argue that historians, scientists and philosophers should view things in their totality?'

'Stop it, Nunis, enough of this distortion!'

'Yes, my friend, this is a distortion. It was to make you say this that I asked these questions. Had I been only a horse trader, I would not have asked any of these questions. But because of the notes I made as an ordinary human being to express my wonder and pain, my well-wishers made a historian of me. A scholar and intellectual, one who knows more than others. And therefore one who has the authority to judge others. Look, Harishchandraji, today, historians like me and litterateurs like you can, if we want, turn Alamgir Aurangzeb into a great, high-principled, generous, non-violent emperor and Dara Shukoh and Baba Sarmad into vulgar criminals!'

Bharatendu looked at him with interest. He said gently: 'Do you know, Nunis, it needed a lowly village rustic like Govardhan to push me out of my mansion. He sent me to witness the tragic event taking place on this street. And yet, he is only a character born from my pen. Tell me, who are the ones pursuing you?'

'Horses! Horses, Harishchandraji. My mind is full of horses today. I see only horses everywhere. The horses that historians sold, that wandered the length and breadth of the country. The horses that drop dead all over Hindustan for princes who fight for kingdoms, for kings who want to build empires. The horses that are going to die tomorrow on the battlefields...'

'What is happening here, Ramchander? What have you brought me here to see? I cannot see anything. Don't you know I have lost my eyesight?' Galileo touched Ramchander with his hands. They were standing on the veranda of a building on the roadside in order to escape the cruel sun.

'Sir, you who increased the size of the universe a hundred thousand times...'

'Yes, my child.' Galileo's throat was choked. Stretching out his hand, he went on: 'Today my world has shrunk into the small circle that I can draw with my hands.'

'Sir, weren't you always blind in a way?' Ramchander took both the scientist's hands in his and said, with the liberty a son feels when he speaks to his father, 'You focussed your eyes on the distance and refused to see the truth of the world. Then, when you began to see the truths nearer you, you denied the distant ones. And now you have lost both.'

'Ram, what is right? To see the mundane that is near us and forget the distant or to see the distant and...'

'How many people have been asking this question and for how long! No one has a final answer... Leave that for the moment. I will now explain to you the things that are happening before us.'

'Tell me, Ram.'

'Throngs of people have lined up on both sides of the streets of the city Shah Jahan built in Dilli. A procession moves along the avenue in the blazing sun, escorted by Shahanshah Alamgir

Aurangzeb's soldiers. They are bringing Dara Shukoh, the emperor's older brother, and his friend Sarmad, the Sufi saint, on the backs of two elephants. The hands of both prisoners have been bound to their backs. Sarmad is naked; Dara Shukoh is clothed in a short loincloth. The crowds are throwing sand at both men's bodies and at the elephants; they are spitting at them and hitting them with long sticks.'

'Stop it, Ram, stop it!' said Galileo, his voice rising. 'This is the same spectacle then, that of leading heretics to the stake.'

'Yes, these men too are being taken to be executed. The procession is moving towards the elevated platform near the ruins of the palace that Firoz Shah built. They will be executed there.'

Galileo released himself from Ramchander's hands, turned away from him and fixed his sightless eyes on something in the distance. He seemed to be listening to the sound of horses' hooves, to the loud cries which were coming nearer. His mind was churning like the sea in a storm.

'What offence have these men committed?' asked the scientist, visibly moved.

'Just one crime, sir—they did not obey the rules of the established religion. One, a shahzada, unmindful of his status, mingled with the common people; the other, a mendicant, abandoned the temples and walked the streets naked, singing songs of love. Both strayed away from their codes of dharma. The scriptures say that it is an unpardonable crime to forget one's own dharma and perform another's—*paradharma bhayavaha*.'

'And why are these people shouting and throwing stones at them?'

'You know that as a scientist, you cannot accept sounds and

sights exactly as you hear or see them. Especially when they are to do with the people. What do people possess that is their very own?'

'I know, I know…'

Galileo left the shade of the veranda and came out into the sun. Not like a blind man but like one with normal vision. He threaded his way with great ease towards the front row. Ramchander followed him like a child, holding his hand.

When they came to the front row, Galileo pushed him forward and said: 'Ram, my child, tell me how these men who are going to be executed are reacting.'

'Sarmad sits on the elephant's back enveloped in dust, bleeding from the wounds the spears and stones have dealt him. He is laughing and singing loudly. Can you hear?'

'Yes.' Galileo listened attentively and repeated the words of the song:

'Inquilabe zamana dekh liya
Hubbe duniya se qualab saf huwa
Jo kali thi khil ke khaq huyi
Jo phool tha kumhala ke khaq huwa'[16]

'Is he mad, Ram?'

'He is a poet, sir.'

'And the shahzada?'

'He does not say anything. He has fallen silent. He sits on

---

[16] I have watched the sunrise and the sunset. I have washed away the stain and deceit of wordly love from within me. I saw the bud give its secret away in its innocent large-heartedness; and that is how it invited calamity on itself—for it withered the next day and turned to dust.

the elephant with his head bowed as if he expects the sword to fall on it any moment.'

'Enough, let us go.' Holding Ramchander's hand, Galileo moved out of the crowd as fast as he had come.

As they broke away from the multitude and left the cities and streets behind, Galileo said: 'Ram, my child, you told me many stories. About your travels, your investigations, about knowledge and science. How exciting it was to listen to you! What a pleasure it is to talk to a scientist! But all the time, I was impatient to ask you something: what did you find out about the weakness of human beings? Did you ever make a study of human weakness?'

Ramchander was about to say something but Galileo stopped him. 'No, don't say it now. I have a lot to tell you before that. In any case, is it not I who should tell you about human weaknesses? I, who went blind after discovering one thing after another, who boasted of my strength and courage endlessly, then finally collapsed and have to hang on to your shoulder now to walk. Come, I will tell you all that, but on another day. Today is the day for processions, torture and beheadings.'

Govardhan, Mariam, Uddakala and Savitri were seated among the people who had found places on the raised platform of the Firoz Shah Kotla at the very end of the royal avenue. None of them spoke to each other. They sat silently, holding their breath, waiting for that terrible last moment anticipating it as their own. And when the swords finally fell, their eyes stayed wide open, as if their own heads were those that had been cut off. The man who beheaded Dara Shukoh and Sarmad was none other than Ali Dost!

73

A li Dost looked at Malik Kafur's body until it became still. He then shook his head and walked up to Malik Kafur's horse which stood on the roadside and caressed its neck and sides. He climbed onto it and kicked its sides gently to make it move.

After a while, the horse picked up speed and began to gallop over the fields, skirting trees and jumping over streams.

As he rode through fields and forests in sun and rain, Ali Dost felt a lightness in his mind. The demons that had troubled him when he had ridden like this once before, through fields and jungles, his clothes spattered with blood from Kamran's eyes, no longer bothered him. He felt the power that Malik Kafur had described as the invisible master hiding behind authority carry him on its back in a manner that even Kafur had not been able to achieve.

As he covered the distance and approached the arch-shaped gates of the city, a huge crowd was waiting to receive him. Soldiers mounted on horses kept watch expectantly, their eyes focussed on the distance. Ali Dost walked into their midst as if there was nothing unusual in all this.

As soon as he came up to them, the crowds began to cry out loudly, one hand on their chest, the other stretched out towards him, beseeching him to behead the two criminals who had blasphemed against their faith. The manner in which they addressed and praised him was as if he was the answer to their prayers. The soldiers who used to pass messages to him from some king or other were now silent. They stood before him with their heads bowed, touching their right hand repeatedly to their forehead in greeting. Having functioned until then as a mere executioner in faraway palaces, Ali Dost felt he was soaring like a saviour into these streets on wings that had sprouted on his sides. All he had done as an executioner was comply with the commands of kings who knew more than he did. Now, without a king to act as a middleman between them, this rabble recognized him as someone who knew more than they did. Ali Dost realized that his journey did not lie between rights and wrongs but between what was right and what was more right, between one who knows and one who knows more.

Ali waded through the crowd towards the platform built over the ruins of Firoz Shah's palace. When he climbed on top of it, the soldiers who stood guard around and the multitude behind them greeted him like a hero. Unsheathing his sword, he raised it above his head in response to their greeting.

Two elephants escorted by soldiers came and stood below the platform. The soldiers dragged the two men seated on them up to the platform, one wrapped casually in a loincloth and the other stark naked, both smeared all over with blood and dust. Wasting no time, the soldiers threw them at Ali Dost's feet.

Ali Dost recognized the two men whom the rabble was

crying out to him to behead for having blasphemed against their faith. One was the emperor's older brother, the other a saint who was greatly loved by the people. For a moment, Ali was stunned by the sight of the victims. All those whom he had executed passed before him in a procession—Prince Kamran, the women of the firangis who ruled the country and the like. Prince Dara and Baba Sarmad, who walked among the people of the country like an ordinary citizen, were not like any of these victims. Kamran had been blinded because of a quarrel among the brothers. And it had been the rivalry between the native princes and the foreign traders that had instigated the massacre at Bibigarh...While now, the citizens were crying out to him, one hand on their chest and the other outstretched, to safeguard the purity of their faith: cut off the heads of the dogs and give them to us!

Ali Dost's sword did not delay a minute longer. The heads of the prince who was a traitor and of the saint who was an apostate fell down and rolled on the ground.

The cries of the crowd and the soldiers showed no signs of dying down. Ali floated above the sound of the cheers, his wings outspread. Finally he had to raise his own hand and quell them.

Ali Dost then picked up both the heads lying on the ground one by one with the tip of his long sword. He climbed down the steps of the platform onto the road. He held the sword up so that everyone could see the heads of the punished men and walked through the centre of the street. He twirled the sword this side and that so that everyone could see it properly. Ali Dost felt that the people had a right to know that the heads they wanted had actually been cut off from the bodies they had belonged to.

But he heard the cheers of the crowd subside as he walked

along. Gradually, the people fell completely silent. Not moving or speaking, they stared at the heads on the tip of the sword, their eyes and mouths opened wide. A frightening silence fell over the street. Ali Dost walked in the middle of the street through the empty path lined on both sides by the motionless crowd with no one in front of him or behind, the heads spiked on the tip of the sword in his hand.

Wasn't it these heads that you wanted? he wanted to ask the crowd that stood before him like a picture this question. But he did not. He remembered that it was he who knew what they wanted more than they themselves did. So, instead of asking them, he said to them: 'I will give you the heads you want. I will give you your own heads! The heads that I decide you should be carrying on your shoulders.'

Ali Dost and the heads threaded on his upraised sword moved slowly along, drawing an isolated line before a world that had become an unmoving picture.

74

Black, jagged, barren hills scowled down at the chasms that divided them. The parched valley twisted and turned between them, now hiding behind the hills, now suddenly emerging in search of the plains. The sun slipped slowly behind the farthest hills.

Noticing a movement on the slope of the hill, the boy stopped and looked at the spot. A group of people with matted hair and beards was peering at him. Rifle barrels pointed at him.

'Who is it?' the boy called out.

'We are each known by the name of our tribe—dakoo,' came the reply at once.

'Don't hide, come down if you want to talk to me.'

'Throw down the bundle on your head and get out!'

'All I have on my head are a few dry twigs,' said the boy. 'I won't give them to you.'

'What's your name, boy?'

'Nachiketas, son of Acharya Uddalaka. My duty is to collect the firewood my mother needs for cooking.'

The boy began to walk on.

'If your duty is collecting firewood, ours is to plunder whatever we can get.'

The dacoits rushed down the hill, snatched the bundle of firewood off the boy's head, pushed him down and ran away.

Nachiketas scrambled up and walked on. He stumbled over something—it turned out to be a corpse. He looked around fearfully and saw that there were many of them strewn around. Some were rotting, some had already rotted and become skeletons, while the blood was still fresh on others. There were the skeletons of long-necked camels from caravans and broken bits from palkis that white ants had devoured.

Further down, the path left the mountains behind and entered a plateau. Death had left its mark here as well. The travellers who came from the opposite side told the boy that the bodies were not those of lone wayfarers or traders journeying in caravans but of armies or civilian communities that had perished in wars or rebellions. Nachiketas looked at the carcasses of horses and elephants among them and at rusted swords, spears and shields, in mute understanding.

He continued down the path till it reached level ground. There he saw green fields, rivers, clusters of huts. The sun had gone down, the shadows were growing longer. He had just begun to feel more cheerful when the bodies appeared again. Travellers told him they were the bodies of refugees. People who had been forced to leave their place of birth and move to foreign lands. They had met one another on this path, fallen upon one another, torn each other apart. Along with the human corpses, Nachiketas also saw the decaying bodies of the animals that had been with them: goats, dogs, cats. The bundles of clothes, cooking utensils, mats and lanterns they had carried with them lay scattered all over the ground. Travellers said to him that the northern highway, the Uttarapatha, which wound down from the high plateau of Gandhara and flowed over the vast plains of the Ganga to the jungles of Burma was always sown with death. They asked him why a boy who had not yet begun to live, who had not fully risen from the level of the ground, was journeying on this road. He had only one thing to say—that he was collecting firewood for his mother so that she could cook food.

The travellers on the road became fewer. Camels, horses and bullock carts disappeared and were replaced by motor cars, loaded trucks, and buses packed with people. The people rushing around in these vehicles had no time to tell him the sagas of the corpses. He walked on, through roads that could tell him nothing, among corpses that knew nothing.

Nachiketas finally came to an empty bus that stood by the roadside. He circled it and saw that all its passengers were lying on the ground. There were children like him, old people, men and women. Some of them were not dead yet. Blood gushed from their bodies, drawing the outlines of fresh pictures on the earth. Some of them trembled gently, others writhed violently. Looking at them, he gradually realized that they were not soldiers or refugees whose bodies he had been seeing, but the very travellers who were narrating to him the fate of the traders, soldiers and refugees along the way. Since their speech was cut off at that point, the knowledge of who had killed them remained inaccessible to him.

75

'What are you thinking about so deeply, acharya?' Savitri asked as she came in with a pot of water. Uddalaka stood in a narrow gap between the huts.

Uddalaka ran his eyes over her torn clothes, her dishevelled hair, the bloodstained scratches on her face and hands. He knew from the way she walked that the pot was not full. Obviously there had been a brawl among the women at the water tap.

He withdrew his eyes from her and ran them quickly over the shabby huts in the slum, saying nothing in reply.

'Kotwalji must be wondering how he's come to a stage where he can do nothing about a squabble at the water tap except watch it helplessly!' she said teasingly.

Not responding to this, Uddalaka asked: 'Where is Nachiketas, Savitri?'

'He went to collect firewood and has not yet come back.' There was anxiety in her voice.

'Salma,' he called her by her old name. 'Whenever he is late, we grow worried. As if guns are being trained at his head as at ours.'

He followed her and sat down on the ledge of the veranda. He took her hand and asked her, 'Salma, can't you see the lines written on his head?'

'We who think we have the strength to protect ourselves, who don disguises, change our names, go into hiding: we could collapse any day before the bullets of a machine gun or stones thrown by bigots. To whom can we entrust this little defenceless boy?'

'To whom except Yama, the god of death, asking him to be kind to him?'

Nachiketas entered at that moment without any firewood. He had hurt his forehead and grazed his arms when the dacoits pushed him down. Going straight to his mother, he climbed into her lap. Savitri put her arms around him and kissed him.

'Who is Yama, mother?' he asked.

'He is Dharmaraja, the lord of dharma, my child. The judge who punishes those who do wrong. But the laws of this world are different. Therefore, he cannot do anything to the living. The world of the lord of Dharma is limited to those who are dead.'

'Father, I think I came walking over the road that leads to the Dharmaraja's palace.' He turned to his father. 'The entire road was scattered with corpses and bones. Do you know why they all died or were killed?'

Uddalaka and Savitri gazed at their child in astonishment.

'A group of people who declared openly that their occupation was plundering...' said the boy. 'They snatched the firewood I had gathered for you, Mother, and pushed me down. I did not die. But all along the road I saw the bodies of hundreds of people who had been looted and killed. Later, when the road came down to the plains, I saw the bodies of soldiers who had been killed in battle. Then of refugees who had been driven out of their own countries. As I went on, I gradually ceased to meet the travellers who told me these stories about the dead. I saw only vehicles that rushed down the road. Then I came across the bodies of a whole busload of passengers who had been pulled out of the vehicle and shot dead. I had no idea why they had been killed so brutally. Father, at which end of the road can one see Dharmaraja's palace?'

'Why do you want to know where Yama's palace is, my son?'

'When I came in, weren't you telling Mother that you were going to hand me over to Yama?'

Savitri tightened her arms around her son, afraid that he might get up and run away. Although he was curled into the circle of her love, his mind was shedding all its barriers and he was moving into a world which was parched and indifferent. That was how he imagined death.

'My son,' said Uddalaka at last, 'Yama's city could be anywhere on the road you came by. It could be next door or here where we stand. We clasp one another's hands—who knows when he will separate them?'

Savitri interrupted: 'Don't say things like that, acharya.'

'How will he know unless I say these things? Where will he hide if he does not know?' Uddalaka knelt down by the boy and looked steadily at him as he continued: 'Do you know how long your parents have been in hiding, wearing these clownish disguises? What means did we have to fight except go into hiding? How many people could we fight? Foreigners, our own countrymen, religious scholars, philosophers, scientists, leaders of cultural movements, judges… all of them wanted our heads at the tip of their spears. My son, you must know all this, learn everything, in order to be able to protect yourself...'

'But father, I don't want to hide from Yama. I want to meet him. I have so many questions to ask him. If it is only in the world of death that I can meet him, that is all right. He is a just man. One who can connect cause to effect.'

In flimsy slum huts made of broken bricks, earth, empty tins and gunny bags, fathers, mothers and children discussed the principles of how to conceal themselves, how to escape, how to put up a fight. Outside, the city sweated, smouldered and shivered. Water pipes that had no water in them, deluges which washed everything away, grains they had no stock of, firewood that was constantly stolen: all these kept them engaged from morning to evening. Processions holding up flags and idols passed by them. They rebuilt the huts that had been destroyed by riots or bombs over and over again. They lay prone on the ground to take shelter from the machine gun bullets that high priests of culture and religion rained upon them. As each calamity took place, the Moinuddins who had become Uddalakas and the Salmas who had become Savitris took their Nachiketases in their arms.

'The only right thing that happened in the life of the policeman that I was,' said Uddalaka, 'was that I took the wife of Govardhan and Ali Dost as my wife and begot a son who asks questions.'

One day, unknown to them, the sepoys of the government came and encircled the slums. They gradually made the circle smaller and smaller until it was directly around Uddalaka's hut. Discovering what had happened, Uddalaka woke his wife and son and said to them: 'Salma and Nachiketas, the yagya, the sacrificial ritual, of my life has come to a close. It is time now to set fire to the yagyasala, where the ritual was performed.

All that there is left to offer to the fire is the yajamana who conducted the yagya and his wife.'

He kissed their foreheads, took their hands, came out and stood before the sepoys. He said to them: 'Come! I am Moinuddin, the rebel kotwal. The noose which did not fit my neck earlier will do so easily now. This is Salma, once Ali Dost's wife, then Govardhan's and now mine—she who evaded the stones the mullahs threw at her many times. This is our son Nachiketas. You did not know of him until now.'

He turned to Nachiketas and said: 'Get ready, child. Your journey is about to begin. Keep all your questions safely in your bag. I am going to set fire to the yagyasala.'

Moinuddin and Salma released his hands and walked towards the soldiers without turning back.

76

Butler Nawab's famous palki was once stolen along with its kahars while going on a journey. Since none of the kahars came back to tell him this news, he could not cut off their heads. He therefore sent his soldiers to the villages where the kahar caste lived and sliced off the heads of all the children there since the adults had gone away to carry palkis. Since their shoulders were more important to the kahars than their heads, Butler thought his action would not put an end to the kahar caste.

Butler's harem suffered because of the loss of the palki. New young women no longer arrived and the rooms vacated by the inmates who died of disease or old age remained unoccupied. One day, Butler was so bored that he had all the remaining women line up in the courtyard and mowed them down in a shower of bullets. The harem, therefore, became empty and the only sign that that it had once been occupied was a cot in each room that was gradually covered by dust and cobwebs. The loss of the women did not affect the nawab too deeply. His interest in sex waned and in any case, he had never been greatly attracted by it. He had very seldom looked at the faces of the women in the harem. Abandoning women, he returned to his old passion for hunting. He converted the harem into a museum for weapons, from ancient bows and arrows, clubs and spears to the most recent kalashnikov rifles. He always carried small pistols and sophisticated automatics with him. The balconies of the harem were transformed into watchtowers. Machine guns fitted with telescopes were installed on them. The harem thus became a fort and came to be known as the Nawab's Fort.

Although Butler used the most modern weapons, the nature of the hunt he pursued became more and more primitive. When he had set out in search of Govardhan after his escape from jail, with the intention of hunting down the mutineers who had destroyed his family and his wealth, a legal and moral sanction had supported his action. Whether it was a question of personal revenge or of the preservation of an empire, certain rules had governed his choice of the victim. Once these rules were set aside and testing the efficiency of the weapons became his main motive, he expended no more thought on whether the victim was guilty or who the victim was at all. On lonely evenings or mornings or afternoons, he would climb to the top of the towers of the fort and order his men to bring him guns and ammunition. He would then fire at the distant horizon. The villagers who lived in the area would panic, for his shots often found their mark on boys grazing their goats on the maidan or farmers working in the fields or washermen washing clothes by the river. Butler did not see anything wrong in this. He was as delighted when a carefully-aimed bullet found its target as when a bullet that had no specific target hit some object by chance.

His attendants sometimes shuddered at the cries that rose

in the distance and on these occasions he would tell them: 'The laws of physics say that whether I fire this bullet from a gun or simply drop it from my hand, it takes the same time to reach the ground. What then is the purpose of my gun? What I regard as achievement is either the distance a bullet covers or the victim who prevents it from falling to the ground!'

One day the sepoys came to the gate of the fort and rang the bell that hung there. This was the practice whenever a culprit was brought to stand trial. The guards opened the gate when they heard the bell. The sepoys entered with two people whose hands and legs were so closely bound to their bodies that they resembled two balls.

Butler heard the bell and got up disinterestedly. Trials in army courts which used to thrill him earlier now bored him. But he put on his uniform anyway with all his decorations, buckled his Sam Browne on it, positioned his peaked cap carefully and went down the stairs.

77

True to habit, Butler did not raise his eyes to look at the two ball-like objects that the guards had laid down in the box for the accused. During a trial, he generally looked at the blank sheet of white paper before him and at the face of the prosecuting officer in turn. He had earned the reputation of being a judge who could conduct a trial in the shortest possible time. Actually, it was not an interest in the trial that motivated him to finish it quickly but his dislike for the odour of the courtroom which was paneled in teakwood and frequently varnished. Since trials in military courts were held in camera and there was no provision for the accused to defend themselves or appeal against the judgment, it was impossible to question the verdicts.

But when the names of the accused were read out, Butler's eyes darted unawares to the box in which they stood.

'Accused number one, Moinuddin; accused number two, Salma Begum.' The prosecutor read out the names a second time.

Suddenly Butler found himself experiencing a long-forgotten emotion—fear. Unable to pull his eyes away, he stared at the two persons in the box. He watched as the guards removed the ropes from their necks and they straightened, assumed a sitting position, and stared back at him.

There were only three kinds of people in the vast courtroom—Butler, who described himself as the court, the prosecutor and his military assistant, and the accused. Despite this, Butler felt that there was a vast assembly staring at him, waiting for him to answer their questions. The idea of justice, which he had not thought of for a long time, invaded his mind.

'These people... what proof is there that these two have committed treason?' Butler asked the prosecutor anxiously, without waiting for him to read out the charges.

'They have not committed treason, your honour. The charge against them is apostasy,' said the prosecutor after the initial moment of shock at the court's untimely question.

'Apostasy?' Butler was visibly relieved. He grew calm and assumed control of himself. Adjusting his uniform, he sat up straight.

'The first accused, Moinuddin, who is a Muslim, disguised himself as a Hindu Brahmin and conducted himself like one. In doing so, he vilified Hindu dharma and its establishments.' The prosecutor read out the charges. 'Salma Begum, the second accused, who is a Muslim woman, received men other than her husband and lived with them, contrary to Muslim law.'

'But these are matters of religion. How is a military court concerned with them? After the Mutiny, did not the Company sarkar give up all involvement in religious matters?'

The prosecutor was unrelenting. 'That is precisely why these people have been brought to this court. As the court observed, the Company sarkar is completely secular now. The government no longer takes interest in categorizing the customs of any religion as good or evil. The trial of these two people is therefore outside the jurisdiction of this court. They have to be tried by the courts of their respective religions. My submission to the court is that they be handed over to their respective religious institutions to be punished or acquitted as they think fit.'

Butler pondered over this for a while. Although he did not look in that direction, he could feel Moinuddin's eyes darting towards him like sharp arrows. This was the man who had taken him to his village when he was at death's door, given him clothes to make him look Indian and saved him from the mutineers. Moinuddin had saved not only him but many other white people from certain death. And he was being tried today for having disguised himself as he had once disguised Butler, for having tried to escape the clutches of the Company sarkar. Butler tried to find a point of law that would make this man's case different from his own. It came to him at last: he, Butler, had disguised himself in order to escape from those who had rebelled against the government. Whereas Moinuddin had done so to escape from the government itself.

This argument was as unpleasant as the odour emanating from the varnished teak panels of the courtroom. But he had no alternative except to hang onto it. Noting his discomfort, the man pulling the punkah began to move his hands faster.

'If that is so, why did you bring this man and woman before me?' Butler shouted, unusually angry.

Although the prosecutor shrank back at first from this outburst, he collected himself at once and made his submission with great courtesy: 'Sarkar, no one can try anyone else in this country without this court's permission. Although other courts can conduct trials or mete out punishment, the permission to carry out such trials can be granted only by a court that belongs to the government.'

Butler glanced at the blank paper in front of him for help. The prosecutor was distressed that the trial was being prolonged. Since the judge remained silent he was forced to prod him after a while: 'Your Honour!'

'Prosecutor!' Butler raised his eyes from the sheet of blank paper. 'The first accused who stands before me is a Muslim. How can I hand him over to a Hindu court for trial?'

The prosecutor bowed his head again. 'We have examined that aspect fully, your honour. The Hindu pandas and Muslim mullahs who are the petitioners in this case came with their families and pitched tents outside and have been waiting there for a long time. In the meantime, they have consulted amongst them and have agreed on an understanding out of court. If the second accused, who is a Muslim, is handed over to them, the mullahs are willing to hand over the first accused to the Hindus.'

The prosecutor placed the papers concerning the out-of-court settlement before the court.

Butler realized that all the doors were closed against him. He ran his eyes over the papers before him for several minutes without actually reading them, darted a quick glance at the accused and sat back in his chair. He then declared the verdict without looking left or right.

'After having listened attentively to all the arguments put forward by the prosecutor and given them due consideration, the court has come to the conclusion that the charges brought against the accused are beyond the jurisdiction of this court. They must be dealt with by the respective religious authorities.

Therefore, in order to try them lawfully and in keeping with the traditions of their respective communities, the first accused, Moinuddin, is to be handed over to the Hindu pandits and the second accused, Salma Begum, to the Muslim mullahs.'

Butler disappeared through the back door without wasting a moment. The prosecutor picked up his papers and went out as well. The courtroom with its panelled walls became even more unpleasant. Although the servant had stopped pulling the ropes of the punkah, it swung for a few minutes more. No one benefited from the breeze.

Moinuddin and Salma did not look at each other while they waited for the policemen to come and separate them. Their tired eyes drifted elsewhere, to faraway fields. Govardhan, who had brought them together, was still wandering over those fields. And Nachiketas, whom they had brought into the world together, was walking barefoot somewhere over the same fields. The light of the burning yagyasala in the distance shed its glow over the sweat and tears on Moinuddin's and Salma's faces.

78

Escorted by soldiers, Moinuddin and Salma were brought out of the court with their hands and legs once again bound to their bodies so that they looked like balls. Beyond the high gates manned by armed guards, the high priests of both religions waited impatiently for them. They shouted excitedly when they caught sight of the victims, hugged each other and danced with delight.

The mullahs who got the ball called Salma ran to the mosque with her. The members of the ulema were already seated there. They opened the trial at once and after indulging in many hair-splitting arguments on various points in the scriptures, they decided unanimously to stone her to death in public. A special audience was invited to view the stoning. Many reporters, members of television crews, intellectuals and feminists, none of whom had been invited, assembled at the spot and the priests did not object to them being there. As they had expected, these persons from the media were so busy recording and documenting the event and taking pictures of it that they did not notice that the ball named Salma was being knocked around so violently that she turned into pulp. When everything was over they regretted that they had not been able to prevent such a dastardly act.

The pandas who got the bundle named Moinuddin carried him away happily on their shoulders. Since they had no written documents or laws with which to conduct a trial, they put him to death on the way.

The law, therefore, both in its existent and non-existent states, dealt with the victims in the same manner.

Butler, who had returned to the fort, was impatient too. He declared a state of emergency in the harem which had been converted into a storehouse for weapons. He ordered all the guards to fall in. All the weapons in the storehouse, from the most primitive ones to the most modern, were taken out. The horses were brought out of the stables. A whirlwind of madness that he did not understand took possession of him. Riding that whirlwind, Butler and his cavalry rushed out of the fort and galloped away.

They eventually came to a small town. A large gathering of people was assembled on the small maidan in the centre of the town. Except for the space occupied by the narrow streets leading to the maidan, it was surrounded on all sides by high buildings. This huge crowd of people, reminiscent of the days of the mutiny, sent chills coursing down Butler's spine. He ordered his men to close off all the streets leading to the maidan. When he was certain that there were no gaps left through which people could escape, Butler raised his pistol and fired three shots into the air. He then commanded his men: 'Fire!'

Butler's soldiers rained bullets on the crowd from every direction. Butler himself shot at them several times.

People dropped dead like moths. Those who escaped the bullets tried to scale the steep walls of the buildings around and slipped down. Seeing no other way out, many jumped into a well in the maidan and died.

When they were exhausted and had no more bullets left, the soldiers lowered their guns. Turning his back on the silent maidan, Butler and his soldiers walked away. As the horses paced slowly along the streets of the silent town under the darkening evening sky, the lights began to come on one by one in the buildings on either side. Inquisitive eyes turned towards the soldiers. The town came gradually to life and sounds became audible. People came out into the streets, gathered in small groups and followed the horsemen.

As the night progressed, the lights in the windows went out again and the noises subsided. Trickling out of their houses one by one, people formed small groups and positioned themselves in front of Butler's horsemen in every street. Surprised, Butler and his men realized that these people were not trying to challenge or obstruct them but demanding something from them. From their outstretched hands, Butler made out that what they wanted were the guns—the guns that had been turned on the helpless, unarmed men on the maidan. They were so impressed by the power of the weapons that they wanted to do what Butler had done: close all the paths to go out, or pack everyone into the marketplace, or detain them while they were celebrating marriage parties, or drag them out of buses or trains or airplanes and shoot all of them impartially. They wanted Butler's guns to use against their own people.

Butler could not refuse these people what seemed to be their destiny. Or it could be that even before he gave the matter thought, his men had begun to hand down their weapons to the people around them. Butler and his men were soon completely unarmed.

Butler did not return to his fort. The forest invaded it. The horses died of hunger and the soldiers took off their uniforms and ran away. Butler himself adopted native clothing and began to speak the local language. His skin grew dark and sunburnt. He eventually went back to his old job of a jailer in a jail situated in a small town.

79

The kumhar fashioned the Kali idol using only clay. He then made it stand on two long, slender legs while the children around him held their breaths.

'Don't fall, Kali-ma, don't fall!' they prayed aloud.

The kumhar comforted them: 'Kali-ma won't fall.'

When the idol was firmly fixed in place, they asked: 'Why did you make the thakur so heavy, kumhar-bhaiya? We would have brought you straw.'

'This thakur is not meant to be washed away in the water, my little friends,' said the kumhar, attempting a smile. 'We won't have a pandal for it; we'll install it in a temple and worship it.'

The children looked at each other in surprise, not sure what he meant.

The boatmen rowing over the river, which was so vast that its farther bank was not visible, were still singing. The breeze blowing over the water made the kumhar, who already had a fever, shiver violently. He made a futile attempt to sing along with the boatmen. The song stuck in his throat and made him cough.

'Are you ill, kumhar-bhaiya?' asked the children affectionately.

It took the kumhar a while to suppress the cough and clear his throat. 'Kali-ma will cure kumhar-bhaiya of his illness, won't she?' he asked, smiling.

'Kali-ma will cure everyone of their illness,' the children repeated the old belief. 'Kumhar-bhaiya, won't you sacrifice a goat for the Kali puja?'

The kumhar did not reply. Burning with excitement, he began to work feverishly on the clay. He transferred Kali's form to it as if it was his own flesh. A majestic figure, leaning slightly backwards. Long, naked legs, the abdomen and breasts—his fingers moved skilfully, shaping them. He stopped at the neck and moved downward again. As he moved upwards, shaping each part and polishing it with care, the children said shyly: 'Bhaiya, you must dress Kali-ma in a beautiful red silk sari.'

'This image of Kali-ma is a naked one, children,' he said. 'It is right and proper that she be naked.'

'Why don't you give the thakur her head, bhaiya? She must have a beautiful face and a crown on her head.' The children's eyes stopped at the neck of the idol which looked as though it had been smoothly slashed with a knife.

The kumhar lifted the head which had already been shaped and instead of placing it on top of the neck, he fixed it to the outstretched left hand, in which there was no sword. Its gaping mouth was turned upwards and the long, thick hair flowed down. He then picked up a length of cane, bent it like a bow and fixed one end to the neck and the other to the open mouth. When he applied red paint to the bow, the children cried out in fear:

'What have you done, kumhar-bhaiya?'

'This is what the Chhinna Mastaka Kali looks like, children,' he explained. 'You may not have seen her before. Kali-ma cuts off her own head and pours the blood that gushes out of her neck like a fountain into her own mouth. Chhinna Mastaka Kali's form is naked and awe-inspiring. But she does not demand that you sacrifice anything to her. She sacrifices herself and disappears; she does not want to be thrown into the Ganga by human beings. A kumhar cannot make her image a second time. This is the last image your kumhar-bhaiya will make, my children...'

When he turned around, the children had withdrawn and were staring wide-eyed at Kali-ma. Their curiosity seemed trapped somewhere between devotion and the vagaries of art. What did it matter whose loss it was—the children's eyes were full of tears.

80

'Ram, didn't you tell me that when we scientists focussed our eyes on the distant bodies in the sky, we failed to see the truths closer home?' Galileo asked Ramchander as he walked beside him, his hand on his shoulder. Ramchander felt the old scientist's exhaustion and the weight of his age in the pressure of that hand.

Galileo went on: 'But that was not true. We scientists did not gaze at heavenly bodies in the distance because we thought that there was no suffering on earth. We believed that deliverance had to come through reason. We wanted to bring science closer to human beings. We thought science would eradicate falsehood and do away with injustice. As you said, the process of finding out the truth was the same as imparting justice. But the law of the world was different. It was the fact that we did not realize that science and justice are two different things in our world that made us presbyopic.'

Galileo stopped to draw breath. Ramchander led him towards a bench in the garden. Seated on it, Galileo measured the space on either side of him with his hands.

Around them were the excavated remains of ancient temples and monasteries. Archaeologists had cultivated a garden, laying lawns in the empty spaces between the buildings.

'Tell me, sir,' Ramchander encouraged him to speak, seated beside him on the bench.

'Ram, there is something as important as knowing the truth and that is being bold enough to tell the truth. I came to understand later that the Church punished me not for making the truth public but for the insolence I showed in doing so. You know that what I said was what had already been said by others before me and that they were things that many people knew... What the Church hates is not the truth itself but the courage people display when they speak out the truth... And yet, how weak, how unreal that courage was! My advice to you, child, is that whatever great things you may discover, do not fail to see human weakness for what it is.'

The scientist stopped again to breathe. Ramchander waited. Galileo went on when he had recovered.

'Do you know, Ram, the barbaric rule of the Church ended with my trial and the thirty years' war. Never has the Church behaved so barbarously—as the fascism that came after or the communism that followed even later did, stamping with their boots on the courage human beings showed in telling the truth. And yet, remember that the philosophies of fascism and communism were built upon the foundations laid by the science we propagated! Scientific materialism did not prevent these philosophies from hating a person's courage to tell the truth as much as the insensitive Church hated it!'

They got up and resumed walking. At the end of the lawn, they came to a path paved with stone, climbed a few steps and reached the courtyard of a ruined temple with an empty sanctum sanctorum and no roof.

'Does not the world say that knowledge is power?' asked Ram.

'Knowledge is just knowledge, nothing more. But those who have it use it to rule over those who do not. They convert their knowledge into authority, into power. Knowledge did not bring salvation to man as we had thought it would. What it gifted us was a group of people who believed they knew more than others, who behaved as if they would never make mistakes. And thus scientists fell in line with magicians, priests, military commanders! All of whom obstructed the deliverance of man... Where have we reached, Ram?'

'These are the ruins of a temple,' said Ram. 'We passed monasteries earlier and like them, this temple has only walls. And broken walls at that.'

Galileo walked along feeling the stones with his hands.

'They are superb carvings, sir,' said Ramchander. 'Every figure on this wall is a masterpiece. Almost all of them are erotic. Sculptures which depict woman at the height of her womanhood, man at the height of his manhood. Each couple does away with the distance between them and melts into one single form!'

'Is it reason or the senses that brings human beings together?' asked the scientist, his fingers searching and recognizing each form. 'If only knowledge had the warmth that emotion has and its ability to melt human beings and mould them into a single shape!'

When they reached the door of the temple, Galileo ran his fingers over the figure of a dvarapalaka, and asked: 'What is this form? It has a weapon in its hand.'

'A doorkeeper. He stands guard to the god's abode. It is

usual to place a statue like this at the entrance to a temple. He has weapons in his hand and a fearful form.'

Galileo smiled. 'One who holds weapons and has a frightening form! God might be an imaginary concept but the security of his abode is a mundane requirement, is it not? Or maybe it is correct that if one can symbolize the saviour God, his doorkeeper can be a symbol as well. A doorkeeper of stone for a god of stone! I suddenly remembered something. Do you know the word for doorkeeper in our language—janitor. Have you heard of the Roman god Janus? Janus is the god of the door. The peculiarity of Janus, however, is that he is a god with two faces!'

'We have gods not only for doors but for directions as well— they are called dikpalas, the gods of directions. One god for each direction, the ashtadikpalas for eight directions. And each of them has an elephant. Just think of it, a dikpala has to guard not just a particular spot but a whole direction, a direction that has no end! Directions that change according to the point at which we stand! A direction cannot be contained in distances or names, it is indefinable!'

Galileo took his hand off the temple wall and began to walk along. He looked as if he had suddenly reached some unknown place. They walked silently along the paved pathway.

When he stumbled against a stone bench, Galileo felt it with his hands and sat down on it. Inviting Ramchander to sit down as well, he said: 'Ram, the thought of another door comes to me. Not the door of a temple, but the door of the torture house of the inquisitors of Rome. As they led me through it, they were taking Kepler's mother out. My crime was science and my friend's mother's was witchcraft.'

Galileo began to tell the story.

81

The torture house was a fort-like structure built of granite on top of a hill. The stone-paved pathway winding around the hill ended at a door and it was there that they met. Katherine was coming out of the torture house. An old woman of seventy-three, weak and emaciated. Her backbone broken by torture, unable to stand erect, her hands and feet in chains. Galileo had crossed seventy. Although he was strong physically, mentally he was shattered. After unbearable torture and rigorous interrogation, the scientist was being taken by the guards for the second stage of his ordeal, to be shown the instruments of torture.

They met and recognized each other. Galileo supported Katherine and helped her sit down on the parapet at the side of the road. He sat down as well. A warm breeze heralding spring blew past them, giving those few moments wings.

'My child!' Galileo heard Katherine address him, her son's friend. She gradually straightened her back and took a deep breath. 'I was brought here for having committed worldly offences. For bringing diseases to people and killing them through witchcraft. Your world is the sky, the solar system, constellations. Do people cause illness and death to others there as well?'

'Mother,' Galileo pressed her hand. 'You were never a witch. Nor have you ever caused illness to anyone or killed them.'

'Who wants to know the truth, child? The inquisitors do not even tell us what the charges against us are. It is we who have to spell out what they are! It can only be that way in a system where it is we who must meet the expenses for the salaries of the men employed to guard us, the judges who try us… The charge against me was that I was a witch. I would not admit that as the truth. You too will not admit to the charge against you: that you are a scientist, and therefore a heretic. That will, however, be a lie.'

Galileo was stunned that Katherine spoke like a prophetess of what he feared most.

'It is true that, for a moment, I doubted the value of truth when faced with the question of staying alive… In any case, what meaning does all this have in our world? Whether the sun revolves around the earth or the earth around the sun, how does it affect the Church? Neither Christ nor the prophets who came before him spoke of these things. It was Ptolemy and Aristotle who were not Christians but pagans, who put forth these theories… This was not the question, Mother. Nor was it a matter of truth and falsehood. It was something else.'

'Do you know what that "something else" is? I'll tell you. When hundreds of women like me were accused of being witches and were tortured and burned, you scientists said nothing. Witchcraft is a superstition, after all. So you had nothing to say against witches being hunted down. You were fighting for science, forgetting the fact that the issues underlying torture and inquisition were not science or superstition but justice and injustice. And now, to escape injustice, you are willing to deny even that science! Did you not ask what value truth has before the issue of staying alive? My child, let this old woman who has seen much tell you this: it is because life is important that justice is important. And because justice is important, truth becomes meaningful.'

'My friend, this was the only reason I fought all alone for six years in the courts for this old, illiterate woman whose name people were afraid to utter and whom they had written off as a victim to be burned at the stake. Because I considered it an injustice.' The voice was Kepler's and Galileo looked around, not sure where it came from. He finally saw him at the window on top of a watchtower in front of the gate.

'John!' shouted Galileo, 'Can't you come down? Can't you join us?'

'I am always on the earth, my friend. While the mind soars through the sky, the body rests earthbound: that is the epitaph I've written for myself. Do you know, Galileo, it was yesterday that I completed my *Harmony of the Worlds*? I wrote it during the six years I spent fighting for my mother in the courts.'

Smiling, Kepler came down the steps of the watchtower. Galileo got up, a weary smile on his face and held out his hand to welcome him.

'I know.' Galileo said, 'Only you can do that—fight for justice on one side, risking your life, and write a book on harmony on the other.'

Kepler came and sat down by his mother on the parapet. Forgetting her own condition, Katherine folded her son's frail, sick body in her arms.

'Yes,' said Katherine, 'He was always a wonder to me, Galileo. The son of a mercenary who had escaped the gallows only by chance and an illiterate woman who was arrested as a witch, tortured and was nearly burned; the brother of a wretched madman who wandered through the streets; himself a victim of all sorts of diseases, full of scabs and putrid wounds—how could such a person have pondered over the harmony of the worlds?'

'Mother, your son has always walked precariously balanced between God and physics, between astronomy and astrology. It was this circus act that John mistook for harmony,' said Galileo.

'Neither the ellipse nor the elliptical paths of the planets were my creations, Galileo.' Kepler's voice was indignant. 'They were always there. All I did was make them known. As for you, Galileo, you saw movement only in straight lines. You who walk without looking left or right, your eyes fixed on certain laws which you think are as constant as the polar star in the sky, how can you discover even plain orbits, let alone elliptical ones?'

'It is possible that my mind, engaged as it was elsewhere, could not perceive the injustice that prevailed around me,' said Galileo, giving Katherine a quick glance. 'But the harmony you saw, John, was not real either. In fact, there is no harmony in this world. While you were drowning yourself in the harmony of geometrical figures, thinking delightedly of geometry as divine or as God Himself, the world outside your room was steeped in cruel wars, plagues, inquisitions, excommunications and deceptions. There is no music in this world, John, there is not even geometry here. You cannot line up completely contradictory things and create harmony. That's just walking across a tightrope. To live without offending anyone—even that is hypocrisy.'

The muscles on Kepler's thin, distorted face tautened. 'Stop it, Galileo,' he shouted. 'It's the exasperation of finding yourself at the stake that makes you speak like this. If my *Harmony* was unreal, let me tell you that your *Dialogue* too was no dialogue, it was a monologue.'

'I agree, John. My dialogue was a monologue and that is what brought me to the stake. But when you wrote about harmony even while fighting to save your mother from the stake, you were only torturing yourself. You were always at the stake, all your life, at the stake you yourself erected.'

Straightening her back with great difficulty, stretching out her upturned hands, Katherine said in a harsh tone: 'Enough! Neither of you must talk about the stake anymore. Look at this old woman, who has just come out of the torture house. I went in as the mother of a scientist, charged with witchcraft. But I have come out as neither of these. I have absolutely no identity now. I am a dry, shrivelled object like a windblown, withered leaf, a grain of sand in the desert.'

'But Mother, your son still stands in front of you as God's representative,' said Galileo.

'And your son's friend as the advocate of certain physical laws that function above God,' added Kepler.

'That is what it is,' said Katherine in a firm voice, full of confidence, ignoring the difficulty she had in breathing. 'The distance between the two of you is only as much as the space between you as you sit on this parapet.'

Their eyes followed her as she stood up. Her wrinkled face became as hard as a stone sculpture. Her eyes grew sharp and her voice firm and deep. It seemed as if she was resurrecting from the wounds inflicted on her by the blows she had endured over the seventy-three years of her sorrowful life, by the incarceration she had endured for a year and by the torture the inquisitors had submitted her to. Blood dripped from her limbs, her dirty, tattered woollen clothes fluttered in the breeze. The chains that hung from her hands and feet clanked loudly.

The illiterate, uncultivated old woman was turning into a prophetess.

'Galileo!' she said, pointing her finger at the scientist. 'Tell me, was it not a friend of yours who once said that God can create a donkey with three tails but not a triangle with four sides? You believe which there are certain physical laws that are universal and that cause each small and big thing in the world to move and to act in a particular manner. And what of your opponents who believe in God? They believe that there is a God who ensures that justice prevails, that the guilty are punished and the good rewarded, and that everything happens in accordance with His laws. The mistake that John made was to think that justice would flow out of faith on its own. We have seen how the believers in God rule the country. We did not receive justice from them. And you, Galileo, what was your mistake? You thought only the laws of science are infallible and that justice would be born from them. But your children and your children's children will find out that this too is not right. Do you know why the beliefs both of you advocated—whether they concerned science or religion, they were just beliefs, children—were wrong? If justice is to prevail, it is not enough that law exist, not even enough that God exist—human beings must have faith in justice. Laws may exist, but there is no law to say that we must obey laws. If there were a law like that, there would have to be one more law to insist that we obey it! And so on, endlessly... Have you watched your children playing football on the playground? The rules of football became valid not because science proved them correct, or because the children had a revelation saying that God formulated them; they are valid because the players accepted them, because they agreed to follow them when they play and because they actually follow them. This is why they play football. Otherwise they would be fighting for the ball on the playground, tearing one another to pieces…'

'Katherine's voice gradually faded away,' said Galileo, concluding the story. 'She was turning back into the old woman who had been shattered by torture. No longer able to stand up straight, she huddled up on the stone-paved path. Since they had finished their task when they brought her out of the gate, the guards removed the chains on her hands and feet and took them away. She stood there alone, without anyone to guard her or keep her company. Then I saw her go down the steps and disappear into the distance. The way of all flesh… Her son Kepler who had been waiting for her at the gate, gradually moved downward as well—along with the epitaph that the body remains earthbound. I saw myself alone at the gate of the torture house that was inside the fort on the hill. With the guards who held me silently. Abandoned by everyone, forsaken by science and reason, my legs weak and unsteady, my mind weeping…'

Galileo waited for a while. Recovering his breath and strength, he went on: 'Ram, do you know why the god of the door has two faces? Why he has only two faces? A door has only two functions to perform, two ways to move: it can either open or shut. It can only welcome or reject. Do you know the meaning of saying that dikpalas guard the directions? Direction is something that stretches out to infinity. What the dikpalas guard is an approach, an idea, a philosophy, a value, all of which extend endlessly.

'In his efforts to see that justice was meted out to Katherine, Kepler tried to interpret a non-existent justice in terms of harmony. Katherine did not obtain justice. After six years of trial, imprisonment and torture, she escaped the stake, that was all. And even though it was after she came out of the prison, the torture killed her. I too only escaped, I did not obtain justice. Kepler's idea of justice might have been faulty but what I did was to buy justice with a bribe. Like Kepler, I burn at the stake forever. As old, illiterate Katherine told me at the gate of the torture house, if we are to receive justice, we must have faith …'

82

It was afternoon when the train stopped at the station. As the distant column of smoke that announced its arrival came nearer, it darkened the platform where the fading rays of the evening sun and the lengthening shadows lay entangled like lovers.

There were not many people in the small station. A little tea shop in which a radio blared non-stop music sold essentials. An old station building with a skeleton of used rails and walls covered with cinema posters. The handful of passengers who got out when the train stopped created a small flutter on the platform.

Mannu looked at the tall, hefty engine driver in blue uniform and cap walking up from the end of the train as if she was expecting him. Actually, wasn't that what she had been doing the last four days, sitting under the banyan tree at the farther end of the platform?

Four days ago, he had taken her down from the train and left her at this spot. He had not told her that his quarters were in this station, or that he would return after four days of duty. In fact, he had not spoken to her at all.

He had stopped the train skilfully just in front of the spot where she had laid her head on the rails in order to die, got down, lifted her up and laid her down by his seat in the engine room. When the train stopped at this station, he had got out and sat her down on the platform around the banyan tree. Then he had said something to the signalman who had been waiting to wave the flag and hand over the key, got into the train and driven off.

Mannu had spent four days under the tree—accepting the kindness the stationmaster and his staff showed her, eating the food they gave her, sleeping under the blanket they provided.

The engine driver came up to her and stopped as if he too had expected that she would be there. Since she had not gone back to lay her head on the rails, he asked her: 'So you've decided to live?'

She nodded.

He held her hand and helped her get up, then led her to his quarters behind the station.

Michael Ramalingam, the engine driver, lived alone. He had no relatives. Once he went out on duty, he came back only after a week. He would rest for two days, then go on duty again. The house was left locked when he was on duty. He had to clean it up and make it habitable again. Even making a cup of tea meant he had to start from scratch.

Michael had no idea who Mannu was, from where she had come or why she had tried to kill herself. Nor did he ask. He needed someone to keep house for him when he was away, attend to him when he came back after work. 'Since you have decided to live, keep this house alive too,' he said to her.

He worked on a train that ran between two famous temple towns. One town was on the seashore, the other was in the interior. The station where he lived was between the two. After doing two trips, he always came back home by the next train.

At some point between these trips Mannu became Michael's wife. Between the cycles of flood and drought, between mutinies and wars, between the darkness that those who disappeared left behind them and the light that people newly encountered imparted, she did not know when the rails bound the earth together on all sides and life began to flow gently and comfortably over them. Generous sunshine, warmth and moisture filled the air around her.

83

Coming down the ladder from the top of the building under construction, Henry saw a man standing on the ground with his eyes riveted on the skeleton of the structure before him. At first, he paid him no attention but after walking a few steps, he came back.

The newcomer did not smile, but there was recognition in the tired eyes. Because of his native clothes and brown skin, it took Henry some time to recognize him. But he finally cried out: 'David!'

'I was looking at the progress of your research. Very impressive! What is more, I have the feeling when I look at this that I have found the answer to a question lying at the back of my mind,' said Butler.

Henry did not ask what the question was. He looked Butler up and down attentively. Meanwhile, the tales of Butler's cruelty which had become legends by now filled his mind. He asked: 'Who is the victim you have come in search of, David?'

'Searching, following and hunting down—there's not much

difference between these pursuits, Henry,' said Butler. 'It is only the intensity of your feelings for the person before you that makes one different from the other. Seen from another angle, it may be the distance between you and that person that creates the intensity. When you are most distant from him, you seek him. As you come closer, you start admiring him. And when he is right before you, you hunt him down.'

'That is a very distorted viewpoint.'

'Henry,' said Butler, placing his hand on Henry's back and forcing him to walk along with him. 'Did I ever have any enmity towards that innocent man, Govardhan, who made me turn from hunting animals to hunting men?'

'No, Butler. It was in the name of the logic of the law that you pursued him—declaring yourself a dispenser of law.'

'In the course of my quest for Govardhan, I once came upon a village. A satsang was in progress there at the time. I saw people singing and dancing in the circle of light made by torches. They were all weeping as well. There was a man standing outside the circle who, like me, was not crying. He was a hunter too. A hunter who was being hunted by his own prey: that was how he described himself. Still, he insisted that he was a hunter. Do you know who he was? Govardhan's older brother!'

'And was that when you yourself began to dress like your victims?'

'It was at a spot on this road, quite far away from here, that I first got into these clothes to escape from native mutineers.' Butler became pensive. 'And then I guided my hunting expedition too into these clothes.'

Henry was uneasy. Deep within him, he felt disturbed.

The sun had become hotter. But instead of going into the shed on the site, they walked among the stone workers.

'What was the question, Butler, for which you found the answer in my architecture?' asked Henry.

'During my long, long journeys, while riding through uncharted areas in the interior of the country scattering blood and fire and corpses around me, the architectural masterpieces on this soil often arrested me. I slept in many sarais built by past rulers. I bathed in their hamams. Mosques, gardens, bazaars, rasois, stables—none of them allowed me to pass by quietly. Henry, have you ever studied the temples, the viharas, the mosques, the tombs, the victory towers that soar towards the sky from this level landscape? Their gopuras, sikharas, stupas, gumbazes, their spires and steeples? Have you worked out how the power of each ruler rose higher and higher, stepping upward on these structures? How every system passed its weight down to the people through its stones and bricks? Each system gives concrete expression to its authority through its architecture. When I stood before the skeleton of this edifice you are building, I felt that just as I transferred the cruelty of my hunt into the hearts of these unsuspecting people by wearing their garments, you penetrated the violence of your quest into them with the phallic tool of architecture. Doesn't the thrill of the hunter's hunger, the explorer's pressure, excite the victim as well, after the first instants of humiliation and pain? Why did you design this structure in the form of a perfect circle, Henry? And surround it with a row of long, thin pillars which are not really necessary? As I observe them keenly, these pillars begin to look like rows of human beings. Human beings eternally condemned to carry loads, creatures who cannot escape being weighed down by the cruel concept of an architect.' Butler paused for a while, then continued emotionally: 'What your architecture does is to freeze reality at a particular stage. Before the hunter that I am flows an endless stream of victims and behind me lies the emptiness of the cremation ground.'

Butler fell silent. For a long time the only sound they could hear were the chisels of the stone workers. Once the workers withdrew for their noon meal, only the blazing sunlight and a hot, heavy silence remained.

Before he went away, Butler sat down and told Henry his story, his voice completely devoid of emotion.

'The expeditions on the plains were the cleverest and most successful phase in the history of my hunting. You will be astonished to know that it was these hunts that inspired my victims to have faith and trust in me. As I finished each operation and was about to leave, people would come out of their houses, their cities, and surround me and my soldiers. It took me some time to understand that they did not come to attack me but to pay me their respects. Impressed with the technical perfection and professional excellence of my operation, they came to ask me for my weapons and my horses. Since I had already decided to close my hunting chapter, I gave them what they wanted without any hesitation. I disbanded my army and retired to the post of a jailer in a small mofussil town. Although it was a small town, it had a large jail. It was like an animal that had swallowed a prey bigger than its mouth could hold. And it seemed as if the prey had been born first! The town had actually grown up around the jail. An isolated town in the middle of a desert, it experienced burning summers and freezing winters. In it lived innumerable prisoners gathered from all parts of the country, who had become lifeless once freedom had been completely drained out of them. Their records had become so jumbled that many had even lost their names. No one knew how many of the registered prisoners had died. The roll-calls there resembled the process of taking a census in the country. By the time the warders reached the end of it, there would have been several new entrants and many deaths. And those who remained would have changed places... Once a terrible famine struck the town. Settling like a cloud over the region, it devoured everything there and moved on to the next district. The government could do nothing to save the inhabitants. Seeing them shrivel up and die in front of me, I asked myself a question: how could one offer the protection one could not give law-abiding citizens to prisoners who had broken the law? I allowed the famine to affect the prisoners as it had affected the townspeople. All the prisoners died and the jail became empty.'

Trying to fight down a sense of shock, Henry asked mockingly: 'So you became unemployed then...?'

'Yes, the famine banished me to the streets.'

'And your staff?'

'Why have a staff if there are no prisoners? I let the famine devour them as well.'

'Why didn't you let the famine take you too?'

'Should there not be guides to direct movement, even if it is that of a famine? Why are you building this beautiful structure? For the rulers who will come after us, isn't it? We can allow emptiness to filter in everywhere else, but there must never be an absence of rulers.'

Without waiting for Henry's reaction, Butler picked up his bag and slung it on his shoulder.

Henry did not stop him. 'You can go, David. When the famine is over, plague will follow. There will never be a state of affairs in which we do not have to point the way to someone.'

Butler laughed. Henry smiled emotionlessly in response as he walked away.

84

Govardhan noticed that the bazaar in the town he and Mariam had arrived in was different from the one he had seen in the earlier town in two ways. While all the commodities were sold at the same rate in the one he had seen previously, the same commodity was sold at varying rates here, even in the same shop. The prices changed according to the mood of the seller and the characteristics of the buyer. The other remarkable difference Govardhan saw shook him to the core. A commodity that had not been available in the old bazaars was sold here: human beings. Men, women, and children sat under the shade of the trees exhibiting their muscles and their tools, waiting for buyers. The market was called the auction bazaar.

Govardhan walked through the bazaar with a heavy heart. Sensing his despair, Mariam asked him why he was sad. 'I feel scared, Mariam, when I see these markets,' he said, placing a hand on her shoulder. 'Although this market is different, it was from a bazaar as absurd as this one that I was picked up one day and lost Salma and Mannu. Let's go away from here quickly, Mariam. These markets are not for us.'

They began to walk fast. But what Govardhan feared happened. The shouts of the sellers and buyers had just started to fade behind them when two policemen suddenly appeared out of nowhere and handcuffed them.

When he recovered from the initial moment of shock, Govardhan saw the gallows clearly before him. At last, at last, he murmured. As for Mariam, she saw the sacrificial animal and the gleaming knife.

It soon became clear, however, that they had been taken into custody for other reasons. Seated in the van, they heard heralds beating drums and making announcements that concerned the laws of the district. The government had declared the town an enclosure. Begging would not be allowed and the police had the authority to arrest vagrants, nomads and unemployed loiterers wherever they were found.

Neither Govardhan nor Mariam understood the announcement. Just as they had never understood the laws which had dragged one to the gallows and the other to the sacrificial lock.

85

The city magistrate's eyes were full of kindness when he looked at the man and woman standing before him with their hands and feet bound. They told him their names when he asked them gently. He asked them what work they did and they said, 'Nothing.' Futher questioning revealed that one had come from a village and the other from the jungle and that, since they had found it impossible to eke out a living, they had come to seek refuge in the city. They did not know that the city had been declared an enclosure. In fact, they did not even know what an enclosure was. When he realized that they did not have a lawyer, the magistrate appointed a lawyer who would plead their case at the expense of the government. The magistrate then asked the government counsel to present his case.

It was an unusually hot day. Drenched in perspiration, the lawyers, the accused, the members of the public who had come to listen to the verdict and the journalists kept wiping their faces with their handkerchiefs. A dust storm had begun to blow outside. The first order the magistrate gave was to close the windows and doors. Although the court employees hurried to obey him, a great deal of dust had already blown in.

The government counsel stood up, wiped the sweat off his face and loosened his necktie furtively. His face was flushed above his French beard and he peered around with eyes that stayed open for long intervals like those of a dead fish. He spoke calmly without gesticulating or showing any emotion. Although he generally spoke in an even voice, he was well-known for dramatics, so people crowded in the court rooms to listen to him whenever he argued a case.

'Just look at this dust which has somehow made its way into the courtroom to make life miserable for us even though we have closed all the doors and windows.' Wiping his face with his handkerchief, the lawyer started to speak. 'Both the persons standing before the court are parasites who do not believe in working to earn a living. They have chosen our city which is an enclosure for their nefarious activities. The honourable court may ask, are not these persons human beings too? Yes, I agree that they are. But their activities are not human, they are bestial. The honourable court knows well that the dust that has got into our noses and eyes, that prevents us from carrying out our duties, is a part of the earth we stand on. But when particles of dust rise from the ground and fly in the air, when they unite with the wind and attack our civilized life, making it difficult for us to breathe, we are forced to close the doors and windows. We have to treat the dust as an enemy.'

The counsel stopped for a moment to wipe his face, then spent a while coughing and clearing his throat, proving the presence of dust around him. Then he continued: 'But these innocent-looking people standing before us are not particles of dust blowing in the wind. This Govardhan is not only a vagabond, he is a fugitive as well. And not just a fugitive but a rebel and a terrorist too. When he was questioned, he revealed shocking pieces of information.'

The courtroom filled with anxiety. The counsel paused, allowing it to grow. When the murmurs of the people became very loud, the magistrate tapped his gavel on the table for silence.

'I request the honourable court to take a good look at Govardhan and his woman, Mariam. It will be obvious to us at first glance that they are criminals. They are members of a notorious criminal tribe. Due to the sustained efforts made by successive kings and the Company sarkar to suppress them and after the popular government began to initiate development projects, these people had to come out of their hiding places and are now weaving their nests in the cities. There is no need to ask a court what the crimes of such people are. They were born with a death-sentence on their heads and the gallows as their final destination. All they need to do in life is choose the particular crime which will earn them that punishment. Their lives are actually only efforts to fulfil the fate they are marked out for. Sometimes they can do so in their own lairs. Sometimes they have to journey long distances, cross continents and arrive in our cities to do so...

'The man standing before the court had already fulfilled it. Yes, a court sentenced him to death long ago. But this arrogant man did not accept it with humility. Submitting to the influence of certain conspirators, he escaped from jail the day before he was to be hanged. From that day, he has been wandering all over, from city to city and village to village, defying the law and dodging the police. Our city can feel proud that it was here that he was finally caught and arrested. This is the story of his escapade. Let us now move to the story of the rebellion he organized.'

The prosecutor took another respite. Impatience showed on the faces of not only the public and the magistrate but on that of the defence counsel as well.

'Although he was a fugitive from the law all this while, this man was never idle,' he continued. 'He used every minute he had for propaganda and sabotage. As soon as he jumped jail, he tried to break into the bungalows of the jailer and the Resident. When he failed in this, he entered a scientist's house, spun him a number of scandalous stories and brainwashed him completely. This renowned scientist, who could have done a great deal for the country, stopped his research, sowed confusion among intellectuals and broke up their association. Meanwhile, this man took to lurking behind bushes and walls and jeering at, accusing and threatening poets and artists. He became a messenger for the mutineers. He drove law-abiding citizens who led quiet lives free of doubts and questions to madness. And here he is now, with some woman he found in the jungle, insinuating himself into an area which has been declared an enclosure, trying to shatter the stability and safety of our urban lives.'

'What was this man's revolt against? Let the government counsel come to the point and not go around in circles.' The magistrate admonished him lightly.

'All I did was draw a circle, since what this man attacked was the centre of the circle. He has questioned the relevance, the legitimacy of the law regarding the declaration of enclosures—that is, the authority of the state to proclaim an area as an enclosed one. History—if I may draw the attention of the court—has only one parallel to this: the well-known rebellion of Robert Kett and his trial. He mobilized the barbarians in the countryside and forests and they surrounded the city of Norvic. What he demanded from the king in return for lifting the siege was that he do away altogether with the practice of declaring any area an enclosure. The court knows what punishment the law meted out to Robert Kett. He was hanged—he and three thousand of his followers.'

'But this man has not done anything like that. And the only person he has with him is this woman who does not even know a language to communicate in. Nor does this man know what an enclosure is, let alone the laws governing enclosures!'

'A born criminal who carries sentences of flogging, internment or even death on his head from the day he is born—does he not challenge the law of enclosures even if he questions the sentence or lays claim to a freedom that is bestowed only on genuine citizens?'

The counsel sat down. The members of the audience began to discuss the point he had raised with one another in hushed voices. The magistrate himself seemed confused, but he quickly took control of himself.

'The learned counsel may enlighten this court further on the government's powers to declare a territory as an enclosure,' he said.

A slow smile of immense satisfaction gradually made its way on the counsel's face, as he got up to answer.

'The court itself has answered this question through its use of the word "power". No matter in however small a measure it is exercised, power divides the space before it into two parts—into the space occupied by the person who exercises it and that occupied by the person over whom it is exercised. That is to say that an enclosure is automatically created at that spot.

'The honourable court knows that, whatever be the political system or political situation, whether it be the government or a rebel, whether it be he who exercises power or he who desires it, each one defines the space that is his and the space that belongs to others. That means that not only governments or invading armies or rebels acquire the power to declare their own enclosures, religious bodies, cultural organizations, science, art and literature acquire it as well.'

The counsel bowed and sat down.

The magistrate went through the usual motions of touching his chin, removing his glasses and wiping them. Then he said to the government counsel:

'The court wishes to know the provisions of the laws governing enclosures and what punishment the counsel wants to mete out to the two accused.'

The counsel rose from his seat again. 'The law decrees that as soon as a territory is declared an enclosure it becomes out of bounds for vagrants. According to the Anti-vagrancy Act which immediately comes into force in that area, an unemployed or itinerant person who is apprehended there becomes the slave of the citizen who caught him and has to work for him. Should such a slave try to escape, his ears will be cut off, the word "criminal" will be branded on his forehead and he will be thrown out of the city. If a person who has been thrown out tries to re-enter the city, his offence will be punishable by death.

'Since the first accused, Govardhan, besides being a vagrant, is also a rebel against the state, the government argues that he deserves no less a punishment than that meted out to Robert Kett—death by hanging. I further submit that, by condemning him to this sentence, the honourable court will only reaffirm a sentence that the king himself had passed earlier. The court has no powers to go against this. Now for the second accused, Mariam. Since this is the first time this woman has been apprehended within the city limits, she must be publicly auctioned in the marketplace as a slave. The statutes do not mention a punishment less severe than this.'

As soon as the government counsel sat down, the magistrate turned to the defence counsel. Exhausted by the government counsel's long arguments, he directed the defence counsel to be as brief as possible in his arguments.

All this while, the defence counsel had been sitting wide-eyed, forgetful of his surroundings, enthralled by the government counsel's eloquence. He had become as emotional as everyone else in the court and was gesticulating wildly. He therefore did not even hear the magistrate's words.

It was only when the magistrate raised his voice again and admonished him that he sprang to his feet. Lean and bent, with a perpetually apologetic look on his face, he was a lawyer who did not have much work to do and who made his living by the few cases that the government gave him. He too wore his beard and hair long—because he had no money to have them cut. The first thing he did when he stood up was to thank the court in an unsteady voice for having appointed him defence counsel, thus providing his wife and children with a meal. He went on to say that although he was appearing as defence counsel, he was fully aware of the interests of the government and would not go against them.

'My two clients, the accused in this case, have already been interrogated in detail. Since my clients have confessed to everything the government counsel has presented to the court, I am left with hardly any arguments to offer. As far as the enforcement of the law is concerned, my clients, like me, are ready to cooperate with the government and the court and are obliged to do so anyway. Therefore, I am going to plead that my clients be forgiven and that their punishment be mitigated to some extent. For my first client, I request that he be given only the second stage of the punishment without going into its third stage—that is, his ears be cut off, the word "criminal" branded across his forehead and he be thrown out of the city. I appeal to the court to give him another chance. As for the second accused, I see no way out for her from the first stage of the punishment. There is no case before this court dealing with the validity of the law concerning enclosures. All that the court has to do is to carry out the law.'

Having said this, defence counsel sat down. The magistrate declared a fifteen-minute recess and withdrew to his chamber.

Once the dust storm had subsided, there had been a good shower and as a result the air had become clean and cool. All the doors and windows of the courtroom were opened and the breeze blew in unobstructed. Glad to be temporarily released from the heat, the lawyers and the audience began to talk about the weather.

The magistrate came back to a more pleasant and relaxed courtroom. He took his seat and began reading the judgment. Even if the first accused, Govardhan, had behaved like Robert Kett, there was hardly any evidence to prove that he had intentionally led a revolt. Besides, people of his type were incapable of leading revolts. Therefore, the magistrate decreed that he be given the second stage of punishment. Once his ears were cut off, and the word 'criminal' branded on his forehead, he was to be thrown out of the city. The court ordered that Mariam, the second accused, be auctioned in the marketplace as a slave. The court specially mentioned that the proceeds of this auction could not be pocketed by anyone but had to be deposited in the government treasury.

86

Govardhan lay on the ground, twisting and turning in excruciating pain. Two lumps of soil and blood had formed at the spots where his ears had been. To some extent, they helped staunch the steady flow of blood. The numbness creeping down the sides of his head lessened the intensity of the pain somewhat. Once he realized that every little movement would aggravate the pain and bleeding, he tried to lie still.

The police had brought him in a vehicle as far as the gates of the city. The driver stopped the vehicle there and the policemen carried him down and sat him in a field on the side of the road. They tied his hands together at the back and his legs in front. A man climbed onto his knees and gripped his head tightly so that it would not move. Two persons stood behind him and, using long scissors of the kind gardeners use to trim plants, sliced off both his ears at the same time so that the torture would not be prolonged. The word 'criminal' had already been indelibly tattooed on his forehead.

His severed ears moved and throbbed on the ground for a

few minutes like fallen lizards' tails and then became still. Govardhan felt affection for them and detested them by turns. Tears coursed down his bloodstained cheeks.

His mind knocked at Salma's door, then at Mannu's. Neither opened. He had known they would not. So he tried another door—Mariam's. It stood open. Govardhan watched as someone dragged her away through it. She would never come back; she would go from market to market and each would take her farther away from him.

Govardhan was alone once more.

When he had been sentenced to death by hanging, there had been someone to smuggle him out of prison. The feeling that there was still hope had given him the courage to ask questions. As he moved from the great scholar Ramchander, who had been writing quietly at his table at midnight by the light of an oil lamp, to the uncouth Mariam who had been led in the fierce glow of burning torches to the sacrificial lock to the accompaniment of drumbeats, the questions had gradually fizzled out. But a certain happiness had come to him, that he could give refuge to someone even though none could give it to him. But now, Mariam too had ended as a closed door.

The belief that his unjustified punishment was an aberration of justice had encouraged him to knock at many doors. However, the court had now made it clear to him that he, Govardhan, stood outside the enclosures of kings, revolutionaries, scientists and artists alike, and that he had been condemned to eternal punishment for no reason. That if not the courts of kings, there were many other courts lying in wait for him on the way with elegant buildings and lawyers and policemen. That the only freedom he had was to choose which crime he was to be charged with and at which court he was to present himself. Salma,

Mannu and Mariam had been small profits he had earned between the courts and the losses he had incurred in each of them.

Govardhan's tears dried up. He shivered with a fever, in spite of the sun which was turning the fields silver. He longed with all his heart for someone near him, but only empty fields stretched around him into infinity.

Two dogs appeared from somewhere. They hovered around him for a while, looking at him and his severed ears lying on the ground in turn. Realizing what they wanted, Govardhan stretched out his hand to pick up a stone, then withdrew it. Emboldened, the dogs slowly advanced. Each picked up an ear in its mouth and ran away.

87

The palki, slowly moving in rhythm to the chant of 'Hai, doli, doli' over the country roads muddied by the first rains, entered a garden by the river. Thereon, accompanied by armed horsemen, it shifted to the track going through the middle of the forest. Much later, cutting through the soft glow of the street lamps, it slowed down and moved along the city streets that echoed with the beats of the tabla and the tinkling of ankle-bells. Its pace became dignified when it came to the royal boulevards lined with flower-laden trees on both sides. The kahars' legs were untiring and their steady humming never wavered. Only the occupants of the palki kept changing, without the kahars even realizing it.

Famine swept in like a swarm of locusts from every direction and settled over an unsuspecting province, greedily devouring every blade of green. Trees and plants were reduced to mere branches and stems, and human beings and animals to skeletons. Historians named the province 1770. After that, the swarm of locusts rose into the sky with the same alacrity with which it had landed and settled, and made its way to the neighbouring province. And all that was left of it were ten lakh skeletons. That province came to be known as 1837. The locusts took off again. To a region where fifty lakh skeletons waited and which would be known as 1858. From there, hungrier and greedier, they scattered north, east, south and west, caressing the thought of a festival where there would be three times as many bones as they had previously left behind. Historians gave a general name to the paths it journeyed on—1889.

The form people gave the goddess of the plague which they experienced as fever, pain and certain death was that of a beautiful woman wearing a white muslin sari. They said that when the clock struck midnight, she could be seen flowing through the cold, deserted streets, her long hair undone, as if she was riding the waves. Next day the plague would attack whichever street she had been seen in. And one night, the few people left in the city, peering through small slits in their barely-opened windows, saw her walking forward steadily until she disappeared beyond the city gates. The next day they heard that the plague had broken out in the neighbouring town which was called 1403 while their own city, 1031, where death had had a long reign, was finally released from it. New life began to blossom in it. After many days, the beautiful goddess of the plague in her white sari went beyond the gates of the city called 1403 and, riding on waves, flowed gently into the one called 1617. And from there into 1836, then 1896, then 1907...

88

One day, between the famines, epidemics and wars that beset Hindustan endlessly, Sarmad, the Sufi saint who was beheaded by Alamgir Aurangzeb, went to see the emperor's father, Shah Jahan, in the prison where his son had confined him. Sarmad was, as usual, naked. Shah Jahan sat on the cot placed near the only window of the cell, dressed in tattered royal robes. There was no one else with him, not even Jahanara, the dethroned badshah's daughter.

Raising his grey eyebrows, Shah Jahan looked at the saint. The inability to believe his eyes and his own discomfiture distanced him from Sarmad.

Aware of the emperor's distress, Sarmad said: 'Do not be ashamed of your condition, emperor. Think of the place I have come from—from beyond death. Not just death either, but a barbarous beheading!'

The emperor lowered his eyes. Two tears rolled down from his eyes and he wiped them away with the back of his hand. 'Tell me something, baba,' he said, with the gentleness that had become part of his voice during his stay in prison. 'How were you able to come back from a place like that?'

Sarmad's face brightened. He laughed, his yellow teeth gleaming through his unkempt beard.

'Prison houses, fetters, sentries: isn't it only the living who have to cope with them?'

'Yes, only we have them. And only we are affected by justice, injustice, anger and sorrow. You who are dead, you are probably not even aware of your condition... but then, even something called a condition does not exist for you.'

'No, it did not exist even when I was alive,' said Sarmad, losing himself in his memories.

A breeze from the Yamuna managed to cross the heavily guarded gates of the fort and enter the cell. A shower seemed imminent. The swollen river reflected the dark, cloudy sky.

Fixing his eyes on Sarmad's nudity and running his hands over his own shabby clothes, Shah Jahan murmured as if to himself: 'They have not removed my clothes and taken them away—at least not yet. And anyway what difference would it make even if they did, in this cell?'

'There are prisons everywhere, Khurram.' Sarmad addressed the emperor by name unwittingly. 'But clothes are for oneself to remove. No one else should do it.'

Shah Jahan suddenly became the prince who had fought wars in the Deccan decades ago and celebrated his youth with the beautiful Mumtaz Mahal.

'You always saw clothes as objects that obstruct reality,' said Shah Jahan with the new sense of lightness he felt. 'While I thought of them as decorative objects that embellished reality.'

'Why should there be anything to hide or decorate between a lover and his beloved, Khurram?'

'I have heard you ask this question many times—I and Prince Dara.' Unmindful of his present state, Shah Jahan still wandered through the world of the past. 'But do you know, baba, the image of Mumtaz that still fills my mind today is of her coming to me dressed in beautiful garments, wearing the most brilliant jewels. Not the naked body I used to hold passionately in my arms.'

'That is why, Khurram, I say that all of you are worshippers rather than lovers. Worshippers of beauty, artists. You could never become one with the person you loved.'

'You are right. Within myself, I have always been an artist who worshipped beauty. While I built mosques and palaces and cities and filled them with decorative objects, whenever I took my beloved in my arms I saw only beauty. Love, as you say, is consummated in nakedness. In shedding all garments and becoming one, in entering into each other... like word and meaning, like the rose and its fragrance. I used to recite these words you wrote... But tell me baba, is not love an art as well?'

Sarmad climbed on to the stool by the side of the emperor's cot and sat down on it with his legs crossed like a Buddha.

'Yes, both of us are artists,' said Sarmad. 'You of beauty and I of love. There is only one difference. The distance between the object and he who views it is the nature of your art. The nature of mine is the obliteration of that distance.'

'But there is freedom in my art. In yours, there is only a denial of freedom.'

'Mine has the warmth of fulfilment. Yours is dry and shrivelled.'

Shah Jahan smiled, got up from the cot and stood by the window. It had begun to rain. The curtain of rain concealed the river and blurred the image of the Taj that he had been permitted to look at through the window as a special favour. All reality seemed to be contained within that curtain. The Khurram in Shah Jahan made way again for the old Emperor.

'What fools we are, baba,' said Shah Jahan, not taking his eyes off the curtain of rain. 'Here I am, a man imprisoned by his own son, compelled to witness the execution of two other sons, his wife dead, the father of a daughter who gave up everything in life to serve him in prison. And you, a saint who sowed love among human beings and who was finally publicly beheaded by the rulers of the country. It was not my worship of beauty or your mission of love that brought us this destiny. We were punished for something else!'

'Not everything that happens or is done in this world need have a reason, badshah,' said Sarmad, going back to the old form of address. 'Most of the victims who suffer atrocities are innocent. And many who are rewarded do not merit it.'

'How then are you able to believe in a just and kind god? How can you love Him? How can you take off your clothes before Him when he cannot take off His or shed any of His pretensions? When all His deeds remain outside human comprehension?'

Shah Jahan walked back, shaking his head, to his shabby cot. He was very agitated.

It was Sarmad's turn now to go to the window and look at the curtain of rain. He waited quite a while before answering the emperor.

'Who told you that I *believe* in Him?' he asked, his eyes still on the rain.

'I know, hazrat, how you tried to play the role of another intrepid Manzur Hallaj and refused to recite the whole of the *kalima* before Aurangzeb and Qazi Abdul Wahab. You stopped at *la ilaha* and would not add *illa Allah Mohammad Rasool Allah.*' Carried away by his emotions, Shah Jahan's language became disrespectful. 'Was that not a cheap trick you played in order to invite martyrdom like your ideal, Manzur Hallaj? Were you not turning from the prophet of nudity that you were to an actor essaying a part on a stage?'

'Jahanpanah,' said Sarmad with mock respect, without turning away from the window. 'The god whom your son, Alamgir Aurangzeb, fears and you worship is yet to be discovered by this poor poet of love, Sarmad. As far as that god is concerned, this brainless fakir is still in the *nafi,* the negative state and has not arrived at the *isbat*, the positive one. I always had only him, my lover, before me. I loved him, *all* I did was love him!'

Shah Jahan looked at the saint's naked back as he stood at the window. His Persian skin which had once been as soft and flushed as a rose petal had become as rough as the scales of a fish with the seventy summers, winters and monsoons it had weathered. Age and fatigue had made not only his shoulders but his whole body sagging and bent.

Realizing that the emperor had fallen silent, Sarmad turned away from the window, faced him and went on: 'There are no doubts or complaints in love, emperor. I do not know what my beloved does or does not do. So the question of faith or trust is irrelevant. Love is just love, nothing else. Tell me, long after Mumtaz, in whom you wished to see all the beauty in the world, was rotting under five feet of earth and had turned into food for worms, did you not build a monument for her? A monument as beautiful as she was?'

Sarmad came up and sat by him on the floor, at his feet.

Sweat glistened on his tired face and he looked weaker, more distressed than when he had arrived.

Shah Jahan's anger had subsided. He kept fidgeting with his shabby clothes.

'Baba, could there not be a form that does not belong to the love you experienced nor the beauty I admired, something that transcends them and belongs to art?'

Sarmad looked at Shah Jahan questioningly.

Shah Jahan tried to explain: 'Something that does not adhere to us like our skin, something that stands separate from our ego, detached, unselfish…'

Sarmad's face grew anxious. Shah Jahan went on, trying to be more precise: 'For instance, the object we adore need not always be beautiful and what we love is not necessarily possessed by us…'

'Go on,' Sarmad encouraged him.

'Hazrat,' said Shah Jahan respectfully, 'you came to India from Persia as a rich merchant who traded in expensive ceramics, carpets and dry fruits. But you abandoned trade and began to learn Sanskrit and Vedanta under the influence of a Hindu youth. You became an ascetic, composed devotional songs and preached the creed of love. You, who once sold garments woven with gold thread for princes and queens, cast off your clothes and walked naked in the streets. In the end, because of your love for your god, you cast off your own body, your flesh and blood and became a naked spirit. Turning away from everything around you, forsaking all worldly things, you journeyed along a path that was narrow and lonely and led to a single point… while I travelled into a steadily widening world. I was a king, you know, and there was nothing in life that I did not see or experience. Wars, revolts, famines, epidemics, the pageantry of palaces, flattery, treachery, intrigue, love, indifference... I was cruel to my own brothers. My sons murdered each other for power. And now, in the end, here I am in this cell, ignored by everyone, bound, deprived of clothing, denied even drinking water. Though I was an artist who admired beauty, I never rejected anything worldly—not pleasures, not even power. My knowledge of the world tells me now that even while we travelled different paths, there was always something similar in our artistic sensibilities, in the ways in which we pursued art. The more we live in this world, regardless of whether we renounce or possess it, the more conceited we become. Conceit rises from within and forces out truth and reality. As I sit here now, I realize that I did not build the Taj Mahal as a monument of my love for Mumtaz. It was a memorial to her beauty, the beauty of her youth. I would have built it even if she had not died. Her beauty would have vanished and the only way I could give permanence to it was to capture it in stone.'

Sarmad's eyes filled with tears. Hoisting up his exhausted naked body with difficulty, he began to pace slowly up and down the room. He said in an unsteady voice: 'Khurram, there is something I concealed from you all this while. You force me to say it now.'

The emperor raised his sad and tired face, furrowed by the battlehorses of experience. He turned to Sarmad, his eyes full of astonishment.

Sarmad went on: 'You were right—when they took me on the back of a she-elephant along the road that passes in front of the Pearl Mosque you built, my mind was full of the memories of Manzur. The followers of Alamgir threw spears and stones at me from both sides of the road. They flung mud at me, spat at me, saying they were trying to cover my nudity. And all that while, I kept building a monument to martyrdom with my body, steeped as it was in pain and blood and filth. I repeated in my mind what Manzur's ashes had chanted after his body was dismembered and burned: *Anal Haq, Anal Haq*... It was at that moment that my eyes fell on a man standing in the crowd. Somehow, the pain on his face mesmerized me. The smile I had been trying to hold fixed on my face suddenly faded. Although the spears had left jagged wounds on my body in several places, I felt that his pain was infinitely deeper than mine. Do you know who he was? Govardhan! A character in a play written by a poet like me, whom the author had set free when he found that he could no longer hold him at the tip of his pen. A man in the street who had been sentenced to the gallows merely because the noose fitted his neck, who was not only innocent but whom the judge himself had declared innocent! In the presence of that man over whose head hung such a cruel fate, I felt that my sufferings and even Manzur's, were nothing. Then a much more frightening thought passed through my mind like lightning. While Govardhan had come down from the stage into the crowd, was not I moving out from among the multitude onto a stage?'

Neither spoke for a while. Outside, the rain had begun to abate, but the sky was still overcast. The faint grey light that filtered into the room cast an uncanny aura around the saint and the king.

'Khurram,' continued Sarmad, 'I feel that I too should have set free the lord whom I had bound inextricably to me with my selfish love, just as that playwright did. Into the world, amidst throngs of suffering human beings to wander endlessly through cruel summers and biting winters and lashing rains, through sorrow and pain, war and famine and plague…'

Shah Jahan got up and went to the window as Sarmad was speaking. Against the dark backdrop of the sky, the white Taj looked like a shower of snowflakes that had blown down from the Himalayas and settled on the banks of the Yamuna.

'Sarmad,' Shah Jahan called the saint by name. 'The thought that I should never have built the Taj has haunted me from the day I completed it. I too concealed the ultimate failure of my art within me, telling no one about it. What monument can there be to beauty, to everything in this world, except life itself? Had Mumtaz lived, I would have watched her beauty evolve and change through that great process of art on which life is eternally at work. I imprisoned her in the memorial that I built. Just as the experience of moving from the midst of life to the stage disturbed you when your eyes fell on that man as you were being taken to be beheaded, the image of the Taj that I see from this prison-house every day wounds me deeply, Sarmad. The Taj took my living Mumtaz away and buried her underneath it. Maybe it is the work of the powers-that-be to throw people into prison, torture and kill them. But the artist is one who fulfils himself by moving along with life…'

89

While Nunis, the Portuguese trader was on his way back after selling horses, he saw a slave girl put up for sale in a market on the road to Vijayanagara. She had a child with her. Nunis was attracted to the little boy who was pointing out to him, perhaps because he was white, and saying something to his mother. He thought he saw the darkness of all space and time in the charcoal-black eyes of the girl. He bought the girl and the child.

Mariam and her child became his friends rather than his slaves. Every time he came back from a trading trip, she would arrange his seat and desk for him as he sat down to write in his diary about the cities and sights he had seen and serve him drinks and food. She delved for answers to his questions and doubts in the deep, dark mines of her slavery and brought them to him.

'The world calls me a historian but it is wrong,' he said to her one day. 'Actually, I know nothing about the past or the future. I just note down the stories and pictures that pass before my eyes on this paper—mere two-dimensional pictures of the present. But everything I cannot see or experience lies flooded within you. From where did you come, Mariam, to that marketplace? From the world lying behind me or the one lying ahead of me? When I look into your eyes, I lose my sense of past and future.'

'What past or future does a slave have, malik?' asked Mariam. 'Time does not exist for a slave. If it did, she would no longer be a slave.'

'I feel it is darkness that speaks through you. The darkness that lies beyond the limits of human vision.'

'I am the darkness, malik,' she said without emotion. She gazed into the distance as if trying to journey into the past and added: 'I saw light for a short while. A man called Govardhan walked with me and taught me language. Then I fell back into the darkness again and lost all sense of direction.'

'Who was he?'

'I don't know—I didn't ask. One day they caught him, branded the word "criminal" on his forehead, sliced off his ears and threw him out of the town. I was sent to the market. And how many markets! In the marketplaces and fields and chambers, they touched me. With ropes and sticks and with their hands.'

Nunis's eyes went over her body. The ropes and sticks had left many scars on it. He looked at the little boy playing on the floor. The sign that her owners had touched her body.

He lifted the boy and put him on his lap. The child tugged playfully at his clothes and his beard.

'Let's call him Satyakama,' he said. 'Let him search for the truth.'

'What does truth mean?' asked Mariam.

'Truth... truth is time. The time that does not exist, for that is denied to slaves. As long as we do not look for it, as long as we do not find it, we remain, as you said, bound in slavery.'

She looked at him wordlessly.

'In one sense, Mariam, we meet at a point.' He went out with the child in his arms and said to her, gazing at the wide expanse of earth before them, 'You walk through a present that is eternal. And I, a trader go from one horse market to another. After each trip, I make a list of the wares and rates in each market... Beyond this point, we are different. However far you go, you remain in the same place. You do not even know whether you are going backward or forward. But whenever I move to a new market, fresh information supercedes the old one. The superceded tables and figures become history... Mariam, this child who does not know who its father is, should not live by outdated tables of figures like a historian. He also should not be bound to eternal present like you. He should surge forward, unlike a historian or slave. Become Satyakama....'

90

Enduku dayaradara sriramachandra ni
Sandadiyani marayitivo? Yindulevo? Ni... [17]

Tyagaraja walked through the narrow lanes of the houses in the agrahara, singing. The fingers of the swami's left hand moved over the strings of the tanpura hanging from his shoulder. The other hand searched for something in the sky. Tears flowed from his eyes.

Not much had fallen by way of alms into the bag hanging at the end of the uttariyam knotted around his neck. Since water had been sprinkled over the earthen path of the agrahara in the morning to purify it, the swami's aged feet moved over it with ease. The women in the houses on either side, immersed in their varied household chores, stopped now and then to listen to his song, before going back to their work. The whole country

---

[17] Why do you not show kindness? Have you forgotten me in the midst of all your work? Or is it that you are not here?

was passing through a severe famine and they seldom had enough rice or pulses to spare for this unchavritti Brahmin who lived by begging and singing every day on his way back from the temple...

Jagela? Yidisamayame gaduchesite
Egati balakavayya srirama! Ni
Vegani dariledayya dinasharanya!
Tyagaraja vinuta! Tarakacharita! Ni[18]

Tyagaraja went past the agrahara and the street where the merchants and the king's servants lived, still singing his kirtana. Here, on this road, the swami had to contend with bullock carts, horsemen and palkis. The road was paved with stones and since it had not been sprinkled with water, it grew warm as the sun climbed higher. Those who lived there had no time to listen to his music. Nevertheless, passers-by who had little to spare and even the beggars dropped something in the bag slung on his back.

Somewhere on this path, a woman began to follow him. He did not notice her. In fact, the swami rarely noticed anything except the image of Sri Ramachandra which he had installed in his heart.

This road too ended at the temple, at its eastern gopuram, a spacious entrance, unlike the southern one where the street to the agrahara started. When he reached there, the swami looked for a vacant space on the platform around the banyan

---

[18] Why are you taking so long? Is it not yet time? Who else do I have to help me? Rama, tell me, I have no one but you.

tree and sat down to rest. It was then that he noticed the woman who had been following him.

He smiled at her. She bowed her head and touched her forehead in obeisance.

'Have you come from very far, amma?' he asked, taking note of her clothes and the way she had paid him obeisance.

'From very far,' she replied.

'Have you come to learn music?'

'This woman too has been earning a living with music, though in a different way,' she said with great humility. 'If it will not offend the swami to hear it, this woman too sang about love. Not love for god, but love for men.'

Tyagaraja's eyes grew sharp and his lips narrowed to form a thin line. But he soon got over his displeasure and smiled again. Then he sang two lines with deep emotion:

Anuragamuleni manasuna sujnana muradu
Ghanulainayantarjnanula keruke gani[19]

'You do not know, swami, I am a fallen woman, a prostitute.' Umrao's voice trembled. But her eyes stared boldly at Tyagaraja.

'I know, amma, I know everything.' The swami smiled again.

'I have heard so much about you, that is why I journeyed this long distance. And when I reached here, I found that all people talk about is you. But it is only when I followed you for this short distance, my feet touching the earth that yours trod, that I really understood you.'

Umrao sat on the ground near his feet. Over them, the

---

[19] A mind that does not know love cannot attain knowledge. Great men who are learned know this truth.

leaves of the banyan rustled wildly in the hot breeze and the flakes of sunlight scattered over the ground danced with them.

'What did you learn about me, amma?' asked Tyagaraja curiously.

'I have seen many singers and poets. But I have never seen a peerless scholar like you who walks barefoot on the streets singing and receiving alms from the very poor, from even beggars. While artists everywhere wait at the gates of kings and nobles with songs to flatter them, why do you wander through these streets, refusing an invitation from even the king himself?'

'You have got it wrong,' Tyagaraja shook his head. 'All wrong. I too am a beggar, amma. Some people take alms from kings who love power. Some from men who are crazy with desire. And I from the people in this street. All of us are beggars. Just as you turned love into a profession, I sold my bhakti, my devotion for god, for a day's meal...'

Tyagaraja's voice faltered. His eyes filled. In a faltering voice that broke from time to time, he said: 'Wicked and shameless wretch that I am, I sold my bhakti for Janakirama for... *janakirama kalushatmudai dushkarmayutudai palumaru durbhashiyai ilalobhaktagresarula veshiyai Tyagarajapujita!*'[20]

Umrao allowed the swami to weep in peace. She too was passing through a stage of deep anguish. They sat there for a long time, drifting silently through their different worlds. One on the platform around the banyan tree, the other on the ground below. Then they got up and walked along the banks of the river. Because of the sudden closeness he felt for her and because

---

[20] O Lord who is worshipped by Tyagaraja who spends his time doing sinful things, who talks ill of others and pretends to be a great devotee!

exhaustion was making his legs unsteady, he placed a hand on her shoulder. The other hand moved over the strings of the tanpura as if picking up the pitch of the ripple of the river. When Umrao's feet touched the waves that unfurled over the sand, they sounded like dancing ankle-bells.

'Swami, dacoits gave me trouble all the way here,' said Umrao. 'People told me that famine and poverty have turned even the good folk of this region into thieves. Those who are not thieves are walking skeletons—mothers weeping for the children whom the sultan, on his way back after an attack, took away as recruits for the army; farmers lamenting over fields that have gone dry because the army destroyed canals and ponds; kings who curse themselves for not having been able to save their people from the armies of sultans and firangis... I saw so many houses, swami, that either lay empty or were filled with the stench of rotting flesh. Do you not see your lifeless country? Do you not hear the sound of its silence?'

'I know, amma, I see and hear it all. Why did I refuse the invitation from the palace and decide to live on the alms the people on the street give me? I felt that my music should gently soothe these broken huts whose walls breathe poverty and disease, not reverberate against the gem-studded walls of palaces. These sorrowing people need god more than the kings do. How many sultans, peshwas and governors tried to rule over them. None of them succeeded, Amma. Only god can bring sound to these silent streets, fill these dead houses with living people. Only god's music...'

'Then why do you keep that god whom everyone needs for yourself? Why is it that you sing of only your sorrows to him?'

Tyagaraja smiled. 'Look at this Kavery river, amma,' he said. 'Mother Kavery who washes your feet and mine. The mother of all of us. Come, your feet have rhythm and my fingers can find the right pitch. Come, the waves are our mother's hands reaching out to us, let us hold them.'

Singing *inta soukhyamani ne jeppajala*,[21] the swami strummed his tanpura. Forgetting herself, Umrao danced on the spreading waves. They stopped when they were tired and began to walk again.

'Look at the Kaveri, amma,' said Tyagaraja, pointing to the wide expanse of the flowing river. 'She divides here into a thousand tributaries that spread outwards like the unfurling feathers in a peacock's tail. It seems as if this beautiful girl who was so shy and modest when she began her journey faraway shed all her inhibitions when she reached here, reaching for the ocean with a thousand outstretched hands. Do you feel she is embracing the ocean? No, her body, spread out like a peacock's tail is taking the vast ocean into herself. The ocean she has always carried within her... I know everything, amma. I have not travelled beyond this little town of Tiruvaiyur, but the ways you walked and the sights you saw are all within me... Is there anything that is not present in music, amma? There is joy in it and pain, hunger, satisfaction, death. Music is a river. I journey over it to reach Sri Ramachandra. I do not make him mine, I do not even embrace him. He comes into me, fills me like an ocean. He claims all the alms I have begged for on my way and makes them his own...'

Unmindful of Umrao walking beside him, the swami's feet moved rapidly over the sand like another river, a river that has found the ocean. His arms stretched out like a peacock's tail. The drone which rose from the tanpura he held high in his

---

[21] How can I describe what a pleasure it is?

hands broke into a hundred pieces like the ripples of the river when they meet the waves of the ocean. He sang:

Intakannanandamemi o ramarama
Santa janula kola sammatiyum degani
Ni japamula vela ni jagamulu ni vai
Rajillunaya tyagarajanutacharita[22]

---

[22] What greater bliss can there be than this? Seated with good people, singing devotional songs to you, all the worlds shine as you.

91

The first one who came out of the pit was Kallu bania. The mason followed him, then the chunewala, the bhishti, the kasai and last of all, the ganderia. They had untied the knots which had tied them to each other and were now separated from one another. However, they still walked and carried out their tasks in the same order. The earth that had been thrown out of the pit lay around in heaps. They lay on the soft, faintly warm soil for some time to rest.

The pit was in the centre of a huge mustard field and was as huge as a pond. Beyond the pit and the heaps of earth that had been dug out, pale white moonlight glistened over the yellow mustard flowers. Once the sounds of digging stopped, a fearful silence enveloped the vast expanse of field. From Kallu to the ganderia, they were all troubled, uncertain how to confront it. Reality, that had been obfuscated by the sheer efforts of their labour, was slowly returning to them. The cool night air revived their bodies that labouring had made hot and sweaty.

After a while, they all sprang up together as if at the bidding of some mysterious force. They moved towards the carcasses of the dogs that had been unloaded by trucks just beyond the pit—dogs that had been shot, poisoned, or simply beaten to death. The blood on their bodies, their protruding eyes and the tongues that hung out were visible even in the faint moonlight. According to the calculations of the municipality, there were a hundred and sixty-four of them. They were the last lot. The authorities had gone from door to door to make sure that not a single one had been left behind anywhere. Pets that had been raised with affection and that children had taken to bed with them had been poisoned by their masters. Volunteers had patrolled the streets with guns and sticks. At one spot, after a bitch that had just littered had been shot, its little pups that had not even opened their eyes had been beaten to death.

The men, women and children of the town had been doing nothing but this the last five days—destroying dogs. Four thousand seven hundred and thirty-four dogs had been offered up for this great dog sacrifice which had lasted five days. The Liberation Army had ordered that the town be completely cleared of dogs within a week. The commander had put up announcements on the walls in several places in town that two human beings would lose their heads for every live, stray or pet dog or pup seen anywhere after a week. The residents proved their subservience by completing the task two days before the stipulated one, such was the fear the Liberation Army generated in the minds of the people. Even the municipality, which was supposed to be on the government's side, extended its support so that the people would not be endangered. For the Liberation Army was sure to keep their word.

It was at night that the members of the army carried out operations like slaying enemies or setting up bombs or booby traps in the town. Supporters of law and order by birth, the dogs would start to bark, exposing them to the police, the arm of the government. This was why the Liberation Army had been forced to issue a fatwa against the dogs.

Kallu bania and the mason began to retch suddenly as they stood before the carcasses. The others turned away in order to control themselves. Somehow managing to overcome their feelings of disgust, they lined up in pairs and began to throw the carcasses into the pit, going from one heap to the next. When all the dogs were in the pit, they picked up their shovels and filled up the pit. When they finished, the night was nearly done. Once it was all over, the six of them stretched out prone over the mounds of fresh earth that covered the pit and wept. They did not see the moon disappear, the darkness dissolve and the town take shape beyond the fields in the pale morning light. Although they were exhausted, they could not sleep. Their hands seemed stained with blood and poison. The cries of the dogs, their convulsive movements, came back to them over and over again. Over the last five days, they had been just murderers— like madmen possessed, out on a spree of hunting and killing. And now they longed to reclaim their old identities. They wanted to begin living the lives they had earned by swimming through a river of blood. But they realized they would not be able to.

'I want to go and open my shop, it has been two days since I did so,' said Kallu bania to himself. It was the first time one of them had opened his mouth to speak since they had arrived there at night with their pickaxes and shovels. After a while he added, 'Or maybe I won't. No one comes now to buy anything from the shop.'

'Half the population has left the town, hasn't it? The houses are empty. I have no work either,' said the mason, getting up.

The chunewala and the bhishti nodded in agreement. The kasai said firmly: 'Even if there's work, I'm not coming. I don't want to do a kasai's work anymore.'

The ganderia agreed. 'I can't catch goats and take them to the kasai anymore either. With the dogs gone...'

'The truth is,' said Kallu, 'we have all been thrown out of our professions.'

The ganderia tried to define their situation more clearly. 'Are we not on the veranda of life already? We were thrown out of houses long ago! We are just veranda-people now.'

They came down the mound of earth and watched the sun rise over the horizon in awe.

The ganderia mumbled to himself. 'The king's declaration forced us to come out of the security of our homes and closed the doors behind us. At that time, all we had for company were these dogs that had been sleeping on the verandas and in the streets.' When he spoke, his voice was choked.

'These creatures were with us even before houses were built.' It was Kallu who spoke. 'They watched over us as we slept on treetops and caves. When we built houses, they stood as sentries on our verandas. And when fate threw us out on the verandas, we pushed them into their graves.'

Stroking his beard, the kasai said: 'The next step from the veranda is to the grave, Kallu. We should have known that. *We* should have known, even if no one else knew.'

'And didn't we know?' asked the mason. 'But we wanted to save our lives.'

'Yes, it was to save our own lives that we ran around the country hunting for Govardhan, who had done no wrong at all, to hand him over to the gallows.' The bhishti's voice was angry and bitter. 'I used to make bags out of the skins of dead goats, fill them with water and moisten the walls to make them strong. And yet the walls collapsed! And it was a goat that died!'

'There is a well inside each one of us, bhishti,' said the chunewala who had been silent until then. 'And it is not water we drew from them but the cries of those whom we betrayed. We listened to them and were glad that our journey was safe.'

The kasai pointed to the ground in front of them. 'There, on our way, I can see a spot where we are all lying dead like dogs. With our limbs stretched out, our eyes protruding, our tongues hanging out...'

They turned in the direction he was pointing to. There was no road there, only fields. All six of them moved towards the field in single file as if sleepwalking. Kallu bania went first, then the mason, the chunewala, the bhishti, the kasai and last of all, the ganderia. No one said anything after that. Nor did they look back. The world they thought they had achieved by wading through blood lay behind them, now someone else's enclosure. Their relatives had abandoned them long ago. They now left behind them their tools and their professions. Only their shadows, which they could call their own, followed them. And even these shortened steadily as the sun rose in the sky.

Although they did not look back as they walked on, they realized that the shadows shortening behind them had taken a certain shape that was becoming alive. They heard the sound of a four-legged creature running on the ground, sniffing and wagging its tail. Their shadows had dissolved into one and turned into a huge dog! Why are you following us, they asked, without daring to turn back.

The dog answered: 'Here's someone asking his shadow why it is following him! It should be the other way round—it's the shadow that should ask this question. It was your own shadows you sliced off and threw away to ensure your safety. Assuming it would make you happy, you killed your own peace of mind. The fault you committed lay in one spot, while you searched to atone for it elsewhere. In what way are you different from those who tortured you?'

92

The mahant saw them coming from his ashram on the slope of the hill—a group of children moving along a brown footpath that the cowherds had trod, slashing through the green grass on the hillside. Each child carried its belongings in a bundle. Their burdens made them stoop forward while fatigue pulled them backward. Still, they kept walking on.

The mahant knew they were coming towards the ashram in search of shelter for the night. The children usually came in the evenings, got up in the mornings and left. He had lost count of the number of times this had happened. Each time, he had failed to give them protection or to make sure they left the way they had come. And yet, every time they came, he would listen to the inner call of dharma and say to them, 'Come, let us try…'

The lost children: that was what the world called them. The youngest was barely seven, the oldest were adolescents. The armies that had attacked their towns and villages year after year had razed their houses to the ground, killed their parents and left them orphans. When there had been no invaders, their parents had fought among themselves, set fire to one anothers' houses and killed one another. Running away from the blazing houses and the world of older people, the children had fled in all directions. Many had fallen prey to wild animals. Some had died of hunger. Others had drowned, trying to cross rivers. Those of them who had escaped from their elders, from wild animals, from hunger and from flooded rivers had met on the road and joined to form groups.

The lost children journeyed with no direction or aim. They flowed along the veins of the earth, making it aware of what it was to be lost. What they gained from their losses was interdependence, the ability to cooperate. They fashioned tents from the twigs and sacks they picked up on the way. They cooked their own food, cut one another's hair, mended their own tattered clothes, made clay toys, nursed those who fell ill and buried those who died.

As they came closer, the children's faces grew clearer—faces that had lost the tenderness of childhood and become indifferent and hard. Fire and blood had burnt or washed out their brief pasts. One of them would hum a tune as they walked along and the others would pick up the melody and make it a song. For a while they would sway along, swinging on the threads of the song, then it would suddenly be cut off. They would fall silent and become the sound of trudging feet, of gasps and sighs. Even as the mahant smiled to see them, his eyes grew moist.

'Baba, can you give us some place to spend the night?' the children asked when they arrived at the ashram.

'Everything I have is yours, my children. But...' the mahant stopped.

'This is only an ashram, there are no weapons here to protect you—isn't that what you wanted to say?' asked the children. 'This is what all babas in all ashrams have to say to us.'

'You can stay here, children,' said the mahant. 'There is a stream nearby. Go and have a bath. Then go to the ashram kitchen and have your food. You can sleep in the hall. I will pray for you all night.'

But none of them could sleep in peace in the cool ashram on the hillside. The children saw it in their dreams as a feeble, decrepit fort. And the mahant as its helpless watchman. Then the night turned into a storm that attacked the fort. Rain and violent winds lashed it. The watchman's lantern flickered like a glow-worm through the rain and the darkness. His futile cries for safety tore the night like lonely wails.

The children listened, holding on to one another. The watchman climbed up the swaying watchtower and called out: 'There's a troop of cavalry coming—and here's a camel army! Watch out, watch out!' The children trembled with fear. They lay down, holding their breath, their arms around one another. 'A town has fallen there!' called out the watchman again. 'Now there's a fort collapsing. Fire is coming out of the buildings inside it!'

During the last part of the night when the starlight had faded and sleep had blessed the children, the rumbling of real cavalry became audible. Chariot wheels groaned. Hoof beats could be heard under the windows, then in the room itself. First one child shrieked, then another... The children's cries faded out along with the hoofbeats in the pitch dark. 'Baba, baba!' the children called out. The mahant lay at the feet of the idol, wounded by sword thrusts, deaf to their plaintive cries.

When the sun rose in the morning in a clear sky empty of clouds, the handful of children who remained and the mahant, who was drenched in blood, met in the ruins of the ashram.

'Children,' said the mahant, 'my ashram too has become a

figment of the imagination like Arjuna's refuge of arrows—a desire that I have, a hope my dharma cherishes. God thinks otherwise. He considers it pride or arrogance. The same god who preaches dharma to human beings punishes those who carry out His directives. The Bhagavad Gita turns into the Book of Job... Let it go, children. Whether it belongs to kings, prophets, revolutionaries or liberators, an army is an army. Who can withstand armies? I am a helpless Partha. Their horsemen came at night, picked up your friends and took them away. For a punishment much more fearful than death: to enrol them in their armies...'

Sitting on the broken steps of the ashram, the mahant watched as the few children who were left took up their bags and bundles uncomplainingly, without crying or speaking, and went down the hill into the sunlight without saying a word to him. His throat was choked and his eyes full of tears. He forgot his own wounds. After all, they were just physical wounds. But the group of children who left had been cruelly decimated to a fraction of the number that had come the day before. Their friends who had been with them until the previous day, who had sung and made toys and played with them, must now be in the process of being transformed into child-soldiers in the regiments of some revolutionary or liberation force, their names erased, all their memories effaced from their minds. And as they moved into towns and villages the thinned stream of children would swell with more like them, orphaned by their own friends of yesterday. Cutting across the green grass and trudging over the brown footpaths cowherds had trod on the hillside, they would arrive at the shelter some other helpless Partha had built in his imagination...

The mahant wiped the blood from his wounds and got up.

He had to build this shelter anew—be it from the imagination or from arrogance. For what did he have except this? He would allow no God to scoff at him and turn him away from his task.

93

Govardhan heard the door open and lifted his head. The man who entered was the smiling, handsome man who had become a constant problem to him over the last two days— one of the three who had kidnapped him. Another person with an assault rifle in his hand followed him in. The smiling man did not have a gun with him now. Instead, he clutched a newspaper which he was using to fan himself.

Both of them came in and checked on the chains that bound Govardhan. The one that secured him to the thick grill of the window did not allow him to move much. The room was long and there were a few chairs and a television set at the other end of it. The emptiness in the rest of the room suffocated Govardhan.

The handsome man opened the newspaper in his hand and showed it to Govardhan.

Govardhan did not know how to read. Whatever the bold letters that ran across it from one end to the other might mean, the three pictures underneath them attracted him. One of them was of Govardhan himself and the others of the two men who had been kidnapped along with him.

It was the first time Govardhan had seen a picture of himself. He had no memory of ever having looked into a mirror. But something told him that this was his photograph. What was more, it had no ears. Even without knowing how to read, he read what was branded in green on the forehead: CRIMINAL.

Govardhan started weeping. When he lifted his hand to wipe his tears, the weight of the chain on his hand pushed him further into despair.

To comfort himself, he glanced at another large picture below, of fourteen mangled and faceless bodies lying dead on the ground. They lay with their limbs twisted, broken, contorted in all kinds of shapes. One of them still held the chapatti that had been in his hand when he was shot. At least Govardhan's condition was better than theirs, wasn't it? Or was it?

Having lost his village, his home, his wife, his child, Mariam and last of all, his ears, wandering by himself through the fields, Govardhan reached a farm. The owner gave him work as a labourer even though he saw the branded mark on his forehead. Besides him, there were sixteen workers on the farm. Huts had been built by the side of the fields for them. They toiled from morning to night and sometimes late into the night as well. They were given rice gruel and rotis three times a day. Govardhan's master said nothing, but his companions pointed to his non-existent ears and the mark on his forehead and laughed at him. He said nothing to them. Whenever there was work to do, he worked with a vengeance, in order to forget everything. When there was no work, he slept through sheer exhaustion. He deliberately distanced from his mind thoughts about other people and memories of those whom he had lost.

Accepting the freedom of this existence as happiness, he felt glad.

One day while the workers were seated together on the ground for lunch, a jeep came rushing up to them. The handsome, smiling man and two others sprang out of it. Govardhan remembered seeing for a moment the smile that had turned into a nightmare and settled in his mind. And then, all three had taken out their guns and begun to fire at the workers. The workers fell to the ground over one another. Fourteen of them died. Three stayed alive, probably because the others had fallen over them. The gunmen dragged them into the jeep and sped away.

The three survivors who were so frozen by shock that they could not even scream, drifted slowly back to consciousness. Beneath the question of how they had escaped was buried the equally unanswerable question of why they had been shot at. Neither the workers nor the kidnappers were in any state to either ask questions or answer them. And after they got here, Govardhan had not seen the other two. It was clear that the three of them were imprisoned in three different places.

The most astonishing thing Govardhan had seen after he arrived was a camera pointed at him. The man who brought it took a series of pictures of him. And they had now appeared in the newspapers.

'Read it,' said the handsome man, smiling at him.

'I do not know how to read, sahib,' said Govardhan humbly.

'Then how did an illiterate fellow like you become a VIP?' asked the man, taunting him. Every time he smiled, Govardhan felt as if a shower of bullets had been released upon him.

For some reason, the handsome man opened the newspaper and began to read out what was written in it loudly. It sounded to Govardhan as if a line of lawyers were standing inside the paper as if in a court, trying him for an offence he could not understand. He learned that the whole world knew of the massacre on the farm and of how the three of them had been taken hostage. The discussion was mostly about Govardhan. It said that Govardhan had been already sentenced to death by a court, that he had escaped from jail and that another court had banished him from the enclosed areas on the charge of being a criminal. The article debated on whether it would be right to meet the demands of his kidnappers in order to have a criminal like Govardhan released. Many learned people and political experts felt that the government ought to wait and not take any action. Especially because the militants had demanded that a hardened terrorist who was responsible for killing many people be released from jail. The Kayastha Sabha had, with characteristic pusillanimity, avoided giving a clear opinion on the matter and taken shelter behind the argument that the government was not any farther behind others in torturing the innocent. Only the spokesman of the government declared in unambiguous terms that they would make every effort possible to have the hostages released, or even forcibly rescue them if necessary. The question of who they were did not bother the government at this moment. It made no difference to them that one of them had been sentenced to death, that he was an escaped convict and a banished criminal. The government believed in justice. If it was necessary to try Govardhan or hang him, they would do it once he was rescued from the custody of the terrorists.

Govardhan dozed off while this long passage was being read. Although it was he who was being tried, he was bored.

'What is your religion, rascal?' asked the handsome man.

Govardhan did not reply.

The man swung his hand and slapped Govardhan at the spot where his ear had been. Govardhan fell to the ground. The man kicked him repeatedly till Govardhan felt blood spilling from his mouth and the sides of his head.

'I don't remember, sahib,' cried Govardhan. 'I will take your religion. And if you teach me, I will speak your language.'

Paying no attention, the man looked at his watch. Then he hurried towards the television set and turned it on.

A woman's face appeared on the screen. She smiled and spoke a greeting. Then she began to speak about the massacre on the farm. Govardhan lay on the ground in his blood and looked at her. The pictures of the fourteen men lying dead on the field and then of Govardhan and the two others who had been kidnapped came up one after another on the screen. The woman said the police were trying very hard to rescue the kidnapped labourers. A man then took her place. He spoke of the threats the terrorists had made. He said that if their demands were not met by the government in the time they had stipulated, they would cut off the limbs of the hostages one by one every day. The remains of the bodies would be dumped in the streets of the city.

It was the announcement that came at the very end that forced Govardhan to sit up, even in the state he was in. The man said the government suspected that Ali Dost's outfit that had already committed many murders was behind this incident. As Govardhan sat there, stunned, the woman who had first appeared came back and began to talk about banks and share markets. And with that, the visitors turned off the television set and left the room.

Govardhan was left alone in a corner of the huge room.

'Ali, Ali, what is this about?' he kept saying as if Ali was standing somewhere inside the room, which slowly turned into a street as silent and deserted as the room itself had been. Ali stood in the middle of it, holding aloft a sword at the tip of which were threaded two human heads. 'Ali, what is this? Don't you know me?' asked Govardhan. Ali did not reply. His eyes did not move. Then he himself became immobile, an image of stone.

The door opened again. This time, besides the handsome man and the gunman who was his bodyguard, three others walked in. One of them had a camera and the others carried varied appliances of torture. Govardhan realized that the time the terrorists had granted the government had come to an end. Terrified, he shrank back against the wall. A cry escaped from his mouth unawares.

'Isn't Ali Dost your leader? Will you tell him I am his brother, Govardhan? If Ali comes here, he can see for himself,' pleaded Govardhan.

All he got in answer was a kick from one of the newcomers.

'I've not done anything to you,' Govardhan cried out. 'I do not even know you!'

They paid him no attention at all. They behaved as if he was really guilty. With their sophisticated weapons, the men tortured Govardhan, cursing and shouting obscenities at him intermittently. Two of them stood on either side of him, twisted his arms and kicked him in the stomach. When he could bear the pain no longer, he begged them to shoot him as they had the other fourteen.

'You are a treasure trove to us. How can we kill you?' they asked. 'We are going to slice you into little pieces, then take a photograph and send it to the government. Only then will those rascals come running to us. They seem to have convinced themselves that only they have a right over you.'

'If the government is your enemy, why did you not kidnap someone who works for it?' cried Govardhan.

'For us, you are the government!' The handsome man laughed loudly. 'Why do we slit the throats of a traffic policeman or a postman or a municipal sweeper? Because they are all symbols of the government! If we torture them, those symbols themselves will abandon the government!'

'But I am just Govardhan. Not a symbol. I'm a poor man, one who has been thrown out of even enclosures.'

The smile on the handsome man's face disappeared and it grew as hard as stone. He came up to where Govardhan stood, his legs shackled and his hands twisted by two tormentors, lifted up his chin and said: 'You are the greatest symbol of the government, Govardhan. You are a prisoner and a man convicted to be hanged. No one else we touch can hurt the government's pride as deeply as you. They will agree to anything in order to get you back. In order to crucify you...'

Ali Dost's face appeared for a minute at the door. But Govardhan did not cry out to him. He only looked at him through tired and wet eyes. He had no one to cry out to any longer. No one to say anything to. He was just a symbol that stood between the government and its enemies. Both were measuring out the blood inside him. He sorrowed and wept symbolically, as only a symbol can.

Ali did not look at Govardhan. He gave his men instructions and disappeared.

The cameraman set up his apparatus. One of the men pressed Govardhan's hand down on a wooden plank. They chopped off his fingers one by one with a knife.

The camera kept clicking incessantly.

94

It was the third consecutive day that the frightening picture had appeared on the television screen. The fourteen labourers lying dead in fourteen different positions, their bodies broken or twisted, their eyes open or shut. Mannu and Michael had been trying to accept the picture over the last two days. And then, on the third day, more pictures appeared.

The first time they heard the news was just as Michael returned from duty in the evening. They watched it, then talked about it late into the night. It was Mannu who started to speak. About her stepfather, Govardhan. For some absurd reason, the king's policemen had come and taken him away one day.

'I've sometimes felt that the difference between a man who dies naturally and one who is killed is that coincidence seems to be ruling in one, while behind the other there may be some reason however absurd,' said Mannu. 'Choupat Raja who sentenced Govardhan to death offered a certain argument for his action, although it was a foolish one. But I do not see even a Choupat Raja behind these killings.'

'How do you know these people have no absurd reasons of their own?' asked Michael, placing his hand affectionately on her shoulder. 'In Govardhan's case, absurd as it was, the reason was directly linked to him: the size of his neck. What we have to find out is the nature of such links where these people are concerned. Life is becoming complex and slipping beyond our comprehension. The links between events and their causes are being made deliberately faulty and complicated by people who are gifted with rhetoric.'

Mannu was journeying through the dark tunnels of her own life. She said, as if she had suddenly found light at their end, 'Maybe it is not so complicated. One could even say it is very simple. The reason is that they are human!'

Michael did not have to go to work the next two days but they did not talk about these things. They allowed the newspapers and the television to parade silently before them. Two days later their fragile peace was broken—Govardhan, the person they had talked about cursorily, appeared on the screen. Mannu could do nothing except cry 'Michael!' and sit stunned, gripping his hand tight.

'Your stepfather, Govardhan?' asked Michael as if he had expected this sudden development in the drama.

Mannu did not say anything.

The drama proceeded, showing no signs of coming to an end. The television stage was embellished by a sketch the police had made of Ali Dost. Accompanied by an announcement that it was Ali Dost, the man who sowed terror in people's minds, and his gang who had massacred and abducted the labourers.

Observing how still Mannu was, Michael asked once again, as if he had anticipated this: 'Your father?'

Mannu pressed her face into his chest.

But she did not weep.

Her eyes were as dry as her mind. But within her flowed a red, hot flood of blood.

Supporting her, Michael turned off the television and moved to the next room. He made her lie down and lay beside her.

'Why do human beings have so much blood in them?' she asked, her head on his shoulder.

'Yes, why? You just scratch your skin and it begins to flow like a stream. We are so brimful of it. But have you ever thought, Mannu, of how perfectly god has fashioned our skin? Every day we move around amidst crowds, in the hustle and bustle of daily living. We work with sharp tools, operate dangerous machines. But it needs violence and fighting to make our blood flow.'

'Has there been no violence in your life, Michael?'

Michael smiled and said nothing. He had never revealed his past to her. He lived in an eternal spring-like present, as if he had never had a past. Like a train that runs from one temple to another. The foot of one could be washed by the waves of the sea and the granite gopuram of the other could soar six hundred feet into the sky. The rails would run between them smoothly, quiet as the surface of a calm lake. Order and discipline everywhere.

'Didn't you have a private life, Michael?' she asked.

'There's nothing private in life, Mannu, except when the human mind confronts certain unique moments. And even at such moments, we install a god or something as important as a god within us. So that they too cease to be private. I come upon moments like that during my journeys. The journey an engine driver repeatedly makes between two points does not take him anywhere in particular. And yet, each time I take a whole world with me. A world complete with men, women, old people and children. Each time it is different from the world I carried with me the time before. And what is more, a part of it is changed and renewed at every station. On every trip I make and at each station where I halt, my privacy becomes inhabited by newer lives... god is the life human beings live through each period of time. The content of god keeps changing with each generation. God changes and grows with the passage of time. If He does not, He would become a Satan. It is gods who have metamorphosed into satans, who are not prepared to give in even an inch, that sit at the head of all religions and rule over human beings. They do not rule, they hunt people, for the reign of Satan is nothing but a hunt...'

Michael took out his Bible and gave it to Mannu to read.

When he walked away next morning to catch his train, his canvas bag slung over his shoulder, Mannu stood at the door watching him. Calm Michael whose mind was always at peace, who liked good food, beer and music. Michael, she said to him in her mind, may you always fill my private moments, you and only you.

95

It was raining heavily. The roar of the rain enveloped Mannu's isolated house on all four sides. Every house that lay beyond that roar had gone to sleep, but sleep evaded Mannu. She opened the window and looked out. The only lights she could see through the swaying curtain of rain were those of the railway station. Their glow shone like threads of gold through the rain. The clamour of a fast train that passed through the station without stopping there rose above the din of the rain and then dissolved into it.

Mannu came back from the window and turned off all the lights except the table lamp. She sat by the lamp and opened Michael's Bible at the page he had marked with a small piece of paper, the eighteenth chapter of the Book of Genesis, and began to read. Her eyes filled with tears as she read. The rain and gale raged outside. Mannu withdrew into the circle of light on the table inside the small house situated in a troubled world. She read, through a film of tears:

... And Abraham drew near, and said, Wilt thou also destroy the righteous with the wicked? Peradventure there be fifty righteous within the city; wilt thou also destroy and not spare the place for the fifty righteous that are therein? That be far from thee to do after this manner, to slay the righteous with the wicked; and that the righteous should be as the wicked, that be far from thee: Shall not the Judge of all the earth do right? And the Lord said, If I find in Sodom fifty righteous within the city, then I will spare all the place for their sakes. And Abraham answered and said, Behold now, I have taken upon me to speak unto the Lord, which am but dust and ashes: Peradventure there shall lack five of the fifty righteous: wilt thou destroy all the city for the lack of five? And he said, If I find there are forty and five, I will not destroy it. And he spake unto him yet again, and said, Peradventure there shall be forty found there. And he said, I will not do it for forty's sake. And he said unto him, Oh let not the Lord be angry, and I will speak: Peradventure there shall be thirty found there. And he said, I will not do it, if I find thirty there. And he said, Behold now, I have taken upon me to speak unto the Lord: Peradventure there shall be twenty found there. And he said, I will not destroy it for twenty's sake. And he said, Oh let not the Lord be angry, and I will speak yet but this once: Peradventure ten shall be found there...

96

Even after it was all over, Govardhan heard the camera click in his mind. Everything had shrunk into the dry, mechanical tick-tock of a clock.

All his twenty fingers had been chopped off; blood gushed from his mutilated hand—and yet he kept staring at that apparatus. As for them, they kept themselves busy setting him up before the camera, holding up his hands on either side of the face with the protruding eyes, the hair that stood on end, the jaws that seemed to have detached themselves from the skull.

Govardhan was amazed at the keenness they displayed in recording the images of his suffering and of the cruelties they inflicted on him. Until now, every agency from the king to the law courts had shown interest only in making him suffer. But these tormentors were equally eager to print and publicize the pictures of their cruelty. Or maybe they intended to convert him into two-dimensional pictures that could be spread out on newspapers. He had been the victim of the rope the king had pulled to hang him; then of the scissors the popular courts had wielded; and now his own brother was pushing him towards a camera so that it could devour him. Govardhan submitted to this as well. Saying tick-tock silently to himself, he withdrew until he fell into an abyss of unconsciousness.

When he recovered his senses, he found himself in a gutter on the edge of a street. He lay face down, precariously balanced on its brick walls. His legs were doubled up under his stomach. Although his head hung down into the gutter, it had not touched the water. Both his hands were in the gutter, washed by the slimy, stinking water in it. The first sound he heard was the gurgling of the water; he thought that was what woke him up.

With the force of a gale, a sudden desire to live possessed him. And with it came a fear of being seen by other people. He did not ask himself why he had this fear. He was afraid of all human beings. He therefore crouched down in the gutter, clinging to its brick walls, making no attempt to stand. Since the gutter was below the level of the road, only his head was visible.

Day had not broken yet. In the semi-darkness, the streetlights cast an orange glow on the empty street and the houses on either side that slept peacefully, wrapped in dreams. Govardhan noticed a stray dog on the edge of the street looking at him with kindness. A thin, brown, bony dog. When he looked back at it, it came closer, wagged its tail and growled as if asking him if he needed anything. He had a sudden desire to embrace the animal but could not raise his hands. They were no longer hands but sacks filled with pain. Govardhan sobbed uncontrollably.

When he had finished weeping, memories surfaced—of where he was, of what had happened to him, was going to happen. He had been a victim of one group of people until the day before and from now on, he was a prey to another group of hunters. The government authorities had assured all media persons and intellectuals that once he was rescued from his abductors, he would be properly tried for having escaped from jail and then hanged. His persecutors had dumped him in this street for everyone to see so that they could prove to the world that they had done whatever they had said they would do and to warn everyone to take their threats seriously. Now you can do whatever you want to do with this man. Govardhan is a common enemy to everyone. Crouched in a gutter with only a stray dog's kind eyes to rely on, Govardhan experienced a moment of enlightenment like the one Buddha had had when he sat under the bodhi tree.

He had no time to think. Using all the strength he had in his heavy hands and legs and in his teeth, he managed to tear off two strips from the edge of his clothes and wrap them over his hands as lepers do. It did not prove too difficult since the cloth was old. The dog, that was closely watching everything he did, came nearer. It bit into the edges of the cloth and pulled them over his head so that they covered the spots where his ears had been. It then moved his hair down to cover the branded mark on his forehead as well. Together they managed to hide all traces of the injustices that had been perpetrated on him. They looked at each other for a while with complete understanding. The dog then went away and after a while, Govardhan got up.

As he walked along the streets which were just beginning to be tinged by the morning light, his hands and ears covered and his eyes lowered, he realized that henceforth, on his journeys, he had to conceal not only his identity but also the traces of the injustices that had been meted out to him.

97

The grey-bearded traveller walked along the rocky, uneven road in the hot sun, his steady pace never varying. He wore a flowing, ankle-length tunic with a singularly huge turban and had a bag slung on his shoulder. A passer-by who overtook him called out: 'Hey, stranger, which country are you from?'

'I am a traveller, my friend,' said Ibn Battuta without slowing down.

'Which country do you come from, stranger?' the man repeated.

'Travellers have no country of their own and no country is foreign to them.'

'How would you introduce yourself?' asked the man, raising his voice and trying to catch up with the traveller, who had moved ahead.

Ibn Battuta laughed. 'People use the names of clans and the colours of the skin in order to identify themselves and others. They search for religions and dharmas. They reach out for languages, cultures, schools of philosophy. We define countries

392   Anand

through our journeys, my friend. Each country we arrive in becomes ours. And those we have not yet gone to are going to be ours as well!'

Ibn Battuta walked on without turning back. The man stood looking at him until he disappeared from sight.

98

The roar of the rain accompanied the camp doctor when he entered the bunker with surgical dressings. Ali Dost flew at him: 'Who asked you to come here? No one is allowed to come in here unless I send for them.'

The doctor, who was drenched, adjusted his glasses, saluted and made an about turn.

Controlling the annoyance which had, unusually for him, got the better of him, Ali called him back and said gently: 'This wound doesn't require a dressing. You can go.'

Ali was cross with himself for doing this. As a rule, he never changed orders that he had issued. Then why had he done so now?

He looked at the wound on the sixth finger of his left hand. It was still bleeding. A six-year-old boy had bitten the hand of the supreme commander of the Liberation Army—he had bitten his sixth finger. The more Ali thought about it, the more upset he felt. And that too was unusual.

He had been inspecting the children who had been recently

caught and brought to be inducted into the famous child brigade of the Liberation Army. Only children between eight and ten years were usually brought in but a six-year-old had been caught by mistake. The boy had suddenly sprung at Ali during the inspection and bitten his hand. It was the sixth finger that hung separate from Ali's palm that the boy's mouth had found. The small teeth had sunk in right up to the bone. The bodyguard's gun had flashed once and the child had fallen to the ground, dead. Ali had thought the other children would spring on him but that did not happen. They had stood dazed, pale with fear.

Ali had watched the blood drop from his finger onto the ground. He had not tried to stop it. His thoughts had wandered to another six-year-old who had walked alongside him long ago, clinging to that finger and slid down from it on the way. That child would no longer be able to cling to him for he lay somewhere now, in a gutter, with all his own fingers chopped off. And this new six-year-old who had tried to catch hold of it today lay on the ground, shot dead.

Ali came out of the bunker followed by the bodyguard.

It was raining heavily. The trees swayed from side to side in the gale. The ground was slippery and wet. But the camp functioned as if it was still day, unmindful of the rain and the late hour. Soldiers with assault rifles and flashlights patrolled the area. Radio sets hummed. The children had been taken away to undergo training. The shouts of the drill captains could be heard in the distance. And the abuses that were being showered upon those who collapsed and fell in the slush on the ground. The rule was that training should be started for the recruits within an hour of being brought to the camp, no matter what the time of day was or what condition they were in. The rule was especially strict where children were concerned.

Ali used to wonder sometimes why he had to live in hiding, in a bunker with a bodyguard, even though he was on liberated territory. The truth was that the supreme commander was not safe even in his house. His own men could be his enemies.

The decision to raise a child brigade had been a turning point in safety innovations. Its soldiers, stolen from their environment before they were old enough to think for themselves, given new names and moulded into new forms, had no history behind them, no relatives. They were solely the products of the training they underwent. Without parents to counsel them, friends to divert them from their path or children to claim their personal feelings or interests, these naked warriors who asked no questions and were as unsullied in their loyalty as the weapons they used came to be relied upon by the Liberation Army for their daredevil operations.

It was one from among this raw, uncluttered material of the child brigade that had dared to reach up and clutch Ali Dost's sixth finger, shattering all the safety barriers around him. The sixth finger that had always stayed outside his palm, a reminder of how far one owned one's actions. Ali Dost's entire life had been this sixth finger's attempt to enter the palm. He had used everything that came his way for it: the mutineers' guns, Malik Kafur's horse, Aurangzeb's sword, the Liberation Army's bombs. But during that attempt, he created many sixth fingers—a whole brigade of them.

The head of the bomb squad came to announce the departure of his men for the next operation. They had selected the most crowded train as their target. It was the time of the Mahamakam temple festival, so the rush was sure to be greater than usual. The bombs placed at four different spots in the train would explode simultaneously. The entire train would be shattered. The deaths would be countless.

Ali Dost did not reply. He watched as the man made an about turn and withdrew. He paced in front of his bunker a few times, then scraped the clay that had adhered to his boots on a piece of wood fixed to the door. He turned to his bodyguard and asked:

'Why did you shoot that child?'

There was a look of utter disbelief on the bodyguard's face. He was forbidden to speak on duty, so he was not sure whether to answer. Finally he said as if quoting from a textbook: 'Does not the movement teach that liberation is more important than the individual? Haven't you, our great leader, taught us that kindness is a revolutionary's worst enemy?'

'What does liberation mean?' countered Ali.

The bodyguard was at a loss for a reply.

'It doesn't matter,' said Ali. 'The boy bit my sixth finger. He believed in liberation.'

The guard was afraid he would be punished for having shot the boy. But the sudden danger signals that the radio set emitted saved him.

Anxiety spread over Ali Dost's face. He went into his bunker and waited for more news.

In a short while, the camp commander came and saluted him. He said that an unidentified army had surrounded the camp, cutting through the radar cover and breaking the intelligence ring of the Liberation Army. They were searching for weak points to enter the camp.

'Whose army can it be?' muttered Ali to himself.

The commander described what the guards had seen with their naked eyes. 'It's an old-fashioned army, mounted on horses with swords and spears as weapons.'

Ali frowned and a shadow spread over his face. Trying to

remain calm, he said: 'Yes, it's an army that our radar cannot detect or our intelligence assess. It is Alamgir Aurangzeb's army.'

'Why should Alamgir Aurangzeb come such a long way in such unpleasant weather in order to attack our liberated territory that neither he nor his army are familiar with?' asked the commander.

'There is no place the emperor is unfamiliar with, commander. Nor is there any war that is not his own,' said Ali, shaking his head. 'In one sense, he has participated in every war in every place. Kamran, the younger brother of his grandfather's grandfather, pioneered a campaign in order to wash away the muck that had crept into politics around the concepts of right and wrong and purify it by placing only two parameters before it: victory and defeat. His disciple, Aurangzeb, is therefore obliged to send his forces at all times in all directions in order to uphold Kamran's doctrine. No one who tries to establish a different principle in politics can afford to ignore the strength of Aurangzeb's empire. We should have expected the arrival of his army.'

The commander was taken aback for he had never seen Ali Dost sound so alarmed and anxious. However, his long experience of battle strategies came to his aid. He said: 'It was Alamgir Aurangzeb who invited you to his capital at the time when you were wandering aimlessly over deserted territory on Malik Kafur's horse, welcomed you at the gate of the lavishly decorated city like a hero and handed over the sword of faith to you—in order to execute his wayward brother, Shahzada Dara Shukoh and the blasphemer Baba Sarmad. Did not that small army of ours that set out with Malik Kafur's horse and Aurangzeb's sword, traverse hills and cities and rivers and pick up from every corner along the way arrows tipped with cultural glory and ethnic pride of every sort, religious kudos and political ideologies to fill its quivers, now so grown in size and strength that the very mention of its name send chills coursing down the listener's spine? Invincible leader, don't you think the emperor has come to you today with his army to offer you his felicitations?'

Ali unsheathed Auranzeb's sword which he still carried around with him proudly and kissed the fresh blood on it. Every time he drew it out of its sheath, fresh blood would spurt from it and he would kiss it with reverence. A purple flame illuminated his face.

Ali said to the commander: 'Aurangzeb gave me this sword in the same way that Humayun once placed a lancet in my hand. This sword is a weapon, but only a weapon. All the campaigns the emperor led were to firmly seal one principle. From the time man began to rule man this principle has been that only the powerful and the clever have the right to rule. Everything else was to the emperor simply a tool to capture power. He hated anyone who begged for power in the name of tradition and pride nurtured on decayed dead bodies, ideologies that took shape from rotting brains. The emperor has not come to felicitate us, commander, he has come to punish us.'

'Why should we worry then, invincible leader? Let the emperor come with his army. They carry swords and spears, while we have the most modern kalashnikovs. We can deal with them in a matter of minutes. All you need is to give the order.'

Ali placed his hand on the commander's shoulder. 'These kalashnikovs themselves are our undoing,' he said. 'When we confront the emperor's swords with our assault rifles, we acquiesce in his doctrine—the doctrine that weapons and force are the mainstay of power. We will be defeated whether we lose this war or win it. All the wars and revolutions we led in the name of beliefs, ideologies, traditions, cultures, nationalities or races, will, without exception, collapse. Or...'

Ali walked to the door of the tent, allowed himself to be drenched in the lashing rain and continued in a cold voice: 'Or, we have already surrendered to the emperor long ago! Because we proved the same doctrine over and over again when we placed bombs in trains, sending hundreds of people flocking to a temple festival to their death, when we created child brigades and dispatched them to the front, when we laid mines of fear all over the country by abducting the innocent and torturing them: the doctrine that our revolutions, our struggles for liberation were the same as Kamran's wars, competitions of strength in order to win power.

'The warrior Humayun was a hollow man. His claims to the right to rule were only meant for show. Like Kamran, he too fought only to win power. In this world, commander, all conflicts are between the strong and the strong. All the rest: ideologies, nationalities, cultural identities and so on are only cosmetic materials for external application... There is no use trying to hide what has already happened. Bring the white flag, commander. Declare a truce with Aurangzeb's army. The Ali Dost who pierced Kamran's eyes with needles now makes a treaty with him. And so Ali Dost comes full circle... There is only one doctrine in war—Kamran's. And only one king in the world—Aurangzeb.'

Ali Dost sent the commander to show Aurangzeb the white flag, walked up to the body of the boy lying face down in the slush and squatted down by it. The rain had washed away all the blood and he was clean and pure now. Silt was flowing down, gradually burying the body.

'Why did you bite my finger?' he asked. 'You bit yourself, actually. You are a sixth finger and can never enter the palm. The palm is power's own land.'

The rain lashed at Ali Dost and at the child's dead body.

99

Mariam was spreading the clothes she had washed to dry on the granite steps on the riverbank when Nunis arrived. He dismounted, drank a mouthful of water from the river and sat down on the steps. Since the sky was overcast with dark clouds, the steps had not yet become hot. The clear water of the river invited him to bathe, but he sat where he was.

Mariam gave Satyakama a bath, sent him up from the river and had a bath herself. She came out in wet clothes.

As he sat by the river watching her climb up the long row of steps, Nunis felt as though she was coming from some faraway place.

'I went round all the streets and the bazaars and did not see a single person. The roads are covered with rubble from the shattered temples and buildings,' he said as if describing the sights he had seen to a visitor. 'I think there are only the three of us now in the city.'

Mariam did not reply, nor did Nunis expect her to. The vacant eyes above the red beard wandered over the river searching for something. Which they found. Movement of some kind! In the city of Vijayanagara, the only thing that moved were the waters of the Tungabhadra!

The victorious army had been camping in the city of the vanquished that Vijayanagara had turned into over the last four or five months and he had watched them bring down the buildings one by one with pickaxes and crowbars. In the end, the army too went back. And meanwhile the inhabitants of the city had either been killed or had fled.

Nunis got up and began to walk with Mariam on one side of him and Satyakama on the other. The horse followed, its reins around his waist.

It was difficult to walk because the roads were completely blocked by debris. In the utter silence, they could hear the sound of their bare feet on the ground and the soft rustle of their clothes.

As they walked along, they came upon a huge pair of weighing scales that had for some reason not been destroyed. The chains carrying the weighing discs were suspended from a stone beam that was supported by two massive carved granite pillars. The empty discs crackled softly as they swung to and fro.

'I have seen the king and queen being weighed in this balance against precious gems and coins on auspicious days. The coins and items of food they used were distributed among the poor afterwards. Now only the wind weighs itself on one or other of the discs.'

The three human beings left in the city—a horse trader from a foreign country, the slave girl he had bought in a bazaar and the boy one of her masters had gifted her—stood looking at the balance curiously, as if they could see the wind swinging on it.

'This empty balance swinging in the wind transports me to a world that lies beyond weights or measures or calculations,' said Nunis. 'Perhaps its name is history. A whole city, vibrant and alive until yesterday, has turned into history, into a book.'

Mariam did not seem to have heard him. She was giving the balance her own interpretation. 'When a slave gets freedom for the first time, what will the state of her heart be, malik? When time begins to throb in it... like a balance that swings gently when a soft breeze blows, peering first into a moment from the past, then fearfully into the future...'

Nunis stretched out his hand to hold hers. But he could not touch her, she had drifted somewhere faraway from him.

'Mariam, where are you?' he asked, looking around anxiously.

'Malik... there's so much noise here. Cries and wails. Can you hear what I say? A country is being split in two before my eyes!' cried Mariam, raising her voice.

'Mariam!' Nunis raised his voice as well. 'A city has been razed to the ground here. Everyone except me has fled the city.'

'Everyone is leaving this country as well. No, not leaving, they are running away in fear, shouting, "Freedom! Freedom!" As if their country has become a wild animals' den. I see people rushing into masjids or hiding in mandirs or gurdwaras or churches. No one wants to stay in his own house... I don't know in which direction to look, malik—into the past or into the future. Is freedom like this, malik?'

'I think you are speaking from the future. And I from the past. Your question itself tells me that time has begun to throb within you. Come Mariam, come to me. Look, Satyakama has driven the wind away and sits on one of the discs of the weighing scales. Don't you want to see?'

Mariam came back to Nunis.

Nunis took her hand and walked up to the scales. Laughing, Satyakama invited them to sit on the other disc. Before Nunis could do so, Mariam ran up to it and it tipped down on her side. Satyakama got up at once and when Nunis climbed on to it, it tipped down on his side. The three of them played like this, swinging in the discs one after another. Their laughter and movements reverberated through the dead stones in the city. The clouds gathered in the dark sky began to roar and the first rain of the summer crashed down. Their hot, perspiring bodies thrilled to it. The burning blocks of granite hissed as the rain swished on them. The scent of fresh earth rose from the ground.

Nunis, Mariam and Satyakama continued their journey happily, dancing as they wove their way over the paths that fleeing horses had galloped along, between the palaces that had become heaps of rubble, the huge sheds emptied of elephants, the royal mints that were now broken walls, the displaced sati stones...

Mariam asked suddenly: 'What lies in the gap between history and freedom, malik?'

'I do not know,' said Nunis. 'I am just a rustic horse trader, what knowledge do I have?'

'I think I know.'

'What is it, Mariam, what is in the gap?'

'A horse trader!'

They laughed.

Mariam went on: 'I passed through many bazaars. Men bought me to offer as a sacrifice, to yoke me to their bullocks, to satiate their lust. Why did you buy me?'

'Perhaps it was destined,' said Nunis thoughtfully. 'Perhaps it was necessary for a horse trader to meet a slave girl in that gap between history and freedom. But it was an unimportant deal. I who lived among the rates prevailing in the market from day to day. And you a slave sold from the past into the future, from the future into the past...' Nunis's face darkened. He continued in a firm voice: 'The mission is over today. We are nearly at the gates of the city. I have to revert to history. And you have to go forward into freedom. It is time...'

Nunis released Mariam's and Satyakama's hands from his own and took the horse's reins. His pace slowed down. Unable to keep up with them, he fell behind. The curtain of rain between them grew thicker.

'Where is uncle, amma?' asked Satyakama apprehensively, tugging the edge of Mariam's skirt.

'His horse has run as far as it could, son,' said Mariam, without turning back. 'It must have collapsed somewhere behind us.'

'Let's go and get him.'

'No, son, the past is behind us. And we are walking towards the future.'

'What is the future, amma?' asked Satyakama with great curiosity.

'You have to find out the answer to that question, Satyakama. I do not have it. My eyes are still filled with the smoke from burning houses. My feet keep slipping in the stagnant pools of blood on the ground, in the slime left by violations.'

Mariam was slipping and losing her foothold. But Satyakama's little feet were firm and steady.

'Amma, who is my father?' asked Satyakama suddenly.

'Why do you want to know that? Even your mother does not know who it is, son. Your mother was a slave. While working with many different masters, I had you. May you be known only by my name—Mariam Satyakama.'

Mariam slipped again and Satyakama helped her up.

'Is not Mariam's son the son of God, amma?' he asked.

'No, Mariam's son is the son of man. You are a man's son.'

Mariam kept slipping and falling down and Satyakama did not notice when her fingers detached themselves from his. He walked on.

Mariam trudged along, watching the curtain of rain blur the outline of Satyakama's figure as he walked farther away from her. Through the rain she saw Truth appear before him as a cross. Saw him shouldering it and stumbling beneath its weight. And being crucified on it. Then rising, resurrected. Then being crucified again, and again...

100

Mannu was not actually searching for Michael's body. Bodies, or the mangled pieces of flesh that could be extricated from the coaches of the shattered train lay all over the ground. People were still trying to piece them together. She did not look at the bodies either. She did not feel that any of them, even Michael's, were different from one another. He had told her when going to work that all the passengers in his train together made up his private life.

The torn and twisted masses of metal which the train had become and the burnt, pulverized bodies of the passengers who had been in it were welded together in such a way that they could not be distinguished from each other. Mannu felt it was unnecessary to separate the flesh, even if it were Michael's, from the metal. Therefore, she simply walked through it all.

'It was a rare occasion, when Mahamakam and Brahmotsavam coincided. There were passengers huddled even on the roof of the train,' people said as they stood around, talking.

'There were four bombs placed in four different spots and they all exploded simultaneously.'

'It was Ali Dost's frightful gang!'

'What did they want? To commit so heinous a crime…'

'Madam,' a railway worker came up to Mannu. 'Michael sahib's…'

Mannu avoided that conversation as well and walked on.

The train and the clamour around it gradually fell behind her.

She walked along the ridges separating the fields where farmers were working and along the sides of ponds where children were washing the buffaloes. She drank water from a river.

A wedding procession accompanied by nadaswara passed her on the village path. And a kavadi procession in the town, with devotees singing and dancing wildly to music. Exhausted at last, she lay down under a banyan tree and fell asleep.

When she woke up, she saw the face of a man who was holding her on his lap and gently stroking her head. The tenderness in his eyes and the smile beneath the grey beard made her eyes moist.

'Your hair is matted with dust and sweat, child,' said the stranger. 'Your face is sunburnt and the soles of your feet cracked. Have you walked a long way?'

Mannu pressed her face into his lap and, for the first time after all that had happened, she wept. He allowed her to weep, not attempting to console her.

He told her then why he had left the kavadi procession and come to her. While dancing and singing in the procession, his eyes had fallen on her. He had realized at once from her expression that something was keeping her sorrow from pouring out. He had felt that it was as necessary for her to weep as it was for him to dance and be happy.

When she had wept enough and the iron gates within her had melted and opened, she told him her story.

'Come, child, let us walk a little bit,' he said.

Mannu did not object.

She saw that all the roads in the city were decorated with bright festoons and banana clusters. Men, women and children dressed in new clothes were everywhere. It was a festival and they were all enjoying themselves.

In a little while they met the kavadi procession they had seen earlier again. A number of new kavadis had joined it— flower kavadis, peacock-feather kavadis, many-layered kavadis. The dancers whirled faster and faster, then slowed down gradually, keeping pace with the rising and falling rhythms of the accompanying drums. Spectators joined in, waving clusters of peacock feathers. The procession made its way to the temple on top of the hill. Mannu and her companion followed along the winding road. At some moment, he began to dance and soon Mannu joined in as well.

The kavadis were lowered to the ground at the top of the hill and the drums stopped playing. The dancers collapsed, exhausted. The image of the deity they had carried was taken into the temple. All grew quiet and soon only Mannu and her companion were left on the hilltop.

'Who have you come in search of all this way, child?' asked the stranger.

'Michael used to say to me that even God changes and grows, that he makes his content larger with the newer and newer lives he takes into himself every day. But my world is so small, baba. So very, very small. I have only one person to search for in it. A solitary person who will no longer grow or change.'

Her voice faltered. Leaning against his shoulder, she sobbed.

'Did you observe the kavadi procession we saw?' he asked. 'At every crossroad, new kavadis joined it. Anyone passing that way could join it and dance. By the time it reached the top of the hill, it had grown as big as the world. The people of this place call it the festival of God. But it is their festival as well. Who is God after all but the devotees who flock to see Him? What Michael told you was so true, child. Just as he used to usher more and more people into the train at every station, you have met so many people who love you. When you take them into you, you too will grow bigger. You must not grow small, Mannu. Those who loved you are greater than those who harmed you. Do not go behind those who make the world smaller. Go with those who make it larger. Make the estate of God that is within you larger...'

'Baba, when they placed me on a burning pyre, when they struck me with swords in the Bibighar, when they ravished my body in the bullock cart, I endured it. But this shattered train has flung me so far into space, I feel that God himself has been blown up. I still have not fallen back to earth!'

'How sad it is that there is no earth to accept this child!' He laughed, then added seriously: 'Mannu, how could you forget your uncle? He has been wandering over this earth for so long, asking questions of all who come before him.'

'Yes, there were always hunters behind him. They ran behind my uncle, who had never done anyone wrong, with nooses, scissors, knives, guns, bombs...'

'And yet Govardhan kept asking questions. Even after his ears were cut off and all his fingers chopped off... It is true that no one answered them, but they all came out onto the road and began to ask questions just like he did. A procession of people asking questions... Come, child, let us go.'

'Where to, baba?'

'I did not say I knew where.'

Mannu laughed.

They went down the hill. The temple on the hill slept by the light of the few lamps that guarded it. But the town that rose before their eyes throbbed with life. People thronged the roads. Music floated out of the houses. The air was fragrant with the scent of jasmine flowers. Lights, glittering fireworks...

101

'Chitragupta!' Yama called out to his friend and accountant. 'Dharmaraja!' answered Chitragupta.

Yama did not go on. And Chitragupta was silent as well, as if he had not expected his master and friend to say anything more.

The two friends had been seated together like this for quite some time, gazing down from the garden of Samyamani on top of the hill at the flat expanse of land below. Meanwhile, the first phase of the night slid into the second one.

Both friends were exhausted. But sleep eluded them. That morning, their henchmen had brought in a load of passengers packed like potatoes in a train that militants who claimed to be freedom fighters had blasted. They had been extremely busy going through the victims' histories and trying to decide whether to send them to heaven or to hell.

'Chitragupta!' called Yama again.

'My lord,' ventured Chitragupta, 'what is it that is worrying you?'

'Do I have to put that into words, Chitragupta? Is there

anything on my mind that you do not know about?'

Chitragupta got up, walked up to Yama, clasped his hands and said: 'We tried one thousand three hundred and thirty five human beings yesterday. They were all victims of ruthless violence. When will those who condemned them to such a cruel death be brought to us for trial—isn't this the question that troubles you?'

Yama looked at Chitragupta, his face full of pain.

Chitragupta went on: 'It is always the victims who come to us first and so we have to try them earlier. Is that not the inevitable order of things? The hunters will come eventually and we will try them as well when they arrive. What difference will it make to the ultimate dispensation of justice?'

'It does make a difference,' said Yama. 'Just as you know all about the problem that makes me anxious, do not I too know what you conceal in your mind? Tell me, friend, does it not make a difference?'

Chitragupta was silent.

'Chitragupta,' continued Yama, 'justice not only demands that we conduct trials but that we do so at the correct time as well. If we cannot do so, the unjust nature of justice will continue to prevail and be sustained.'

A strong wind began to blow from the valley. It reached out into every corner and crevice of Samyamani. The anguish and restlessness that it held within it did not fail to affect them.

'Chitragupta,' Yama went on, 'all the accusations that people have been spreading about Samyamani have been proved true. Samyamani is stricken with disease. Its functionaries are cruel, its judges heartless pen-pushers...'

'Enough, my friend,' said Chitragupta, 'Enough!'

'Who knocks at the door of Samyamani?' asked Yama, turning

towards the sound at the door. Concentrating his divine power of vision on the spot, he said: 'It seems to be a little boy.'

Chitragupta could see the boy knocking at the door as well. Rapidly going over the account books, he concluded that it was not yet time for this boy to be here. No messenger had been sent to fetch him. He had come on his own.

'Who is this boy?' asked Yama.

'He is Nachiketas. A little boy who has come to us on his own.'

'Bring him in.'

'That is not possible, my lord. It is not yet time for him to enter our city. We will have to go to him.'

'What does he want?'

'Come, let's find out.'

Yama moved towards the gate of Samyamani with Chitragupta following him.

Standing on the steps near the gate, a little boy whose large eyes were filled with impatience greeted them respectfully.

'I am Nachiketas,' he said with great humility, 'the only son of Moinuddin, known as Acharya Uddalaka, and Salma, known as Mata Savitri.'

'Why have you come here?' asked Chitragupta, his tone full of annoyance. 'And that too, at this unearthly hour? I did not send anyone to fetch you.'

The boy did not answer. With the curiosity of a child, he gazed at the crumbling walls of Samyamani with peepul trees sprouting out of the deep cracks in them, at the rotting doors which had been so badly eaten by termites that anyone could push them open and at the watchman who was dozing, dead drunk, next to it.

'Why has your city decayed so badly, uncle?' the boy countered with a question of his own. 'Every wall, every gate, every watchman, is a symbol of decay. I have heard that death follows decay. Is that why your city has the face of decay, Uncle?'

'Be careful of what you say,' Chitragupta warned the boy angrily. 'This is a city of justice, not of death as the scandal mongers say.'

'Then what am I doing here? I am a child. What offence can a child be charged with?'

Yama touched Chitragupta's hand and he fell silent. Yama said gently to the boy: 'Child, we did not bring you here. You came of your own accord.'

The boy smiled. 'Who walks to death of his own accord, Uncle? Either you bring a person here or he is pushed here by someone. As for me, I have come with questions that my father said only you can answer—you, Dharmaraja. Tell me, uncle, what form of justice is it that pushes countless children like me into the city of suffering and death while they are still young and incapable of committing sin? Why are we made the targets of vicious machinations? Why are we used as weapons to target others? Uncles who are so just, look into your books. What sins have we committed? The sin of having been born?'

'Child, whether you were brought here or sent here or came on your own, you stand now at the door of Samyamani. Our books do not record anything against you. Therefore, do not step in here. But since you have come here anyway, forget the world below. We will send you straight to heaven. To a heaven where the palaces are made of gold and filled with dancers who have music on their lips. We will arrange for chariots and horses to take you there.'

Exasperated by the temptations held out to him, Nachiketas said angrily: 'Keep your chariots and horses, your dancers and their music, for yourself. Just tell me, for what fault are we innocent ones pushed into the city of death and denied life?'

'*Nachiketo maranam manuprakshi*.[23] Death is a phenomenon that even the gods have not been able to understand.'

'Uncle, I know what death is, even if you do not. I do not want to know what death is but what the nature is of the justice that drags the innocent into it.'

'Child, knowledge cannot be earned by argument, it has to be handed out by a great teacher. It is because they do not understand this that the wise in their arrogance and fools in their ignorance grope blindly in the darkness that is the world.'

'I am neither a fool nor a learned man. I am just a child. I seek the truth from you, who are a great teacher.'

'Then know, child, that the soul does not die nor is it born. It does not take shape from anything, nor does it give anything shape. If the slayer thinks that he slays or the slain that he is slain, they think so because they are ignorant.'

The boy was visibly bored by Yama's answers. Irritated, he said: 'Dharmaraja, I did not ask you about my soul. I asked about life in the world. About streams of blood, the cries and screams that rise along the roads, about knives and guns…'

Yama went on with his diatribe, paying no attention to Nachiketas: 'The wise say, child, that you cannot understand the body without understanding the soul. If the body is the chariot, it is the soul that is the charioteer.'

The boy sat down on the ground. 'Who is driving my chariot towards death then, uncle? My own soul?' he asked tearfully.

'The essences lead the soul and the mind directs the essences. Intelligence directs the mind and the soul directs intelligence. Beyond the soul…'

---

[23] Nachiketas, you must not ask me about death.

'Uncle, uncle…' Nachiketas's voice grew fainter.

'The soul is indefinable, child, and beyond understanding. To know it…'

'Uncle,' the boy's eyes began to close.

'Son, *kshurasya dhara nisita duratyaya durgam pathastatkavayo vadanti. Uthishtata, jagrata, prapyavarnnibodhata…*'[24]

The boy was fast asleep.

Yama sat next to him, leaning against the frame of the gate. His eyes were full of tears. The muscles of his face had sagged and his skin had become wrinkled. Chitragupta supported his friend. Under the grey sky, the night grew older, slumbering on the shoulder of the tired earth.

'What age are we in now?' asked Yama, his voice sounding as if it came from a distance.

'What kind of question is that, my lord?'

'You are right, Chitragupta. For many years now, I have only asked what time it is. Today, when I put this child to sleep, unable to answer his question… I don't know why, I thought of our childhood. Of how far we have moved from the children that you and I were, my friend.'

'We were annoyed with our forefathers because they merely chronicled events in time without recording their nature. And now, not only the nature of events but time itself has vanished from our scrolls. We are watching events acquiring a timeless nature right before us.'

'Time takes shape and moves in justice. Injustice is beyond time, after all.'

'We argued that time acquires meaning because of events.

---

[24] Sharp as a razor's edge, hard to cross and difficult is the path, so the sages say. Arise, awake, get the best teachers and learn from them.

But when events themselves lose their meaning, what can we do? When the dispensation of justice slips out of our control, when injustice becomes law, when innocents are punished in place of the guilty...' Chitragupta stopped and began to stroke the sleeping boy's head.

'Time itself becomes meaningless,' Yama completed Chitragupta's sentence. 'It then becomes possible to lift an event from anywhere and place it somewhere else. And to pick up a human being from any spot and place him elsewhere. He will begin to walk again... in this world from which time withdraws, Chitragupta, it is Yama who grows old! Yama is about to die. This boy came to ask the god of death, who himself faces death, questions about death. That is why I could not say anything to him. May he forgive me...'

Leaving behind Nachiketas and Chitragupta, who sat with his eyes closed, caressing the boy's hair, Yama walked slowly back to Samyamani.

102

Another group of people went past Satyakama. He moved to the edge of the road to observe them. They were the same kind of people he had seen—ranging from the very old who walked leaning on sticks to babies straddled on their mothers' hips. Sick and healthy. Poor and rich. With boxes on their heads, bundles on their backs, bags on their shoulders. Some clutched boxes containing valuables close to them, others struggled with unwieldy charpoys, mattresses that had been rolled up, mats and hurricane lamps. Fowls perched in baskets while cats and dogs trailed behind.

When the group had gone past, Satyakama walked on. Yet another group came along before he reached the crossroads. This one came from behind him and went in the opposite direction.

He stopped at the crossroads, waiting for more to turn up. And he was not disappointed. Groups of people came pouring in through the four roads that converged like the spokes of a wheel at the roundabout. Each group picked one of the four roads and disappeared down it.

Satyakama saw that the city was almost empty. There was no traffic and the clamour had ceased. The jets of water spraying from a fountain at the centre of the roundabout grew thinner and slower as the pressure of the water decreased and finally stopped altogether.

The dead bodies of human beings and horses and the upturned vehicles that lay scattered over the road made the journey difficult. The young boy was fed up of seeing houses where the doors lay wide open, windows with no lights in them, chimneys with no smoke.

He went past not one but four cities like this.

And then he came to a riverbank where a man was seated under a banyan tree with his eyes closed in meditation. He was emaciated—no doubt because of continued starvation—and insects, birds and animals moved freely around him. Plants had sprouted so close to him that they brushed against him. Tired of having seen only people who were in flight, the boy was astonished and fascinated by this man who seemed to have sprouted from that spot and was now one among the living creatures surrounding him.

The man who had seemed to be deep in meditation opened his eyes when Satyakama went up to him. Two eyes whose brightness did not match the emaciated body darted towards Satyakama.

Satyakama greeted him respectfully and said: 'Bhagavan, I am charged with the mission of taking away your four hundred weak and skinny cows and bringing back a thousand sleek, fat ones. But all along my way, I saw only violence, killings, people in flight. The yadavas who are supposed to raise cows are fighting among themselves and destroying one another.'

'Young man, I am not the Gautama Haridrumata you seek,'

the man answered, his tone infinitely kind. 'I am Gautama Siddhartha. A mere seeker of truth, like Mariam Satyakama.'

'Whoever you may be, bhagavan, I accept you as my guru.'

'How can one seeker of truth become the guru of another seeker of truth, child?'

'All along the way I came, I saw only people fleeing, abandoning their cities, their houses, their own families. They were seeking refuge in temples, mosques, gurdwaras and churches. Some were even going back to the caves where their ancestors used to live. Some, instead of using their languages to communicate were making prisons of them instead, to shut themselves in. While everyone was running away trying to find somewhere to hide, I came upon you, seated in the company of not only human beings but also animals, birds and plants, refusing all refuge, utterly at peace with yourself. Each of us may or may not find the truth. But one seeker of truth is different from another, guru.'

Gautama Siddhartha smiled. 'That is why you are Satyakama and I am Siddhartha,' he said. 'Let me be only Siddhartha to you and you only Satyakama to me. I too arrived here after travelling a long way like you, Satyakama. Let us talk about the paths we travelled.'

Satyakama sat down beside Siddhartha on the carpet of leaves that had fallen from the banyan tree. 'Tell me, Siddhartha,' he said, 'is freedom this state of peace and calm that you have achieved or is it what the people I saw in flight were seeking?'

'You saw four cities, Satyakama, and people being pulled in four different directions at the crossroads of all four. Did you see happiness and satisfaction on their faces?'

'No, their faces were terror-stricken.'

'Each of the four cities you saw is one of the four parts of human existence. Human beings live in four cities: those of their beliefs, their customs, their clans and their languages. The inhabitants of each city fear and detest their neighbours. So each of the people you saw running away was fleeing his neighbour. Each thought freedom lay in being freed from his neighbour. But is that freedom?'

'That is not freedom, Siddhartha.'

'I will tell you now about the city I saw. Leaving the pleasures of my palace one day, I walked through the streets of my city. And I saw there four other states of human existence: disease, old age, injustice and death. If the people you saw were the slaves of fear, those that I saw were victims of suffering. I set out on my journey seeking a way to free them from their suffering.'

'And what was the truth you found, Siddhartha?'

'The first was that there is sorrow in the world; second that there is always a cause for sorrow; third that it is possible to liberate oneself from sorrow; and finally that the way of liberation is nirvana. But Satyakama, I will not counsel you to take the path of nirvana.'

'Why, Siddhartha?'

'When I awoke from meditation this morning and looked at your face, I lost my faith in nirvana. When I heard you talk of the people you saw fleeing, I realized that the path of nirvana would only be another flight like that. To free oneself from one's neighbours, from one's body—that is not liberation. The freedom we seek should be from fear and sorrow. And that cannot be achieved by abandoning one's neighbours or one's body. On the other hand, we should realize freedom within ourselves and in our neighbours... We have no alternative but to carry the four-armed cross of our existence, to be nailed to its four arms. We must lie upon it and suffer... Come, Satyakama, let us continue our journey. Let us go back to our cities and make them inhabited places again.'

They rose and Siddhartha said to Satyakama, who seemed hesitant to proceed: 'Go first, Satyakama. I started this journey before you, so my legs may give way. And you have much farther to go than I have.'

103

When the first rains were over and the soil became cohesive again, the children began to shape figures with it and play with them. They sat in the vast fields under a sky filled with dark clouds and kneaded the earth, enjoying the cool breeze blowing over them. Ramchander noticed that most of the shapes they made were cones with circular bases. They first made cylindrical shapes with the soil, then slanted the cylinders and rolled them on the ground until one end grew pointed. They made clusters of cones like this, big and small, and piled them up at different spots. Although they were not meant for worship, he realized that they were part of some ritual. One of the surprising things Ramchander had noticed about this human habitation was that people there did not worship anything. They only observed rituals.

The cones the children had fashioned reminded Ramchander of the drawings of the ellipses he had seen in an old book that the elders of the community had shown him. They did not know how to read the book. Turned into nomads because of their endless flights, they must have lost their language somewhere along the way. They now cultivated the land, lived in their houses, raised animals and wove their clothes, but they had no idea whether the language they spoke was the one in the book. And yet, they had carried the book, the script and perhaps even the language of which they had lost, everywhere they went.

This habitation, a small and fertile oasis that Ramchander had come upon in the middle of a vast expanse of arid land, had amazed him in many ways. No one in the community could tell him in what state they had been when they fled from their original home or where it had been or what kind of life they had led there. While talking to these people who had forgotten their own history, Ramchander felt that his own memory was fading and that he had forgotten how he had reached this place. He asked himself what whim of destiny had brought him to these people. Into a community that had drawn amnesia close around it like some disease and created gaps between cause and effect at every stage.

Drawing out a thread from his clothes, Ramchander used it to cut through at an angle one of the cones the children had fashioned. When they saw the elliptical figure he had made, the elders rushed in excitedly and brought out their book. But the initial enthusiasm they had experienced soon vanished from their faces. Looking in turn at the ellipses in the book, then at the one made by cutting through the cone, they fell silent and grew sad. Their eyes vacant, they searched for the relationship between the drawings in the book and the rituals they observed. Failing to find it despite repeated attempts, they closed the book, got up and quietly went their ways. Ramchander was left alone. Gradually, it began to rain and the cones the children had made became wet and dissolved once again into earth.

Long, long ago, when Apollonius of Perga cut through a cone as Ramchander had done now and constructed an ellipse, the people of Greece had seen it only as a funny, crooked form that would serve no special purpose. Indeed, some had even derided it, considering it a mockery, a distortion of and a deviation from what was then thought of as the perfect form, the circle. Two thousand years later, a scientist had discovered that it was the shape of the orbital path the planets take around the sun. Kepler himself had thought earlier that the orbital paths of the planets were perfect circles. It must have been an intensely painful experience therefore for Kepler, who had seen geometry in everything and worshipped geometry as God, to have to stretch his dream of perfection in order to make a compromise with reality.

Before Apollonius drew one, the planets had drawn ellipses around the sun billions and billions of times. But analytical geometry, which helped create the equation for drawing an ellipse, was a mathematical device that the mind of Descartes gave form to. To the question of whether analytical geometry existed before Descartes invented it, the answer might perhaps have to be no. For it was not a truth, but rather an experience attained by a seeker after truth.

Ramchander felt that the human mind constantly journeyed over innumerable helixes in the universe like truth, perfection, reality and dream. Even as man's dreams assiduously gathered materials to bridge gaps, the languages lost to memory opened up cracks that gaped before him.

One of the languages humankind had lost in the course of its long journey was that of justice, the longing for which had actually triggered off the process known as civilization. It was the language of justice that had given meaning to the voices of civilization. But civilization had forgotten its language. It had needed an illiterate villager to tell Ramchander this.

The rain poured down on that small habitation surrounded on all four sides by arid land. Thunder roared, lightning flashed, a gale tore over it. The rain dissolved countless things and returned them to the earth and also spurred awake many things within the earth.

104

Standing at the crossroads with a lighted torch held aloft in his hand, Kabir sang:

Kabira khada bazaar mein
Liye luathi hath
Jo ghar phuke apna
Chale hamare sath[25]

No one paid him any attention. People came from the bazaar up to the crossroads, took different paths and went their ways. It was beginning to grow dark, the clamour of the bazaar was dying down and shopkeepers were preparing to go home.

Kabir's eyes were moist and glistening, his voice full of

---

[25] Kabir stands at the crossroads of life
With a torch of love in his hand
Oh brother! If you want to follow me
You must set your house on fire.

eagerness. His hair flew in the wind. He turned like a madman to every man and woman, young and old, exhorting them:

Jo ghar phuke apna
Chale hamare sath

No one wanted to go with him. The torch in his hand began to burn out. As its flame descended, Kabir himself caught fire and became a torch. He stood at the crossroads, burning.

105

The faint coolness of autumn that hung in the evening air brought a little comfort to Govardhan. He was completely worn out. He sat down on the ledge of the culvert on the roadside to rest his legs.

The shadows of the trees on the roadside had grown longer than the trees themselves. Darkness had fallen over the paddy fields. All that could be seen of the village that lay at the end of the road beyond the fields was a cluster of trees and the tips of a few houses that showed through the foliage.

It was not often that he arrived in a village in the evening. Whether he reached one or not, night would fall. And since the night always arrived, Govardhan would somehow go through it. He therefore sat idly on the ledge, allowing his legs to recoup and watching the sun go down, not overly anxious about the proximity of a village.

He ran the palm that had no fingers over the surface of the ledge. The plaster had cracked in places. At one spot it had completely crumbled and a plant with a few leaves had grown in the crevice. He fondled the plant with his palm as well. While doing so, he noticed a column of ants moving along the path he had traversed. He lifted his feet so as not to obstruct them.

A father passed by him followed by his child. There was a faint clatter from the bag that hung from his shoulder, probably from the tools he carried. Neither of them talked to Govardhan, nor did they glance at him. Govardhan's eyes followed them until they disappeared from sight.

Govardhan felt an emptiness within him when they were lost to view. Why had they not noticed him? Why had he not been able to talk to them?

A loudspeaker from the village began to blare out a song. A film song. Although distance muted its sound considerably, he could still hear it clearly in the stillness of the evening. It was probably from a wedding reception or a birthday celebration being held in some house. A yard covered with a carpet, decorated with banana leaves and festooned with coloured streamers. Lights everywhere. Guests trooping in. The hosts greeting them with smiles and leading them to seats. Bearers moving around with drinks and snacks... The sense of family warmth, of the affection of relatives and friends that the faint melody wafting from a distance had carried him into now became a lump that choked his throat. He experienced an infinite longing to go and participate in the reception, to be in the company of human beings. But he did not get up. Sitting there without moving, not even bothering to wipe away the tears in his eyes, he listened to the song.

The colour of the earth on the road had darkened. But he could still see the column of ants that had been walking tirelessly along it all this time, that continued to go on tirelessly. He wondered whether, attached to the surface of the road as they were, walking steadily all day and all night, they were any less lonely, any more secure, than he was.

'Shall I come with you?' he asked the ants. 'We can walk along talking to one another.'

The ants said: 'If you join our column, you may not reach a village at night.'

'That does not matter. Some night, I am sure to reach some village or other!' he said.

'But there may not be a reception there that day.'

'That doesn't matter either.'

So they walked along together.

On the way, the ants said: 'Govardhan, this thing you call speed is a strange phenomenon and treacherous too, when you come to think of it. It makes distance quarrel with time, turns what is going to happen and what has already happened upside down. See now, you must have noticed as you began to walk with us that many of the paths you have already traversed are those you will have to traverse again.'

'That too does not matter,' said Govardhan. 'I can also see it the other way: that many of the paths I have to traverse are those I have already walked over.'

epilogue

The truth is that, in the end, there is no end. I do not stop this narration at this point because it is over. For even if I stop, Govardhan's travels are not going to end here.

I have never concluded any novel in the belief that the story ended at that point. All I have realized is that the writer has to withdraw at a certain stage. At the stage when he is sure that the reader can take over the work and carry it farther. And when he feels it is right for the will of the reader to operate from that point.

Actually, no literary work is a compact solid body. Nor is reading a slavish action imposed on the reader by an autocratic writer. A finished work is a collection of many pieces of work. And reading is a flexible activity that is free to take off from the work at any point and slip into something else. A work that is good is one which inspires the reader to do this. And a good reader is one who is able to take off and slip away in this manner.

There is a reason for me to say this, one that is especially relevant to this work. It is not my aim to immortalize injustice and cruelty. Nor did the original author of this work do that. However, he cut through the knotty problem in an ingenious way. And when he later chose another path, our protagonist, the traveller on this journey, in his role as a character, was left stranded as a man sentenced to eternal punishment. But did he too not change as a character in the course of his long travels? I find I lack the courage to look at the Govardhan who stands in the hundred and fifth chapter as a mere character. And where am I? Both the original author of this story and this humble follower of his have been left far behind. You may not even find it possible to hear our voices now!

An engine driver appears at a certain point in this narrative. A new group of passengers joins him on every trip he makes. At each station, a part of that group is replaced. He fills the spaces in his private life with the presence of these groups of people who are being constantly renewed. Every time he comes back from duty, he realizes that another area of his privacy has ceased to be private. The point here is not whether this is a loss or a gain (his own view is that it is a gain), but that it happens. That we are constantly shared.

As a work progresses, areas of a writer's privacy cease to be private. And so it goes on until, at a certain stage, an intimacy is established between the writer and the reader. They have to leave each other at that point.

As far as Govardhan's travels are concerned, we have perhaps reached that point.

———— • ————

Characters from the Puranas, from history and from other creative works who appear in this novel (though not necessarily in the same form or role)

Bharatendu Harischandra (1850–85): known as the father of modern Hindi literature and author of a large number of works including plays, poems and essays.

Govardhan: a character in a play by Bharatendu Harishchandra entitled *Andher Nagari Choupat Raja*

Choupat Raja: another character in the above-mentioned play.

Ramchander: Ramchander Mathur (1821–?), mathematician, researcher and journalist. A prominent member of the famous group of intellectuals in Delhi that included Mirza Ghalib and Syed Ahmad Khan.

Mahant: a character in the play *Andher Nagari Choupat Raja*.

Ali Dost: the soldier who was commissioned to blind Kamran, brother of Mughal Emperor Humayun.

Ibn Battuta (1304–69): the world famous traveller from Morocco who visited India during the reign of Muhammad Bin Tughluq.

Chitragupta: Yama's minister and friend, the keeper of the accounts of the sins and virtues of human beings.

Yama: known as Dharmaraja, the son of Surya. He tries the souls of human beings, assesses the merit of their deeds and assigns them to heaven or hell.

Dandi: Surya's assistant, described as the one who is seated beside Surya in his chariot carrying a pen and an ink bottle.

Kamran: younger brother of Mughal Emperor Humayun. He fought against Humayun who defeated and blinded him.

Humayun (1507–56): the second Mughal emperor, the son of Babar.

Mirza Ghalib (1797–1869): well-known Urdu and Persian poet.

Mirza Mohammad Ruswa (1857–1931): famous Urdu writer who lived in Lucknow and Hyderabad, author of the novel *Umrao Jan Ada*. He also wrote penny dreadfuls for sustenance.

Umrao Jan: a dancing girl who lived in the mid-nineteenth century in Lucknow. Ruswa's novel was based on her life.

Moinuddin: a controversial personality, the kotwal of Paharganj Thana, Delhi, at the time of the great Mutiny. He was instrumental in saving several innocent lives on both sides during the mutiny. He finally joined the mutineers. He was believed to have escaped to Arabia after the British suppressed the mutiny and launched the great hunt for all those who had sided with the mutineers.

Rani Kamla Devi: the queen of King Karnadeva of Gujarat.

Sultan Alauddin Khilji (?–1316): defeated Karnadeva in war and made Kamla Devi his favourite and principal queen.

Malik Kafur (?–1316) Alauddin's trusted eunuch and slave, later his commander and wazir. He took over as the sultan after Alauddin's death but was soon killed.

Amir Khusrau (1253–1325): Persian poet and musician who was court poet at the courts of Balban, Kaiqubad, Jalaluddin, Alauddin, Mubarak Shah and Ghiyasuddin Tughluq.

Sankaracharya: the great Hindu philosopher who lived in the eighth century, the exponent of Advaita Vedanta. The story goes that Lord Shiva appeared before him as a pariah in order to remove the caste prejudices that were rooted in his mind in spite of being a great scholar.

Kalidasa: famous Sanskrit poet who is believed to have lived in the third century.

Aurangzeb (1618–1707): the sixth Mughal emperor, who ascended the throne after imprisoning his father and killing his brothers.

Dara Shukoh (?–1659): Shah Jahan's eldest son. He was friendly with Sufis and with preachers of other religions and popular among the common people. He was beheaded by Aurangzeb.

Sarmad (1590–1657): a Sufi poet who walked naked. He was beheaded by Aurangzeb.

Nunis: a Portuguese trader who visited Vijayanagara during the reign of Krishna Deva Raya (?–1530). He wrote elaborate accounts of his experiences in India in his diaries which became the main source of information for this period.

Nachiketas: a Brahmin boy who appears in the *Kathopanishad,* famous for the searching questions he asked Yama about death and kindred subjects.

Galileo (1564–1642): astronomer-scientist who was arrested by the inquisitors in 1633. Threatened with the death penalty, he surrendered and recanted.

Katherine (1548–1621): Kepler's mother. The inquisitors arrested her at the age of seventy-three on a charge of witchcraft and tortured her. Kepler fought courageously with the authorities for six years and finally got her released.

Kepler (1571–1630): astronomer-scientist who stands between Copernicus and Galileo in the history of Western astronomy.

Shah Jahan (1592–1666): the fifth Mughal emperor. He was imprisoned by his son Aurangzeb and he died in prison.

Tyagaraja (1767–1847): great musician and composer in the tradition of Karnatic music, author of innumerable kirtanas and ragas. He lived in Tiruvaiyur near Tanjavur. It was during his time that Hyder Ali attacked and ransacked Tanjavur and destroyed its famous irrigation systems, bringing on a famine of unprecedented severity and many deaths.

Satyakama: the son of Jabala, a housemaid in the *Chandogya Upanishad*. He approached the guru Haridrumata to acquire learning.

Gautama Buddha: the founder of Buddhism. He lived in the sixth century before Christ.

Kabir: the well-known sufi saint who lived most likely in the fifteenth century.